Love Finds You

in

Last Chance

CALIFORNIA

Love Finds You

in

Last Chance

CALIFORNIA

BY **MIRALEE FERRELL**

summerside
PRESS

Cover and Interior Design by Müllerhaus Publishing Group

Published by Summerside Press, Inc., 11024 Quebec Circle, Bloomington, Minnesota 55438

Fall in love with Summerside.

Printed in the USA.

Dedication
....

This book is dedicated to Kim Vogel Sawyer.
My heartfelt thanks for your friendship,
your confidence in my writing,
and your prayer support.
I'm truly humbled and blessed.

Acknowledgments

....

This story, and the opportunity to share it, was placed in my path by the Lord. The idea of a strong young woman trying to succeed in a man's world in the Old West rumbled in my heart for months. The story of Kittie Wilkins, a woman who lived in the 1800s and ran one of the largest horse ranches in her area and time period, fascinated me, but I had no idea how it might be born. One day I got a note from my friend and fellow author Kim Vogel Sawyer, saying she'd recommended my work to a new publishing house that was starting a romance line. She offered the information a bit apologetically, half afraid I might not be pleased. Not so. I felt honored that someone of Kim's caliber would endorse me. Thank you, my friend; I'll forever be in your debt.

A huge thank-you to Rachel Meisel and Jason Rovenstine from Summerside Press, along with the rest of the staff who helped make this book a reality. You gave me an opportunity to be part of this awesome new line, and I'm grateful for your encouragement and support. You guys are the best!

Tamela Hancock Murray, my wonderful agent, has watched over my career and championed my work from the very beginning. She's stood beside me when prospects looked dim, prayed for me when we were unsure of an outcome, and cheered when prayers were answered. I so appreciate not only the professionalism she brings to her job, but the friendship and personal touch she offers, as well.

My husband and I journeyed to Last Chance, now just a wide spot in the road with a few tombstones, foundations, and hundred-year-old fence posts rotting in the woods. We discovered two wonderful sources

of help in the Foresthill area. Nolan Smith, District Archaeologist
for Tahoe National Forest, drove with us over three hours round trip
from our B and B up to the high mountain site of Last Chance. He was
invaluable, showing us the area and providing wonderful bits of insight
into the local history. While we were there, we spent three nights at the
Christmas Tree Vineyard Lodge, a wonderful B and B owned and run by
Claudia Raco. Her hospitality, knowledge of the area, books she lent me,
and suggestions of whom to consult were a tremendous help. The great
people who volunteer at the Foresthill museum also have my thanks.

I couldn't write an acknowledgment page without touting the
praises of my family, especially my wonderful husband, Allen. He listens
patiently when I'm stressed, puts up with scanty meals when I'm pushing
a deadline, and celebrates with me when each book is contracted and
released. My grown kids, Marnee and Steven, along with their spouses,
Brian and Hannah, have been staunch supporters, as has my sister, Jenny,
and brother, Tim. Sylvia Gould, my mother, gets a special word of thanks
for taking the time to be a proofreader for me and for being a constant
source of encouragement.

Some of the inspiration for my character of Alexia came from my
strong, independent daughter, Marnee. She's my best friend as well as my
riding partner; the girl was practically born on a horse. And don't worry,
Steven—one of these days I'll weave a story around your personality, as
well. God has blessed me with such an incredible family network.
No author can succeed alone. I have some of the best critique partners
and knowledgeable advance readers. A huge thanks goes to my crit
partners who labored and brainstormed with me: Kimberly Johnson,
Sherri Sand, and Teresa Morgan. You gals rock! Blessings on my three
faithful advance readers who gave me honest feedback. Tammy, Kristy,
and Amanda, you're awesome and I hope you'll stick with me for a few
more books.

And finally, my heartfelt thanks to the rest of my family, church body, and friends who so unfailingly cheer me on in this exciting and challenging journey called writing. I'd never make it without your prayers and love surrounding me. My greatest source of inspiration is from the Lord, and all praise, honor, and glory go to Him. I'm nothing without Jesus, and my writing would be hollow words without His touch. May He always receive the glory for every word that I write.

LAST CHANCE HOTEL, 1860's
LADDER TO 2nd FLOOR DORMITORY

LAST CHANCE, CALIFORNIA LIES ABOUT TWO AND A HALF hours northeast of Auburn, California, deep in the Sierra Nevada mountains. It's now a ghost town with only one small shack and a cemetery attesting to the thriving mining town that once existed. The town is almost totally obscured, and the encroaching forest hides the remnants of several hand-dug cellars. In the late 1800s, the main street contained a hotel, a candy store, a butcher shop, a dry goods store, and possibly more. Visitors can still see the spring and nearby glade that once boasted a small apple orchard, all tucked behind the scattering of homes that backed main street. The mule team routes into the town were steep, dropping nearly 5,000 feet in elevation from the top of the ridges to the bottom of the canyons, making for treacherous travel. It took a hardy miner or pioneer to traverse the rugged mountains and make his home in Last Chance.

Miralee Ferrell

Prologue

....

June 1877—two miles outside of Last Chance, California

Benjamin Travers trotted his horse across the mesquite-dotted meadow that was just beginning to show patches of green. Spots of snow still clung to protected areas under the spreading boughs of cedar trees where the sun hadn't yet stretched its warm fingers. The nearby ridges of the Sierra Nevada mountains failed to stir his appreciation today. Getting to town and ridding himself of his heavy burden filled his thoughts and drove him forward.

A bright glint flashed, pulling his gaze to the tree-covered hill nearby. He reined in his horse and stared but didn't see it again. His unease deepened and his horse seemed to sense it, snorting and sidestepping. He picked up his reins, determined to get to town, and the sooner the better. Once he'd paid for the horses, dropped off his ore samples, and headed back home, he'd breathe easy again.

The loud bark of a rifle report struck his ears a split second before a bullet pinged off a nearby rock, scattering bits of flint. His Morgan gelding snorted and jumped to the side, dancing and rearing.

Ben jerked on the reins, pulling his horse back to a standstill. "Easy, Ricky." He patted the gelding's neck and removed one foot from his stirrup. He had started to swing off when another shot erupted from the hillside above. The bullet whistled by, only inches from his head, and struck bits of flint from a large boulder a few yards away.

Ricky screamed and reared, landed hard, and kicked out. The horse tucked his head low between his front knees, and his hind feet lashed out high. Ben never regained his seat. Ricky's tremendous lunge threw him hard, and he landed next to the rock outcropping on a shallow wash of loose gravel and small boulders.

His heart hurt. The pain crept up his neck and down his arm, growing so intense that he groaned and gripped his chest. He sucked in a deep breath, gasped, and choked. A sharper pain somewhere in the region of his heart struck again, sending an agonizing ache all the way up to his jaw.

Somehow he managed to drag himself the few feet to the base of the rock-strewn bluff. He fumbled in his pocket and withdrew the leather pouch, shoving it under a small jumble of boulders and branches. Every breath hurt. He waited a moment, praying that the pain would pass. Fighting to finish his task, he piled small stones up in front of the shallow cleft where the gold lay. If the rider still waited, he'd find the spot, but if not, Alexia or Joe might discover the hiding place later.

The last rock dropped into place and Ben dragged himself away. No sense in someone finding him close by, if he did pass out or die. He managed to crawl twenty feet or so, when another fierce pain rocked him back on the sand. He uttered a deep groan and slid forward onto his belly, his face lying against the rough pebbles. A vision of Alex and her cheerful smile flashed across his mind before everything around him grew hazy and faded into darkness.

* * * * *

The man sheathed his rifle with a satisfied grunt. Travers had taken a hard fall, and after crawling a few feet, he hadn't moved. His body lay partially hidden, with only his legs in view. He'd like to put a bullet into the man's skull, but the presence of the law in the area stayed his hand. Too bad his bullet had missed, but it might be better this way. He'd best get away from this spot fast, before a passing miner came to investigate. If no one stopped by and Ben didn't get up, so much the better. He'd wait an hour or so and come by again to see what had transpired.

Chapter One

....

Early July 1877

"He did what?" Alex couldn't believe the banker's words. "My father wouldn't put me in that position. I'm sorry, Mr. Elton, but I have a hard time believing this." She leaned against the straight-backed chair and crossed her arms, trying to keep the fear out of her voice.

The clink of coins at a teller's window not far from the bank president's desk sounded loud in the room. Only a short wall divided Clarence Elton's private space from the foyer, and Alex saw the familiar faces of three townspeople doing business a few yards away. She dropped her voice, hating the idea that inquisitive ears might try to pry. "Why didn't you tell me sooner? Dad's been gone almost three weeks."

Heavy brows lowered over Clarence Elton's eyes, a sharp contrast to the normally gentle expression on the older man's face.

"I'm sorry, Alexia. I should've taken care of this right after his passing. I knew this would add to your grief, so I kept putting it off." He leaned forward and propped his elbows on the top of the well-polished desk that served as his work space in the diminutive office at the back of the town's only bank. "I witnessed his signature myself."

Alex felt the blood rush to her cheeks and thought her high-necked dress might choke her.

Time. She needed time to absorb what she'd been told. Mr. Elton sat without speaking, the warm light in his faded blue eyes testifying to his sympathy.

Why would her father do this without her knowledge? "The ranch has been doing well. We've been selling a steady stream of horses to the cavalry, and smaller lots are selling in the cities. Why would he mortgage the ranch?"

Mr. Elton steepled his fingers and rested his chin against their tips. "He'd planned a substantial increase of your stock. He told me he'd contracted for some fresh blood, as he put it. A Morgan stallion was to ship from Los Angeles, along with a few blooded mares. He didn't discuss his plans with you?"

Alex shook her head and frowned. "He didn't. Can I turn over the funds in our account and cancel the note?"

"I wish it were that simple—but there isn't enough to clear off the loan. He borrowed more than he needed for the horses. He asked for gold coins and planned to take them home until he decided what he needed. No money was found on his…er, I mean…" His face reddened and he dropped his gaze. "I'm sorry."

"I understand. I'll check his safe, office desk, and bureau drawers when I return to the ranch. I'll pay you as soon as I find the money. How long ago did he take out the note?"

"The day before his accident. Knowing Ben, I'm sure he would have put the gold in a secure place at home."

Alex gazed around the tidy bank, trying to take in all that she'd learned. The familiarity of the pine walls and polished floor brought some sense of normalcy but did little to quiet the tumult in her mind. She rose, shook out her skirt, and met his gaze.

"Let's hope so." She started to speak again, but her voice caught in her throat. She walked over to the window with her back toward Mr. Elton. Nothing made sense right now. This was wrong, all of it. Papa shouldn't be dead; he was only sixty-two. Why, he'd been as healthy as a wild mustang and had never been sick a day in his life.

She turned around and met Mr. Elton's eyes. "His horse arrived home a couple of hours after he left, and from what I've discovered, he never made it to town. It's possible he may have sent the wire to the people in Los Angeles the day before—in which case, I should find a receipt for the new stock. Either way, I'll see that the note is paid."

"It isn't due for a year. There's plenty of time to build your herd."

"Thanks, Mr. Elton, but I'd prefer to pay it now if the gold can be found."

Mr. Elton leaned his elbows on the desk and clasped his hands. "Martha's getting up in years," he observed, seemingly trying to lighten the mood. "How's she doing? She rarely makes it to church anymore, and I haven't seen her since your father's service. She's been with your family—what, about twelve years now?"

Alex nodded, and a smile touched her lips. "Since just after Mother's death. You'd never know she's seventy years old. She can work circles around me in the house and still find time to bake bread and pies. She doesn't do well sitting long spells in the buckboard, though, and when her back bothers her, she has devotions at home."

A wide smile brightened the banker's face. "Ah, yes. Martha's famous pies. What I wouldn't give for a slice of her Gravenstein apple pie right now."

"You'll have to come out sometime. Papa would…"

Sudden realization hit so hard that she felt like a shod mule had kicked the wind right out of her lungs.

"I miss him," she whispered.

Mr. Elton probably did, as well. He and her father had been close friends, and the older man had spent a number of hours eating pie in their kitchen over the years. She turned away for a moment and then swung around, all trace of emotion wiped clean.

"I know as much about running the ranch as Papa did. I can make it succeed on my own."

Mr. Elton's bushy brows drew together, giving his normally serious face a more somber look. "It was one of your father's dearest wishes that you settle down with a young man from the area. It's not seemly for a young single woman to run a ranch and boss a crew of rough wranglers."

Alex frowned. Why did people always assume she wanted a husband? Had her mother lived, her softening influence might have tipped her toward more domestic tasks, but her father had trained her in every aspect of running the ranch. They'd spent hundreds of hours riding the hills and caring for the horses that supplied their livelihood. She'd idolized Papa and the other cowhands as a girl, and her constant interaction with the men only strengthened her desire to make a success of the ranch. She didn't need a husband to run it for her.

She felt a little guilty for glaring at the banker, but she didn't much care. "And exactly who am I supposed to marry?"

A smile tugged at the corners of Mr. Elton's mouth. "There's Charlie Danson on your neighboring property—his father has a prosperous gold mine—and Walter Sloan's been sweet on you since you wore short skirts. Both are good, hardworking young men who'd be proud to court you."

Alex took two strides toward her chair and flopped into it. "Charlie can barely stay on a horse, and Walter is a big baby. Do you know that when we were in the second grade I showed him a snake, and he almost fainted?"

A small chuckle escaped Mr. Elton's lips and he wiped his mouth with the back of his hand. "Sorry, my dear. I can't imagine what I was thinking. But I'm sure if you take some time and study on it, you'll find there's at least one eligible man in the area that might suit you. I've certainly heard of several who think they're in love with you." The twinkle in his eyes was unmistakable and served to irritate Alex even more.

"This is not funny, Mr. Elton."

"Of course not. I apologize. I realize it's a serious matter." He sank back into his chair and sobered. "You have a year to settle the note, even if you don't find the gold. You might check with Rob at the telegraph office and see if anything came in about the horses' arrival."

"I'll do that. I'd better be going."

"One more thing." He held up a hand. "Your cousin Carter Foster stopped in not long after your father's passing. He indicated an interest in purchasing your ranch, should you have any trouble making it succeed."

"Carter Foster?" She cocked her head to one side. "He's not my cousin, you know. He's barely related by marriage. Besides, I have no desire to sell."

"Of course you're under no obligation, but I thought you should know."

She nodded, pushed her chair back, and stood. "I need to check on that gold and try to get this mortgage off my back. Thank you for your kindness, Mr. Elton. Please come out to the ranch anytime. We'd love to have you."

He leaned his knuckles on the desk and pushed himself to his feet, a small grunt escaping his lips. "Thank you, my dear. I'll do that."

* * * * *

Alex stepped out of the small wood structure and shielded her eyes against the glare of the early summer sun. Somehow the sights and smells of Last Chance seemed different after hearing Clarence Elton's tidings. No longer did the view of the magnificent pines and cedars dotting the landscape make her heart swell with joy or the green of the trees remind her of childhood days racing through the woods on her pony. Today they only brought a sense of loneliness and isolation. She looked across the canyon separating the distant Deadwood Ridge from their little town. Long, hard toil was required to reach the nearest settlement by wagon, and she hadn't been out of Last Chance for more than a year. With her father gone and Uncle Joe's health failing, she doubted she'd see the sites of a large town any time soon.

Not that she hadn't loved the years she'd spent here—Last Chance was her home. But life was a constant struggle for most of its one hundred or so inhabitants. The town's survival depended on the productivity of the half dozen mines dotting the landscape within a mile or two of town, and it was rare to see a wagon roll into the area. Mule teams brought most of the goods, and Alex doubted that a stagecoach or train would ever wend its way up the steep, forested canyon walls or along the dense ridge tops. Last Chance was truly the end of the trail in more ways than one.

Her childhood had been happy, tagging after her father while pretending to be a wrangler. Friends hadn't come easily, and many of the other children viewed her as arrogant or stuck-up. Many a day she'd gone home to her mother, and later to Martha, crying over mistreatment by the other girls. She'd eventually learned to ignore teasing, turning an uncaring ear to those who didn't understand.

While her mother had taught her manners, Alex had always preferred riding a horse or helping birth a new foal to attending a church social. Time hadn't altered that desire, and her current lack of friends among the female population of Last Chance proved that little had changed.

Except for Elizabeth Anders, her best friend these past couple of years. Alex still had a hard time believing that the tall, elegant brunette who'd arrived by mule team to help run her ailing uncle's dry goods store had befriended her. The men coming in from the mining claims were smitten with the green-eyed beauty, and a few of the women had been catty at first. But Elizabeth's sweet, accepting nature swayed public opinion and produced a grudging acceptance among the women, which soon turned to respect and even admiration.

If only she had time for a quick cup of tea with Elizabeth before
heading back to the ranch. She sorely needed someone to talk to, but the
urgency of her errand pressed her forward. A gray-striped cat raced out
the door of the nearby mercantile, apparently relinquishing his mousing
duty at Ike's general store. Loud laughter and tin-panny music drifted
through the open door of the saloon at the end of the street.

Alex shaded her eyes and stared at the distant figure who'd appeared on
the walk outside the saloon. It looked like one of her wranglers. She shook
her head—the men knew the saloon was off-limits during the day. Her
father hadn't tolerated his hands drinking during work hours. In fact, he'd
had very little sympathy for that behavior at any time of the day or night.

Alex stepped off the boardwalk and headed toward the man, but
he swung the opposite direction and disappeared around a corner.
Following a strange man into an alley didn't appeal to her at the moment.
Instead, she turned and directed her steps to the minuscule clapboard
telegraph office across the street.

The dark-clad figure of a portly, middle-aged man emerged from the
office and surged toward her. Parson Moser smiled and raised his hat as
he approached. "Alexia, how are you today? Haven't seen you at church
recently. We've missed you."

Unlike some preachers whom Last Chance had tolerated in the
distant past, Bill Moser was the genuine article. He lived what he
preached, and he cared for his flock as if they were his own children. The
warmth he exuded drew Alex a little closer to God, but a few gossiping
women in his congregation caused her to steer clear of attending church
on a regular basis. They didn't approve of her lifestyle or the freedom her
father had granted her.

She slowed near the edge of the boardwalk a few feet from the
telegraph office and smiled. "Thank you, Pastor, I'm doing well. I'm
on an errand, or I'd love to chat."

He patted her arm. "That's fine, my dear. You've been on my heart lately. Anytime you need to talk, my door is open."

"Thank you. I might stop by sometime soon—and I'll try to make it to church a bit more regular. Business at the ranch has been pressing since Papa passed."

"I understand, but that's even more reason why you need your church family." He patted her arm one more time and smiled before moving away.

Alex watched the ambling form. Did he truly not see what some of the women put her through with their petty comments, or did he simply choose to believe the best of everyone? Was there something deeper to the man's belief in God and mankind than she understood? She shook her head and stepped over the threshold of the tiny one-room shack that served as the telegraph office. Better get her mind back on business.

Rob Bartlett raised watery hazel eyes from the paper lying on his rough-hewn table and smiled. "How can I help you, Miss Travers?"

One step took Alex to the front edge of the table. A rumbling wagon passed by the open door, and dust rolled into the tiny enclosure.

"Aaa-choo!" Alex pulled a hanky from her pocket, covered her mouth, and sneezed again.

"Bless you. Feel free to pull the door to, if you'd like. It gets a mite dusty in here so close to the street. Guess I've gotten used to it." Bartlett waved a hand in the air, but his red-rimmed eyes testified to the truth of his statement.

"That's all right, I won't be long. I need some information, if you'd be so kind."

He sat up straighter, and his toothy smile lit up his homely face. "Certainly. Anything."

"Do you know if my father sent a wire to Los Angeles about purchasing a stallion and mares?"

"Yes, I recall that he did."

"And did he wire instructions to the seller about payment?"

"Hmm…" He stroked the stubble on his narrow chin and looked up at the board-covered ceiling. "Let me think. Ah—I remember." He smacked the palms of his hands together. "He planned on sending the money later. The buyer said he could wire the funds when it suited him. Guess they'd done business before and the man trusted him."

"So he didn't come back?" She leaned a trembling hand on the table and willed her voice to remain calm.

"Nope. Shore didn't. In fact, I believe it was the day before he…" He cleared his throat and dropped his gaze.

"He died. Yes. I know. You've been most helpful, Rob."

His head jerked up and his Adam's apple bobbed. "Thank you, Miss Alex. Wish I could'a helped more."

Alex mustered a smile and stepped from the room, clear on one thing. She had to get home and talk to Martha and Uncle Joe, her two oldest and best friends. Maybe they could help cast some light on her darkening world.

Chapter Two
....

Justin Phillips wiped the sweat from his forehead with the back of his leather-gloved hand and jammed his hat onto his head. The sun in Nevada territory always felt twice as hot as it did near the Pacific coast.

"Blame it all," he muttered to himself. "Why'd Ben have to saddle me with this mess?" He pulled the creased telegram from his hip pocket and read it through again.

> *Need help. Ranch in trouble and life in danger. Come quick and keep quiet. Alex hates interference. Debt will be settled. Benjamin Travers*

Looked like there was nothing to do but hit the trail. But what about Toby? Justin tugged off his gloves, pocketed them in his denim jacket, and stored his tools in his wagon. At barely three years old, Toby might have a hard time holding up on a prolonged trip. And once they arrived, how would he care for the child?

Time for worrying later. A good meal, a hot bath, and a shave might clear his mind. He'd better round up what Sam owed him for repairing the saloon door—again. It was a good thing he handled a hammer as well as a rope and a rifle, as there weren't a lot of wrangling jobs around lately.

It sounded like Ben Travers needed a hand on his ranch—as well as help corralling the person causing him trouble. Justin didn't like that last part. Trouble had dogged him the past couple of years, and he didn't need any more. Especially trouble of the female variety. Justin tended to steer clear of women, but an especially persistent one had been dogging him here in town. Molly had only been gone a few months, and he had no desire to get mixed up with another woman. Might be a good reason to move on.

The promise of steady work and repaying an old debt to a friend drew him. He'd better check on Toby. If he helped Travers and started over on his own, it mightn't be so bad.

He stepped into the small, dark boardinghouse owned by Mrs. McGavin and headed for the kitchen. He probably shouldn't have left Toby in the care of the elderly woman. She claimed she'd not yet seen seventy, but it was common knowledge that eighty years had come and gone and possibly more. If it weren't for her widowed daughter Mary, Justin doubted Mrs. McGavin could've kept her boardinghouse open.

A loud howl cut through the air and propelled him down the hall and into the deserted kitchen. Toby sat on the floor in the corner, scrubbing his eyes and crying. The little boy lifted his arms. "Papa. I hungry. Want some dinner, Papa."

Justin scooped up the boy and stroked his tangled dark curls. "Papa will find you something to eat."

The three-year-old wrapped his arms around his father's neck. Had Mrs. McGavin left Toby alone? He'd feed the boy, get him to bed, and see what was going on. Maybe it was just as well Ben's message came when it did.

He lifted the lid on a pot shoved to the back of the stove. A comforting fragrance wafted out, and his mouth watered. Chicken soup. He placed Toby in the chair he'd fashioned, pulled it close to the table, and ladled soup into a bowl. A piece of buttered bread completed the meal. Justin tied a dish towel around the little boy's neck and handed him a spoon.

The sound of footsteps in the hall turned him in that direction. Mrs. McGavin's bulky form came panting into the room. "Land sakes. What's all the squallin' about?"

Justin clamped his lips together and then took a deep breath. No sense in taking his anger out on this woman. "Toby was hungry. I found him on the floor, crying. Alone."

Mrs. McGavin bustled to the stove and placed the lid back on the pot. "I just stepped out of the room for a minute. I planned on feedin' the boy soon as I got back."

Toby grinned as he slapped his soup with his spoon.

"That's enough, Toby. Don't play with your soup." Justin bent over, wiping soup from the boy's face.

"You need a wife. I can't take care of this young'un whilst you go off to work." Mrs. McGavin turned with her hands on her ample hips. "He's too much for me."

Justin straightened and faced her. "His mama died not long ago. I'm not ready to marry again."

"Humph. I heard she was a saloon girl. Looks like you could'a done a better job pickin' a mama for the boy."

Justin clenched his jaw and rolled his shoulders back. "I did what I thought best." He bent over Toby and fed him the last few spoonfuls of soup.

"Humph. I'da given her some money and put her on a train back to her mama, if you'da asked me."

Justin ignored the comment. He hadn't asked Mrs. McGavin for her opinion, but that had never stopped her from voicing it.

"So she died not long ago and left you with the boy?"

"Yes."

"Leaves you in a fix, and me as well, way I see it."

Justin untied the towel from Toby's neck. "I need to put Toby to bed. I'll come down later and settle up for my board. I'll be leaving tomorrow."

Her chin jerked up. "Now, I didn't mean nothin'. I'd be happy to have you stay. Mary can watch the boy. Just pay a little more for his care. No call for you to leave."

Justin shook his head and looked over the top of Toby's curls at the fawning woman. "I'll be pulling out in the morning. Got a job offer in California."

"What about the boy? You got no one to care for him."

"I'll care for him. We'll be leaving tomorrow." He nodded and stepped out of the kitchen. Toby needed a nap, and he needed to pack.

* * * * *

Justin reached over the top of the buckboard seat and patted the squirming child lying on the pile of blankets. Toby settled back into a restless sleep, one chubby hand clutching a ragged blanket. The two of them, along with his stallion Durango, had traveled by train from Truckee to Colfax, where three days ago he'd purchased a wagon and team for the rest of the trip. From the look of the surrounding country and the report he'd gotten in Colfax, he must be less than a day from the small town of Last Chance.

The sturdy team of horses was an asset. His Arabian stallion would've struggled to pull the load up the steep canyon trails. They'd made it through the area around Robinson Flat without incident, but the sharp, winding grade the past few hours challenged even him. Earlier he'd spent more than an hour cutting and limbing a pine tree and rigging it to the back of his wagon. The extra weight had created enough drag to slow their forward progress down the hill, and it kept the wagon from running over his team. Word at Foresthill said the shorter route through Michigan Bluff was even more treacherous and impossible for a wagon. In places, the trail cut into the side of a sheer cliff. One spook or misstep of a horse could send the beast and rider plunging to their deaths. Although still hazardous in places and a couple of days longer, the route he'd chosen was worth the extra time—he'd not take a chance with his son or his gear.

Justin heaved a sigh and flicked his reins. The drooping horses picked up their heads and leaned into the harness. Toby slept on, unaware of the excitement just behind him. Justin almost envied the boy. No worries at this young age except a full belly and a toy to play with. Still, he knew the child missed his mother. It had been hard for both of them to adjust to being together full-time. What had made Justin think he could raise Toby alone, with Molly gone?

Justin had long abandoned the ritual of prayer, but the pressure of his situation urged him to reconsider.

"Lord, I haven't been much on speaking terms with You the past few years, but I need Your help with this boy. I can't stand the thought of giving him up, and I can't see raising him on my own. Any help You give would be appreciated."

A few miles later a rough signpost boasting LAST CHANCE, POPULATION 101—FOUR MILES peeked out through the dense brush alongside the dusty road. Justin had formed no concrete plan beyond meeting Ben, but a town this size might have a boardinghouse with a woman willing to help care for his son.

Justin sighed wearily. Too bad he'd left Auburn a year ago and headed to Nevada. Coming from there would've been only a couple days' journey. It had been a long pull from Nevada and up into the Sierra Nevada mountains to this little mining town with the strange name.

At his stop in Foresthill, a talkative old miner had shared the story of the naming of Last Chance. Legend had it that a group of miners had searched the ridge for days and, discouraged by their lack of success, decided to return to the valley where they'd started. One miner dolefully remarked this was their last chance to find gold on the west side of the mountains. Before breaking camp, one of the hunters scouted a flock of quail a short distance away. He took aim and shot, knocking one from a tree. In its dying struggles, the bird scratched away the leaves, exposing the bare ground. The miner stooped to pick up the bird and noted a rock. Upon closer inspection, he concluded that he'd found gold. The group set up permanent camp and, remembering the earlier dejected remark, they named the place Last Chance.

The road wound along beside a meandering stream, and the shafts of sunlight glinted off the water like prisms dangling in a window. Whispering pines lined the edges of the stream, interspersed with flowering brush and mesquite. The past few days must have been dry, as dust puffed up from the horses' hooves as they plodded along, pulling the wagon astraddle the ruts cut by carts and wagons before him. Glimpses of small meadows were visible through the branches of the trees, inviting Justin to pull over and stretch out in the nearby shade. But the gurgling stream splashing and singing over the rocks in its bed urged him on, drawing him toward the future that lay ahead.

Justin slapped the reins against the dusty back of his team. "Giddap there! Time enough to rest when we reach the town."

Chapter Three

....

Alex clucked to the mare pulling her small buggy and glanced at the sun slanting westward. It was nearing suppertime, and yet chores remained. The faint road wended its way along a flat, heavily treed area. The horse slowed her pace as she began the climb to the higher elevation of the mountain plateau where the Circle T ranch was nestled.

Towering fir trees lined each side of the narrow road, mixed with cedar and pine. The sound of tinkling water alerted Alex that the ford across Grouse Creek lay ahead. Due to late snows and spring runoff, the water level was high, but it was nothing the hardy mare couldn't handle. They topped a rise and descended into the shallow gully, where Alex halted the buggy. She hitched up her skirt and then stepped onto the wheel and down onto the road.

Grasping the mare's bridle, Alex led her to the shade of a spreading oak a few yards from the stream. The mare greedily ripped at the long tufts of grass, and Alex sank down onto the cool green patch nearby.

Everything had happened so fast at the bank that she hadn't taken in the implications of her father's actions. She needed time to absorb the information before facing Martha and Uncle Joe at the ranch house. They'd both be curious to know why she'd stayed so long, although Alex would bet that Joe knew about the bank loan.

Papa and Joe had been close friends since their early days of driving cattle to market. Joe had signed on at Papa's struggling new horse ranch right after Papa had filed the homestead papers. Papa hadn't met Mama yet, and Joe was a first-rate cook and horse wrangler. Over the years, the two men had grown closer than brothers.

Had Joe encouraged Papa to take the loan or argued against it? Uncle Joe loved Alex, but he loved the ranch, too, and he wanted to see it grow and prosper as much as her papa had. But if he'd known and not told her? She shook her head, guilt swamping her for allowing even a spark of distrust to enter her mind. Uncle Joe would never betray her or her father. He and Martha would like nothing better than to see her settled, married, and happy. They were the only people she knew without a doubt that she could trust.

Frowning, she tore at a clump of grass and twisted the blades, shredding them and watching them fall. There might be a man somewhere worth caring for—but if there was, she hadn't met him. Decent men lived in these mountains, but none that set her heart pounding. Her parents had enjoyed a vibrant, special bond, but not all marriages were established on this sort of mutual love. Hers would be, if she ever married. She'd never settle for friendship and simple respect.

There were one or two men whom she could tolerate, but let him take charge of her ranch and tell her what to do? While she tended the house, cooked meals, and sewed? Not likely.

Alex pushed to her knees. She needed to get home. Now. No more foolishness.

A light rain began to fall, spattering the dust on the trail. A gust of wind kicked up last year's leaves pooled under the tree and sent them scattering from her side. She glanced at the sky, worried at the sudden shift in the weather. At this altitude, a fast-moving storm could transform the brightness of day into gloom in the space of a few minutes. A rumble of thunder sent a tingle of fear through her. Somewhere high up in the mountains, a serious storm brewed. Time to get home before she got soaked.

The dapple-gray mare had inched away to the far edge of the grassy patch and looked to be heading for the stream. Alex hurried down the slope to the buggy as the rain turned from a soft drizzle to a steady downpour. She climbed up onto the seat and slapped the reins.

"Let's go, Glory. Time to get home."

Glory blew a soft, whiffling breath and moved forward, seemingly just as eager as her driver was to get home. Alex directed the mare to the water and looked upstream. It had surged to a higher level since she'd stepped out of the buggy. There was no time to lose—a flash flood could hit this gully and sweep everything in its path. She didn't care to get caught in the oncoming water or to be stuck on the town side of the stream. No telling how long it would take to abate once it overflowed its banks.

Alex clucked to the snorting mare and urged her forward, but Glory didn't like the look of the fast-moving water.

"Let's go, girl. You've crossed hundreds of times."

Glory backed up a couple of steps. Alex tapped the reluctant mare with the tip of her whip, and she settled down and surged ahead. Alex felt a flood of alarm when she saw that the water had reached the mare's belly, more than a foot higher at the center of the stream than when they'd crossed earlier.

Just then a rumbling sound from around the bend caught Alex's ears. Her breath caught in her throat and she lifted her whip, cracking it over the mare's back.

"Let's go! Giddap!" Glory shook her head and emitted a loud whinny but kept the buggy moving toward the opposite shore. "You can do it, girl. Come on." Alex spoke in a calm voice to the agitated mare and glanced upstream again.

A hundred yards away, a wall of water rose, flinging small trees and debris in its wake. It bore down toward the buggy. The wheels felt mired in quicksand, so slow was their forward progress.

"Hurry, Glory! Come on, girl, hurry!" Alex stood and plied the whip, a feeling of raw terror coursing through her veins.

The mare bolted forward, her feet scrambling on the rocks of the streambed. Finding secure footing, she lunged up the slight incline on the other side. A few seconds later the buggy emerged safely on the water-soaked bank. Alex pushed the mare on, gaining higher ground before turning to look back. The wall of water swept just below, sending the roiling trees ahead of it like the blades of a windmill driven by a heavy wind.

Alex sat for a moment, not caring about the rain blowing against her face. A few seconds longer and Martha and Uncle Joe would have been planning another funeral. Her body shook as she clutched the reins and stared at the churning water. Gratitude swept over her. God was indeed good.

Again she slapped the reins on Glory's back. This time, the mare didn't hesitate but moved forward with a toss of her head. Minutes later the ranch came into sight, and Alex heaved a sigh of relief.

Home. A sense of peace and safety filled her heart. She loved this place and could never turn it over to anyone else. The ranch would remain hers, whatever she had to do to keep it.

* * * * *

Alex pulled the mare to a halt in front of the barn.

"Frank? You in there?" She stepped down from the buggy and walked to Glory's head, patting her sweaty neck.

A burly man strode from the dark mouth of the barn and stopped a few feet away. He wiped a hand down his overalls and tipped his head. "Howdy, Miss Alex. Glad you made it back before supper. Miss Martha was startin' to worry."

"It took longer in town than I expected, and I hit a patch of swift water at Grouse Creek." Frank was a new hand, and she didn't care to give him any details about the ranch's business. "Unhitch Glory from the buggy, would you? She brought me through some high water and she'll need a good rubdown."

"Yes, ma'am. I'll take care of her." He took the side rein and urged the mare into the cavernous barn.

Alex would have normally dealt with the mare herself. She hated asking her men to do things she was capable of doing; they had enough work of their own. But she had one thing on her mind: finding Martha and Uncle Joe.

She headed across the open space in front of the barn and onto the packed dirt surrounding the house. The structure wasn't overly big, but it boasted a large wraparound porch on three sides. Martha's green thumb was evident here, with the rows of flowers lining the ground in front of the porch and extending several feet into the smooth dirt area. A spreading oak that must have been three hundred years old cast its shade over the two-storied house, giving a welcome respite from the hot summer sun.

Her papa's touch showed in every board and shutter of the house. He had loved well-lit rooms, and while he'd paid dearly for them, he'd brought in a number of windows. A porch swing hung on the front veranda, a thoughtful gift from her papa to her mother years back. He'd brought his little daughter out in the cool of the evening and rocked her to sleep while telling her bedtime stories.

A longing to feel his strong arms around her swelled in Alex's chest. Why did God take him so soon? Didn't he know she still needed her papa?

A deep-throated bark sounded, and a huge black-and-tan form dashed around the corner of the house. Alex smiled and braced for the big dog's greeting.

"Hunter! Sit."

The massive animal immediately plopped himself onto the ground at her feet, but his expressive eyes clearly stated his desire to greet her in a more exuberant canine fashion. Alex laughed and hugged her friend.

"It's good to see you, too, Hunter." She waved an arm. "We'll play later."

He took off across the yard and immediately returned with a thick stick.

"Not now. You'll have to get one of the wranglers to throw it." She watched the dog turn, hang his head, and cross the yard to the barn, the stick still gripped in his mouth.

A movement caught the corner of her vision. One of the hired hands, Davis, stood just inside the barn door watching the interaction. She raised her hand in a brief wave, and the man stepped out into the sun. Something about his eyes didn't look right, and Alex stepped closer and squinted. Bloodshot.

Had Davis been drinking? Her thoughts flew back to the man she'd seen leaving the saloon. Could he have arrived here ahead of her? Yes— she'd stopped at the telegraph office before heading home.

"Davis?"

He pulled his hat from his head and looked at his feet. "Yes, ma'am?"

"Have you been at the ranch all day?"

"Uh…" He glanced up and met her eyes. "I've been checkin' the mares in the east pasture."

She folded her arms and tilted her head. "You haven't been to town?"

"No, ma'am. Not today." He turned his hat in his hands. "Did you forget somethin' you want that I should get for you?"

"No. How were the mares?"

The sudden shift in topic seemed to catch him off guard. He jerked his head up and met her stare. "Oh—fine—just fine, Miss Travers. No problems a'tall."

"Okay, thanks." Checking on him might be an option, but she'd let it go this time. To her knowledge, Davis had never been dishonest or slacked in his work. Besides, the men had been working doubly hard since her father's death. Maybe he just needed a break.

The front door swung open and a tall, gray-haired woman stood on the stoop. "Alexia? I didn't hear you ride in. You been home long?"

Martha's familiar voice sang across the lawn, its welcome tones warming the cold places her father's passing had created.

Alex swung away from Davis and crossed the gravel to the porch. "Hunter wanted to play, but I told him to wait." She trotted up the steps. "I declare, only a year old and that dog's as big as a pony. Is Uncle Joe in yet?"

"Yep. He just finished his chores. Dinner will be ready in ten minutes. I began to think you'd miss it." Martha wiped floury hands on her apron and gave Alex a quick hug. "You all right?" She stepped back and examined the younger woman's face, worry and love evident in her eyes and mouth.

"Right enough, I guess." Alex grasped Martha's hand. "Come on, let's have some of your famous coffee. After that drive, a cup sounds good."

They crossed the foyer and entered the parlor. A large fireplace lined one wall, with horsehair chairs and a sofa flanking the other. It opened into a dining area containing a wooden table large enough to seat twelve people. Flowers stood in a vase in the center, and three place settings sat at one end.

Martha bustled to the stove in the nearby kitchen, lifted the coffeepot off the grate, and returned to the table with the pot and three steaming cups balanced on a tray. She hurried back to the stove, lifted a lid, and sniffed.

"Stew's ready. Help me dish up?"

The two women carried the stew pot, a plate with big slices of bread, and a crock of home-churned butter to the table. Alex never failed to feel gratitude to their old friend Jonesy, who kept a milk cow. The thought of hot bread without butter seemed almost a sin.

A door slammed and a whistle sounded at the rear of the house. Alex would know Uncle Joe's special brand of music anywhere. A moment later, the short, lanky man stomped into sight. He leaned on a cane and moved with care, but his eyes lit when he spotted Alex. He removed his hat to reveal white hair badly in need of cutting, curling as it was over his collar.

"Hi there, darlin'. How'd your meetin' with the banker go?" He pulled out a chair and slipped into it.

Alex loved the man, but in that moment her feelings toward Uncle Joe weren't very charitable. From his guarded expression, she knew that her father had confided in him. To what extent, she didn't know, but the truth would come out soon enough. "Mr. Elton was kindness itself, but I can't say much good about his message."

"Uh-huh." Uncle Joe leaned back and crossed his arms, but a compassionate look filled his faded blue eyes. "He told you about the note Benjamin took out."

Hurt shimmered from Alex's voice. "So all this time you knew and didn't tell me? Why?"

Sorrow clouded his face. "Wasn't my place. Your father was my best friend. I couldn't betray his trust."

A gentle hand squeezed her shoulder and Alex looked up at Martha. "Honey, don't you go blamin' your uncle Joe. Your papa told him to keep quiet. He didn't want you getting riled at Joe."

Alex sat up straight and felt her scalp bristle. "You both knew? I can't believe this!"

Martha sank into her chair and straightened her dress before answering. "Yes, and if he hadn't died, it would've been your father's place to tell you, not ours. Your papa was a strong man and once he'd made up his mind, one didn't go against his wishes."

"Not even after he died? I went into Mr. Elton's office blind. Felt like I'd been tossed into the creek in the middle of winter." Alex laced her fingers around her mug of coffee but didn't lift it to her lips.

Joe fingered his mustache and cleared his throat. "I'm sorry. Martha and I discussed it, and we planned on tellin' you. But then Clarence asked you to come and we knew you was about to find out."

Martha raised her hand. "We'd best pray and then eat. Joe, would you bless this food?"

Joe uttered a short prayer and then raised piercing eyes that looked straight into Alex's heart. "We didn't mean to hurt you."

Alex picked up her spoon, took a bite of stew, and sighed. "I'm not angry. Well, maybe I am a little, but I can't stay angry at you two for long." She smiled weakly. "But I'd like to know what Papa was thinking. It's not like we need more breeding stock. We're getting along fine."

Joe's snow-white head shook from side to side. "He wanted more than just gettin' along for you, darlin'. He wanted to make sure you'd be provided for proper-like, if'n anything should happen to him."

"And look where that's gotten me." Alex took a deep breath and blew it out. "I'm sorry. I hate this. Why couldn't Papa have left things the way they were?"

Joe stretched out his short, dusty legs and reached for his mug. "Life can't stay the same forever, Alex. Ever'thing changes some time or other."

"But I don't understand why he'd choose to go into debt. Papa meant the best, but this mortgage puts me in a tough position. I don't know if the horses have been paid for, and Mr. Elton says Papa left the bank with a bag of gold the day before his accident. Did he leave it with either of you?"

Martha sat upright and stared first at Alex, then at Joe. "Gold? I had no idea he was carrying gold." She turned a distraught face to the quiet man. "Joe?"

"Don't remember seein' or hearin' about any gold. I reckon it's possible he kept it on his person for safe keepin'. Your papa told me about the bank loan, but I figured he'd send payment straight to the breeder in Los Angeles." He drummed his work-roughened fingers against the polished surface of the pine table. "There's one more thing…."

Alex leaned forward and narrowed her eyes, not liking his tone. "Yes? What else don't I know?"

"Your father was carryin' ore samples to the assayer at Last Chance the day he died. He wasn't seen in town, so it's a safe bet he didn't make it before he fell off his horse." He scratched his whiskered chin and frowned. "Not sure why I didn't think about that 'fore now."

Martha gasped and clasped her hands over her heart. "What you talkin' about, Joe? Why would Ben have ore samples?"

Joe scraped his spoon across the bottom of his bowl and then wiped up the broth with a slab of bread. He took a large bite, chewed, swallowed, and shook his head. "You know Ben's had a hankerin' to find gold. That's what brought him to this country. Sure, he turned to ranchin', but that didn't keep him from hopin'. He told me the night before he died that he'd found what looked to be a likely spot somewhere on his land. Told me he'd show me where after he got the assay results."

Alex gripped Joe's hand. "Do you have any idea where he found it, Uncle Joe? He didn't tell you the general area?"

Joe shook his head and squeezed her hand. "Nope, 'fraid not. Guess somebody should check with Samuel at the assay office. Might be a false alarm."

"I'll check." Alex sighed and leaned back in her chair. "He raised me to help run this ranch, and I don't understand why he kept this from me. I'm not a little girl anymore."

A loud thumping at the kitchen door interrupted the small group. Alex turned her head and Joe pushed to his feet, grasped his cane, and hobbled to the door. He swung it open and peered outside. "Tim. What can I do for you?"

A rawboned cowboy stood holding his hat, spinning it round in his calloused hands. Alex slipped behind Joe in time to see Tim raise troubled eyes to the older man. "I need to give my notice."

Joe scowled. "What for?"

Tim dropped his gaze to the floor. "Got me a better job offer."

"What d'ya mean? Don't we pay fair wages?"

"It's not the wages, Joe."

"What's the problem, then?" There was a pause. "Spit it out, son."

Tim hesitated and then glanced at Alex. "Since Ben died, things been gettin' shaky around here." He turned his attention back to Joe. "You're stove up and can't ride, and we got no boss."

Alex stepped forward and put her hand on Joe's arm. "I'm taking Papa's place."

"I know, ma'am, and that's just it. I just don't think I can work for a woman. No offense. Some of the other men feel the same. Foster offered me a job, and I told him I'd take it."

Alex sucked in her breath. "Carter Foster? He's trying to hire our men behind our backs?"

"No, ma'am. I ran into him at the saloon one night and we got to talkin'. I told him my concerns. He said you'd be a fair person to work for, but I told him I planned to move on. He's runnin' a few more head of horses and doin' some mining, as well. He offered decent wages and said he'd put me in charge, if I do a good job."

Joe nodded. "So after workin' here for nigh on to three years, you're quittin'."

"I'm sorry, Joe."

Joe's expression hardened. "Stop by in the mornin' and draw your pay. And tell the other men if anyone wants to leave, they can do the same."

Alex stepped back from the door as Tim hurried away. She crossed her arms and glared at the closed door and then swung around toward Joe. "I know as much about running this ranch as Papa did."

Joe patted her shoulder. "I know, honey." He glanced at Martha and she gave a sparse nod. "Gus quit today, too."

"Gus? But why? He's been with us as long as Tim."

"I heard him talkin' to Tim about you bein' in charge when I walked up behind him. We had words and he up an' quit. Gus and Tim are old pards."

Alex leaned against the doorjamb and groaned. "Great. Two hands gone in one day. That makes it tough, since Frank's so new. What if some of the others leave? I'm surprised Davis hasn't, seeing how he's a buddy of Tim and Gus."

Joe leaned on his cane and shook his head. "Guess you'll have to take the reins and prove you can do the job. You've been ridin' and breakin' horses since you were little. Some of the men might not want to work for a woman, but a few will give you a chance. I'll help all I can, but this hip won't let me do as much as I'd like."

Martha wrapped her arm around Alex's shoulder and squeezed. "You can do it, Alexia, but you need to trust God. He's the one in charge, not you."

Alex drew a deep breath and let it out slowly. "I know, but it's my responsibility, not His. The men won't see God giving the orders; they'll see me. It's not like I can turn it over to Him and sit back."

Martha reached out a gnarled hand and stroked Alex's hair, running her fingers through the tangles teased by the wind. "No. You shouldn't sit back, but you do need to trust Him. There's a difference, and it's one you'll have to figure out if this ranch is to succeed—and if you're to have peace."

"I know, but I'm not sure how to get from where I am to what you're suggesting. It sounds easy to trust God, but it's hard when the person you always leaned on is suddenly gone." She ducked her head and whispered to herself in a low voice, "And God's the one who took him."

Joe cleared his throat and tapped his cane on the floor. "Reckon I'll go sit for a spell, if you ladies don't need me?"

Alex gave him a quick peck on the cheek. "Thank you both. I'd better check Papa's office and see if I can find any sign of that gold." She walked

out of the roomy kitchen and across the small foyer into her father's
pine-paneled office to the left of the front door. She paused and drew
a deep breath, taking in the sparse masculine aspects of the room and
inhaling the scent of his leather chaps still hanging on a hook nearby.

This had been his sanctuary and work space, all in one. It was the place
where the young Alex had run for comfort with her bumps and bruises or
when her heart was sore from the teasing at school. Papa had always made
time for her, always put aside his work and taken her on his lap.

The large oak rolltop desk sat under the window overlooking the
front yard. Alex squatted down and raised the hinged section, which
was inset into the wooden floor next to the desk. The lid of a safe lay
beneath the surface. She spun the dial one direction, then rotated it back
the other, repeating the process again. She grasped the handle, pulled up
the lid, and reached into the vault. A few envelopes and a small number
of bills. She set them aside and then thrust her hand back into the dark
hole. Empty.

"Find anything, hon?" Martha's worried voice coming from the foyer
preceded her into the room.

Alex stood and placed her hand on her hip. "Not yet, but I haven't
checked the desk, the bookshelves, or the closet." Alex rolled up the top
of the desk and rummaged in each cubbyhole then directed her search to
the drawers beneath.

Martha bustled over to the closet and threw the door open wide.
Guns, ammunition, old hats, coats, and boots stood in a jumble. "I'll
help. Your father never let me organize this mess, so it might take awhile
to wade through it."

They worked in silence for the next thirty minutes. The search
yielded childhood drawings of hers, which Papa had kept, and
storybooks they'd shared—items that brought a sting to her eyes. Alex
squashed her emotions and kept searching.

Finally, she sank back into her father's swivel chair. "I can't imagine anywhere else he'd have kept ore samples or a bag of gold, but they don't seem to be here."

Martha's forehead furrowed and she shook her head, worry clouding her normally calm face. "Maybe he took it to the bank?"

"No. Mr. Elton didn't see him again. Rob said Papa sent a wire to the seller saying he'd pay for the horses later."

"You don't suppose…" Martha stopped.

Alex tipped her head to the side and thought for a moment. "That maybe someone discovered the gold after he fell from his horse? I've been wondering the same."

"But Doc said he hadn't been dead long when John Sellers found him."

"I know. Besides, I can't imagine anyone robbing Papa and leaving him. Not in our little community. Most of the miners stay at their claims, but if one found him, they'd have stayed till help came."

Martha nodded and sighed. "We may never know. Send a wire to that breeder and see if your father paid him. And if not, try to stop those horses from shipping."

Alex groaned. "It never occurred to me they might still be coming. I'm headed to town first thing in the morning. I'll get a wire off, check with the assay office, and maybe stop to see Parson Moser or Elizabeth. I wouldn't mind getting someone else's opinion."

"Good idea, dear. You could use a friend right now."

Alex hugged the older woman and held her close for a moment. "I love you. Have I told you that lately?"

Martha patted her shoulder and smiled. "I think you have, dearie, but I do enjoy hearing it. You be careful. One accident in our family this year is enough."

Chapter Four

....

Alex rode Banner, her Morgan-Mustang cross, into Last Chance and
pulled him to a stop at the fir-sided telegraph building. She swung down
and shook out her split skirt, then tossed the buckskin's reins over the
hitching rail and stepped into the small office for the second time in as
many days.

Rob raised his head and a confused look clouded his face. "Miss
Travers?"

Alex leaned her palms on the table and smiled. "Sorry to keep
bothering you, Rob. I need to send a wire. Do you still have the address
for that breeder my father contracted with?"

"Sure do. I keep all those important records." His narrow chest
swelled with pride. "I'm a government employee, you know, and I do
my job right."

"I'm sure you do it wonderfully." She smiled at the beaming man.
"I'd like to send a wire to that same address. Would you copy it for me?"

"Certainly, Miss Travers." He reached for a pad and pencil, adjusted
his eyeglasses, and poised the pencil above the paper. "Go ahead."

"Hmm, let's see…" She pursed her lips and thought for a moment.
"Ben Travers dead. Stop. Are stallion and mares paid? Stop." She tapped
a finger against her lips. "If not, halt shipment. Stop. Please advise. Stop.
Alex Travers."

Rob finished scribbling and raised serious eyes. "I'll get that right
out. You goin' to be in town for a while, case an answer comes back?"

Alex nodded and stepped toward the open door. "Yes. I'm stopping
by the church to speak to Parson Moser and then the dry goods store

to see Elizabeth Anders. If the reply doesn't come today, I'll be back tomorrow."

A dreamy smile covered Rob's face. "Miss Anders?" He sighed. "She's a lovely lady."

Alex bit back a grin. "She certainly is. Thank you, Rob."

She stepped eagerly onto the boardwalk. A conversation with her parson and a meal with Elizabeth were just what she needed. She reached for her horse's reins then hesitated. It wouldn't hurt Banner to stand tied for an hour or two. She patted his neck and swung away from the rail. The church was a short walk, and the exercise would do her good.

She tapped on the office door near the back of the church building. "Parson Moser, would you have a few minutes?"

The door swung open and Bill Moser's portly form stood framed just inside. "Certainly, my dear. Come in and have a seat."

Alex spent the next few minutes sharing her predicament with her parson, who listened attentively and sympathetically. Unburdening her load felt good. Leaning back in the overstuffed chair, she asked him, "So what do you think, Parson?"

Bill Moser linked his hands behind his graying head. "I'm not quite sure. It doesn't sound like Ben to do something irresponsible. I can't imagine him sending for those horses without paying for them first." He twisted his mouth to the side and sighed. "You'll more than likely get word that the horses are paid in full."

"If Papa promised to buy them, I'd rather see them paid for than not. But while I'd love to introduce new blood into our herd, I can't say it's the best time, with Papa gone and the gold missing. Of course, maybe I can locate the spot where he found the gold." She shook her head. "But the country surrounding the ranch is rugged, with so many canyons. It would be like trying to find a mouse in a hay field. I sure hope God's got a plan for helping me pay off the note on the ranch. It's going to weigh heavy on me until it's paid."

"I'm sure He does, Alexia. Your part will be trusting Him and keeping your eyes and heart open."

She nodded. "You'll keep this to yourself, won't you?"

"Of course. But it might not hurt to let Sheriff Ramsey know. He could keep an ear to the ground, just in case."

She nodded and pushed to her feet. "Guess I should be going. I'm hoping to catch Elizabeth since it's about time for the store to close."

Parson Moser rose and came around his desk. "I think that's just what the doctor, or the parson, ordered," he said with a chuckle. "Nothing like a little woman-talk to set your heart at ease." He wrapped his arm gently across her shoulders, drawing her into a brief hug. "Don't worry, my dear. The Lord will make a way out of this turmoil. Try to trust Him."

Alex returned the hug for a moment. "I'll try." She stepped back and gave him a wry smile. "But you've known me for most of my life, and you understand how hard it is for me to depend on anyone."

The parson's response was cut short by a loud shout from somewhere outside. Alex jerked open the door without thinking. She bolted out of the office in time to see Ralph Peters, their huge blacksmith, racing across the small sanctuary and blasting through the front door, his massive legs devouring the distance.

* * * * *

Justin heard a loud holler and footsteps pounding the dirt behind him.

"Hey, you!" A man's voice split the air of the hazy summer afternoon. "Hold up there." The voice bellowed again.

He swiveled his head around. A lumbering man who appeared to be twice his size launched himself into the air. *What in the world?* The impact of two hundred and fifty pounds of solid flesh slammed into his side, nailing him to the dusty ground.

"Get off me, you oaf!" He struggled to move, but his arms were pinned.

The giant glared, his brows drawn together over angry eyes just inches from Justin's face. "You ain't going nowhere, buddy. Lie still and you won't get hurt." He tightened his grip on Justin's arms. "Pastor! You'd better get over here." He called to the man hurrying across the front of the church.

The arm beneath him started to tingle. Once again Justin attempted to shift his weight, but he couldn't budge. "What's the problem?" he asked angrily.

"Save it till the sheriff arrives." The gruff voice sounded inches from his ear. "Johnny, run and get the sheriff, would you, boy?"

"Sure, Mr. Peters." The high-pitched tone of an adolescent boy spoke out of range of Justin's sight, and light feet scurried across the hard-packed ground and onto the boardwalk beyond.

Justin desperately wanted to holler at his captor, but he doubted that would improve his standing. "Ease up, all right? You're about to break my arm."

The pressure lessened and Justin took a deep breath. *The sheriff'll sort this out.*

A door slammed, and again footsteps thudded across the wooden boardwalk. Justin gingerly turned his head. A pair of well-worn boots underneath black canvas pants strode through the dust two feet from his face.

"What's going on here, Pastor?" The gruff voice of the stranger reached Justin's ear.

Another voice answered. "I don't know, Sheriff. I was escorting Miss Travers out of the church when Ralph shouted something about the church being robbed. I got here in time to see this man lying on the ground with Ralph sitting on top of him."

Justin's thoughts ran wild. *Rob the church?* He'd done no such thing! He wriggled to free himself when he spied black-laced shoes peeking out from under the hem of a dark blue skirt. He turned his head with an effort. His eyes traveled up the fabric and fastened on the flushed face of a young woman staring down at him. Long, wavy brunette hair cascaded several inches beyond her shoulders, flying loose rather than secured in the customary bun. No bonnet adorned her glossy head, but the edge of a straw hat poked out from under her bent arm. Large blue eyes looked quizzically from a perfect oval face, but her lips were pursed in a tight line. He groaned at the injustice of his position and made one more futile attempt to free his arms.

The first voice spoke. "I'll take it from here, Ralph. Let this fellow up."

Ralph grunted and rolled off to the side then placed his meaty hands on the ground and heaved himself to his feet.

A calloused hand reached down and gripped Justin's, pulling him to his feet with a heave. "I'm Sheriff Carl Ramsey. What's your story?" A pair of gray eyes under bushy white eyebrows drilled into Justin.

"I'm not sure." Justin picked up the hat lying upside down in the dirt and slapped it against his pants, raising a cloud of dust. He glanced at the young woman standing on the fringe of the small group in time to see her avert her eyes. "This guy jumped me. That's about all I know."

The sheriff pivoted toward the large man, who stood with his arms across his chest. "Ralph?"

"Yeah." Ralph jerked his chin toward Justin. "I was comin' through the back door of the church to speak to the parson when I seen this character takin' off out the front door. Don't he look familiar?"

The sheriff scratched his chin and shrugged. "Can't say that he does. Who you think he is, Ralph?"

The big man glared at the stranger. "He's the spittin' image of Clay Ives, the horse thief. You got his Wanted poster on the wall at the jail. It says he's tall an' well built with blond hair and a black horse. This feller has a black horse tied to his wagon, and the rest fits, don't it?"

The sheriff turned his gaze on the silent man and waited for a response, but none came. "Want to tell me where you're from?"

Justin shrugged. "Nevada. And I'm no horse thief."

Ralph pushed his bulk forward and thrust out his chin. "So why'd you run when I hollered at you to stop?"

"I didn't run." Justin drew himself up and glared back. "I walked; you ran. You slammed into me, remember? I was heading to my wagon, minding my own business."

Ralph reached out a massive hand and wrapped long fingers around Justin's wrist. "I saw you stuffing somethin' in your pocket when you left the church. You steal somethin'?"

The scowl on Justin's face deepened. "What's in my pocket doesn't concern you." He wrenched his wrist free and took a step back, turning to the sheriff. "I went looking for the minister and didn't find him. I stuffed my handkerchief back in my shirt and started to leave when this loudmouth yelled at me." He glared at the blacksmith.

Parson Moser stepped between the two glowering men when a cry from the buckboard startled the group. Justin slapped the hat on his head and scowled. "Now look what you've done. Toby didn't get a long enough nap, and he's going to be cranky."

Ralph gaped, his mouth hanging open so far that his chin almost touched his chest. "You got a kid in there? Why didn't you say so?"

Justin put a foot on a spoke of the wheel and swung up into the buckboard's seat. "When would that've been? When you were sitting on me?" He leaned over the back of the seat and plucked a small boy out of the bedding. "Toby's missing his mama and needing a meal, and that's why I stopped at this church." He glared at the small group assembled below him. "Anyone care to help me, or do I keep on driving?"

* * * * *

Alex released her pent-up breath. She'd been afraid for a minute that the disagreement might lead to blows. The newcomer looked like he could care for himself, but Ralph was a broad-shouldered, stout man, and his work at the smithy had hardened his muscles till they resembled the iron he hammered each day.

At the sound of the little boy's cry, Alex stepped behind the parson, hoping she wouldn't be noticed. This man's troubles didn't concern her, but she couldn't help but gaze curiously at the newcomer.

Dust from the trail covered his frame. Broad, powerfully built shoulders tapered to a muscular chest and slim hips. Dark blond hair in need of a trim flopped into his eyes, and at least two days' growth of beard covered the firm jaw. A pair of angry brown eyes glared from under the broad brow, and a straight, strong nose sat above grim lips.

As he'd pushed to his feet, his shoulder muscles had rippled through the fabric of the sweat-stained shirt. When he was on the ground, she'd assumed he'd be shorter than Ralph's five-foot-ten height, but when he straightened, he'd topped Ralph by almost an inch.

Alex dropped her eyes before he caught her staring and averted her gaze to the stranger's horse. If the stallion tied to the back of the buckboard was any indication, he was a good judge of horseflesh. Deep liver-chestnut—almost the black that Ralph had claimed, with a long, tangled mane and a tail nearly sweeping the ground. Looked like he might have Thoroughbred in him, along with a strong strain of Arabian. Now there was a stallion she wouldn't mind using to build up her herd.

If the horse belongs to him, that is. She mentally shook herself, annoyed at the thought. Ralph's accusing him of stealing didn't necessarily make him a thief.

The fussing child drew her attention. The man was bouncing the boy on his lap to quiet him. He'd called the little chestnut-haired boy Toby, but what was *his* name? Toby plopped a dust-covered thumb into his mouth and laid his head against the man's chest. *Strange that he has a child with him but no wife. He said the boy was missing his mama. Is he meeting her on the trail?*

The sheriff stepped forward and placed a hand against the side rail of the buckboard. "What's your name, son?"

"Phillips." The terse answer seemed to be torn from the man's lips, and no smile softened the words. "I'm Justin Phillips, and this is my son, Toby."

Sheriff Ramsey stretched out a hand toward the stranger, who hesitated before grasping it.

"You just passing through our little burg or staying for a while?" The sheriff doffed his hat and wiped a sleeve across his brow then shoved it back on his gray head.

The man on the wagon shrugged. "Haven't rightly decided. Thought I'd try to find a meal for me and the boy, maybe get a bed for the night. I've no set plans." He glanced toward Alex, his dark brown eyes giving her a small start.

"Will your wife be joining you soon?"

"No. She passed away a few months back. It's just me and the boy." He looked down the street. "Is there a hotel around?"

Ramsey nodded and fingered his mustache. "Sorry to hear about your missus. There's the Last Chance Hotel, but it's no place for a child. Just one big bunkroom on the second floor. Mostly miners use it, and you have to climb a ladder from the outside. Saloon is downstairs but there's a nice little restaurant to the side, and there's a candy store and barber shop t'other side. The hotel can get a mite rough at times."

"Nothing else?" Justin patted the little boy's back and whispered something in his ear.

The sheriff nodded and pointed up the street. "There's a boardinghouse on the edge of town. Miz Alice Rice runs it. She's a spinster—and a good Christian. She don't tolerate no drinkin' or swearin' in her establishment, and she serves a right fine meal if you're a mind to spend the night. Real reasonable, and she'll even allow you to draw a bath."

Justin nodded, settled the child deeper on his lap, and reached for the reins with his right hand. "Thank you. I'll swing by Miss Rice's place and see if she has a room for me and Toby." His eyes shifted toward Ralph as a hint of a smile touched his lips. "After my welcome in Last Chance, I wasn't sure I'd get any help."

He cast a glance toward the parson, gave a sparse nod, and then looked straight at Alex. "Ma'am." He tipped his hat, but his eyes lingered for a moment and a quizzical look touched his features.

Alex stared back, feeling powerless to break the gaze. A slow blush rose up her neck and warmed her cheeks. She opened her lips, unsure of what she should say, when the slap of the reins on the horses' rumps snapped them shut again. She spun toward the church and ducked her head. She could hear the buggy moving down the road but didn't look back. The sheriff and parson could see the pair off.

Alex directed her steps toward her waiting horse. The visit with Elizabeth would have to wait until tomorrow. She'd been gone long enough.

* * * * *

The man stood in the shadows of the blacksmith shop, his mind replaying the scene he'd witnessed in front of the church. A stranger in town wasn't part of his plan, but from the looks of things, he was a drifter and would probably be moving on. The man slipped around to the back of the building and untied his horse. Time to go stir things up a bit. Alex didn't need to get too comfortable out at that ranch, no sir.

Chapter Five

....

Justin slapped the reins on the team's haunches and turned the wagon in the direction the sheriff pointed, toward the other side of the small town. He'd keep his eyes open and get the lay of the land. It wouldn't hurt to look around before heading to the ranch. Ben Travers's request for secrecy kept him from telling the sheriff his business. Time for that after he got Toby settled and spoke to Travers.

His thoughts drifted back to the attractive woman he'd seen at the church. She'd met his gaze without flinching and with no hint of coyness in her eyes. Molly had flirted with every man she met—offering empty promises and stirring men's pulses. Somehow Justin didn't get the same impression from the girl at the church—she didn't seem the type to put a lot of stock in her looks.

The horses' hooves raised little puffs of dust in the wide street that stretched between the buildings scattered along each side. A sign announcing CRAMER'S DRY GOODS STORE swayed in the light breeze that swept down from the surrounding cedar-and-pine-dotted hills cradling one side of Last Chance.

Justin's eyes were drawn to the saloon and gambling hall across the street. Such establishments used to be his home away from home. Never again, not with Toby in his life. He'd made a pledge that no liquor would touch his lips after he assumed care of his boy, and he'd see that the promise remained intact.

The batwing doors of the establishment swung open, and a young man in rider's garb fell onto the wooden boardwalk. Justin slowed his rig. A ruddy-faced man with red hair and a bartender's apron stepped out and looked down at the prostrate figure. "No fightin' in my joint, you hear? Come back when you're feelin' better."

He grasped the man by the wrist and hauled him to his feet then gave him a none-too-gentle shove toward the horses hitched at the rail. "Climb on yer horse and head out. No sense in getting yerself beat to a pulp—or shot."

The man dusted his shirt with a curse and then untied the reins of a sorrel gelding standing relaxed at the rail. He pulled the horse's head around and stuck the toe of his boot into the stirrup then swung up into the saddle without another word. Justin shook his head, remembering the days when he'd been in the man's situation—though never as early as mid-afternoon.

The aproned man turned his head and glanced at the slow-moving rig. He met Justin's gaze and tipped his head. "Nice stock you've got, stranger." His booming voice held a hint of an Irish brogue. "Passin' through, or stopping for a while?"

Justin brought the team to a standstill. "Thanks. I'm stopping at Miz Rice's boardinghouse."

"Riley is the name. Mosey back and join us for a drink after yer settled." A broad smile lit the man's round face and crinkled the skin around the blue eyes.

Justin shook his head and picked up the reins. "Sorry. I've a son to care for and can't be leaving him." Toby had curled up on the seat of the buckboard with his head on Justin's leg, sound asleep.

Poor little guy. The past two weeks had tuckered him out, with no time to play and few regular naps or healthy meals. Last Chance seemed friendly enough, and if Miss Rice had a room for more than one night, he'd settle there while he checked out the situation at Travers's ranch.

Riley raised a hand and turned back toward the doors. "Aye. Good afternoon, then."

"Afternoon." The creak of the wagon's wheels muffled Justin's reply, and the man disappeared back into the dimly lit interior of the saloon.

A huge yawn closed Justin's eyes for a second, nearly causing him to miss spotting a young boy bolting across the road in front of his team. "Ho, there! What's your rush, son? You about got stepped on."

The boy he remembered as Johnny bounded up on the boardwalk, paused, and turned back. "Nope. I'm pretty quick, and no horse will get me. Miz Rice give me a nickel for some eggs at the store, and I'm supposed to hurry. She's baking somethin' for her boarders." Johnny's freckles stood out against his sunburned face, and his mischievous eyes sparkled.

Justin's mouth watered at the thought of eating something home-baked instead of dry biscuits and jerky. "You'd better get a hustle on, but be careful of those eggs. Miss Rice mightn't be too happy if you bring them back broken."

"Yep, she'd lick me for sure." Johnny waved then darted through the rough-hewn door of the general store.

Justin clucked to his team and smiled at the space of time it took to travel the short distance to the boardinghouse. Quite a busy, friendly little town. A hand-painted sign posted above the door of the clapboard building next door read Doctor Is In. He shook his head in amazement. You didn't often find a doctor in a town that boasted so few people, but the surrounding mines and ranches probably brought in a fair amount of business. A small hotel on the far side of the doctor's office and a barbershop across the road completed the picture, and he guessed that the church might double as a school on weekdays.

A weathered gray-and-white house at the end of the street was identified by a sign nailed to the picket fence in front as Miss Rice's Boardinghouse. Colorful flowers hung in a bucket from the rafters of the small covered porch, and the tidy path to the house boded well for the cleanliness of the place. Green gingham curtains fluttered in front of the half-open windows to the left of the porch, and a hand-lettered sign reading WELCOME hung on the front door.

Justin pulled his team to a halt and moved Toby's head from his knee. Placing a bedroll gently under the boy's cheek before stepping down from the wagon, he tied the horses to the nearby gatepost and lifted the sleeping child into his arms.

His knock at the door brought the sound of rapid footfalls landing on a wooden floor, and seconds later the door swung open. A small, birdlike woman peered out from under bright red hair peppered with gray, which billowed around her face in unrestrained clouds. A pair of spectacles perched on the tip of her thin nose, and a long, slender finger reached up to push them back in place. She might have been forty, or she could've been fifty-five. It was hard to tell. Life could be hard on women in this country.

"Yes?" Her wary gaze swept over him in an instant, but when it landed on the sleeping child in his arms, her expression softened. "Come in! You've got your hands full, mister. Come lay the boy down in my parlor."

Justin stepped over the threshold onto the well-worn fir floor and followed his hostess two strides down a short hall to the doorway of a side room. His glance took in the green curtains and half-raised window. This must be the room he'd seen from the road. Clean and tidy like he'd expected, it was sparsely furnished with a small sofa, two button-backed rosewood chairs, and a round side table. A picture of a farm graced the mantel above the fireplace in the middle of the far wall, and a large braided rug claimed the room's center, its deep green and yellow hues bringing both color and a sense of tranquillity to the area.

Miss Rice bustled into the room and beckoned Justin over to the flowered sofa under the window. She reached up and drew down the sash, dimming the evening light, and patted the seat. "Lay him down here."

Justin bent and placed his sleeping son on the brocaded surface. The tiny woman placed a knitted afghan over the boy, tucking it under his chin with gentle fingers. She touched her finger to her lips and nodded toward the door. Justin followed her back into the hall, still within sight of Toby.

Miss Rice swung toward him and crossed her arms over her bosom. "What's your name, young man? You wanting a room for the night?"

Justin swept his hat off his head and wiped his brow with the back of his sleeve. "Yes, ma'am. The boy and I would like to stay for a few days, if you have room and don't mind taking a child."

Her eyebrows shot up into her unkempt hair, the only thing that appeared out of order in what he'd seen of this tidy home so far. "Mind? Of course I don't mind. I'd never turn a child away. Never. Can't say as much for a lot of parents, but children have to come first. Yes, sir, they do." She jerked her head down the hall and crooked a finger at him. "Follow me. What'd you say your name was?"

"Phillips, ma'am. Justin Phillips." He followed her down the hall, glancing into another small room. A table set for six nearly filled the space opening onto the roomy kitchen.

"It's Alice Rice, not ma'am. But you can call me Miss Alice. Most folks do." She stepped through the kitchen doorway that led into the dining room and pulled out a straight-backed chair. "Have a seat. Coffee?"

"Yes, ma'am—I mean, Miss Alice. I'd appreciate that." He placed his hat on the neighboring chair and took the seat offered. "Nice place you have here." Lace-edged curtains trimmed the window, and the glass sparkled in the late afternoon sun. The top of the pine table was waxed to a high shine, revealing the craftsmanship and care someone had lavished on the sturdy piece of furniture.

Miss Alice bustled into the kitchen and pulled open a cupboard door, exposing a stack of plates and bowls. She reached for two dark brown mugs and stepped across the kitchen to the wood stove in the corner. A coffeepot sat on the metal grate. Grasping the handle with a towel, she poured the mugs to the brim and set one in front of Justin.

Finally, she pulled out a chair and sank onto its hard surface with a sigh. "My feet aren't what they used to be." The cup of coffee sitting beside her went untouched, but she waved at Justin, urging him to drink. "What brings you and the boy to town?"

"We've been traveling for the past two weeks, and this looked like a nice spot to stop for a while," he hedged. The woman's eyes narrowed, and she seemed to catch the fact that he'd avoided answering her question directly.

"That your boy?" Her tone sharpened and she leaned her bony elbows on the table, peering at him through her eyeglasses.

Justin took a sip of the hot brew and set the cup back on the table. "He is. His name's Toby and he's just three. His mother died awhile back and I'm hoping to find someone to help with his care." There. He'd said more than he'd planned or wanted, but this woman didn't look like someone who'd give up easily when on the hunt for information.

She tilted back in her chair and clasped her hands in her lap, her face relaxing out of its harsh lines. "Too bad. I'm sorry you lost your missus." Her tone turned brisk. "I serve breakfast, lunch, and dinner, and you can have a room with two beds, if you'd prefer, or one full-sized instead. I have five rooms to let, with three of them filled. No smoking in the house, no chewing or spitting, no swearing or taking the Lord's name in vain, no drinking, and no lady friends in your room. That clear?"

"Yes, ma'am." He sat up straight. She didn't seem to mind that he'd used "ma'am" this time. "How much does each room cost?"

Her posture relaxed. "The room with one bed is cheaper, as there's less linen to care for. It's eight dollars a week, and the room with two beds is nine. That includes board. I won't charge you any extra for your little man since he won't eat much. 'Course, you can save a little if you pay by the month." She reached out and patted his hand. "Don't mind me, son. My bark is worse than my bite, although I don't tell everybody that. Pays to keep them guessing, know what I mean?" The hazel eyes twinkled and a small smile softened the strict lines of her face.

He grinned at the perky little woman. "I reckon I do. Don't worry, I won't give away your secret." He pushed back his chair and stood. "One bed is fine. I'd better get Toby up to our room where he can get a proper nap. Would you have any place I might give him a bath? I'm afraid it's been awhile since either of us have cleaned up proper."

"I do. I have a big washtub in the shed off the back of the house. I'll heat water on the stove, and when you're ready, you say the word. You can pack the hot water outside and draw cold water from the well and make you a right fine soaking bath."

She walked to the back door of the kitchen and pulled it open, stepped outside, and pointed a few yards down the porch. "Right back there is the tub, in that little room on the end, and back yonder"—she beckoned across the small yard to where a small, circular brick wall sat, a wooden framework above it—"is the well. I'd let you pump it here in the kitchen, but it's faster to draw out a bucket and dump it into the tub."

Justin nodded and smiled. "Thank you, Miss Alice. I haven't had a sit-down bath for longer than I can remember. Toby'll think he's in heaven."

"Come on. You can bundle up the child and I'll take you to your room. You'll meet the other boarders at dinner." She started to exit the room then swung back around and raised her hand. "One more thing—visitors are allowed in the parlor."

"Yes, ma'am. But I don't intend to have any visitors." A vision of the brown-haired girl at the church rose in Justin's mind, but he pushed it back down. He'd been down that road once before and found little to recommend it. No, a hired woman willing to care for his son while he worked would be the best thing for Toby. A wife wasn't in the picture.

He followed Miss Alice back to the parlor, a feeling of relief sitting firm in his chest. Rest. He'd almost forgotten what it felt like.

Chapter Six

....

Alex peeked through the small, dirty pane of glass next to the door of the assayer's office. Seeing no one, she pushed the door open then stepped over the threshold into the dimly lit room. In a building this small, kerosene light and a tiny window had to suffice. Lumber was easy to come by with the mill just outside of town, but windows were scare.

Her gaze drifted from the cluttered desk to the rough-hewn shelves covering one wall. An empty chair rested a few feet from the worktable, which was strewn with ore samples. Instruments lay where their owner had dropped them, and silence blanketed the room.

It didn't appear as though Samuel would be gone long, with the room unlocked and in disarray and his assistant, Fred, nowhere in sight. But still, Alex didn't like to wait. She wanted an answer to allay the worry growing inside.

Alex stepped out the door and peered up the dusty street, hoping to spot Samuel's stooped form heading her way. The sauntering figure of a man coming toward her drew her attention.

"Miss Travers." Sheriff Carl Ramsey paused to tip his hat, exposing his shaggy gray locks. "Business with Samuel?"

She hesitated then pulled the door closed behind her and joined the sheriff on the walkway. "Yes, but he's out right now. May I speak to you in your office?"

His gray brows rose but he nodded and gestured for her to move ahead. "Certainly." He adapted his long stride to her shorter one. How she hated wearing a skirt. Trousers gave a sense of freedom that this tangled mass of fabric could never do. She was sorely tempted to

65

disregard her father's wishes and wear them to town, but Martha would scold her if she tried. Wearing men's pants while working on the ranch was one thing, but doing so in town was another.

Sheriff Ramsey ushered her into his office. He waited until she had seated herself and then sank behind his desk, sticking his long legs out to the side and propping one foot over his knee. "To what do I owe this pleasure?" His smile crinkled the corners of his mouth and reached up to his twinkling eyes.

Sunlight streamed through the small window positioned above his desk and threw sparkling rays over the scattered papers. Sarah must have cleaned again; the shining windows testified to her handiwork. Alex sniffed, taking in the scent of freshly scrubbed floors. "You're lucky to have a wife who loves to clean."

He chuckled and straightened the pile on his littered desk. "Yep. Sure am. Drives Sarah plumb batty that I won't let her touch my desk. I know she's itchin' to come in when I'm gone and make everything neat and tidy, but I told her 'Hands off.' She don't need to be worryin' about who's busted out of jail or wanted by the law."

Alex grinned. "Sounds like Sarah. You're lucky to have her, you know." She removed her straw hat and placed it on her lap then smoothed her hair back from her face. "You heard about my father taking out a note against the ranch?"

His eyes widened a bit then narrowed. "No, sure haven't. Surprises me, though. Your pa didn't seem the type who'd go in debt."

She nodded. "Exactly. You asked about my business with Samuel. It seems Papa may have found gold on our land."

The sheriff's mouth dropped open. "Ah-huh. Well, now." He sucked in a breath and shook his head as though trying to clear it. "Who'da guessed it."

"He dropped ore samples off to be assayed, and I'm hoping to get the report. I was hoping he might've mentioned it to you, maybe given you an indication where it was located. With the gold gone that he borrowed from the bank..."

"Gone, you say?" Sheriff Ramsey leaned forward and placed his large hands flat on the desk. "What do you mean, gone?"

"Mr. Elton said Papa borrowed money and took it in gold. It wasn't found on him, and I've not found it at the house. I've searched the area where he fell but didn't find anything. Uncle Joe knew he'd found gold, but Papa never told him where."

"Uh-huh. That might bear lookin' into some. Yes, sir. Think I'll take me a little ride out to where he fell for another look-see around."

"Thanks, Sheriff; another set of eyes would help."

The sheriff held up his hand. "One more thing, Alex. You've known Carter Foster for years. His pa and yours were friends and neighbors. He might be a good man to turn to if you keep havin' trouble."

She placed her hat back on her head and tied the ribbon under her chin. "I'll keep that in mind, but I don't think it's anything Uncle Joe and I can't handle. Just thought you should know, you being the law and all. I'd best get back and see if Samuel's returned."

He pushed up from his chair, making it creak in protest as his lanky frame rose. "I'll let you know if I find anything."

* * * * *

Samuel kept his head down for a full minute after Alex stepped into the room, his gaze intent on a chunk of ore he turned slowly in his hand. A heavy magnifying glass hovered in one large hand, and he studied the rock from several angles before carefully placing it back on the table and raising his eyes.

"Miss Travers. May I help you?"

Alex stood in front of the desk, her hands clasped in front of her. "Good day, Samuel. I understand that my father brought in some ore a few weeks ago. Do you have the report?"

Samuel adjusted his eyeglasses and reached for a stack of papers on the corner of his cluttered desk. "Hmm. Ben Travers. Let's see…" He shuffled through the stack, one paper at a time, placing each one down before peering at the next.

Alex gritted her teeth and clenched her hands to keep from grabbing the stack and flying through them herself. Samuel might be thorough, but he wasn't known for his speed. A snail could flounder across the street before Samuel finished considering whether to step off the boardwalk.

He reached the last several pages and his hand paused in its search. "Ah…here's the paperwork. I knew I'd find it eventually." He pulled his eyeglasses from his face and waved them in the air. "I distinctly recall Benjamin bringing the samples in. However, he asked that I not disclose the results without his permission." He shoved the eyeglasses back into place and gave Alex a suspicious look over the rim.

She did her best to school her features into somber lines and not roll her eyes. "As you might recall, my father is no longer with us. He can't give his permission, and as I'm his daughter…" She braced her fingertips on the edge of the desk, leaned forward, and smiled. "I'm sure you won't have a problem giving me the report."

Samuel cleared his throat. "I suppose it would be appropriate, as you're his only kin." He adjusted his eyeglasses then glanced down at the paper and back up at her. "Hmm… Fred, my assistant, notes here that it was already picked up. Well now"—he rubbed his chin and squinted at the paper— "Fred writes that your pa gave us permission to give it to another gent."

Alex jerked upright. "What other gent? Uncle Joe?"

"I'm not sure. Fred didn't clear this with me." Samuel shoved his chair back from the rough-hewn worktable and set his eyeglasses down.

He swung around and stared at the door in the back of the room. "Fred. Come on out here." His bellow filled the room and Alex winced.

The door opened and a young man with a dirty mop of light brown hair shuffled into the room. He glanced at Samuel then his gaze darted to Alex. A wash of red crept up his neck and flooded his cheeks before he dropped his head and stared at the floor. "What'cha needin', sir?"

"Got a question for you." Samuel thrust the paper at the boy. "I found this receipt with your name on it. Says someone stopped in here with a paper from Ben Travers. You wrote down"—Samuel waved the paper under Fred's nose—"that he picked up the report on the ore. That right, boy?"

Fred's eyes rose to the level of the paper under his nose, and he stared at the words. "Yessir."

Alex tried to still her pounding heart. "When exactly was this?" Who had asked after her father's business? Had he empowered someone besides Uncle Joe? If so, why didn't Joe or she know about it?

"Hmm…let's see." Samuel scratched a spot on his fleshy cheek. "It don't say here on the paper what day he came by." He jerked his attention back to the red-faced young man. "Fred. You're not supposed to give out paperwork 'thout showin' me first. 'Sides, I told you to always date these things. It's important to date 'em." He shook the paper again and Fred took a step back.

Alex moved forward and lowered her voice. "Fred, do you remember who the man was and what day he picked up the report?"

Fred peeked at her. "I–I–I think it was the day your pa died. Your pa signed a paper sayin' it was all right to give it to the man."

"But that doesn't make sense. Papa planned on dropping the samples off that day, and he never made it to town."

Samuel drew himself up and dropped his hand to his side. "No, ma'am. Ben dropped off the samples a few days earlier so's we could get the assay done…."

Alex extended her hand and gripped the edge of the desk. "What do you mean? Uncle Joe told me he brought them to town that day."

"No, that was the second batch. He brought in the first bunch a week before. I tol' him I'd like more from another spot nearby, so's we could know the extent of the find. But he never arrived with the second batch. I don't believe the ore samples were found on him or his horse." He leaned back in his chair and folded his arms.

Alex looked from Samuel to Fred. "Do you still have that note—the one the man gave you?"

Samuel turned to Fred, eyebrows raised. "What about it, boy? That man give you the paper from Ben?"

"Yes, sir. But he asked for it back. The gent came a couple of hours a'fore your father's accident. He had a paper and said Mr. Travers sent him. He asked me to sign it so's he could show Ben he came by. Sounded reasonable, since you said Ben was wantin' the assay report in a hurry. I signed it and give it back." Fred clasped his hands in front of his waist and wrung them. "I asked him to sign a paper sayin' he took the report. That help you any?"

Alex nearly threw herself at the young man. "You have his name and signature? Yes, please show it to me."

Fred shuffled over to the worktable and reached underneath. He slid out a wooden crate, pried open the lid, and stood up with a paper clutched in his hand. "I tol' him we couldn't let no reports leave outta here without bein' signed for." He thrust the paper at Alex.

She reached out an eager hand and gripped the paper, her heart rate accelerating with hope. Maybe they could put an end to this mystery. She ran her eyes down the single sheet and stared at the bottom. "There's nothing here but a statement that someone picked up the report for my father, an X, and the name 'Tom' beside it."

Fred nodded. "I put down on the paper that the report was bein' picked up at Ben Travers's request and asked the man to sign it. He put his mark at the bottom."

Alex stifled a groan and rocked back on her heels. This was growing worse by the moment. "Can you describe him?"

Fred narrowed his eyes and looked up at the board-covered ceiling. "Let's see. About yea tall." He held a hand up to his own height. "Brown hair, maybe in his twenties, and not too heavy. Looked like a miner."

"That fits a few dozen men in the area. You didn't recognize him?"

"Can't say that I did. I'm sorry, Miss Travers. He said it was Mr. Travers's signature and I didn't question it, since Mr. Travers was waitin' on the results."

After scolding Fred one more time, Samuel waved him out of the room. He waited till the young man disappeared through the back door then pasted on a smile. "I'm sorry, Miss Travers. If he weren't my sister's boy, I'd never keep him on. He's a good boy, just don't always think."

Alex tapped the toe of her boot against the wood floor, working to stifle her irritation. "Do you remember the assay findings?"

"Oh yes, I certainly do. The ore showed a strong indication of gold. That's why I wanted a second bunch of samples, to confirm his find. But it looked like he'd hit a decent pocket. You find that gold, Miss Alex, and you'll be sittin' pretty. Yes, ma'am."

Alex headed out the door. She'd left her patient gelding waiting at the hitching rail long enough.

Chapter Seven
. . . .

The next morning Justin took advantage of Miss Alice's offer to watch Toby. He could think of one person he could ask about Ben Travers's location. His hard-heeled boots made deep thudding sounds on the rough-hewn boardwalk as he directed his steps toward Sheriff Ramsey's office.

The town looked only slightly different from ground level. Trees flourished on the edge of town surrounding Miss Alice's abode; some farsighted individual must have seen the value that shade would add to the home. A scattering of wildflowers dotted the landscape around a nearby house, and an old oak spread its magnificent boughs over the cedar-shake roof. According to Miss Alice, many of the trees suitable for timber had already found their way to the local sawmill. Three large oaks stood in front of the Last Chance Hotel, but only a few of the smaller pine, cedar, and fir trees lingered on Main Street.

"Mornin." Justin tipped his hat to a woman gripping the hand of a young boy as she stepped out of the mercantile and into his path.

"Who's that, Ma?" The youngster's voice carried back to Justin, but the mother's reply was lost in the tramp of feet heading the opposite direction.

Not a lot of people in town this morning, which suited him fine. He strode to the end of the boardwalk and down to the street below. A light rain had fallen during the night, settling the dust. He drew a deep breath, enjoying the smell of the freshly washed air.

He rounded the far corner of the mercantile and stepped up onto the walk. The door swung open and a woman stepped out. Justin altered his stride and attempted to swerve, but she did the same—right into his path.

His shoulder struck hers, and the box she carried careened toward the ground. Why hadn't he been watching more closely?

She took a stumbling step. "Oh, gracious." Her hands shot out, grasping at the air.

Justin abandoned his quest for the box and lunged toward her, clutching her shoulders and setting her upright. He retained his grip until she stood firm on her feet, staring down into the same pair of beautiful eyes that had peered at him as he lay in the dirt in front of the church. He groaned, released her, and stepped back. "I'm sorry, miss. I should've been watching my step."

A slow blush colored her cheeks and she swung her head, tossing her long hair to the side. "No, it was these miserable skirts. Why I have to wear so much fabric is beyond me."

He raised his brows and smiled, but he couldn't think of a thing to say that wouldn't embarrass her further or dig him a deeper hole. "I see."

"I'm sure you don't, but it doesn't matter." She shook out the folds of the offending skirt and then tipped her head and met his eyes. "Oh. You're the man that Ralph—" She stopped herself with a roll of her eyes. "Now I must apologize. I put my foot in the hem of my skirt and then in my mouth. Papa wouldn't be happy if he'd heard me."

"No need, ma'am." He retrieved her box and brushed the loose dirt from its sides. "I hope this wasn't something breakable."

"It's only sugar, so no harm done. But I'm glad it didn't burst, or there'd be no pie or cookies any time soon." A quick smile flashed across her face. "I've got more errands to run. Good day." She tucked the package under her arm and headed across the street toward the dry goods store.

Justin shook his head. First he'd landed in the dirt in front of her, and now he'd nearly knocked her into the street. *Hope I never have to see her again,* he thought, and then realized that his wish wasn't entirely genuine.

Justin forcibly turned his thoughts toward what had brought him down this street in the first place. He stepped off the walkway and across to the sheriff's office, just in time to see the man himself step out of the door. He picked up his pace.

"Sheriff?"

Carl Ramsey spun around, an alert look in his sharp eyes. "Phillips, right? Wasn't sure I'd see you again, after your reception at the church the other day."

Justin removed his hat, running his fingers along the wide brim. "That's what I'd like to talk about."

"Ah-huh." The sheriff peered from under shaggy brows and wagged his head toward the still-open door of his office. "Come inside."

They crossed the threshold in silence, and Justin waited till the door shut behind them. "Thanks."

Ramsey motioned with his head toward a chair and took the wooden one behind his desk. A loud squeak emanated and he winced. "Keep meanin' to oil that, but I never think of it when I'm up. How'd you find things over at Miss Alice's?"

"Nice lady. Offered to watch Toby so I could talk to you. Good food, too. I'm beholden to you."

The sheriff flashed a broad smile. "That woman sure can cook. My missus and I stop by there 'bout once a month and take a meal with her. Gives my Sarah a break from cookin'. Now, what's on your mind?"

Justin ran his fingers through his hair, wondering where to begin. The letter from Travers residing in his hip pocket was a constant reminder of why he'd come, but the need to move slowly had kept him silent until now. Sheriff Ramsey struck him as a fair man and a decent judge of character, based on the way he'd sized up the situation at the church. Travers hadn't indicated where the trouble lay, but Justin doubted that the man sitting across from him played a part in it.

He leaned forward and met the sheriff's interested gaze. "First, I need to tell you that Benjamin Travers sent for me. He asked that I not make that known, but I believe I can trust you. I don't know the area or where Travers lives, and I figure you've the right to know why I'm in town."

Ramsey's chair protested again as his weight shifted forward and his eyes bored into Justin's. "Travers, you say. Ben Travers sent for you? Why?"

"That's between him and me. If he cares to tell you, fine. All I need is some direction to his place."

"Afraid he can't tell me anything. Or you, for that matter. Ben Travers is dead."

Justin jerked up, nearly toppling his chair. "Dead. What do you mean? I have a telegram from him. He sent it a month ago."

"'Fraid his heart gave out. At least, that's what Doc Stevens thinks." Sheriff Ramsey crossed his arms and leaned back. "He just invite you out for a friendly visit?" He tipped his head at the vacant chair and waited until Justin settled back down.

"Travers said his ranch was in trouble and thought someone might be threatening his life. He asked me not to let anyone at the ranch know he'd sent for me. Said someone named Alex wouldn't appreciate interference."

The sheriff frowned and pulled at his mustache. "True, Alex is a mite strong-willed. Strange Ben didn't mention anything to me. You sure of your facts?"

"Yes. I kept his telegram." Justin shook his head, hoping to clear it of the shock that burrowed its way into his mind. "I can't believe Ben's dead."

Carl Ramsey sobered. "You say Ben told you the ranch was in trouble?"

Justin nodded and waited. The serious look on the older man's face indicated that his mind appeared to be mulling over a problem.

"He say what kind of trouble?"

"No, sir. I figured he'd tell me more when I arrived. He just asked that I get here quick."

The sheriff stretched out a leathery hand and smiled. "Care to let me read that telegram? If people ask questions about what you're doing here, I can answer honest as to your intentions."

"Guess it couldn't hurt." Justin pulled the creased and worn missive from his pocket and handed it over, watching the inscrutable expression on the sheriff's face. "Sheriff, I know it's an awfully bold thing to be asking when you hardly know me, but do you think his death might be more than it appears?"

Ramsey shrugged and shook his head. "I'd not go that far, leastwise not yet. There wasn't a mark on Ben's body; saw him myself. 'Sides, Doc Stevens is good as it gets 'round these parts. If he thought it was Ben's heart, I'm liable to take his word for it." The sheriff's gaze appraised Justin. "What're your plans now?"

"I'm not sure. I came expecting to meet Travers, but with him gone, I can't just go out to the ranch."

"You got a point there." The sheriff leaned back in his swivel chair and stared at the ceiling. "Let me think on this."

Justin got to his feet and slapped his hat on his head. "Toby's apt to be awake, and I promised Miss Alice not to be long."

The sheriff's chair came forward. "I'll be in touch. Think I'll talk to the reverend, if you don't mind. He and Ben were good friends."

"As long as he keeps it to himself. No way of knowing what direction the trouble came from."

Ramsey stood and stepped around his desk. "No worries there. The reverend knows how to keep his mouth shut." He stretched out a work-hardened hand. "Dealing with folks' lives day in and day out in a small town teaches you that much."

Justin shook the sheriff's hand and then headed toward the door. "Let's hope he can shed some light on it."

Chapter Eight

....

Alex stepped into Cramer's roomy dry goods store situated on the corner across from the bank and glanced around for her friend. The front counter was empty, but Elizabeth's voice drifted up from the end of an aisle. "I'll be there in a minute."

"It's just me, Elizabeth. Take your time." Alex walked to a table covered with bolts of fabric and fingered a blue-sprigged muslin. While she preferred men's pants on the range and for horseback, she wasn't completely averse to dressing up when necessary. She didn't like to think of herself as vain, but the glints of admiration she got when visiting Auburn went a long way toward dulling the pain caused by the catty tongues of the women in Last Chance.

Elizabeth emerged from the household goods aisle with Sarah Ramsey on her heels. The sweet-faced wife of their sheriff was a favorite to all, and one of the few women who always tried to draw Alex into the feminine circle in town.

"Alexia, how wonderful to see you." Sarah's beaming smile crinkled clear up to her eyes. "What brings you to town this fine day?"

"I'm hoping to talk Elizabeth into sharing a meal with me at the hotel." Alex raised her eyebrows at her friend and smiled.

"I'd love to. I'll join you for dinner when I finish Sarah's order. Want to wait for me, or should I join you there?"

"I'll wait. I'm not in a hurry."

Sarah Ramsey placed her handful of items on the counter and reached for her small reticule. "I won't keep you girls. How much do I owe you, Elizabeth?"

Elizabeth rang up the spool of thread, two pounds of sugar, and four yards of calico. "That'll be one dollar." The *ding* of the cash register and clink of the silver dollar dropping into the tray filled the quiet store. "Have a good day, and thank you for coming." Elizabeth walked Sarah to the door.

After the older woman stepped outside, Elizabeth flipped the sign on the door. She removed her apron and shook it then walked back to the tall wood counter and hung it on a hook. "I'm so glad you stopped, Alex. I've been thinking about you all morning."

Alex linked arms with her tall, willowy friend and smiled. "I've so much to tell you, but first things first—I'm starved."

Elizabeth drew the shade, pulled open the door, and locked it behind them. The street was quiet this time of day, as the miners only came to town on occasional trips and typically headed for the dining room next to the hotel or the saloon. New Caledonia mine lay a short distance from Last Chance, and Alex noticed a scattering of miners seated in the little dining room when she and Elizabeth walked through the door.

She nodded at a big bearded man seated across from a tall, angular woman at a small table just inside the room. "Mr. and Mrs. Gurney. How are you today?"

Clive Gurney looked up from his meal, and his heavily laden spoon paused midway. "Fair to middlin', Miss Travers. Mabel, you remember Miss Travers?" He turned to his dour-faced wife and nudged her when she didn't reply. "Mabel?"

"Ah yes, Alexia Travers." The woman's lips curved into a grin, but her unsmiling eyes appraised Alex from head to foot. "Wearin' blue 'stead of black, I see! Done grieving your pa already?" She glared at her husband and chortled. " 'Least she's not wearin' men's pants today!"

The skin above Clive's beard glowed red and his eyes blazed. "Mabel! You apologize to Miss Travers."

Alex held out her hand and shook her head. "Please. It's all right. I'm sorry if I bothered you. Have a good evening."

Elizabeth slipped her hand into Alex's and drew her across the room to a quiet corner away from the gaping crowd. "I'm sorry, hon. I don't know what's wrong with some of these women."

Alex slid into her chair and dropped her head into her hand. "Mrs. Gurney thought I was flirting with her husband." She lifted troubled eyes to her friend. "I've always known they thought I was standoffish because I don't attend the women's socials and I wear pants when I ride. But I had no idea they thought I had designs on their men!"

Elizabeth put her hand over her mouth and stifled what sounded like a choking sob. "Oh, my!" she gasped, trying to smother her laughter.

"What can possibly be funny?"

Elizabeth leaned back in her chair, lifted the napkin from the table, and covered her twitching mouth. "I had this rather sudden image of you and Clive Gurney running away together. Bushy, bearded, balding Clive Gurney, who's at least twice your age and three times your weight. Tell me that's not amusing!"

Alex stared at Elizabeth, but then the absurdity of the picture struck her and she began to giggle. It was the first time since her father died that she'd been able to laugh, and in spite of the strange circumstances that induced the laughter, she had to admit that it felt good.

A rumpled young waitress hurried to their table, wiping her hands on her apron. "What can I get for you gals? Ma made some tasty beef stew and biscuits, and she's got a big pot of beans, along with pie and coffee."

Alex leaned her elbows on the table and looked up. "Hmm, that sounds good, Lacey. And maybe a cup of coffee and some pie later."

Elizabeth nodded and smiled. "I'll have the same. Have you been busy today?"

"Yeah. Seems like when one person decides to come eat, a whole passel troops in. Dinner kept me runnin', but Ma's glad for the extra business." She sighed and turned to go. "I'm glad things've slowed now, but I'd best hustle 'fore anyone else drops by. I'll get your meal right out."

Elizabeth watched the young girl hurry back toward the kitchen on the far side of the crowded room. "Lacey's a nice girl. Too bad her mama's too cheap to get more help. It seems like she lives her entire life here."

"Miss Travers!" Rob Bartlett rushed into the room, waving a slip of paper above his head. "There you are," he wheezed as he trotted over to her table. "It came—your answer came. The horses—they're comin', Miss Travers. Looks like they'll be here in just a few days!"

Alex groaned then pasted on a smile and thanked the excited man. She waited until he headed back across the dining room before turning to Elizabeth. "Just what I need. More debt and horses I know nothing about. Why is God letting this happen? Wasn't it enough that Papa died? Can't He let me have a few weeks of peace?"

Elizabeth reached across the gingham cloth and patted Alex's hand. "Don't blame God. You know He loves you, no matter what's happened. You need to trust Him, Alexia."

"But it seems so unfair. It wouldn't be so bad if Papa hadn't taken out the mortgage on the ranch. But to have the gold disappear and these horses coming and my hired hands questioning whether I'm capable of running the ranch…" She drew a long, deep breath and shook her head. "I don't understand where God's supposed to be in all of this."

"Right beside you, where He's always been. Does the Bible promise that life will always be fair after we give our lives to Him?" Elizabeth smiled and tipped her head to the side. "You know it doesn't. But He promises to give you the strength and grace to get through the tough times, if you'll trust Him."

Alex sighed. "I know. You're always right, Elizabeth. I'm sorry to burden you with my complaints."

Elizabeth's warm brown eyes softened. "You can complain to me anytime you want to, as long as that independent streak of yours doesn't take over and make you decide to do something foolish."

Alex bit her lip and tried to look serious. "Who, me? Independent? Why, honey, I'm just as sweet-natured and compliant as they come."

Elizabeth covered her mouth and giggled. "Yes, and I'm going into seclusion at a monastery soon." She dropped her voice. "But truly, Alex—God really will take care of things if you'll just quit fretting." She propped her arms on the table and leaned forward. "Now tell me all about this handsome stranger who stopped at the church the other day. The whole town's been talking about it."

Alex shrugged. "Good looking or not, I don't think he intends to stick around. He seemed like more of a drifter to me."

Elizabeth narrowed her eyes and a sly smile crept around her lips. "Ha! So you did notice his looks."

Alex felt the heat rise up her neck and stain her cheeks. "Well, I'm not blind."

The two girls laughed and turned at the sound of footsteps stopping nearby. Lacey stood next to their table, coffeepot in hand and a dreamy look on her face. "I'm not blind, either. He stopped in for coffee yesterday evening, and he sure does clean up right fine." She let out a heartfelt sigh and refilled their cups then floated away to the next table.

Alex looked at Elizabeth and put her hand over her mouth. "Lacey's got it bad. She might be the answer to that man's prayer. She'd make a great mama to his little boy and get out from under her mother's thumb all at the same time."

Elizabeth shook her head and leaned back in her chair. "From what I've seen, I don't think so. He looks like a man who knows what he wants, and I doubt it's a dreamy girl hoping to escape her mama."

Alex placed her napkin on the table and pushed back her chair.

"I guess it's a good thing God didn't put us in charge of the world *and* matchmaking, huh?" She fingered the gold locket hanging on a slender chain around her throat.

"A very good thing." Elizabeth leaned across the table and touched the locket. "Your mother gave you that, didn't she?"

"Yes, and my grandmother gave it to her. When Mama knew she might not live through the birth of my little brother, she slipped it off and put it around my neck. I've not removed it since."

"One of these days you'll need to put a special photograph in there." Elizabeth rose and stepped around to slip a hand through Alex's arm. "Come on. Let's take a walk. You've never seen the gent in question 'all cleaned up,' as Lacey says. Maybe we'll bump into him."

Alex felt grateful that Elizabeth's head was turned. The reminder of her encounter with the handsome stranger on the sidewalk not long ago sent another flood of color to her cheeks. "I'll walk with you for a few minutes, but not because I'm interested in seeing the drifter again— whether he's 'cleaned up' or not."

Elizabeth didn't reply, but a smug little smile clung to her lips as she tugged her friend out of the room.

Chapter Nine

....

Alex sat on Banner and leaned her hands against the pommel of her saddle. The knoll where she'd stopped stood several hundred feet above the high plateau and gave her an excellent view of the ranch.

She'd ridden to the far side of the property not long after sunrise, needing time alone. Over the years, she'd discovered that her mind worked best when on horseback, so she'd saddled Banner, whistled to Hunter, and headed for her favorite lookout.

Distant bay, sorrel, and black horses dotted the plateau floor, and occasional puffs of dust rose under the hooves of young foals racing across patches where the grass hadn't yet returned. The ridges of the Sierra Nevada range loomed over it all, casting impressive shadows over the high mountain plateau. The sound of the wind whispering among the sugar pines soothed Alex's agitation.

She swung from the saddle, slipped her horse's reins around a low-hanging branch, and whistled sharply. Before long she heard a crashing in the dense mesquite as Hunter bolted through and dashed to her side, his big pink tongue lolling and his sides heaving. "What've you been hunting, you big goof?" She stroked his black ears and looked into his soulful eyes. "Where's your stick? Go find it."

Hunter streaked away and began a frantic hunt under the nearby trees. A few minutes later he returned triumphant, a large stick clamped in his jaws.

Alex held out her hand, and the dog obediently placed it on her palm. He stepped aside, his gaze never leaving the stick. She leaned back and heaved her entire body into the throw. Hunter's long strides covered the distance almost before the stick landed near the stream bank.

Alex continued the game for a few minutes then sank onto the grass and patted the ground beside her. "Down, Hunter. That's enough— no more."

The quiet of the spot reached out and embraced her, wrapping tendrils of peace around the trouble still surging in her mind. While her father's decision to mortgage the ranch and keep it a secret baffled her, another part of her heart admitted he'd known her better than anyone. He'd understood her dread of change and how hard she'd fought against it all her life. She'd been her father's daughter for so many years, and an independent woman besides. He must have realized she'd want to succeed on her own.

He'd had high hopes she'd meet a man and marry someday, and he used to tease her about becoming an old maid. In her heart she admitted to occasional loneliness, but she didn't feel the need for a husband. She could break a young horse, deliver a foal, shoot as well as Uncle Joe or Papa, mend fences, ride herd at night, and track with the best of the hands. About the only thing she couldn't do was cook, and she cheerfully left that to Martha. Nobody cooked like Martha anyway, so she saw no sense in trying.

A wet nose and soft whine brought her back to the present, and she stroked Hunter's head. "I'll keep this ranch and make it succeed on my own. I don't want to share it with anyone but you, Martha, and Uncle Joe."

Hunter crept a little closer, laid his head on her knee, and gazed into her face, his ears cocked forward. "Do me a favor? Chase off any men that come courting and I'll throw a stick for you anytime—deal?"

He tipped his head to the side and his entire body wriggled.

"Good boy. We'll keep life the way it is now."

Alex pushed to her feet and the big dog jumped up, watching her every move. "Guess we'd better go check on the foals. Nothing will get done while we sit here moping." She untied the buckskin's reins and swung up into the saddle. The view from this hill never failed to satisfy her continual longing for freedom.

Why couldn't she have been born a man? Running the ranch alone wouldn't be an issue. Why in the world couldn't women be treated the same as men? She shook her head, knowing that wouldn't happen in her lifetime. At least she still wore the pants on her ranch. She grinned and looked at her legs. Quite literally—and if she had her way, that's how it would remain.

* * * * *

Two hours later Alex rode onto the ranch and swung down in front of the barn. They'd covered some distance and she'd given the gelding his head, allowing a fast gallop across the valley floor. Banner loved the freedom, and the run had somewhat loosened the hard knot lodged in her chest.

"Alexia? You have visitors, dear." Martha's strong voice floated across the open area between the house and the barn. "Charlie and Walter both arrived a few minutes ago and are inside washing up. I told them I'd bring tea and cookies to the front porch. You can join them there when you're finished."

Alex groaned and rolled her eyes, not excited about the prospect of visiting with either of the young men. She'd known them since childhood, but in the past few years they'd tried to transform themselves from playmates into suitors. She'd humored them in the past, always keeping them at arm's length.

She unsaddled and rubbed Banner down in record time then left him munching grain in his stall. One of the ranch hands could've cared for her horse, but the few extra minutes gave her time to adjust her attitude from annoyance to graciousness before she met the men waiting on the porch.

"Hey, Alex!" Charlie Danson waved a big-boned hand that protruded from a rumpled shirtsleeve. "Did you have a nice ride?" He sat sprawled across a large wooden bench in the shade of the veranda, looking every bit the unkempt miner's son she remembered from his preceding visits.

Alex sighed. Just an hour ago she'd wrestled with her not wanting to change, but as she looked from untidy Charlie to prim and proper Walter, she wished for a teensy bit of change, just this once. These two young men had been trying to court her for months, and each of their visits was a virtual replay of the one before.

Charlie's aversion to riding a horse appeared to have driven him on foot from his father's nearby claim. Mud caked his rough work boots, and dried sweat had cut little rivulets through the dirt on his face. Walter's fastidious appearance stood in sharp contrast, his neat black suit brushed and his hat shining.

Walter peered over the top of his eyeglasses at her clothing and frowned. "Aren't you going to change, Alexia?"

"No." She stepped up onto the porch and sank into a nearby chair. "I've been checking the foals in the upper pasture and I'll be heading back out after you leave, so I see no reason to change."

She glanced at his crestfallen face and felt a twinge of guilt for her harsh tone. Patting his hand, she added, "I'll get you both more tea." She reached for their mugs and headed into the house, leaving two very quiet young men on the porch.

A few moments later she slipped back onto the long porch, her tray laden with refilled cups and a heaping plate of cookies. She reached the corner and started to turn when a loud whisper slowed her steps.

"Why don't you head home, Charlie? You know Alexia's always been interested in me, not a big overgrown kid like you." Walter's severe words brought Alex to a halt.

"Aw, shucks. That ain't true, and you—you—you know it." Charlie's slow, rather pained speech caused Alex to wince. "She's my friend, too. I've knowed her longer than you, and my pa runs a mine. He don't just work at the mercantile."

"My father doesn't work at the store, he owns it," hissed Walter. "It's not doing you any good hanging around here. I mean to court Alexia proper. You don't know anything about what ladies want—all you understand is dirt and rocks."

Alex rolled her eyes and groaned. Charlie and Walter had been rivals since grammar school, but this was ridiculous. The last thing she wanted was for either of them to court her, and the sooner they realized it, the better.

She stepped around the corner of the covered porch and crossed the last few yards in long strides. "Here you go! More cookies and tea." A swift glance at Charlie's red face and Walter's sullen countenance gave her resolve. "I'm sorry to leave you boys, but Dad's passing left a lot on my shoulders. Not that I can't handle it, of course," she added as a look of sharp triumph crossed Walter's face. "It leaves me less time to socialize, and I really must get back to my chores."

Both young men started to protest and rise, but she waved them back. "Never mind getting up. Sit and finish your cookies. I'm sure you haven't chatted with each other for some time. Feel free to ask Martha for anything you need." She stepped off the porch and headed for the barn, trying to hide a grin.

"But...wait!" Walter sprang to his feet and swung to the edge of the porch. "I wanted to take you for a drive in my buggy. It's going to be a fine evening. I'm sure your ranch hands can take care of the chores, Alexia."

"I'm sure they can, too, but what kind of example would that be, asking them to do my work?" She shook her head, keeping a straight and solemn face. "No, sir. That's not what they're used to, and I don't intend to change. Would you give Charlie a ride home? I'm sure he'd appreciate the offer." She didn't try to hide her grin this time, as her pant-clad legs carried her the last few strides to the barn.

* * * * *

Justin nodded at a few friendly faces on his way from the boardinghouse to the church, but he didn't slow to chat. He had to make a decision about Toby.

A freight wagon loaded with bulging burlap bags pulled to a stop in front of the general store, and the driver jumped down to tie up his team. Justin veered around the end of the wagon and stepped over a wide stretch of mud.

The loud bark of a dog preceded the screams of a young boy, as a brown-speckled hound dashed down the middle of the road with a ragged youngster on its heels. "Hey, you! That's my hat! Bring it back." The boy's tousled curls shone in the sun and his shirttail whipped in the breeze as he disappeared around a corner close on the hound's heels.

Justin chuckled and shook his head, remembering his own youthful antics. He'd bet the youngster wouldn't give up until he'd caught the hound and then all would be forgiven. Boys and dogs seemed to have an understanding, and their upsets often turned to play.

He crossed an open grassy area and slowed in front of the church, suddenly remembering the humiliation he'd suffered at the hands of the local blacksmith not many days ago. The big brute had better not try anything today. Tackling him when his back was turned might have worked once, but that wouldn't happen again.

The church looked like a recent addition—the cedar shakes on the roof hadn't grayed from the sun, and the paint on the siding hadn't peeled. Clean windows sparkled in the morning light, and caring hands had planted flowering bushes near the front door. A bell high up in the steeple hung silent, but it held an air of expectant waiting.

He stopped near the double front doors and reached for the handle when it suddenly swung open and a man pushed his way through. Justin drew back, wondering at the determined expression on the man's face. Parson Moser followed as far as the open door and stood without speaking. He nodded at Justin.

The man jerked at the reins tied to the rail and loosened his horse. "Pastor, I'd appreciate your help—a woman's going to have a rough time making a success of that ranch." The dark-haired man shoved a broad-brimmed hat onto his head. "Never mind; I'll ride out and tell her myself." He raised a hand to the parson, ignoring the man standing nearby, then swung up into the saddle. A jerk pulled the horse around, causing him to stamp and snort. The rider touched the gelding with his spurs and cantered toward the hills.

"Mr. Phillips, I'm sorry for the poor welcome. Won't you come in?" Parson Moser stepped toward Justin, his hand outstretched.

Justin shook the man's hand and nodded. "Don't mind if I do. Something's weighing on my mind." He stepped ahead of the parson into the cool darkness of the small sanctuary. "And I'd be pleased if you'd call me Justin."

"Certainly." The parson motioned Justin toward the back of the church and ushered him into the tiny room that served as an office.

The area appeared neat, and the aroma of fresh leather filled the air. Justin sniffed appreciatively and glanced around, drawing a chuckle from the older man. "Even preachers have to care for their gear. Never know when you're going to get called out to a ranch or a mine. I just oiled my bridle." He nodded to the simple leather headstall hanging on the back of a nearby chair.

"You don't use a buggy?" Justin settled into the chair across from the small wood desk. "I'd have thought—"

"That it's more fitting for a man of my age and station?" Parson

Moser smiled. "I do if the weather's bad. But I grew up on horseback. My father owned a ranch, and I rode herd before becoming a preacher. I guess straddling a horse is still in my blood."

Justin relaxed, liking this man even more. "I'm hoping for your help."

The parson leaned forward, clasping his hands on the worn desk. "Name it."

"It's about my son." He drew a deep breath. "I need to find work and I can't care for Toby at the same time."

"I see." Parson Moser nodded and met Justin's gaze. "What are you thinking?"

"Are there any families in your church who'd consider taking in a little boy?" He winced as the words left his mouth. "I don't mean permanent, just for a short time till I can get a job and figure out a way to care for him at the same time...." His words trailed off and he bowed his head, certain he'd see censure in the preacher's eyes.

Parson Moser cleared his throat. "Hmm. That may not be the only option, if you love the boy and want to keep him."

Justin's head jerked up and he almost glared. "Of course I love him. I didn't have much say in his raising, but I'd do anything to keep him. If there's another option, let's hear it."

A smile crept across the older man's face, crinkling his mouth at the corners and lighting up his eyes. "There might be, if you wouldn't mind working at a ranch owned by a woman."

"A woman?" Justin shook his head. "I don't follow."

"Miss Alexia has a large spread a couple of miles out of town. Her man Joe helps run the place, but I'm guessing they might need help."

"Where does Toby fit in?"

"Martha's the housekeeper—she's been there for years. She loves children and might care for your son if you were hired. Talk to Joe Todd—he's been on the job since the ranch started. I think he does the hiring, and he's a good man. Tell him you stopped here and that I sent you." He leaned forward and met Justin's eyes. "One thing, though. Can you ride, rope, and break a horse?"

A slow smile spread across Justin's face. "Yes, sir. That I can."

"Then pack your duds and offer your help. I can't imagine Joe'll turn you down. Ride east out of town about a mile and a half. Cross a stream and head up a hill. The ranch is on a long plateau." He pushed back his chair and rose, offering his hand. "Good luck. You may be the godsend that ranch is looking for."

Justin nodded. "Thanks. I'll take your advice." He shook the parson's hand and jammed his hat back on his head. Time to get Toby and head out. Maybe his luck had changed and he'd find one last chance at the ranch up the road.

Chapter Ten
....

Alex shaded her eyes, looking toward the sinking sun at the man on horseback riding up the lane. His seat in the saddle looked familiar, but the glare of the sun in her eyes didn't allow clear visibility until he'd almost reached the porch.

Carter Foster pulled his horse out of its slow trot and rested his hand on the pommel. His smile lit up the serious planes of his face. "Alexia, I haven't seen you in some time. Sorry to hear about your father's passing."

She allowed herself a brief nod and a small smile. "Thank you. What brings you out this late in the day?"

He rested his hands on the pommel of his saddle, and a pained expression creased his handsome face. "I've been worried about you since Ben died. I'd have attended the service, but business took me east for a spell. I only returned a few days ago."

She crossed her arms and leaned against a nearby pillar. "So you came to offer your condolences?"

He shook his head and smiled. "Aren't you going to ask me to step down?"

She had no desire to entertain him, but common courtesy demanded it. "Of course, and I apologize. I'll ask Martha to bring some coffee to the parlor. Have you eaten?"

He stepped down from his gelding and knotted the reins around the rail. "I've eaten. Coffee would be fine, thanks. But it's a lovely day. How about having a cup with me here on the porch?"

"I don't mind taking a break. I'll be right back. Help yourself to a chair." She hurried to the kitchen and nearly bumped into Martha in the doorway. "Do you have a pot of coffee on?"

The bustling woman wiped her hands on a towel and then tossed it on a hook. "Of course. When don't I have hot coffee? Who's here, and why don't you bring them in?"

Alex opened a cupboard door and pulled out an earthenware mug. "Carter Foster. He prefers to stay on the porch."

Martha grunted and frowned. "Strange him coming here now. We didn't see much of him when your pa was alive. Wonder what he wants now that Ben's gone?"

"Now, Martha, that's not fair. You know Carter travels to Auburn on business. I'm sure he'll be around more, now that he's running his pa's place the way I'm running mine." Alex wrapped a towel around the handle of the coffeepot sitting on the stove and poured the hot brew into the mug. "Besides, you know that Papa and Mr. Foster were old friends—and distant cousins to boot. Papa always said we should be kind to family."

"Sure, and I agree with that, when they're *family*. But Carter Foster is so far removed you can't rightly call him that. He's after one thing. This ranch. And I'd not be surprised to learn that he'd like *you* in the bargain."

Alex turned so fast she almost slopped the coffee. "Martha! Carter's always been decent to me. But I'm not in love with him, so you don't have anything to worry about."

Martha picked up a big pot of steaming water from the back of the stove and poured it into the washbasin. "He may be nice enough, but he's too old for you. Even if his daddy left him a big ranch and enough money to buy this place three times over, it don't make him the right man for you."

Alex patted Martha's shoulder. "Clarence Elton did tell me he offered to pay off the note and buy the ranch if I had any problems. But don't worry," she hurried when Martha turned a grim face her way. "I do not intend to sell him the ranch. But I need to hear him out."

Martha sighed. "I reckon we'd best be polite, even to those who think they're better than the rest of us." She plunked dishes in the water so hard that Alex winced. "But don't you be inviting him to dinner."

Alex laughed and hugged Martha then headed toward the front porch with the coffee. Carter reclined in the swing, pushing off against a post with his dust-covered riding boot. His black broadcloth suit and matching hat looked new and appeared little worse for the ride from his place.

He stretched out a hand that hadn't seen much hard labor and grasped the mug of coffee. "Thank you, Alexia."

She sank into a padded wicker chair a few feet away and sipped her cold tea. "I'm curious as to what brings you out this way. It's not like you to visit without a reason."

He shot her a direct look and laughed. "Never one to hide how you feel, are you, my dear? Can't I make a social call without raising suspicion?"

"I doubt a social call brought you here, Carter. Clarence Elton told me you stopped by the bank."

"Ah." He lifted the mug to his mouth but didn't drop his eyes. "I'll get to the point, then. I'd like to buy the ranch." He raised a hand when she started to protest.

Alex drew a deep breath, released it slowly, and nodded.

He set his mug on a table nearby and laced his fingers in his lap. "I can offer you top dollar for the land and the horses, and I'll keep on any wranglers who care to stay. You can't run this place by yourself. I understand you've already lost at least two hands, and others will probably follow. If you can't keep up with the ranch, you may lose your contract with the cavalry. Why not sell now? Move yourself and Martha into town. You'll have enough to keep you in a nice little house for years, or at least until you find a husband." He grinned and leaned back in his seat.

Alex shifted in her seat, suddenly wishing she'd listened to Martha about inviting Carter to stay. An offer for her ranch didn't bother her so much, but the ongoing insistence that she needed a husband was growing old. She raised her gaze and kept it fixed on Carter's smiling face. "No thanks, Carter. It's not that I don't appreciate the offer, but Papa taught me enough to make a success of the ranch. This is my home, and I have no intention of moving." She set her glass down on the arm of her chair with a little more force than she planned, and liquid spilled over the side.

"I know that mortgage will be hard to meet. I could offer an alternative that would solve your problems and allow you to keep the ranch."

Alex picked up her tea and took a sip. "And what would that be?"

"Marry me, and the ranch would still belong to you. We'd run it together, and with my ranch adjoining yours, we'd be the largest force between here and Auburn."

She gasped and nearly choked on her drink. "Marry you? But—I don't love you."

A smile softened his features. "I care for you, Alexia. I wanted to court you properly instead of rushing this, but with your father gone… well, I thought I should declare myself."

Alex clasped her hands in her lap and bowed her head, trying to sort her thoughts. Carter wasn't like Charlie or Walter—he was older, more mature, and with a spread almost as big as her own. A bit of a dandy, perhaps, and content to slide along on family money, but a decent sort nevertheless. She looked up into his handsome face. The offer wasn't distasteful, just unexpected. If she never found someone to truly love, could she marry to save the ranch and all she'd grown up loving? She drew a deep breath and squared her shoulders. "That's kind of you, Carter, but I can't say yes to something this sudden. I've never considered you in that regard."

"I'm sure you'd come to care for me. I'd be good to you, Alexia. And think of the land we'd own between us. You control one of the best water sources within a hundred miles. My place adjoins yours and is covered with good timber. Besides, I have enough money for both of us, and your worry about the mortgage would be over."

She set her glass on the porch and rose. "I'm sorry. I'm not prepared to make a decision like that based solely on finances."

The eager light dimmed in Carter's eyes, but he maintained his smile. "Life would be much easier for you."

She shook her head and stepped away. "I won't say yes, Carter, but I appreciate your offer and I'm honored that you care."

He settled his hat on his head and straightened his bow tie. "Since you didn't say no, the proposal stands," he said softly. He stepped off the porch, untied the reins from the hitching rail, and swung into his saddle. "I'll stop by again. I'd hate to lose touch with my great-uncle's only surviving family." His face lit with a stunning smile. "And I'm not giving up hope that you might change your mind."

"You're welcome to stop in again." She watched him turn his horse and trot from the yard before he laid a spur to his horse's flank and urged him into a canter.

A small part of Alex feared that Carter might be right. According to Uncle Joe, unrest seemed to be stirring among the few wranglers that remained. She'd have to find a way to rally them, prove her mettle as a boss. And somehow she'd find a way to raise the money to pay off that mortgage. She had to. Losing the ranch wasn't an option—and right now, at least, neither was marrying Carter Foster.

Chapter Eleven

....

Justin lifted Toby from the security of Miss Alice's arms, placed the boy
on the saddle, and then swung up behind him. He'd almost left his son
at the boardinghouse but then reconsidered. Joe Todd deserved to know
the package he'd be getting if he hired him. Besides, the housekeeper
should meet Toby and decide if she wanted to care for him. If she wasn't
interested, Justin would move on. He'd made that decision in the small
hours of the morning. Although he'd not spent much time caring for the
boy in the past, he knew he wanted a place in Toby's future.

"Ready to go for a ride?" He ruffled the boy's hair and picked up
the reins.

"Want to wide the horsey myself, Papa." Toby's small hands reached
out toward the reins.

"Maybe later. We'll see what we can do about teaching you to ride
soon." He touched his heel to Durango's flank and the stallion moved
forward. The horse's hooves made small plopping sounds in the mud that
had accumulated from last night's rain. He kept the stallion at a walk,
avoiding the small cluster of women who skirted around a large puddle
in the middle of the street.

As he neared the edge of town, a squawking rooster flew in his
path, causing his horse to sidestep and snort. "Easy, Durango." He
clucked to his mount and picked up the pace. The cool morning breeze
made him thankful for the warmth of his buckskin jacket. A quick glance
reassured him of Toby's comfort, as well. Miss Alice had bundled him
in a small woolen coat and cap she'd found discarded by a previous
boarder.

The parson's directions pointed him onto a road that climbed a sharp incline and headed up through the scrub pine.

Justin recalled that Benjamin Travers had homesteaded a high mountain plateau a few miles from town. He'd have to ask if it adjoined the ranch where Joe Todd needed help. Parson Moser had mentioned a woman owning it, but it sounded as if Todd was likely the manager, seeing as he did the hiring. Justin figured the owner must be a widow. He'd heard stories of other women who'd been left alone on cattle ranches and had to call on outsiders to ramrod the hands after their husbands died.

His mind turned to Ben Travers. He knew that Travers's grazing area covered a section several miles long, where he ran numerous horses and only a scattering of cattle for beef. Well he remembered the older man's love for fine horseflesh. He'd turned his eye toward developing one of the finest bands of horses in the western half of the country and had become the envy of ranchers across California. What a shame the man had passed on before he could realize his dream—or uncover the root of the trouble he'd hinted at.

A small hand tugged on his arm and Justin looked down into Toby's upturned face. The boy pursed his lips and crinkled his brows. "Where we go, Papa?"

"To see a nice lady who lives on a horse ranch."

"Toby wide a horsey?" He sat up straight and smiled, and Justin wondered how anyone could resist the winning blue eyes.

"We'll see, son." He encircled the small shoulders and pulled the boy close. "Let's talk to the lady and see if she'd be willing to take care of you while Papa works."

"Okay. I ask the lady to wide the horsey." Toby's mouth set in a determined line and he gave a decisive nod, bringing a hearty chuckle from Justin.

"I'll bet you will at that, my boy." He pulled the horse to the right at the fork then headed for the ford in the small stream. Must only be a short distance from here. Stately Douglas fir trees dotted the countryside, interspersed with smaller pines. Early summer flowers peppered the small open field and cascaded the area with a beautiful array of color. Molly had always loved bright, vibrant colors, and she would have loved this scene. What a perfect place for a home.

He shook his head. No sense in pining over something that was never meant to be. The past was over, and the future still waited to be written. Today was all he'd been promised, and he'd make the most of what he'd been given. Toby was his family now, and nothing would break that bond.

A black-tailed deer jumped from the brush fifty yards ahead and sailed across the hard-packed road. The chattering of a squirrel in a pine caught Justin's attention. He watched with amusement as the small creature attacked the base of a pinecone and dropped it to the ground. It raced to a nearby limb, repeating the process, and cones continued to fall. Wise little creature, getting his stores in early for winter—better than some men Justin had met.

He rounded a corner and pulled to a halt as the panorama of the high mountain plateau spread before him. More than a mile of rich grazing land dotted with occasional mesquite brush and small sugar pine trees encompassed his field of vision. The summer sun glinted off a stream running along the eastern side, and to the far west perched a two-story house, barn, and outbuildings. He shaded his eyes against the glare of the sun and squinted into the distance. Not far from the barn, a small band of mares grazed and a number of foals bucked and reared in play.

He turned Durango toward the house. Someone had done a fine job, setting the attractive home back in the shade of large oak trees, with fir just beyond. What looked like bunkhouses lay on the far side of the clearing. An older man with a heavy limp opened the big door at the front of the barn and headed toward the house.

Durango slowed to a stop in front of the house, and a gray-haired woman stepped out onto the long covered porch.

She glanced at Justin, but when her eyes found Toby, they lit with what looked like sheer delight. "Get down and come in, stranger. I'll bring some cookies for your boy while you hitch your horse to the rail." She nodded then turned and hustled into the house.

Justin swung down from Durango and reached up for the smiling boy. "You hear that, Toby? The nice lady has cookies." He set the squirming boy on the ground.

A deep voice turned Justin around. The man he assumed to be the boss drew close and stopped, leaning heavily on a hand-hewn cane. "You must'a rode out from town? I see your horse hasn't broke a sweat, and it don't look like you're packed for a long ride." He extended his hand. "Joe Todd."

Justin liked the look and sound of the older man and shook the proffered hand, pleased by the strong grip. "Justin Phillips, and this is my son, Toby."

A pair of sober blue eyes looked up at Joe. "Eat cookies, and Toby wide a horsey?"

Joe bent down to Toby's level. "We'll see what we can do, young man. But the cookies first. Right?"

Toby bobbed his head and grinned. "Wight." He took Justin's hand and pulled him toward the porch.

The front door opened with a light squeak, and the gray-haired woman bustled out carrying a heaping plate of sugar cookies in one hand and a tray with pitcher and glasses in the other. "Here you go, gentlemen. Cookies and milk. Can't have one without the other."

The next few minutes passed in companionable silence as the group consumed a large portion of warm cookies and cold milk. Justin sat back with a sigh and patted his stomach. "No more for me. Best cookies I've had in a long time, but don't you go telling Miss Alice that. She'd have my hide."

The woman introduced as Martha sat up straight and a grin crinkled her cheeks. "You mean our Alice Rice, over in Last Chance? You know her?"

"Sure do. Me and Toby been bunking there the last couple of days."

"Well, why didn't you say so? That makes you practically family. Alice is my second cousin, and a finer cook I never met." Martha patted Justin's knee then reached to brush a crumb from Toby's chin.

Joe grunted and shook his head. "Nope. Second best. We got the best one sittin' right here on the porch."

Martha chuckled and tipped back in her chair. "Shucks, Joe. I didn't realize you could cook."

Joe scratched his head and burst out with a guffaw. "Land sakes, woman. You do beat all." His laughter died and he turned to Justin. "Now, young man, what brings you out? You lookin' for a job?" His shrewd eyes seemed to size up Justin in one glance.

Justin set his glass on the table. "Yes, sir. Parson Moser suggested I stop. He said you were the person in charge."

"Nope, not me. The boss'll be here soon, though. From the looks of your outfit, I assume you're a rider?"

"I am. I've worked both cattle and horses over the years."

Martha touched his arm, her eyes serious. "The boy." She dropped her voice. "His ma? Will she be along?"

Justin met her steady gaze and shook his head. "No, ma'am. She passed away a few months ago, and Toby is all I have. Where I go, he goes. That's the rub. I'm not sure any ranch will want to take on a man with a youngster underfoot, but I can't give him up."

"Of course you can't." She crossed her arms and huffed. "No man should give up his son for a job." She glanced back at the boy and a smile softened her face. "He's a right pert little boy. Smart for his age, and a good eater, as well."

Justin grinned and moved the plate of cookies out of the little boy's reach. "No more, Toby. You won't have room for supper." He ruffled the boy's hair and turned back to Martha. "Yes, ma'am. He's a good boy. Wants more than anything to ride a horse. We've been on the road for a couple of weeks in the buckboard, and I didn't have a quiet horse back in Nevada. The stallion's too high-spirited for a child, but Toby's been pestering me something fierce."

Joe tapped the base of his cane on the porch. "I'll bet I can take care of that. We have an old pony that's out to pasture, but with a little work, he'd be a solid child's horse again. What d'ya think, Martha?"

Martha sat up and beamed. "I think that's a wonderful idea. And I could care for the boy while you're at work, if you get hired. That is, if this old coot here," she nodded at Joe with a grin, "has the energy to teach the boy to ride."

Joe chortled and winked. "Old coot, huh? Last time I checked, you was eight years my senior. But as long as you keep making these cookies, you can call me whatever you want." His faced sobered. "But I'm afraid we're gettin' a mite ahead of ourselves. It's Alex's decision, not ours."

As if on cue, the sound of horse hooves on the nearby road pulled their attention around. Joe rose to his feet. "Here comes the boss now." He waved an arm and raised his voice. "Come to the house before you put your horse up. Got someone for you to meet." He reached for a cookie while he waited, took a large bite, chewed, swallowed, and then coughed. "Sorry. Guess I'd best slow down." He wiped his mouth and took a drink of cold milk. "Alex, this here is Justin Phillips and his boy, Toby. I'll let him tell you why he stopped in."

The young woman looped her horse's rein over the hitching rail and climbed the porch steps then extended her hand. "Alex Travers."

Justin rose to his feet. His jaw worked but no sound came out. He cleared his throat and tried again. "Alex Travers? But how…what…

you can't be…" A quick glance at Joe Todd's confused face mirrored the expression cloaking Martha's and the young woman's, who was still standing with her hand extended.

The woman he'd seen at the church and bumped into on the street dropped her hand and frowned. "I beg your pardon? I can't be what?"

"Alex Travers," he said again, emphasizing the last name. "I–I guess I didn't expect a woman!" He narrowed his eyes and tried not to stare at the beauty standing before him. "And you most certainly are not a man."

* * * * *

Alex bristled and choked back an exclamation of irritation bordering on anger. The nerve. And to think that when she'd bumped into him she'd thought him shy and a bit charming. Ha! His comment did nothing to her pulse now but send it simmering.

She remembered Ralph's accusation that he looked like a horse thief on a Wanted poster. The sheriff had waved that aside and believed the stranger's explanation, but what did he know?

"I'm Alex Travers. My given name is Alexia, if that makes you feel any better, and my father was Benjamin Travers. May I ask why you're here? I assumed you'd be riding on after the incident at the church."

Uncle Joe gazed from her to Justin and back. "What incident you talkin' about, Alex? You know this man?"

She shook her head. "No, but I saw him at the church a couple of days ago when Ralph mistook him for a horse thief on a Wanted poster."

"Horse thief, huh?" Joe swung his gray head toward Justin. "You don't strike me as a man who'd stoop to thievin', but you cain't always judge a horse by his color." He scratched his chin. "What you got to say for yourself, young man?"

Justin looked from Joe to Alex. "Not much needs sayin'. I came to this country hunting a job, and I've never been in trouble with the law. I've ridden for some good outfits over the years, both cattle and horses, if you need a reference."

Alex nodded her head. "I'd appreciate that. Your resemblance to the man on the poster is striking, but I doubt he'd have a child with him if he were on the run from the law."

She glanced at the little boy snuggled on the nearby seat. What a captivating smile, and the blue eyes looked capable of thinking up more mischief than the average adult could imagine. The dark curls tickled the tops of his ears and draped over his collar. His father wasn't bad looking, either—and his shoulders looked like he was no stranger to hard work. The firm handshake he'd offered and the calluses on his palm only confirmed this impression.

Justin nodded and seemed to relax. "Thanks, ma'am, and I apologize for my surprise. Guess when I heard the name, I assumed that *Alex* would be a man." He waited for Alex to sit and then followed suit, pulling Toby onto his lap. "I'm here because I'd like a job." He held up a hand when she started to reply. "One thing, though—Toby is part of the deal. I won't give him up. If that's a problem, I'll keep moving." He settled back and wrapped his long, muscular arms around the boy, who appeared content to hold still for the moment.

"I see." She glanced at his boots and then at his horse tied to the hitching rail. "Do you know horses? And—are you willing to work for a woman?" This time she held up her hand. "Just a moment. Let me clarify. I've lost a few hands who didn't think a woman should be running a ranch. I assume you can ride, or you wouldn't have a horse. Same with the rifle in your scabbard. But I don't just need someone who can sit a saddle. I need someone knowledgeable about horses who will take orders from a woman without question."

A small smile cut across the somber planes of Justin's face and then deepened, creating a dimple at the corner of his mouth. "Reckon I can, ma'am, if they're sensible orders. But I can't promise not to question. I wouldn't promise that to a man. And to answer the riding and shooting, I think I'll do."

Martha leaned forward and broke her silence. "I'll take care of the boy, if you want to hire him. It would be a mercy to have a little one scampering around under foot again."

Alex frowned and tilted her head. "Are you sure that would be wise, Martha? You have a lot of energy, but chasing a child around on top of all you do now?"

Joe cleared his throat and tapped his cane against the porch. "I'll help. The boy can help me around the place, can't you, boy?" He reached out to Toby and tweaked his nose, eliciting a giggle.

"Toby help. I wide the horsey." He pointed across the grassy area toward the pasture where the mares and foals grazed.

Joe laughed and slapped his knee. "I declare, the boy has a one-track mind. Sure, lad, you can ride the horsey, if Miss Alex gives your pa a job." He turned his gaze to Alex and raised bushy brows.

Alex grinned and shook her head. "Sounds like I'm not being given much of a choice…." She glanced at Justin, but her words came to a halt at the sound of a horse running up the lane. She pushed to her feet and shaded her eyes. "Uncle Joe, can you see who that is?"

Joe leaned on his cane at the edge of the porch and stared at the figure coming into sight. "Looks like Frank. He's been out at the west pasture checkin' on the stock. What's got him so riled?"

Silence blanketed the group until the rider pulled his lathered horse to a sliding halt, throwing chunks of grass and gravel. "Joe, the horses…" He paused, drew a deep breath, and tried again. "I just came from the pasture on the far side of the valley. The geldings—they're gone."

Chapter Twelve

....

Alex grabbed the snorting horse's bridle and stared at Frank, certain she'd heard wrong. "Gone? What do you mean, gone?"

Frank drew a soiled handkerchief from his pocket and mopped his sweating neck. "I left them for an hour or so when I tracked one that wandered off. I found him, but when I got back, the rest was gone."

Joe shook his head and rapped his cane against a nearby post. "Don't make sense. You check for prints? See where they headed? Somethin' must'a spooked 'em."

"Yes, sir. I done that. Found shod prints pushing the herd into the brush. Tracked 'em for a while but figured I'd best get back here and let you know."

Alex stepped closer to the rider. "You're sure? How many shod horses? Could they be our riders?"

"I don't think so. I didn't recognize the tracks, and most of the boys are fixing fence right now. Davis and Will are on the other side of the plateau with the main band. There were only about thirty head, mostly geldings, and it looked to be only two riders pushin' 'em."

Joe started limping toward the steps, but Alex reached out and grasped his arm. "Uncle Joe, where are you going?"

"After those horse thieves, girl." He brushed her hand off and turned away.

"No. I won't have you riding. Doc said your hip won't hold up. My horse is saddled and I'll take Frank back with me."

Justin took off his hat and ran his fingers through his dark blond hair. "You haven't said whether I have a job, Miss Travers, but you can count me in." He threw a glance at Martha, who held Toby's hand. "That is, if Miss Martha will keep an eye on Toby."

Martha nodded. "I'll care for him, and my prayers go with you all."

Alex threw her a grateful glance and turned to Justin. "I appreciate the offer, Mr. Phillips. You do this for me and you've got the job."

He slapped his hat back on his head and met her eyes. "I'll do it whether I get the job or not, ma'am." He stalked to his horse, pulled the reins, and swung into the saddle. He turned his attention to the silent child standing by Martha. "You be a good boy, you hear?"

"Yes, Papa." The little boy leaned his head against Martha's skirt, and she stooped to place an arm around his shoulders.

Alex strode to the other end of the rail and untied her horse. She pulled a pair of gloves from her saddlebag and slipped them on. Catching movement from the corner of her eye, she jerked her head in time to see Joe sidle up next to Justin's leg. She barely caught the low rumble of the older man's voice.

"You watch out for my girl."

Alex swung into her saddle and pulled her gelding's head around. "I can take care of myself, Uncle Joe. You'd best tell him to watch out for himself." She jerked her head toward the two waiting men. "Enough talk. Let's find my horses." She touched Banner's flank with her heel and didn't have to ask twice. The spirited gelding broke into a trot that quickly changed to a ground-eating canter.

* * * * *

Justin rode his liver-chestnut stallion in silence and watched the slim figure a few yards ahead. He'd made a fool of himself for the third time. After nearly knocking over the woman he now knew as Alexia Travers, he thought he'd done everything possible to make a bad impression. Why hadn't he kept his shock to himself? Why hadn't he paid attention when the parson referred to Alexia? He thought back to Ben Travers's telegram mentioning Alex. All this time he'd assumed Alex to be a son, not the attractive woman riding in front of him like she'd lived most of her life on horseback.

She sat astride her mount wearing trousers, with no skirts to impede her movement, and a hat atop her small, attractive head. Her long, rich brown hair lay in a braid down her back, but a few strands had pulled loose and tossed in the breeze created by the fast-moving horse. She seemed focused on their task, riding with confidence and purpose.

He'd seen something in her face back at the ranch when Frank delivered his news: Vulnerability and a quick flash of uncertainty, both appearing for only a moment and gone so fast he'd almost doubted their appearance. A complex woman for sure—the kind he liked to avoid.

He turned to check on Frank. The wrangler lagged behind on his big chestnut gelding, allowing the horse to recover from his hard run across the valley floor. Or could there be another reason the man didn't seem to be in a hurry to return? His mind flashed back to Travers's warning that he keep quiet. Had some of his own wranglers been working against him?

The hill on the far side of the plateau finally came into view. Alex continued the brisk gallop across the grazing land, skillfully skirting the manzanita brush and gopher holes along the way. He'd doubted the wisdom of a woman riding along on a potentially dangerous mission, but she handled a horse as well as any man—better than most, in fact.

Alex slowed her horse and held up a gloved hand. "Frank." She turned and waited for the wrangler. "Is this where the horses were when you headed into the hills after the stray?"

He drew up beside her and glanced around. "Yes, ma'am." He pulled his horse to the side and pointed. "And there's the tracks of the shod horses. I trailed them for about a half mile into the hills then doubled back to the ranch."

Justin nudged his mount forward and leaned over the side, staring at the prints on the churned-up ground. "Looks like two shod horses loped into this area and swung around the band."

He kept moving. Alex and Frank followed, but he didn't look back. The band of horses was easy to trail, but the shod tracks appeared intermittently when a hoof landed on a bare patch of ground or chunks of grass were dislodged. "They're headed toward the hills, all right, and being careful." He gestured toward the direction Frank had indicated with a nod. "Want to go after them, Miss Travers?"

She shot him a glance and moved ahead. "That group of geldings was shipping to the army next week, and I can't afford to lose them." She touched a spur to the horse's flank and surged forward. "Let's go."

The small group stayed close together for the next half mile, following the tracks as far as Frank had gone. Then they slowed to a trot. Alex scouted ahead, with Frank and Justin fanning to each side. As far as they could tell, no stragglers had dropped out or headed into the narrow canyons branching off to the right.

As the ground became steeper and rockier, the tracks grew less distinct and the riders were forced to slow to a walk. Alex waved an arm and brought the men to a halt. "There's a shallow valley up over this ridge." She pointed to the hills above them. "Move slow and keep your ears open."

Justin loosened his rifle in its scabbard. It went against everything in his nature to allow Alex to take the lead, but seeing her determination, he kept quiet. It certainly wasn't common for a woman to take charge of a ranch, but it wasn't totally unheard of, either—especially when a death in the family forced her hand. But a woman leading a hunt for missing horses that could lead to a shoot-out? He shook his head. As much as he wanted a job, this might be more than he cared to tackle.

Of course, working for Travers's daughter would enable him to settle his debt once and for all. And it seemed that Alex needed all the help she could get. The missing horses might have spooked and the shod-horse tracks been made by the other wranglers, but Justin doubted it. What was it that Travers had written? *"Ranch in trouble and life in danger."* Was there more to his death than a heart attack and a fall from his horse? The doctor didn't seem to think so. But something about the horses' disappearance didn't sit right with Justin.

They worked their way around loose boulders and skirted a small section of shale, slowing the ascent. Justin watched the trim figure ahead with grudging admiration. She hadn't done anything foolish so far, and hopefully there wouldn't be a problem on the far side of this ridge.

Alex pulled up her horse before she crested the ridge. She stepped off and hunkered down against the ground. Smart. She didn't plan on sky-lining herself where a potential attacker on the other side could take a shot.

Justin eased himself from the saddle and looked around at Frank, who spat a stream of tobacco against a rock before stepping down, as well. Justin led his horse the last few paces.

Alex looked from one to the other. "Ready?"

Frank let loose another stream of tobacco and nodded. Justin pulled his rifle from his saddle and moved to her side. "Let's go."

She glanced at the rifle then turned to her horse and withdrew hers. "Right. Keep a sharp eye out."

They ground-hitched their horses and moved on silent feet for the last few yards, bending low and keeping their heads down. No one spoke for several minutes as they crested the ridge and surveyed the small valley below. Finally Alex eased back and dropped down on a rock. She glanced from one to the other. "The horses aren't there."

Justin set his rifle butt on the ground and nodded. "Want to wait a few minutes and then take a look?"

Frank bit back a curse. "I tell you, the riders moved them horses into this valley. You seen the tracks."

Alex pulled off her hat and plunked it on the rock nearby. "Well, they're gone now. There's no rocks or brush big enough to hide them."

"So whadda we do now?" Frank let loose with another stream, which hit a small pebble, making it bounce.

She brushed loose hair from her face and shrugged. "We follow their tracks." She stood and walked to her horse, sliding her rifle back in its sheath.

Justin kept a firm grip on his rifle and strode back to the ridge. Nothing. He narrowed his eyes. No wrangler worth his keep would move a herd from good grazing to rocky terrain. He swung back toward Frank. "You sure you didn't see anything else?"

Frank pushed to his feet and stuck his face up against Justin's. "Don't make no never mind if you're new, you'd best watch yer mouth." His eyes narrowed. "In fact, you could'a stole those horses your own self, 'fore you come to the ranch."

Alex jerked her head at the man. "Enough, Frank. No one is accusing you of anything, but I want to know the same thing. Is there anything else you saw?"

He swung his head from side to side and glared. "No, ma'am. I didn't see nothin' more than I said, and I don't know nothin' about them missin' horses."

"Fine." Alex swung into her saddle. "Let's head out. I can't afford to lose that contract with the cavalry."

They covered the first half mile toward the ranch in silence with Alex leading the small band of riders and Justin trailing. He squinted against the sun and shaded his eyes toward the horizon. It looked like a rider was darting through the clumps of mesquite and heading their way. The cloud of dust kicked up by his cantering mount increased as the rider drew near. A heavily lathered bay gelding pulled to a stop a few yards in front of Alex and the rider raised his arm. "Alex. I've been hoping I'd run into you out here. I stopped at the ranch and Joe sent me out."

Alex kept a firm grip on her restive horse's reins, forcing the jigging gelding to a halt. "What's the trouble, Carter? Looks like you've been running your horse pretty hard."

"Yeah. I was coming from my ranch, cutting through over the hills on the other side of this pasture, and saw some men driving a band of your horses."

Alex leaned forward, her back stiff and eyes intent on the stranger. "You saw them?"

He took off his hat, wiped the sweat from his forehead with the back of his sleeve, and then replaced the hat, giving it an extra shove onto his head. "Yeah. I didn't think anything of it, as I wasn't close enough to see if they were your men. But it looked suspicious when they spotted me and moved the horses from a trot into a run. They headed down into a gully. I thought about following, but they had a pretty good lead. Figured I'd do more good letting you know."

Alex pressed her palms against her forehead. "I'm so mad I could… I could…" She dropped her hands, drew a deep breath, and let it out slowly. "Thank you, Carter. Frank brought word earlier." She nodded toward the silent wrangler sitting nearby. "You must have come along after Frank headed back to the ranch to alert us. We didn't get there in time, either, but I intend to find out where they went and who took my herd."

Carter picked up his reins and swung his horse's head around. "Anything I can do to help, just name it."

Justin followed Alex and the two men but kept well behind. He needed time and space to think about what just happened and how it all might play into Ben Travers's telegram. Travers's warning of trouble reared in his memory again, and Justin's gut told him this could be just the beginning.

Chapter Thirteen

....

Alex slapped her gelding on the rump and waited as he trotted out to roll in the pasture. She swung the gate shut and turned to the silent man standing nearby. "I can't believe we didn't find those horses."

"That bank of shale and the heavy brush made tracking difficult. Not much more we could do."

She shrugged. "I'm sure your son is wondering about you. You're welcome to walk to the house with me."

Justin slapped his hat against his leg, making the dust fly, and then settled it back on his head. "Thank you."

"You're from Nevada?"

"Yeah."

She was silent for a moment, wondering what to say next. "Your little boy must look like his mama."

"Yes. He favored her."

Alex sighed and headed to the house. Another man of few words. Her father was much the same, and at times it had irritated her. What was so hard about saying more than two or three words in a row?

They'd gone three strides when Davis swung around the end of the barn into sight and then abruptly pulled to a halt. Something flickered across his face, but then it stilled and grew passive. "Miss Alex." He nodded and tossed a curious glance at Justin.

"Davis, did you happen to move the herd of geldings from their pasture to the small valley over the hill?"

"No, ma'am. I been workin' on the far side of the ranch. Didn't go anywhere near the geldings today. Why?" He stuffed his hands into his pockets and leaned a hip against a nearby post.

"They're gone. We found tracks of two riders, but they disappeared in the rocks. I want you to question the rest of the wranglers and tell me what you find out."

"Sure thing, ma'am. Happy to help." He touched his fingers to his hat brim and moved away.

Alex had taken two steps before she realized that Justin wasn't beside her. She looked over her shoulder. He stood staring at the open barn door where Davis had disappeared. "You coming?"

"Yeah." He turned and moved forward. "How long has he been with you?"

"Davis? I don't know. A year or so, I guess. He came some months after Tim arrived, and that was well over two years ago. Why?"

Justin shrugged. "I'm not sure—he looks familiar."

"Papa!" A small figure flew off the porch and launched himself at the legs of the man striding beside her. "You comed back."

Justin swung the youngster up and hugged him. "Yes, I came back. I told you I would, didn't I?"

Toby nodded but pursed his small lips in a frown. "But Mama said she'd come back, too, and she goed to heaven."

Justin pulled the boy to his chest and buried his face in Toby's hair. "I know. But Papa will take care of you. I promise."

Alex's footsteps faltered. Toby's plaintive question cut to her heart. She drew a deep breath, suddenly certain of what she needed to do.

She stepped up on the porch and drew the door open, holding it for Justin and Toby. He nodded and took one long stride across the threshold then paused inside the roomy foyer that spanned the front of the house.

Toby wriggled down from his arms and pointed toward the kitchen then tugged at Justin's hand. "Cookies over there, Papa. Come on."

Alex bit back a chuckle and smiled. "That's where we're headed, young man. To the kitchen." She beckoned Justin forward and saw him glance around then carefully wipe his boots on the rug inside the door.

Justin grasped Toby's hand and slowed the boy's rapid pace. "You've had enough cookies for now. We'll take you back to town and get a proper meal."

Alex swung around and paused. "Martha cooks enough for a small regiment. Why don't you plan on staying for supper so we can discuss the terms of your employment?"

His brows rose. "I didn't tell Miss Alice I wouldn't be back."

"She won't worry. Her boarders come and go and oftentimes skip meals."

Justin nodded. "Thanks."

Alex stepped into the large, sunny kitchen and glanced around. "Martha?" She noticed a pot bubbling on the stove, which meant Martha couldn't be too far away. A wonderful fragrance rose from the pot, making Alex's stomach rumble in anticipation.

"I'm in the pantry, child." Martha appeared in the door in the back corner of the kitchen, clutching a large jar of strawberry preserves. "Found it." She paused, glanced from Justin to Toby, and then leaned down to the little boy. "Do you like bread with preserves?"

Toby's blue eyes lit up and a big smile covered his face. "Uh-huh! Toby loves bread 'n' jam." He turned to tug on Justin's sleeve. "Papa want some?"

Martha chuckled and straightened. "Yes, Mr. Phillips, do you? Or should I say, would you care to try my homemade bread, along with roast beef, mashed new potatoes, and a slice of apple pie?"

Justin's eyebrows rose, and Alex noticed that he didn't hesitate to respond. "It's Justin, and yes, ma'am. Much obliged." He glanced around the room. "Where would you like me to wash up?"

Martha motioned toward the back door. "There's a pitcher with soap and a towel outside that door. Help yourself and come back hungry."

A big smile crept onto Justin's normally serious face, and Alex realized that it was the first time she'd seen the man grin. How amazing, that a smile could transform a face like that. She'd thought him a handsome man before, but after that smile....

Alex shook her head, annoyed at herself for entertaining such thoughts about one of her cowhands. Didn't she have enough to think about? Besides, the man was grieving his dead wife and had a small son to care for. That was not a triangle she cared to get caught in.

She slipped away to change out of her riding clothes and into a dress. Martha had begged her years ago not to come to the table in her riding gear. Usually it irked Alex to have to change for dinner, but for some reason she couldn't quite decipher, a dress appealed to her tonight. Besides, the idea of sitting down with Justin while wearing men's pants caused her a twinge of embarrassment. She didn't know what he'd thought when he'd arrived and seen her wearing them, but she could only imagine.

She drew a simple, pale blue cotton dress over her head, buttoned the front, and ran a brush through her curls. After another quick glance in the mirror, she slipped back into the kitchen. "Where's Uncle Joe?"

Martha put the lid back on the pot she'd been stirring. "I think he's taking a nap. Would you wake him, dear? It's almost time for supper."

Alex could count on the fingers of one hand how many times she'd heard of Uncle Joe napping, and most of those were in the days after his fall.

She headed for his room and tapped on his door. "Uncle Joe? It's Alex. May I come in?"

An indistinguishable reply sounded inside. The bedsprings squeaked, and she heard feet thump on the floor. "Sure. Door's open."

A rumpled Joe met her gaze when Alex pushed open the door. "Are you all right?"

A scowl crossed his face, but then it faded and a small smile took its place. "I'm fine, darlin'. Just a mite tired. My hip's been botherin' me and I haven't been sleepin' too well. I'm right as rain now, though, after that little rest." He tugged on his boots. "Supper ready?"

She sank down on the cotton-ticked mattress beside him and slipped her hand through his arm. "Yes. It's on the table, and we've asked Justin and Toby to join us." After a short pause, she asked, "What do you think of him, Uncle?"

His serious eyes couldn't quite hide the twinkle threatening to escape. "I think Toby's a right fine little boy and this old place could use a little scamp like him runnin' around, livening it up again."

She shook his arm. "You know very well who I meant. I'll tell Martha not to feed you any pie, if you keep that up."

"Oh, you meant Phillips senior? Well, now. From what I could tell, he seems an all-right fella. You thinkin' of hirin' him?"

"I am. As long as you agree. But I'm still not sure about the boy…."

Uncle Joe drew himself up. "You leave the boy to me and Martha. I think that young'un could use some motherin', and Martha's just the one to do it. And you'd best be asking his father to stay in the house, as well."

"Why? Our wranglers don't stay in the house. That's what the bunkhouse is for."

Joe shook his head and peered at her. "Not when they have a child that age. It's no fit place for a youngster. Some of our men are rough, and the boy's too young to be around them. 'Sides—what about the times his pa will have to help with foaling at night or some other chore? Who's goin' to care for the boy if he wakes scared or needs to be tended for some reason?"

Alex tipped back her head and looked at the ceiling, hating the logic of his words but knowing they were sound. "What will the rest of the men think? Won't they see it as favoritism? And how about the townspeople? They already think poorly of me. Not that I care." She shrugged. "But he's not married, and it might be unseemly having him in the house."

Joe stood, gripped her arm, and lifted her to her feet. "You're the boss now, Alex, and you'd best remember that." He gently turned her to face him. "It don't matter what others think, if you decide it's the right thing to do. Besides, Martha and I are enough of a chaperone to suit anyone. Don't question your decisions or allow others to, neither. Stand firm and take charge, or you'll have more men quittin'."

"You're right." She stood on tiptoe and kissed his cheek. "Thank you. Now let's go to dinner, before Martha decides that neither one of us deserves any pie."

He chuckled and shooed her out the door. "Right you are, my girl. Right you are."

* * * * *

Justin stood behind his chair. His head felt as if he were swimming and he'd not quite come up for air. The vision in blue that had drifted into the room a few minutes earlier didn't in the least resemble the woman who'd ridden out after the horses. Her long hair hung loose around her shoulders, and the setting sun coming through the windows had cast a golden-red glow on the brown curls. A flash of pink tinged her cheeks, and her skirts swished around her slender hips when she entered the room.

He shook his head. No time to get sentimental over a woman. Hadn't he learned his lesson with Molly? Maybe he'd made a mistake, coming out here and asking for a job. But he'd promised Travers, and he'd never once broken his word. He didn't plan to start now, no matter how many pretty daughters appeared.

Martha came into the room with Toby in her arms. "We've not had a little one at the table for many a year. Guess Joe'll need to build the boy a chair so's he can reach his plate." She sat the toddler down on the bench and turned to pull a couple of books off of a nearby shelf.

Justin lifted Toby from the bench and waited for Martha to slip the books under the boy before setting him back down. "There's no need for that, ma'am. I have a chair in the wagon that I built, back at Miss Alice's. Besides, I don't imagine we'll be taking regular meals with you."

Martha left the room and returned shortly, her hands filled with a steaming platter of roast beef that made Justin's mouth water. She set the platter down and beckoned to Alex. "Let's get the rest of the food on the table. Joe's starvin', and I reckon so is this young man." She rumpled Toby's hair and winked.

"Yep. Toby starvin'." the little boy parroted with a grin and a big nod.

Martha waved Justin to the seat beside Toby and walked briskly back to the kitchen. Joe slipped into his seat across from Justin. The ladies brought the rest of the food and took their seats.

Justin waited, not sure if he should begin. The creamy mashed potatoes almost drew his hand to the serving spoon against his volition, but he kept his arms by his sides. This wasn't his house, or even the boardinghouse, and he had no desire to shame himself in front of strangers.

Joe reached for Alex's hand, and she stretched her other one out toward Martha. Justin watched, puzzled at the move, but he gripped Martha's hand when she reached for his.

"How 'bout me?" Toby waved his small hand in the air. Justin chuckled and grasped the boy's fingers.

The rest of the heads at the table bowed, and Joe's booming voice filled the quiet room. "Father, we thank You for this wonderful food. We thank You for these visitors in our midst and for our family. Bless this food, we pray. In Jesus' name, amen."

A soft murmur of amens filled the room, and Martha's firm grip relaxed, allowing Justin's hand to drop. He should've guessed they'd pray before the meal. It had been years since he'd thought to thank God for food—or for anything else—but something about the gesture warmed his heart.

"Papa?" Toby tugged on his sleeve. "I hungry, Papa. We eat now?"

Martha passed the bowl of potatoes to Justin with a sweet smile. "Serve your boy first then yourself."

The next few minutes were spent passing the food and sampling the variety of dishes. Homemade applesauce tasted like heaven with warm bread right out of the oven. Miss Alice could cook, but this went beyond simple good cooking. This was a feast.

It had been awhile since Justin had sat with ladies such as these at a supper table. He tried to remember the niceties his mother had taught him, and he took care not to talk with food in his mouth or place his elbows on the table—two things that would earn him a thunk on the head by his father when he was growing up.

After two servings of pie, Justin laid his napkin on the table and sighed. "That was the best meal I've eaten in months. No—make that years."

Martha's face shone as though illuminated by the midday sun. "Why, thank you kindly." She glanced at Toby and back at Justin. "Looks like your little man is starting to droop. Want I should take him in the parlor and rock him for a bit?"

Justin stood and reached for Toby, drawing him to his chest. "We should be getting back to the boardinghouse." He nodded at Alex and Joe. "I appreciate your hospitality." He turned toward Martha and smiled. "And thank you for your kind care of my boy, ma'am."

Alex rose and glanced at Joe then back at Justin. "I wonder if you'd mind having a cup of coffee with us in the parlor, while Martha rocks Toby? We'd like to talk about the job."

Justin rubbed Toby's back and ran a hand over the tousled hair. "Sure. Guess a few more minutes won't hurt, if you're sure you don't mind." He looked at Martha.

The older woman beamed. "Not at all. Just bring him on in." She led the way across the dining room and into a cozy parlor near the front of the house. A cheerful fire burned on the grate, and brightly colored knit throws lay over the backs of the chairs and the sofa.

Justin placed the dozing boy in Martha's lap and took the chair Joe offered.

Alex settled into an upholstered chair near the fire and turned her face toward Joe. The firelight cast a soft glow on her face and magnified a somewhat wistful look that hovered around the finely chiseled mouth. "Joe, I'd appreciate it if you'd explain to Mr. Phillips what we discussed."

Joe sank into the sofa near Alex and nodded his gray head. "Yep, just gettin' to that." He trained his serious gaze on Justin. "We're offerin' you a job and a place to live. Both you and the boy, if'n you care to accept."

Justin ran his hand around the rim of his hat and met Joe's eyes. "I do, and I thank you. We can move our belongings into the bunkhouse tomorrow, if that suits you."

Joe wagged his head and tapped his cane on the braided rug at his feet, making a dull thump. "No, sir. No bunkhouse for you or the boy. Both of you will stay in this house. We have a big room upstairs that'll do right fine. The boy needs to be where Martha can help look after him."

He held up a gnarled hand when Justin started to speak. "Hear me out. Martha can't be trottin' back and forth to the bunkhouse at night when you're on duty, and a boy that age don't need to be around our wranglers." He grunted and shook his head. "Leastwise, not in close quarters. You take the job, we'll expect you to stay in the house." His bushy brows lowered over the piercing eyes, and his hand gripped the head of the cane.

Justin held back a smile, and his thoughts turned to Ben Travers. He understood how the two old codgers had become such friends. They shared the same bulldog tenacity and an expectation of getting their own way. He hazarded a glance at Alex and, judging by the firm set of her mouth and tilt of her chin, guessed she'd inherited some of the same.

He sat back in his chair and nodded. "Fine. The house it is. But I'll be returning to the boardinghouse tonight to pick up the rest of my things and to let Miss Alice know I'm moving."

Martha continued her rocking but spoke in a quiet voice. "Why not leave the boy here? You've mentioned he's used to staying with strangers. He's asleep and won't know you're gone till tomorrow."

Justin hesitated, hating the thought of leaving Toby again. But he saw the wisdom in the housekeeper's suggestion and relaxed. "I agree. We'll get him tucked in, and if he doesn't wake, I'll let him stay."

Chapter Fourteen

....

Alex raised her hand to knock on Miss Alice's door. Conflicting thoughts raged in her mind and nearly spun her back to her horse. Maybe Frank would've been a better choice to help with this chore than Justin. But she needed Frank at the ranch, and Justin was already in town. She shrugged and lifted her hand to knock, following through this time.

She glanced down at her worn boots and snugly fitting trousers. She'd left her town dress hanging on its hook in her bedroom, breaking one of her father's earliest rules. But it couldn't be helped. The new horses were arriving today and she couldn't handle an unknown stallion and mares in a dress.

Miss Alice threw open the door with a flourish and emitted what sounded like a high-pitched little crow. "Well, I never. Alexia Travers. What brings you to my door so early?" Her glance traveled from Alex's long-sleeved shirt down to her belt, pants, and boots and back up again to her braided hair. "Looks like a right smart outfit. Wish I could get away with it," she chuckled. "I declare—these skirts sure do get in the way of a body's work sometimes." She stepped back from the door and beckoned. "Come in, come in. And pardon my chatter. I've got a pot of tea on."

Alex grinned and gave the tiny woman a warm hug. "Thanks. I came by to talk to my new employee, Justin Phillips."

"Oh my, he's already gone." The sparrowlike woman shook her head. "I think he's over at the stable, getting his horse. He told me he's moving to your ranch today."

Alex glanced out the front window and then back to Miss Alice. "I'm sorry I can't stay and visit. I'd best catch Justin before he heads out of town. I'll come back when I have more time and take you up on that cup of tea."

She stepped out the door and down the steps to her waiting horse. Swinging into the saddle, she turned the horse away from the hitching rail and onto the hard-packed street toward the stable. The early hour hadn't discouraged a few hardy souls from venturing out. Most of the miners were busy at their diggings, but a half dozen locals moved in or out of businesses along the town's main street.

The crisp, high mountain air tickled Alex's neck and made her thankful for the warm woolen jacket. Nights could still be crisp at this elevation.

She drew abreast of the blacksmith's shop and pulled her horse to a halt. The large wooden door squealed as someone rolled it aside.

Justin stepped out, squinting against the bright morning sun, and paused when his gaze landed on Alex. "Well, howdy, Miss Travers. I was just headed to your place."

"I hoped I'd catch you. The stallion and mares my father purchased are arriving this morning, and I need your help. They came by train to Auburn. Since we're short-handed, I hired drovers to bring them up the trail."

"Uh-huh." Justin swung up into his saddle. "I assume they'll be coming up the trail through Foresthill and on through Robinson Flat the way I came. If so, there's no danger of missing them."

Alex clucked to her gelding. "No. That's the long way. The drovers will bring them through Michigan Bluff and across to Deadwood. It's less than half the distance, but the trail's only used by pack trains and horses. Too rough for wagons. We should meet up with them in the next hour or so."

* * * * *

The man standing beside the hotel watched Justin and Alex trot out of town then spat and cursed. Something had to be done. Rumor had it her new horses were arriving today, and that cowboy was settling in fast. He saddled up his horse and headed down the trail for Auburn.

* * * * *

Alex and Justin urged their horses into a trot as they hit the edge of town and kept up the ground-eating pace for several miles with sparse conversation. Alex fought the temptation to ply Justin with questions; his past wasn't her business. Instead, she clamped her lips shut and concentrated on the rocky terrain as they descended in elevation. Small rocks rolled under their horses' hooves, and they reined the animals around trees downed by the last big windstorm that hit the mountains.

Finally, Alex's curiosity got the better of her. "So, you and Toby traveled here from Nevada?"

He threw a glance her way. "Yep."

She averted her gaze and sighed. "What kind of work did you do there?"

He checked his mount at a steep declivity in the trail then eased the horse forward at a slower pace. "Ranch work mostly, with a little carpentry from time to time."

"Carpentry? You're handy with tools?"

He shrugged and smiled. "Don't know how good I am, but I get by."

"I'll remember that, if you don't mind. Papa had a knack for building, but Uncle Joe hates swinging a hammer—unless Martha pushes him hard."

"Sure. Glad to help," he drawled and then lapsed into the familiar silence that had accompanied them the first few miles.

Alex knew she'd have to content herself with the little information Justin had chosen to give, as his impassive face didn't encourage her to ask more. Maybe after he'd been on the ranch for a while, she'd venture a question or two more. She shrugged. Folks round here said all that mattered was what a man was now—not what he'd been. But a small voice still niggled in the back of her mind. She knew Justin had been married, and she couldn't help wondering what had happened to his wife. Did he lay awake at night missing her?

Alex lassoed her thoughts and drew them close, not willing to travel any further down this imaginary path. Justin Phillips was a stranger who'd more than likely move on before long. He probably needed a grubstake and nothing more. Besides, he'd made it clear that he'd been widowed only a few months. It wouldn't be very kind of Alex to start asking about his deceased wife.

Justin drew to a stop ahead of Alex and held up his hand. "Horses coming."

Alex mentally kicked herself for being so deep in thought that she'd missed the approaching riders. It was certainly not the image she wanted to present to the new hand—that he could lead while she spent her time daydreaming. She spurred her horse and trotted up alongside. "Yeah, I hear them. Let's wait in that meadow."

They reined their horses onto the grassy patch of land on the right side of the trail but didn't dismount. A man's voice shouted something indistinguishable, and then two men driving three horses trotted into view, with a haltered stallion behind.

Alex urged her mount forward and swung in beside the lead mare. She noted Justin doing the same on the far side. With the help of the drovers, they turned the small band into the meadow of lush grass. A black bay mare snorted and rushed past Alex, heading for the open trail and back down the way they'd come. Alex swung her gelding around but then drew to a stop. Justin had spurred his stallion into a run and circled around the mare, turning her back to the stamping, restless band.

He sat back hard in his saddle and slid his horse to a stop beside Alex. "That mare is quick. She'll produce some fine, fast foals that'll cover some distance."

Alex stared at her new hand, amused at the number of words he'd strung together. She grinned. "Yeah. They're supposed to be in foal to the stallion, and they're due early next spring. If we like what we see, we'll stand him to a few dozen of our mares."

She glanced over at the pawing, snorting stallion straining at the rope. He shone almost black in the sun, but the deep red cast to his coat made him a liver-chestnut, her favorite color of Morgan. The long tail nearly dragged the ground, and his cascading mane fell several inches below his arched neck. A strong head with a large jaw and wide-set, liquid brown eyes topped the massive neck. She noted the well-defined muscles in his hindquarters with pleasure. Morgans were bred to haul heavy loads, and this one didn't look to be an exception. At four years old, he appeared stronger than any she had at the ranch. Maybe her father hadn't made a mistake—she'd rarely seen the stallion's like anywhere in the state.

Justin leaned his gloved hands on the pommel of his saddle and smiled. "You like him."

She turned to meet his level gaze. "Sure. What's not to like?" She gestured at the milling group. "But we'd better get them back to the ranch. The drovers look to be tired and they'd probably like this herd off their hands."

Alex drew alongside the wrangler who appeared to be in charge and extended her hand. "Alex Travers."

The man's eyebrows rose in apparent surprise and he glanced from her to Justin. "You're Alex Travers?" He swept his hat off his sweat-drenched hair and tipped his head.

She pursed her lips, too familiar with his reaction to be amused. "Yes.

That's Justin Phillips, one of my hands. I'm Alexia Travers, the owner of the Circle T." She swung her gaze to the loose horses then raised her brows at the drover. "The mares aren't haltered."

He cocked his shoulders back and raised his chin. "Nope. We drug them behind us for miles and they got plumb tuckered out. Figured this close to town we could turn 'em loose and drive 'em ahead of us with no trouble."

Alex nodded. "We're only a few miles from the ranch, and I'm sure our cook would be happy to rustle up some dinner."

"Much obliged, ma'am. The name is Tom Riley." He jammed his hat back onto his head and beckoned to his companion. "Daniel, we're taking the horses on to Miss Travers's ranch and gettin' a bite of grub before we hit the trail back to town."

Daniel swung his lasso and turned a mare back into the meadow. "Sounds good. But I wouldn't mind stoppin' at the saloon first, if they have one."

"They do." Alex gave a curt nod. "Justin and I can take them the rest of the way to the ranch if you decide to stop in town." She moved forward. It was time to get home.

Alex glanced back once more at Justin and felt an unwelcome stirring. The man knew his job and sat a saddle better than most men she'd known. Not only sat it better, but looked blamed good in it, too. Those long legs and small hips fit neatly into the saddle leather. His broad shoulders and muscular arms swinging the rope at the flank of a mare were dust-covered but hard and fit.

She spurred her gelding and moved back to the rear of the plunging herd. Time to get back to the business of saving the ranch. From now on, she wouldn't let anything—or anyone—distract her.

Chapter Fifteen

....

Christy Grey stepped down off her horse and groaned. Her body ached from the thirteen long miles over some of the roughest canyon country she'd ever traversed. Why Sanders hadn't let her come the long way around on a wagon, she couldn't fathom. The stagecoach from Auburn to Foresthill had been bearable, but the mule train across the final miles of toll road was downright terrifying.

She reached up for the small bag tied behind her saddle and surveyed her surroundings. Last Chance was a fitting name for this place. The little clapboard town at the end of the road didn't appear to have much to offer. From her place in front of the Last Chance Hotel, she could see a saloon, a candy store, a barber, and a butcher shop. She turned her gaze away from the saloon. Her occupation would take her to that place of business soon enough.

What appeared to be a blacksmith shop sat on the edge of a meadow with a scattering of cedar and pine trees separating it from the road. On the ride through the short street, she'd counted fifteen homes dotted haphazardly among a few straggling trees. Judging from the abundance of stumps lining the hillside, it appeared that someone with an axe had mowed down anything with timber value.

A sudden high-pitched whine sounded on a hill above the town. She'd heard that noise before—the buzz of a large circle saw cutting through logs to feed the ever-growing need for lumber.

She sighed, picked up her satchel, and stepped up onto the nearby boardwalk. Turning to the man holding the lead pack mule, she asked, "Can you take my trunk off the mule and place it against the wall?"

The burly driver leered at her curly auburn hair and allowed his gaze to slide over her shoulders and hips to the tips of her dust-covered boots, which peeked out from under the hem of a deep green traveling gown. "Sure thing, ma'am. But your boss said you'd want them dropped off at the saloon."

She stared back at him, holding his gaze until red crept up his neck and he dropped his eyes. "Here will be fine." She turned on her heel and kept her back to the man, stepping aside as he tossed her trunk against the nearby wall with a grunt. A few moments later, she heard the creak of the boardwalk as his massive weight stepped off the planking in front of the hotel. The crack of the whip and the sound of plodding hooves attested to the team's retreat. The only passenger on this trip, she'd been forced to rebuff the driver's advances ever since their stop in Deadwood.

She shivered and pulled her bag close to her side. Sometimes she hated her life and all it entailed. This town wouldn't be any different from the rest. The townspeople—particularly the upstanding women—would shun her as soon as they found out what she was. Dance hall girls weren't looked on with kindness, even by those claiming to practice Christian charity. In fact, the religious folk often treated her the worst.

There were many times when she longed for something different, longed for a chance to start over, but she knew no other life. No, she'd do what she'd been told to do and then move on somewhere else.

She'd need to avoid Phillips for a few days until she got established. Her orders had been clear, and she dared not disobey. Too much was at stake.

A young boy thumped down the boardwalk, kicking a pebble before him. Christy held out her hand as he drew near. "Can you help me?"

The boy skidded to a halt and turned wide eyes to meet hers. "Sure. Whatcha need, lady?" He appeared to be about nine years old and not husky enough to carry her trunk.

Maybe she should've accepted the mule driver's offer to drop it at the saloon, but she couldn't abide the man a minute longer. She'd left more than one saloon whose owner had pushed her to "fraternize" with the patrons. She'd serve drinks, dance with the miners or cowboys, even sing a song when requested, but she'd never allowed a man to take her to his room. Her sister had made that mistake, and she didn't intend to end up like Molly.

"If I give you two bits, can you find someone to take my trunk to the saloon?"

He stared at her modest traveling dress. "You goin' to work there? You don't look like no dance hall girl. You got awful pretty red hair, though."

She smiled, not minding the compliment from this young admirer. "Yes, I'll be working there."

He nodded. "You bet." He spun on his toe, dashed up the street, and disappeared into what appeared to be the livery stable. A couple of minutes later he reappeared with a huge man in tow.

"This here's Ralph Peters. He'll tote your trunk." The boy held out a grubby hand. Christy placed a silver quarter into it and pressed his fingers around the coin.

"Thank you. May I ask your name?"

"Johnny. I run errands for people. You ever need anything, just holler. I'll help you out." He puffed up his small chest and grinned.

"Why, thank you, Johnny. I'll be sure to do that." She turned to the big man standing quietly beside the boy. "You're Mr. Peters?"

A flush crept up the big man's neck and stained his cheeks. He dropped his eyes and twisted the hat clutched in his large hands. "Yes, ma'am, but just Ralph is fine."

She drew a deep breath and let it out slowly. Men were such strange creatures. So often they were bold when they discovered where she worked, but occasionally she'd find a shy one like this. Most of them took one look at her and fell over themselves to please her. She wasn't vain, but she'd been around too many men to be naive about her appearance. "If you take my trunk to the saloon, I'd be happy to pay for your trouble."

Ralph picked up the heavy trunk, hoisting it easily and carrying it like a child would cradle a favorite toy. "No trouble, ma'am. My pleasure." He gave her a quick glance out of intelligent, soft gray eyes that shone with a gentle light, and then he turned away.

"I'll be along soon. If you could please tell the owner that the trunk belongs to Christy Grey. He's expecting me."

"Yes, ma'am," Ralph called over his shoulder.

She sighed, uncertain of her next move. Would Sanders approach her? Or was she to find him? She had no idea where she'd look. She shrugged.

A tantalizing odor drifted out of a nearby hotel, and her stomach rumbled. A bowl of soup and a biscuit sounded tempting. She drew her valise close to her side and stepped off the boardwalk. Might as well enjoy a few minutes of living like a respectable woman—it wouldn't be long before word spread that a new saloon girl had arrived.

Chapter Sixteen

....

Justin sat his horse and drew the sweetly scented air into his lungs. The fragrance of pine and mesquite lingered on his clothing from the ride through the dense stand of scrub, which he and Alex had encountered on their ride to the south pasture.

"This sure is pretty country, Miss Travers."

Alex nudged her horse and drew alongside his stallion. "Yes, it is." They rode for a moment in companionable silence. "It's Alex, by way. No one on the ranch calls me Miss Travers."

"Alex, not Alexia? It's a pretty name."

She shrugged and patted her gelding's neck. "It's nice enough, but Papa always called me Alex, and it's what I prefer. There are a few people who insist on calling me Alexia, whether I like it or not. I don't mind Martha and Elizabeth using it, but they're special."

"I see. Then Alex it is."

Silence fell again as they moved out of the brush and started across the pasture with Alex once again in the lead. Justin glanced at the woman sitting her buckskin gelding a few yards away. This morning she looked too young to be running a ranch, with her hair pulled back in a braid. The fitted waist, men's trousers, and tall leather boots rising to the top of slender calves accentuated the slim figure relaxing in the English saddle. He frowned, wondering about that saddle. Most riders in these parts preferred Western saddles to the skimpy, nearly flat English contraptions.

Alex dropped back and drew her horse to a halt next to Justin's stallion then turned wide, inquisitive eyes his direction. "What?"

He jerked his head. He'd been staring. "Sorry. I've been working for you for almost a week, and you always ride that saddle. Just wondering what you see in that pancake."

Her lips turned up and she chuckled as she glanced at his heavy saddle. "When I know I'll be herding horses and may have to throw a rope, I use one with a horn—but I prefer this for everyday use." She patted the spot where a horn should reside. "My father always wondered what I saw in it, too. He told me I'd pitch over my horse's neck if I didn't watch out."

Justin couldn't restrain a small, answering smile. "So…?"

"I feel more secure in it. I rode bareback for most of my childhood, but when I graduated to a bigger horse, Papa insisted I use a saddle. I saw one in a catalog and begged Papa to buy it. He humored me but placed a bet with Uncle Joe that he'd be selling it after the first couple of rides. I fell in love, and he lost the bet."

She shifted her weight and patted her horse's neck. "This is as close as I can get to bareback. I like to feel my horse under me—to be aware of what he's going to do before he does it and move with him." She turned away and stared out over the band of horses, not seeming to expect a reply.

Strange as it might seem, Justin did understand. He'd been raised on a horse. His papa had been a wrangler and had ridden with the young Justin in front of him on his saddle since almost before Justin could walk. Horses were in his blood, and he couldn't imagine a life that didn't include them.

But though he could identify with her at times, Alex was still a puzzle to him. In one moment she seemed too young and feminine to run a ranch, and in the next she'd show a strength and wisdom beyond her years. Most wranglers would balk at working for a woman who insisted on meddling in every aspect of the ranch. Sure, a woman acting as the figurehead after her husband died wasn't too uncommon, but in such cases, the foreman ran the show. Joe wasn't healthy, so Alex had little choice. Yet somehow he doubted she'd sit at home and tend to the house even if Joe were perfectly fit.

His thoughts drifted to Molly. She'd been pretty—not stunning, but attractive in her own way, with her large hazel eyes and long, thick hair. He couldn't see her giving orders to a bunch of men. No sir, she'd needed men to show her attention. Pretty as she was, Molly hadn't been much of a wife. But at least she'd given him Toby.

He knew he hadn't been much of a father to Toby, and he shook his head, shame blanketing his emotions. He'd failed in all the ways that mattered most to a man. Years ago he'd believed in the concept of a loving God, but not anymore. He didn't really blame God, but he felt that his prayers often fell flat.

The sound of a snorting horse roused Justin from his ruminations of the past.

Alex stared at him. "You all right?"

"Yeah. Just thinking." He drew a deep breath, wondering how much, if anything, he should tell her. He didn't want her sympathy. Besides, women often couldn't be trusted. A pretty face and sweet words wouldn't fool him again.

She waited a moment, eyebrows raised, and then swung her horse around. "Let's check the mares and see which ones we'll bring in to the stallion."

He nodded and settled his hat more firmly on his head. Work would keep his mind off the past and, hopefully, off the young woman who'd appeared in the present. No telling what the future held, but he could say with a certainty it wouldn't be Alex Travers. He hadn't been able to hold his wife's interest, and he didn't care to take that risk again.

Work and Toby—those would be his salvation. That and keeping his word to Ben Travers.

* * * * *

Alex loped Banner across the flat grassland toward the grazing herd then pulled him down to a trot. No sense in stirring up the mares and having them bolt. She heard the pounding hooves of Justin's mount as he swung to circle the mares. Good—she'd rather not be near him at the moment, after what she'd seen on his face.

Pain, pure and simple. Had he been thinking about his wife? Earlier, she'd sensed that he'd begun to relax, and their conversation about her saddle had to be their longest yet. But then he'd closed up again and grown painfully silent.

What made her think this man was different from any others that drifted through their high-mountain town? Sure, he was more handsome than most, and the way he looked in his denim trousers and snug-fitting shirt....

Alex reined in her thoughts but couldn't help glancing across the meadow to where Justin patrolled the mares. He barely talked, he had a small son, and he was still in love with his wife. With these drawbacks and possibly more, why did she constantly find her eyes drifting his way? Papa had always told her that character mattered most in a man, and what did she really know about Justin's? Nothing other than his obvious love for Toby.

Her thoughts drifted to the men who'd shown a recent interest in her. Charlie, Walter, and Carter. Her nose wrinkled and she shook her head with a sigh. To be fair, Charlie and Walter were hard-working, dependable young men who'd make a couple of girls fine husbands— but neither of them ignited the smallest spark of attraction in her. Carter? She'd never thought of him in that regard. He'd been courteous— even charming—when he'd stopped by the ranch a few days earlier, but nothing about the man drew her.

It didn't matter—she didn't *need* to marry. Papa had seen to that. As long as the ranch was successful, her future was secure. Sure, many girls were married and expecting their second or third child by her age. But she'd never been like other girls. Maybe that's why Elizabeth was her only close friend.

She sighed and shifted her weight in the saddle. A shout drifted across on the breeze and she jerked her head around. Justin wasn't where she'd last seen him on the far side of the herd. She scanned the grassy terrain then let her gaze drift farther back to the edge of the meadow, where the foothills climbed up toward the peaks. A rider stood in his stirrups, waved his arm, and shouted again. Justin. What in the world?

Alex laid her spur to her horse's flank. He jumped into a lope then moved into a driving canter. Justin swung down off his horse and headed for a clump of brush. Banner plunged into the clearing where Justin had stood. She sat back in the saddle and reined him in, stopping not far away. Something dark and bulky lay under the branches. A movement behind a nearby tree caught her attention, and she noticed a chestnut mare standing on three legs, her head hanging.

The dark form under the brush didn't move, and Alex sucked in a sharp breath when she saw the still outline of a dark sorrel foal with wide-open, blank eyes.

"What happened? Is the mare hurt?" She swung down, ground-hitched her gelding, and strode over to the silent man standing over the foal.

His raised eyes met hers. "Looks like it could've been a cougar. The foal is hamstrung, and something's been gnawing on his hindquarters. We may have spooked the cat not long after the attack."

"A mountain lion? They don't normally trouble the herd with so much game around. We keep the stock close to the ranch house and barn in the winter." She knelt down to examine the foal. "I hate losing the babies."

Justin nodded, stepped to his horse, and unhooked his rope from the back of his saddle. "If it's an old or crippled cat that can't run anymore, it'll keep killing the foals." He shook out a loop and walked quietly toward the mare. Her nostrils flared and her eyes widened as she backed away. It was obvious she didn't want to leave her foal, but she'd been on the open range long enough to be leery.

"Whoa, girl…easy. It's all right. Come on, Mama, we need to take a look at that leg." He kept talking, keeping his voice low but creeping ever closer.

Justin shot the loop out and it settled over the mare's head. He tightened the rope, dallied it around a nearby small tree, and walked the length toward the snorting, plunging mare. "Easy, girl, easy."

He edged forward, his gaze intent on the mare. Nothing about his demeanor spoke of speed or urgency. Instead, a sense of calm purpose seemed to emanate from him. The mare stopped pulling against the rope and it loosened around her neck. One more time she snorted and lunged. At Justin's continued quiet words, she finally settled and stood.

Justin reached for the rope dangling from her neck and made a quick loop over her ears and around her muzzle, creating a makeshift halter. Alex walked over and stopped a few feet away then eased up to the mare's injured side. "She must've pulled something, from the look of the swelling in that fetlock joint." She ran her hand down the horse's leg to the swollen area. "It's hot. Might take awhile to get her back to the ranch." She looked up and found Justin's eyes on her.

He moved his gaze to the injured leg. "I'll take her in."

Alex shook her head. "You bring the colt. There's a canvas roll behind my saddle—pack him in that. If we leave him here, the cat will return. No sense in putting the rest of the herd in danger."

Justin nodded and reached behind Alex's saddle, unbundling the roll and heading for the downed colt. "Good idea. I'll come back later and push these horses closer to the ranch. It might not hurt to have them away from this area."

"Thanks. We need to find that lion, as well." She stepped into her stirrup and swung astride, keeping a tight grip on the rope that haltered the mare.

Justin lifted the canvas-wrapped foal and placed it across his saddle then secured it with a rope running under his stallion's belly. The big horse swung his head toward the object and snorted, but he didn't shy or pull away. "Since we'll be traveling slow, I'll walk. I can keep a better eye out for the cat, in case it's still around."

Alex tugged at the rope attached to the injured mare and clucked. They walked the animals in silence for nearly a mile, all the while casting glances around the rugged terrain. The grassy area had ended sometime back and they traveled single file along the top of a ridge, with rocky outcroppings and trees dotting the landscape. A hawk circled above, casting his shadow briefly over the ground before soaring out of sight over the edge of the bluff.

An uneasy feeling tickled Alex's nerves, and she felt the hair on the back of her neck rise. She looked over her shoulder at Justin in time to see him pull his horse to a stop. "What?" She tugged on the reins and drew to a halt. He held up a hand and pointed.

She stared in the direction his finger indicated. Standing on top of a nearby rocky point about thirty feet away was a tawny cat. It was a big one, even for these parts. Its amber eyes stared with an almost hypnotic quality, and one of its ears twitched. A front leg hung at a strange angle. The lion must've been kicked by one of the horses while bringing down the foal. Somehow she didn't think the injury was going to stop this big predator from attempting to finish its dinner.

The big cat's tail ceased its twitching, its ears flattened, and its body seemed to coil and bunch together. Alex slowly dropped her hand to her rifle scabbard and drew out her gun, bringing it up against her shoulder. Her finger hovered over the trigger.

Boom! A loud report sounded beside her, and the cat leaped into the air. His body crashed down to the bottom of the small abutment, not fifteen feet from her horse's hooves. Her gelding snorted and jumped sideways. "Easy boy." She tugged on Banner's reins and quieted him then struggled to draw the prancing, spooked mare close alongside.

She glanced at Justin—how'd he get a shot off so quickly? She'd barely gotten the big cat in her sights when he'd fired. The cougar had been ready to spring—she'd seen it in the crouch of its body and the flattening of its ears—but Justin had beaten her and brought down the cat in one easy shot.

"Nice shooting."

"Thanks." Justin handed her the reins and walked up the boulder-strewn hillside, keeping his rifle extended and trained on the still form. He leaned over the cat, nudging it with the toe of his boot. "Dead center. Heart shot. I doubt he knew what hit him."

Alex nodded. "It's a shame to kill something so magnificent. But once these cats get old and can't hunt deer or rabbits, the horses become fair game."

Justin stepped down onto level ground and grasped his stallion's reins. Alex moved Banner forward, genuinely thankful the man was good with a rifle *and* with the stock. Still, she forced down a twinge of irritation that he'd gotten his shot off before she had. One thing she prided herself on was her ability with a rifle, and he'd topped her.

She clucked to her gelding and moved past the spot where the big cat lay. No sense in feeling jealous of someone else's ability—that was childish. Besides, as the new boss of the Circle T, she'd best count her blessings that God saw fit to bring her a skilled wrangler who'd take orders from a woman.

Alex shifted her weight in her saddle and turned toward Justin. "We need to hunt for those missing horses again. I can't afford to keep losing stock. I'll want you and Frank to try tracking them again and let me know what you come up with."

Justin gave a silent nod and patted his stallion's neck. "Good plan. I'll get on it first thing in the morning. There won't be enough light to head out again after we get back to the ranch."

"Thanks." Alex swung back around. The mortgage against the ranch felt like a lead weight on her mind, pulling her into a dark place where she didn't care to venture. Martha was right. She needed to trust God and give this mess to Him, but the loss of valuable breeding stock made it hard. Her mind drifted back to Carter's offers of marriage and financial security, but the thought only lasted a moment. No. She'd make it on her own, whatever it took.

* * * * *

Alex laid her ledger aside and pushed to her feet. "Martha, did you need any help before I check on the mare we brought in today?"

Martha's voice floated out from the kitchen. "I'm fine. Just setting the sourdough for flapjacks tomorrow. It looks like there's still enough light. I surely do love these longer days."

"It's only July—still plenty of time before winter sets in." A quick peek out a window showed the sun dipping toward the horizon, but enough light remained to get a good look at the mare. Alex headed outside and across the cleared space between the house and the barn. A horse snorted in the nearby corral, and the sound of pounding hoofs retreated from the rail fence.

An indistinguishable figure moved on the far side of the enclosure, and Alex pulled up short. Frank often checked the stock at night and must have had the same idea. "Hey, Frank, you headed for the bunkhouse?"

"It's Justin. Thought I'd check on the mare." His tall figure emerged from the shadows and into the softening light.

Alex rested her arms on the top bar of the corral. "How's her leg look?"

"I just turned her loose. Still a bit of heat in the fetlock joint, but it doesn't appear any worse for the trip home. Her milk bag is pretty swollen since she hasn't been able to nurse."

"She'll be uncomfortable for a while. We don't have any orphan foals right now, so we'll need to keep a close watch." Alex shifted her weight on the fence and turned to face him. "Is Toby asleep?"

"Yeah. He's pretty excited about the promise of a horse ride, so it took a little longer than usual." Justin's smile relaxed his face.

"He's a sweet little boy—you're blessed to have him."

Justin leaned a shoulder against the nearby post, giving her a shy smile. "Thanks. I think so."

Silence settled over the area, with only an occasional stamp of a horse disturbing the evening. Justin glanced up, and his deep brown eyes caught her staring. She felt a slow blush creep up her neck and dragged her eyes away from his, grateful for the lowering dusk. "Um, I wanted to thank you for your help with the mare and foal today."

He met her eyes again. "Glad I could help." They were silent for a few more moments until Justin surprised her by speaking again. "You get lonely this far from town?"

"I didn't, until Papa died. But Martha and Uncle Joe mean the world to me, and I'm grateful they're here. The ranch has been my life—all I've cared about since I was little, when I put on my first pair of britches and rode on my first roundup." She dropped her gaze and ran her hand down the side of her trousers.

His chuckle brought her head up, and his grin caused the dimple in his cheek to appear. "You must've caused some tongues to wag, wearing boy's britches and riding on a roundup. I'll bet you were a handful for your mama."

She matched his grin and nodded. "I can't tell you how many times

I overheard her scolding Papa. She wanted me raised a lady, but since Papa didn't have a boy, he taught me to ride like one."

"I'll bet you were a cute little girl." His dry laugh filled the air. "So you just kept on all these years. Does it ever cause you a problem with the other women?"

She shrugged and tried to keep the bitterness out of her voice. "Sometimes. I've gotten used to it, though. There are a few women in town that don't agree with my choices. I steer clear of them whenever I can."

"Too bad." He straightened. "Running a ranch from horseback while wearing a dress seems like a tall order to me." A smile creased his face. "But then again, I've never tried it."

Alex threw back her head and laughed, the thought tickling her funny bone. When she glanced up again, the laughter died on her lips. Why was Justin looking at her that way?

"Guess I'd best get back and check on Toby." Justin pushed away from the fence and tipped his head. "Good night."

She raised her hand and slowly let it fall as he strode away. "Good night."

His long legs took him away from the corral in a matter of seconds, and before long the sound of the front door opening and closing met Alex's ears. She lifted her gaze to the moon peeking through the parting clouds. The thunderheads were breaking up and drifting apart. There would be no lightning strikes tonight—at least not in the sky.

Chapter Seventeen

....

Alex swung open the door of the dry goods store and heard the bell's gentle tinkle. She stood for a moment, allowing her eyes to adjust to the harsh light filtering through the front windows. She wiped her hand across her brow. Summer heat had come with a vengeance these pasts few days.

Elizabeth's head lifted and she smiled over the shoulder of the woman standing in front of her counter. "Alex! It's good to see you. I'll be with you in a few minutes."

"Thanks, Elizabeth. Take your time." She stopped to examine a rack of leather gloves on a shelf near the front, lifted a pair to her nose, and drew in a breath. *Mmm.* New leather had its own special fragrance, one she'd come to love over the years.

The clink of coins hitting the drawer of the cash register drew her attention back to the front. She'd never seen this woman before. Possibly a miner's wife up from Auburn? Doubtful; her taste in clothes wasn't something most miners' wives would choose. A deep green dress of fine cotton hugged her trim form, showing off the curves of a youthful figure. Ruffles at the throat and wrist lent a feminine touch; red curls pulled back from sparkling eyes and a pretty face completed an attractive picture.

Elizabeth waved Alex forward, and the stranger turned her way. "Alex, meet Christy Grey. We don't have many young, single women in our town. Christy, this is my best friend, Alexia Travers. She owns the Circle T ranch a few miles from town. Maybe she can answer your question."

Alex extended her hand and found it met by a firm grip. Clear brown eyes met hers, and a tentative smile curved the red lips. "I'm pleased to meet you, Miss Travers."

"Please, call me Alex." She grinned at the raised eyebrows and curious look. "My father wanted a boy and tried to hide his disappointment by naming me Alex. I'll answer to Alexia, but I'm partial to Alex."

"And I'm Christy." The redheaded girl tipped her head and her smile grew.

"You had a question?"

"Yes. I'm looking for someone, and I understand he may be in town. Justin Phillips. He has a little boy named Toby. Miss Anders thinks you've met him."

Alex's heart jolted. Could this be the boy's mother? No—Justin said she'd died. A sweetheart? She shook herself. It wasn't her business. "Yes. I hired him at my ranch. We lost a couple of wranglers and I've been shorthanded."

"Toby's with him?" Christy gripped the narrow rail lining the front of the tall wooden counter.

"He is. Are you a friend?" Alex hated to pry but couldn't seem to bite back the question.

Christy shrugged and gave a small smile. "Something like that."

A chill brushed Alex's skin. The woman standing in front of her seemed self-possessed and certain of her standing with Justin—and she was beautiful enough to turn any man's head. Finally, Alex lifted her chin and smiled. "You're welcome to come visit any time."

A subtle change passed over Christy's face—a brief flash of wonder, with a cold mask settling in its place. "Thank you. But I see you haven't heard about me yet. Once you know, you'll retract the invitation." Her chin lifted with a hint of rebellion.

Alex frowned. "I don't offer hospitality lightly."

Just then, the bell on the door tinkled and two middle-aged ladies stepped inside, their laughter and chatter filling the space at the front of the store.

Elizabeth stepped around the counter and smiled. "Mabel, Clara, how may I help you?"

Mabel Gurney glanced at Christy Grey and nudged her shorter friend. "There she is, Clara," she whispered in a too-loud voice. "Told you they'd hired another one over to the saloon, didn't I?"

Clara crossed her arms over her ample bosom and stared at Christy. "Humph. Indeed you did." She gripped Mabel's arm and drew her in a wide circle around Christy and Alex. "Come on, dear, let's go to the back of the store so these *ladies* can have some privacy." She glanced from Christy to Alex and back again then snickered and drew her companion down the nearby aisle.

Alex felt the blood rise in her face and started to reply, but Elizabeth reached across the counter, placed a hand on her friend's arm, and squeezed.

Christy drew herself up and squared her shoulders. "See?" She spoke softly, addressing Alex. "You didn't realize you were inviting a dance hall girl to your home. Want to take it back now?"

Alex stood for a moment without speaking, gazing at the young woman holding herself so rigidly against the nearby counter. The hard look on her face spoke of deep pain—pain that Alex knew too well from her own past, caused by repeated rejection and criticism. "No, I don't. You're still welcome. What you do for a living is no concern of mine." She saw Elizabeth cast her a quick glance and wondered what her friend might be thinking. Understanding and support would be nice, but she wouldn't back down on her stance, regardless.

Christy dropped her head, and Alex saw the muscles in her neck jerk as she swallowed hard. "Thank you. I'd hate to tarnish your reputation."

"Believe me, Miss Grey—having you come by the ranch couldn't possibly tarnish my reputation any further." She gave the girl a grim smile. "As you can see, there's more than one woman in this town who doesn't care for *me*. If you decide to come, it's fine by me."

Christy nodded and picked up the small bundle lying on the counter. "Good day, ladies. I'm glad to have made your acquaintance." Without waiting for a reply, she walked briskly to the door and slipped out.

Elizabeth stood silent for a moment, and Alex waited for a scolding. Finally, Elizabeth slipped around the counter and wrapped her arm around Alex's waist. "I'm not sure what you're trying to prove, but I admire you for offering." She spoke in a low voice and her gaze shot to where Mabel and Clara were laughing in a far corner of the store.

"I'm not trying to prove anything. She wants to see my new wrangler and I invited her to the ranch." Alex shrugged. "I can't see that it's anything to boast about."

Elizabeth squeezed her shoulder. "You know how tongues wag, and inviting her out will give them more ammunition." She dropped her voice to a whisper and nodded toward the back of the store. "I had no idea when I introduced you that Miss Grey worked at the saloon, but clearly Mabel and Clara did. Word spreads fast around here. Just keep that in mind."

Alex sighed wearily. "So be it."

Elizabeth smiled, walked back behind the counter, and sank onto the three-legged wooden stool. "What did you think of her?"

"Christy? She's beautiful. But I think there's more to her than she's willing to show."

Elizabeth nodded and tapped her fingers on the wood surface in front of her. "I agree. She expected you to reject her. I'm sure that's happened to her a lot."

"Which is why I didn't. I know what it's like." Alex drew her eyebrows together thoughtfully. "I wonder how she knows Justin…."

"Does it worry you?"

Alex stared at Elizabeth's upturned face. "Why should it?"

Elizabeth shrugged and smiled. "Oh, I don't know. He's single, handsome, and living on your ranch, and she's single, beautiful, and asking after him."

Alex crossed her arms over her chest. "And he's newly widowed, still grieving his wife, and raising a small child. Although I must admit I am curious to know where she fits into the picture."

"It's a small town. I'm guessing it won't be a secret for long."

The sound of staccato footsteps heralded Mabel and Clara's approach. "Is she gone yet?" Mabel stopped near the counter and peered around the front of the store.

Elizabeth smiled at the woman. "Yes, Mrs. Gurney, she's gone."

Mabel drew herself up and lifted her bony chin. "A word of advice, young lady. That one's a scarlet woman. It's not seemly to talk to someone like her." She cast a disdainful glance at Alex. "Not that it bothers some people, I'm sure." She sniffed and turned away. "I need a spool of thread." She placed it on the counter and stood with her back to Alex.

Elizabeth glanced at Alex and back at Mabel. "I don't think there's anything wrong with showing Christian charity to a stranger. Jesus taught that, you know. He sat with publicans, tax collectors, and sinners, and He willingly forgave them."

Clara placed her plump hands on the counter and leaned forward. "I'll bet we won't see her darken the door of our church coming to ask forgiveness."

A shocked look crossed Mabel's face. "I certainly hope not. If she does, I'd expect Parson Moser to ask her to leave. People like her don't belong in polite society."

Alex stepped forward, her hands clenched into fists. "Well, if you two represent 'polite society,' I don't blame her for staying out of it."

Mabel glared and took a step back. "Well, I never." She sputtered and spun toward Elizabeth. "I'll get that thread later. Good day." She seized Clara's arm and dragged her from the store.

Alex sagged against the counter, shame engulfing her. "Oh, Elizabeth, I'm sorry my temper made you lose a sale."

Elizabeth shrugged. "I don't care." Her face lit with a small grin. "It's not like they have a choice. Michigan Bluff is too far to ride for a spool of thread."

Alex smiled in spite of herself, and Elizabeth squeezed her arm. "I have an idea. How about we get a bite to eat?"

"You bet; I'm starved."

* * * * *

Elizabeth's elbow bumped Alex's side and she leaned close to hiss in Alex's ear. "Is that Carter Foster coming out of the hotel?"

Alex looked in the direction Elizabeth was gazing and saw the well-dressed, tall figure standing near the door. "Yes. He's stopped by the ranch a couple of times recently and been quite nice." She sensed Elizabeth's curiosity bump up a notch, but she'd wait until they were alone to answer for that statement.

A smile lit Carter's handsome face. He slipped his hat from his head and bowed as Alex stepped onto the boardwalk a few feet away. "Miss Travers, Miss Anders. You're both looking lovely today."

Elizabeth smiled and tipped her head. "Mr. Foster, what brings you to town? I heard you've taken on some new hands and expanded business out at your place."

His eyes narrowed just a mite, but then a smile replaced the shadow of a frown that had started to form. Had Alex imagined it, or had Carter taken Elizabeth's comments as a reprimand for hiring two of her wranglers?

"Just taking a break to eat some of Georgia's cooking. How about you ladies?"

Alex laid her fingertips on Elizabeth's arm and squeezed. "We're stretching our legs. Elizabeth's been cooped up in the store and needs fresh air. I wish you a good evening, Mr. Foster."

"It's Carter. We're friends, remember?" A lazy grin creased his face. "In fact, I wonder if you'd mind my calling on you sometime in the next few days."

Alex drew back a half step and furrowed her brows. "Call? On me?"

He chuckled and crossed his arms over his chest. "On the prettiest lady in the Sierra Nevada mountains. Present company excepted." He nodded at Elizabeth and smiled.

Alex didn't reply but simply stood, feeling glued to the boards under her feet. Call on her? Whatever for? She'd already told him she had no intention of entertaining his proposal of marriage. No matter what he'd said, she knew Carter well enough to understand that business was foremost in the man's mind. A small shock shot through her arm and she jumped, realizing that Elizabeth had pinched her.

"Oh, I suppose so, Carter…." Her voice drifted off. Entertaining Carter wasn't something she looked forward to, but hospitality demanded a certain degree of civility.

"Wonderful." He placed his high-brimmed hat on his head, grinned, and nodded. "I'll leave you to your stroll, ladies. Have a good day." Without a backward glance, he stepped off the boardwalk, unwrapped his reins from the rail, and swung into the saddle.

Alex stared after him. Why hadn't she said no? Because Papa would've expected her to be cordial. One visit wouldn't obligate her, and her sense of duty would be fulfilled.

* * * * *

The wire cutters caught on the inside seam of his pocket and lodged there. The man cursed and pushed them in deeper then yanked hard. The sound of ripping fabric increased his venom. He'd ruined his last pair of decent trousers. The boss had better be willing to kick in some extra money for this job. The tightly stretched wire would be tricky to nip without springing back and wrapping him up in its treacherous spines. He'd best hurry—no telling if someone might come down the trail. He'd been warned not to get caught, but he didn't need the reminder. They still considered horse theft a hanging offense in some parts of the country. He might not be stealing and selling 'em off, but a Travers wrangler might not see it that way.

Gripping one section of the wire with pliers and cutting the adjoining section, he moved it aside, careful to not let it whip out of control. With the last strand nipped, he pulled all three and wrapped them around the nearest post. His horse had wandered a few yards down the fence line, and he trudged over and caught up the reins. He hated fences, hated working, hated taking care of someone else's nags. He deserved his own ranch.

Finding gold would be better—then he wouldn't have to work. The horse snorted and sidestepped, earning a hard yank on the bridle. Time to go. He swung into the saddle and laid his spurs to his mount's sides. His gelding lunged forward, covering the ground between the freshly cut fence and the small band of horses milling a hundred yards away. Good. Looked like they were rarin' to run. A loud shout and a swing of his rope accomplished what he hoped. The horses took off through the opening and, seconds later, disappeared into the trees.

One more notch in his boss's belt for pulling this off. He'd rather have kept the horses moving and taken them to a buyer. The sale of a few dozen of these horses would bring in quite a sum. He rubbed his chin and grinned. Maybe…

No. He'd seen what the boss did to those who double-crossed him.

Better keep to the plan. No sense gettin' himself killed—no amount of money was worth that.

Chapter Eighteen

Alex hurried down the staircase, intent on getting to the kitchen in time to help with supper preparations. Ranch chores had consumed most of the day, and she'd barely had time to clean up and slip into a dress.

She met Uncle Joe at the bottom of the stairs, where it opened onto the entry. Approval sparked his gaze as he took in her feminine garb. "I think your ma had the right idea when she insisted you be trained in the ways of a lady. You look mighty fine tonight."

"Why, thank you, Uncle." Alex stretched up and planted a light kiss on his cheek. "I guess it's nice to be noticed once in a while."

"Huh. Seems like you've been gettin' plenty of noticin' these past few days."

Her eyebrows rose and she took a step back, inspecting his face. "Meaning?"

"That young man, Justin. Don't tell me you haven't seen him peekin' at you whenever you wear a dress to the supper table."

"No, I haven't. And I think you've got quite an imagination."

He shook his head and grunted a negative. "Figured you'd seen it your own self, or I'd not have mentioned it. But don't let it go to yer head, Alex. He's more'n likely passin' through. Wouldn't want you settin' your sights on him and havin' your heart broke."

Alex grabbed his arm and pulled him into her office. "Uncle Joe! What if he'd heard you? I'm not setting my sights on him, and my heart is not in danger."

"Humph." The old gray head wagged, and Joe rapped his cane on the floor. "I'm not blind, lass. I've seen you lookin' at him when you think no one's watchin'. I'm just warnin' you, that's all. Hate to see you hurt." He slipped an arm around her shoulders and gave her a brief hug then left the room, his cane echoing off the wood floor.

* * * * *

Justin hung his lariat on his saddle and swung the saddle onto a rack on the wall of the barn. He'd rubbed his horse down and turned him out in the small pasture allotted to his stallion. From the sounds emanating from his stomach, it must be near suppertime. His mouth watered. No matter what the fare might be, it would be good. No doubt about it, Martha was the best cook he'd encountered. He'd made a point of telling her how much he appreciated her care of Toby the past few days along with her excellent meals.

Hoofbeats in the lane leading to the house drew his attention. None of the wranglers were due in this early, but something could've happened. He tugged off his gloves, tucked them into his hip pocket, and headed out the open barn door.

Alex emerged from the house wearing a soft yellow dress, and the sight of her feminine appearance jolted his heart. Not that she wasn't attractive in her ranch garb, but he was partial to the way she looked now. Her face turned his way for a moment, and he caught his breath when their eyes met and locked. What did he see in those blue eyes before they swung back down the lane? She didn't return her gaze to him but kept it fixed on the rider approaching the house.

Davis rode at a hard trot into the yard and pulled his sorrel gelding to a halt in front of the house. "Miss Travers?" He glanced at her dress before his eyes found her face, and then he swept off his hat. "Got unsettlin' news, ma'am."

Alex shaded her eyes against the sun and looked up at the wrangler.

"What's happened?"

He swept his sleeve across his glistening forehead. "Found the fence over on the north side of the ranch cut. Horse tracks leading out toward Carter Foster's place."

"Cut? You're sure it was cut, not broken?"

"Yes, ma'am. Nipped as clean as you please. Found a set of boot prints and a place where someone set his knee in the dirt to cut the bottom strand."

Justin narrowed his eyes and stared at the man. The day he'd come, Frank had reported missing horses—now Davis. Frank had gotten angry when pushed for information. Davis hadn't given him any reason for suspicion. Except...

A memory tried to surface, and Justin dug a little deeper. That day in town. The saloonkeeper had told Davis to head back to the ranch when he'd had too much to drink. That wasn't a crime, and lots of cowhands drank. But that wasn't the only time he'd seen the man; he was sure of it. He shook his head. It might pay to keep an eye open on Alex's wranglers.

Alex crossed her arms and frowned. "Did you go after the horses?"

"No, ma'am. Thought I'd come report in first. Sorry; guess I should'a taken off after 'em."

She waved her hand in dismissal and then signaled to Justin. "Davis, you've met Justin Phillips. He's a good hand at tracking. Take him and find those horses."

Davis tossed a glance at Justin and gave a bare nod. He settled his hat back on his head and jerked his horse back a few steps.

Justin nodded toward Alex, glad she'd chosen to send him. "I'll saddle my horse." He swung around and headed toward the barn.

Dust rising down the lane and the dull thud of horses approaching stopped his progress. Two men pulled dusty, sweat-caked horses to a stop near the porch. He didn't recognize one, but the other man looked familiar. He gave a small nod as the memory returned. It was the rider of the bay gelding they'd met while returning from their hunt for Alex's missing horses.

The two men doffed their hats as Alex stepped to the edge of the steps. "Alexia, someone's cut your fence." The dark-haired man on the bay spoke in a ringing voice that carried to where Justin stood near the barn.

Alex raised her hand and motioned. "Justin, can you step over here, please?" She turned back to the man riding the tall sorrel gelding. "I'm sure you know my wrangler, Davis. He rode in a few minutes ago with the news." She tipped her head toward Justin. "Carter Foster, this is my new hand, Justin Phillips. Justin, Mr. Foster has a ranch that borders mine."

Justin gave a curt nod but didn't speak. Foster didn't appear interested in Alex's wranglers and ignored the introductions. He sat erect in his saddle, a firm grip on the restive horse sidestepping in front of the porch. The man appeared almost a dandy in his dark-brown brushed trousers and matching jacket. The russet-colored hat perched on his dark hair looked new, and the boots showed little to no wear.

Alex rested her hand against a post. "I appreciate your letting me know, Carter. Did you find any of the horses?"

Foster nodded and kept his gaze on Alex. "Some of the stock drifted to my place. Tim here found them and reported to me."

Alex glanced at the man but did nothing else to acknowledge his presence.

Justin took a step forward. "Tracks?" He doubted the man worked his own ranch, much less had the ability to track a lost horse.

"Nothing that lasted after Alexia's band of horses went over the top of them."

She nodded. "I'll send Justin and Davis over to bring them back and mend the fence. Any idea who might be responsible?"

Foster braced his hands on his pommel and leaned forward. "None.

But there's no need to send your hired men. I put two of my men on it already. Your horses are back on your land, and my men are repairing the fence. I figured you'd want to know as soon as possible."

"Thanks. You've gone out of your way to help, and I appreciate it." She gave him a warm smile. "You've got a bit of a ride back to your ranch and I'd hate to see you make it on an empty stomach. Can I convince you to stay for a cup of coffee and some pie?"

Foster cast a quick look at Justin and then smiled. "Don't mind if I do. Tim can care for our horses." He swung down off his horse, handed the reins to Tim, and stepped up on the porch in one long stride. "Maybe your man can unsaddle and turn them out?"

Alex turned to Davis. "Consider yourself off for the night." She swung toward Justin as though she'd only now remembered his presence. "Would you put up Carter's horses?"

Justin nodded and turned away, but Foster's voice covered the distance. "What do you know about Phillips? He's new here, isn't he?"

Alexia's reply was unintelligible, but Justin slowed his steps just the same. "Regardless, you need to be careful." Foster's clear words continued.

Justin swung around, a hot retort on his lips, but the two on the porch stood with their backs to him. Foster offered his arm to Alexia and gave a slight bow. "I must say I can't remember a time I've seen you looking more beautiful." She placed her hand in the crook of his elbow, and they turned toward the door.

Justin covered the distance to the barn with eyes that barely registered the sights around him. Foster's wrangler had preceded him with the horses and stood just inside the barn door. "Here." The man shoved the reins into Justin's hand when he approached. "I'm takin' a smoke. This is your job, not mine." He swung on his heel and disappeared out the door.

"Just as well," Justin muttered. He needed time to think. He took the two geldings into the barn, swung a stall door open, and released the first horse. After securing the second gelding, he stripped off the saddle and started to work. Thankfully, he didn't need his mind on this task. He turned his thoughts back to the house.

Could the man be more to Alex than just a friend? It wasn't his concern who courted Alex—she was his boss, not his sweetheart. But something about Foster rankled even though the man had appeared helpful enough.

The question remained, Who had cut the fence? Justin had no reason to suspect Alex's wranglers. He'd not form an opinion yet, but he planned to inspect the ground surrounding the cut portion of fence. Fences didn't cut themselves, and someone stood to gain.

First, missing horses the day he'd arrived, and now the fence. Something wasn't right, and Justin intended to find out what.

Chapter Nineteen

....

Alex left the church on Sunday afternoon unsettled by her conflicting feelings. The sermon had challenged her heart and the gentle music had soothed her emotions. But the coolness of a number of the women as she'd taken her place in the pew near the back of the sanctuary had put a damper on her spirit. The stress of the past few weeks had taken its toll, and she felt no desire to visit. She picked up her skirt and stepped off the porch. A solitary walk in the woods would give her a chance to think.

She'd gone only a few dozen yards when a soft voice wafted across on the breeze. "Alexia…" It sounded like Elizabeth. Alex paused and turned to shield her eyes from the early afternoon sun. Elizabeth stood on the porch step with one hand raised.

Alex waved back and cupped her hand to her mouth. "I'll come by later. I'm going to take a walk."

Elizabeth nodded and turned back inside. What a blessing to have a friend who understood and didn't judge. Alex hitched her skirts above her ankles, not caring who noticed. She headed through the scattered trees and down a slight hill behind town, toward the spring-fed meadow. The sound of water gurgling into the pond soothed Alex's spirits. Her eyes drifted over the apple trees near the edge of the meadow which hung with almost-ripened fruit, the wildflowers blooming near the water's edge, and the bees buzzing from flower to flower. A breeze blew the fragrance toward her, and she sucked in an appreciative breath.

Alex walked the length of the meadow away from the spring, passing behind the blacksmith shop and the corral housing the horses. Several mounts plunged away from the fence when she drew near then settled back to picking at scattered bits of hay. She drew her skirts up higher, no longer afraid of being seen this far from town.

The thought of her father tugged her up the hill to the cemetery. He'd chosen to be buried on his beloved ranch rather than here on the edge of town, but the peace and tranquility of the place drew her just the same.

She walked through the lightly forested glade, running her fingers along the tops of the white marble headstones marking the dozen or so graves. The town had been established only twenty-five years before and, thankfully, not many had died and been buried here in that time.

She sat down beneath a tree, careful not to disturb the nearest grave. So much had happened since her father's death, and she still had so many unanswered questions. Not just about the recent trouble at the ranch, but about Justin and Carter and even Christy Grey.

A gray squirrel scampered up a tree, drawing her attention from the nearby headstone to the swaying branches above. He chattered his displeasure while racing back and forth on a low-hanging limb.

Alex leaned her head against a tree. "Hey, little fellow. I'm not going to hurt you."

His antics continued and the volume increased. A nearby crow added to the cacophony with his deep-throated squawk, and a neighboring jay joined in the chorus.

"Quiet, please!" Alex laughed and picked up a foot-long sugar pine cone, lofting it into the tree. The heavy cone landed against the trunk with a thud and fell back to earth. The squirrel ceased his chatter but the birds continued their cry. She started to rise, determined to find a quieter place, when a rock zipped through the air and struck the tree inches from the crow. The bird spread his black wings and swooped down the hill, retreating into the distance.

Alex looked around and her eyebrows rose. Justin stood a few yards away, a smile lighting his face. "Mind if I join you?" He nodded toward the spot beneath the tree beside her. "Or would you prefer to be alone?"

She couldn't stifle a grin. "After rescuing me from that racket with your wonderful display of marksmanship? Please." She patted the ground.

He dipped his head and moved forward then settled down a couple of yards away. "Is your father here?" He looked around at the nearest headstone before his gaze traveled across the small glade.

"No. He always said he'd want to rest at the ranch. I came here after church to think."

Justin nodded. He picked up a fallen twig and snapped it between his fingers. "I needed a few things at the store."

"You don't attend church?"

He shrugged. "Guess I got out of the habit a few years ago."

"Have you thought about starting again, now that you have Toby?"

"I hadn't, but it's a good point. He might enjoy it, and I do want him trained to know right from wrong."

"I agree. I think a parent's guidance, combined with the help of a good church, does a lot for a child. Did you bring Toby to town?"

He shook his head. "No, Martha offered to keep him. Joe's giving him a ride on the pony this afternoon." He glanced up and met her eyes. "The boy sure loves that pony. I'm grateful you allow us to use her."

She shrugged and dropped her gaze. "She was getting fat. Besides, Toby's a sweet boy and I love watching him learn."

Silence settled over the glade. Alex plucked at the grass growing next to the tree trunk. What brought Justin up to the cemetery, and why had he sought her out? She couldn't deny the pull of attraction she felt when he was near, but there'd been no indication that he experienced the same.

Justin stuck a long blade of grass between his teeth and leaned against the rough bark of a tree. His soft voice broke the stillness. "You miss him a lot, don't you?"

"Papa? Yes. More than you know."

He winced, and she bit her lip. How stupid of her to forget. "I'm sorry, I didn't think…"

Justin shook his head and glanced at her. "No, it's all right. I was actually thinking more about my pa than Molly."

She sat up straight and folded her hands in her lap. "You and your pa were close?"

"Very. He and Ma raised me on a small ranch—he taught me everything I know. Not just about ranching, but about life." He emitted a harsh laugh. "Seems I've forgotten or walked away from much of what I learned. He'd not be proud of some of my decisions."

Justin swung a leg under him and pushed to one knee. "That headstone." He pointed to a large white stone a few feet away. "That who I think it is? It says E. Allen Grosh. Would that be the man who first discovered the Comstock Lode but didn't live to claim it?"

She shook herself, trying to keep up with the swift change of topic. "Yes. Ethan Allen Grosh. He died here in Last Chance."

"How'd he get so far from his gold claim?"

"Papa told me the story—he heard it from folks who knew Mr. Grosh. It seems he was on his way to San Francisco in hopes of raising money to fund his mining operation. His brother had died a few weeks before, and Grosh got a late start leaving the mountains. He and his partner, Buck, got caught in a bad snowstorm and were lost for days."

Justin looked at the tombstone with interest. "They found their way here, then?"

She shook her head. "No. They wandered for days without food, after having to eat their donkey. Frostbite set in and they'd given up, lain down, and figured they'd die. Some miners found them and built a sled of sorts then dragged them into town. They had to cut off Buck's leg and part of one foot, but they couldn't save Grosh."

"What happened to the silver he found?"

She raised her eyes to the faraway hills. "Buck said Grosh stashed the ore samples and the map to the claim in a leather pouch at the stump of a fallen tree and marked it with a cross, but no one ever found it. Papa heard that Grosh left a man named Comstock to watch over his cabin. Two years later Comstock found a large vein of silver not far up the hill from Grosh's cabin and struck it rich."

"Huh. Poor Grosh."

"Papa said some men aren't meant to have treasure; it ruins their lives and poisons them against God. But it's sad that Grosh died and never had a chance." She leaned back and wrapped her arms around her knees. A longing to blurt out the secret of her father's find before his death caused her to open her mouth, but she snapped it shut again. Martha and Parson Moser had counseled her to pray and trust God, but what about trusting Justin? Maybe that should be a matter of prayer, as well.

"It is, at that." Justin rose to his feet and brushed his hat against his legs, removing the pine needles and bits of dirt. "I'd best be getting back. I hate taking advantage of Martha's kindness."

Alex put a hand against the tree and started to rise. "Martha's in her element. She loves caring for Toby—it brightens her day and livens up the house."

Justin extended his hand and Alex grasped it. A tingle started in her fingers, shot up her arm, and warmed her chest. She wanted to drop his hand and run, but Justin didn't loosen his hold for several seconds. He looked down into her eyes. "Alex…"

She met his gaze. "Yes?"

He released her hand and took a step back, clearing his throat. "I'd best go. Thanks for letting me sit with you a spell." He swung away and covered the distance to the bottom of the hill in a few long strides.

Alex stood with her hands clasped. Was she the only one who'd felt something when their hands met? What had he almost said?

She needed to talk to someone about Justin Phillips, and she knew just the person.

* * * * *

A peek through the window showed the figure of Carl Ramsey moving about, so Alex pushed open the door. "Sheriff? Mind if I come in?"

Ramsey finished placing a long-barreled rifle up on the rack next to the door then turned a smiling face her way. "Alex. It's good to see you. Come in, come in."

"Thank you."

"Just gettin' back from church, are you?" He waved to the chair in front of his desk and took his own.

"Yes, but I took a walk up to the cemetery afterward."

"Ah. It's a nice place to visit when you need to think. Peaceful." He cocked his head to the side and raised one eyebrow. "Missin' your pa a powerful lot, I reckon?"

Sudden tears sprang to Alex's eyes but she batted them away. As much as she missed her father, she hadn't come to discuss him. "Yes. But I hoped to ask you some questions."

He leaned back and folded his arms. "Sure. Go right ahead."

"You remember the man Ralph tackled at the church? He had a wagon and a little boy."

"Uh-huh. Sure do. Justin Phillips."

"You've seen him since then?"

"Yes, ma'am, I have."

Alex rested her hat on her lap. "I hired him. Now I'm wondering if I made the right decision."

"You havin' a problem with him?"

"No, it's not that. I'm just wondering—Ralph thought he resembled a man on a Wanted poster, and I wondered—

"—if Phillips might be that man or might be on another poster?" Ramsey stretched his legs out to the side of his desk.

She met his direct gaze. "Yes."

"You got a reason to be worryin' about him, do you?"

She shook her head. "I'd like to think I don't. When I first met him, I didn't question his story. And of course, his having a child and all..." She shrugged.

"Now you think he might be a thief—or worse?"

"Well, not really. But after some of the things that've happened lately, I'm not sure what to think. He's a wonderful father, and he's been a big help at the ranch, so I feel guilty even asking. But now that I'm in charge, I need to make certain I've not hired someone who's running from the law."

"Why don't you tell me what's bothering you? Somethin' happenin' I need to be aware of, Alex?"

"Some horses disappeared the day Justin arrived on the ranch. We never recovered them. A few days later a fence was cut. Carter Foster had some of his men drive my horses back on my land and fix the fence."

"Ah-huh. Well, some of your land isn't fenced at all. I s'pose that first group could'a wandered off from the main herd and disappeared in the mountains for a spell, but it don't sound good."

"If it weren't for Ralph's accusation about the Wanted poster, the rest might not have bothered me. Justin showing up the day my horses disappeared worried me a little, but I've not had any complaints since hiring him."

"I'll tell you this much. Justin spoke to me and gave me the same details about the horses. To my knowledge he's not wanted anywhere." Alex started to interrupt, but he held up his hand. "It's good that you're bein' cautious. I'm not worried about Phillips being a horse thief, but it pays to go slow sometimes. How 'bout I look into his background and get back to you?"

She fingered the brim of her hat then placed it on her head and rose. "Thank you. That's more than I'd hoped for. I'll take him at face value until I hear different from you."

Sheriff Ramsey stood and escorted her to the door. "Glad to help. Come by any time. And Alex?"

She turned and looked up into his serious eyes.

He stood with his hand braced against the open door frame. "You be careful. I don't think this is a case of someone playin' a prank. Listen to Joe and keep your eyes open. I'll do the same."

Chapter Twenty

....

The sound of hoofbeats an hour before supper drew Alex out to the porch. She groaned. *Carter.* She'd pushed his request to come calling to the back of her mind. She knew she had no choice—she'd have to ask him to supper. Spinning on her heel, Alex hurried to the kitchen. "Martha? Can you set one more plate?"

Martha shut the door to the wood cookstove and raised a flushed face. "You know I always fix plenty. Who's coming?"

"Carter Foster is riding up the lane."

"What's that man want now?" She planted her hands on her hips and huffed.

Alex sighed and leaned against the cream-colored pantry standing near the washbasin. "I saw him in town awhile back, and he asked if he could call."

Martha's eyebrows shot high on her forehead. "Well, I declare. I was right. He's wantin' to court you."

Alex rolled her eyes and smiled. "Don't get all fired up, Martha. I'll turn him down if he wants to come again."

Martha cocked her head. "Joe's gone for the evening, so you may want to make sure Justin and Toby sit down to the table. The boy likes to take his meals outside with his papa sometimes. Might do you well not to be alone with Carter or to let him stay long after supper."

"Carter's a gentleman, and I'm not worried about appearances. But I guess you're right—it might be better to have more people here. I don't want to encourage him by spending time alone." Alex gave Martha a quick hug and headed for the door. "I'd best see what's holding him up. I thought he'd be at the door by now."

* * * * *

Justin swung around at the clatter of hoofbeats approaching the open barn door. Joe had ridden out to check on Frank and the mares around mid-afternoon and didn't plan on arriving home until sundown. The older man's joy at being in the saddle again, even for one short afternoon, touched Justin. He couldn't imagine the misery he'd feel if he lost the ability to ride.

Carter Foster reined to a stop and swung down from his saddle. "I've come to call on Miss Travers. See that my horse gets a good rubdown and a bag of grain." He thrust the reins toward Justin.

Justin took a step back and folded his arms. "I've got work to see to." He nodded toward the nearest stall, just inside the gaping doors. "Help yourself." The last thing he cared to do was coddle Foster or his horse. The man wasn't helpless—or his employer.

Carter's laugh was more like a snort. He reached out a hand and tapped Justin on the chest. "You need to remember your place, cowboy. You're Miss Travers's hired hand, not the owner of this place. I happen to be courting her, and if I ask you to care for my horse, it's your job to do so."

"Justin? Carter?" Alex's voice pierced the tension. "What's going on?" She stepped forward and looked from one to the other. "Carter, I heard you ride up and thought you'd be at the house by now."

Carter's hand fell to his side and a smile melted the hard angles of his face. "Your wrangler was just offering to stable my horse." He tipped his hat at Justin and held out the reins. "Much obliged, Phillips."

Justin hesitated then took the proffered reins. "No problem." He nodded at Alex and started into the barn, but her voice halted him two steps later.

"Be sure to bring Toby to supper tonight. Mr. Foster will be joining us, and I'm sure he'd enjoy meeting your son."

Justin slowly swung around and his gaze lit on Foster. A strange look passed over the man's face, and just as quickly it disappeared. He glanced at Justin then turned his back and walked Alex to the house.

"Come on, horse." Justin clucked to the gelding and led him to a stall. "You deserve a good rubdown after hauling that *hombre* around all day." Foster reminded Justin of a barn cat playing with a field mouse, or maybe a snake slithering after an unsuspecting bird. He shook his head. What did Alex see in the man? He hadn't seen any signs of interest on her part, but then, what did he know? Foster was right—he was only the hired man.

"Papa, you here?" Toby's dark head poked around the edge of the stall divider. "Miz Marfa said come to dinner."

Justin grinned at the boy and swung him up onto his shoulder. "What's my boy been doing all day?"

Toby giggled, bouncing up and down. "Unca Joe help me ride the horsey. And Miz Marfa fix me cookies. I play wit' the wagon Unca Joe made."

"You're gonna be plumb spoiled if they keep that up." He grabbed a flailing leg as the boy tipped backward. "Whoa there. Hold still, or you'll fall on your head."

"Sorry, Papa."

Justin set Toby back on the ground and knelt in front of him. "Did you say 'Thank you' to Miss Martha and Uncle Joe for all the nice things they did for you?"

"Uh-huh. I mean, yes, Papa."

"Good. Now we're going to clean up and go to dinner. Miss Alex has company, so you be on your best behavior, all right?" He patted the little boy's back and directed him toward the front door.

"Yes, Papa. I be good."

A few minutes later Justin lifted Toby into his chair at the far end of the table and took a seat beside him, just across from Alex. Carter

Foster sat to her right and Martha hovered over the table, placing the last steaming dish in the center.

Carter sniffed the fragrant aroma of the fried chicken and sighed. "Smells heavenly, Martha. I'm envious of Alexia, having you as a cook."

Alex glanced at Martha. "She's the best cook in these parts, if not the entire state. But most important, she's family."

"Martha, you've been a godsend to the Travers family over the years. They're blessed to have you with them."

Martha raised her brows and something resembling the shadow of a smile touched her lips. "Why, thank you." She passed the plate of chicken then some fresh-baked biscuits and a plate of corn on the cob. Silence prevailed as the hearty meal made its way onto each plate.

Alex set down her corncob and wiped her fingers on a napkin. "Have your ranch and mining claim been keeping you busy, Carter?"

He set down his coffee and nodded. "Very. My herd has grown steadily over the years—so much so that I took a band of geldings to Auburn recently to ship to the cavalry. You know they occasionally ask me for a few extra horses when they're short. They mentioned you'd not been able to meet your quota after your recent loss." He hesitated a moment. "They've...offered me a contract. I'm sorry, Alexia."

Alex frowned. "I didn't realize they'd be making a decision so soon. This is the first time I've not delivered an order on time. It would've been nice if they'd have let me know before reassigning the contract." She reached for her mug of coffee. "I'm sorry; my problems aren't your concern." She put on a smile and straightened her shoulders. "It's too bad Uncle Joe couldn't be here to visit with you. He and Frank are checking on the mares and won't be in for a couple of hours."

"I'll see him another time, but I didn't come to visit Joe. I hoped you and I might have a little time to ourselves this evening."

Alex blushed and reached for her mug of coffee, but she was saved from having to respond when Toby dropped his fork with a loud clatter.

Carter turned his gaze on Toby and stared for several seconds before he chuckled softly. "You're right, young man; we shouldn't be ignoring you." He cleared his throat and spoke a little louder. "How old are you, son?"

Toby held up three fingers. "Free. I a big boy." A sweet grin lit up his face.

Alex beamed at the boy. "And a sweetheart he is, too. His father has done a wonderful job raising him."

Carter's cold eyes bored into Justin, but his posture remained relaxed as he leaned his shoulder toward Alex. "Poor little tyke. I understand that he lost his mother. Must be hard for 'im."

Something in the statement put Justin's senses on alert, but Alex turned her compassionate gaze from Toby to Carter. "I know what it's like to lose a mother, and you're right; it is hard."

"I'm sure he'll benefit from your presence, my dear." Carter laid his hand over hers resting on the table, and it seemed to Justin that she didn't withdraw it overly fast. Maybe it was the supposed sympathy he'd shown for Toby or the memory of her own loss, but Alex appeared captivated by his charm. Whatever the case, Justin couldn't stand sitting at the table much longer.

He laid his fork by his plate and pushed to his feet. "Martha, Alex. I hope you'll excuse me. I have something I need to tend to in the barn." He laid a hand on Toby's hair for a moment. "I'll be back in time to settle Toby into bed."

Martha picked up a cloth and wiped a dribble from Toby's chin. "Sorry you can't sit with us awhile longer, but you do what you have to. Don't worry none about your boy. He'll be fine."

Justin nodded and strode from the room feeling as though the soles of his feet were on fire. He'd done it again—been tricked by a pretty face. He suddenly realized that despite his resistance, he'd allowed himself to believe that Alex might someday care for him. And as unwilling as he was to admit it, it stung to discover that she was interested in someone else. *Women.* Why'd he think this time might be different?

Disappointment turned bitter in his mouth, and he wanted to choke and spit. He'd keep his distance, be a good employee. Even a friend, if Alex showed she needed one. But he'd not set himself up for the depth of hurt he'd experienced in the past. He'd do the favor Travers had asked of him and then move on. No matter how much his heart yearned for a home, it wouldn't be here.

Chapter Twenty-one

....

One week later, Alex stood at the bottom of the stairs and raised her voice a notch. "Martha? Uncle Joe wants to know if you're ready. He's got the horses hitched to the buggy." Filtered sunlight cast soft beams over the polished wood floor, and not a speck of dust lingered on any of the pine furniture in the entry just off the parlor. Martha had risen early to leave her household spotless before she ventured off to town.

"Yes, dear. Tell Joe I'll be down in a minute." Martha's excited reply drifted from her open bedroom door. "I'm trying to decide which hat to wear. The blue is my favorite, but Alice has never seen the green one. What do you think?" She stepped out of her doorway and leaned over the banister running across the landing at the top of the stairs.

Alex bit her lip to quell the grin that threatened to escape. Martha and her hats. She gazed up at a straw creation perched on the gray hair. "The blue feathers are pretty, but since you haven't worn the green one, I'd choose it." She glanced out the front door. "But you'd best hurry. Uncle Joe gets testy when he has to wait."

"Oh, balderdash. It's not going to hurt the old coot to sit in the buggy for another five minutes." Martha pulled the hat off, leaving small tufts of hair sticking up in several directions. She swung on her heel and headed back to her room. "Please let him know I'm on my way. The green will do."

A few minutes later Martha bustled down the stairs, carrying her canvas grip in one hand and her hat with the other. "Can you fasten the hat pin a little more securely, Alexia?" She set the grip down and turned her back.

Alex secured the hat firmly in place then gave the older woman a quick hug. Martha pulled back, her hands on Alex's shoulders. "Maybe I should stay home. It's going to be too much, you taking care of Toby and doing the cooking." She reached up to undo the hat.

"Nonsense." Alex picked up the small canvas grip and headed for the front door. "We'll be fine. Justin will be here for part of the day. I've cooked more than a time or two, and I can handle things. Besides, you don't get to visit Alice very often, and she's expecting you and Uncle Joe."

The horses hitched to the buggy in front of the house whinnied and stamped. Martha looked outside to where Joe patiently sat on the front seat. "Perhaps one of the hands can drive me. That way Joe could stay around here."

Alex laughed and reached for Martha's hand. "Come on, you old dear. I'm not six years old; I'm a grown woman. Frank is here, and Justin and Davis are both working close by. Now go—or Uncle Joe will unhitch the horses and sit on the porch."

"Oh my." Martha rushed for the door, stopped, and then trotted back to plant a kiss on Alex's cheek. "Thank you, love. I'll try not to worry."

"Good." Alex walked her to the front steps and handed her off to Joe.

He helped Martha into the seat then stepped up and grasped the reins. "We ready to go, ladies? Or do I sit here another hour or two whilst you decide somethin' else?"

"Oh, pshaw, Joe. You didn't wait on me no time at all. Let's get a move on, or we'll miss havin' tea with Alice."

Joe rolled his eyes at Alex and winked. "Git up there, boys. You heard the lady. It's time to go to tea." He slapped the long reins against the team's haunches and clucked, sending them surging forward. "Have yourself a fine day, Alex," he called back over the sound of the rumbling buggy.

She waved and didn't suppress a chuckle this time. Those two characters bickered at each other half the time, but truth be told, they were the best of friends. Martha behaved like a big sister to the crotchety old Joe, and while he loved to tease her, Alex knew he'd defend her to the death.

Time to get to work. It would be up to her to prepare lunch for Toby today—and Justin, if he got back from checking the mares in the south pasture. She reached up to rub the gold locket hanging around her neck. "Mother, you would've loved Toby." The precocious little boy was hard to resist—as was his father.

He'd seemed to be warming up to her until the evening Carter came to call. She frowned, trying to remember if anything untoward had happened that day. Justin had stabled Carter's horse and joined the group for dinner. He'd been silent through most of the meal, even though Carter had gone out of his way to be charming and pleasant. In fact, even Martha had thawed toward their guest.

So what was Justin's problem? She walked to the kitchen and pulled open a cupboard. Maybe some of Martha's bread and a slab of meat for a sandwich would do, with some fried onions and potatoes on the side. She'd have to make a trip to the cellar for the vegetables.

She shook her head. Men were beyond her understanding, especially the ones who kept to themselves. She narrowed her eyes and her hand stilled in its work cutting slices of bread. Carter hadn't put out an effort to speak to Justin, come to think on it. Could Carter be jealous? She'd didn't want to think of that possibility.

She sawed at the bread, not paying close attention to the blade. "Ouch!" She dropped the knife and stared at the blood dripping from a cut in her finger. "I can't believe I did that."

A tap sounded at the open front door. "Anyone here?" Justin's deep voice vibrated through the entry and back to the kitchen.

"Come in." Alex stared at the deep cut, walked to the basin, and pumped the handle. A gush of water flowed over the cut, spreading it open to reveal a patch of white beneath the blood. A faint feeling settled over her, and the room darkened and spun. She tried to grab for the counter but instead caught air and felt herself sinking toward the floor.

"Whoa, there." A pair of strong hands clasped her under her arms and lifted her off her feet. "You're bleeding. Alex...Alexia! Don't faint on me!"

The dizziness faded, and she heard Justin's strong heartbeat beneath the light cotton shirt where her ear lay cradled against his chest. "I'm— I'm all right." She struggled weakly and felt his arms tighten around her.

"No, you're not. Now hold still so I can take a look at your hand." He gently deposited her in a nearby chair and reached for a towel. He held it under the dribbling waterspout and pulled the handle down. "What'd you do?"

Alex couldn't tell if the dizziness had been from his embrace or from the cut. She sat up straight and tried to control her trembling voice. "I cut my hand while slicing the bread. I–I've never fainted before."

"You would've hit the floor in another second. You faint at the sight of blood?" He knelt beside her and held her hand, his touch making her arm tingle. "Let me take a look." The damp towel mopped at the blood and he kept pressure on it for another few moments. "Hmm...it's pretty deep."

"Not usually."

"Huh?" He looked up, confusion written across the face that was only inches from hers.

"I don't faint at the sight of blood—not even my own. It was strange. I looked at the cut while it was under water and it spread open. I guess I thought I saw the bone. For a second I thought I'd severed my finger." She waved her other hand in the air. "The room started to spin." She laughed in embarrassment. "It's silly."

Justin kept pressure on the towel around her hand and looked right into her eyes. "No, it's not silly at all."

Alex caught her breath. His eyes were clear and direct. They seemed to pull her in, drawing her closer. Her heart began to pound and she felt sure the dizziness would overwhelm her again—but for an entirely different reason this time.

Justin cleared his throat and his eyes dropped. "Well, now. I think we'd better get some salve on this and wrap it tight. You might have a scar if it's not stitched. You want me to drive you in to see the doc?"

Alex pulled her hand out of his grasp and held the towel with her other hand. "No. I'm sure salve and wrapping will be fine. Thank you." She leaned back in the chair and closed her eyes, not wanting to meet that compelling gaze again. She chided herself for acting like a young schoolgirl smitten with her first crush. The man likely hadn't felt a thing as he'd leaned close—except maybe sympathy and a little amusement that a woman who claimed to be capable of running a ranch would get woozy over a cut. "If you don't mind helping. I don't think I can wrap it by myself."

Justin found the supplies and wrapped the cut without a word. Finally, he pushed to his feet and stood staring down at her with concerned eyes. "If you think you'll be all right, I'd best check on Toby. He should be waking from his nap."

Alex jumped to her feet and gasped. "I can't believe I forgot." She started for the door but stopped and clutched the back of a chair, dropping her head.

Justin glanced back, turned, and walked to her side. "Sit." He placed a strong arm around her waist and guided her back to her chair. "Stay." He leaned her back and kept his hands on her shoulders.

She chuckled and looked up. "That's what I say to Hunter. 'Sit. Stay.' I'm not a dog, you know."

"Not hardly." He grinned and headed for the door then swung around. "But I mean it. Stay put. I'll check on Toby, and when I come back I'll finish those sandwiches."

"I can do it." She started to rise, but his stern gaze deterred her. "All right, I'll wait."

"Good." He turned at the door to the kitchen and glanced back. There was something indefinable in his glance—a hesitancy or caution that she couldn't quite fathom. He turned and disappeared up the stairs.

Boots clumping down the stairs alerted Alex to Justin's return moments before he rounded the corner with Toby in his arms. The little boy rubbed his eyes and yawned. "I waked up." He looked at Alex, and a sweet smile pulled at his plump cheeks.

* * * * *

Justin placed Toby near Alex on the elevated chair and handed him a half slice of bread. Toby stuffed a piece in his mouth and stared at Alex's finger wrapped in the bandage. "You got a owie?" He didn't wait for her reply but held up his own small hand. "Toby got a owie, too." He pointed at an invisible spot on his thumb. "Papa kissed it and made it better. Papa kiss your owie, 'Lexie?"

Justin cleared his throat and ruffled Toby's hair, anxious to turn the attention away from Alex's glowing cheeks. "Eat your bread, son, and I'll make us a sandwich." He turned toward Alex with twitching lips. "He has a one-track mind if he gets something stuck in his head."

Alex laughed. "I've noticed. Like the day you came, when he begged to ride a horse."

Toby's head snapped up and his eyes grew large. "Toby ride the horsey?" He began to squirm in his chair. "Please, Papa?"

Justin rolled his eyes and shook his head. "Now we're in for it."

Alex leaned back in her chair and cocked her head to the side. "Sure, why not?"

"I beg your pardon?" Justin stopped cutting the bread and stood with the knife poised in the air.

She grinned and pointed at the knife. "Watch what you're doing, or you'll be next. Uncle Joe's been leading the pony in the yard, but I think it's high time Toby had his first real lesson. I was riding all over the barnyard at his age."

Justin took the lid off the crock of butter and spread a liberal amount on each slab of bread. "I'd be obliged, if you really don't mind. Now, what do you want between these slabs of bread?"

"The meat is in the cellar. We carved out some ice this winter and wrapped it in burlap. Uncle Joe slaughtered a steer last week, and the ice has kept it fresh. There's a crock of cool milk down there, too."

"I'll get it." Justin turned to Toby. "You be good and don't get down. When we're done eating, Miss Alex says you can ride her pony. But you have to eat your dinner first."

Toby's dark curls bobbed as he nodded. "I be good. I eat all my dinner."

"I'll be right back." Justin headed for the door and pulled it shut behind him, turning Toby's words over in his mind. *Kiss her owie and make it better.* Part of him had wanted to bolt from the room, while another part had wanted to laugh and raise her finger to his lips.

* * * * *

The meal passed in silence, but Alex had no sense of the discomfort that she'd felt with other people when conversation lagged. This felt right— safe and companionable—like a family should. She jerked her thoughts back—she didn't need a ready-made family. She took a quick gulp of milk and choked.

Justin grabbed a towel and stuffed it into her hand. "You all right?"

She raised wet eyes to his and nodded then gave a final cough and smiled. "I hope that doesn't become a habit—your having to ask if I'm all right."

A sly grin crept over his face. "Yeah. Wouldn't want the hired hand taking care of the boss lady. Might not be good for your reputation."

She stared, hardly able to believe her ears. He was teasing—actually teasing. She grinned back and narrowed her eyes. "You'd best watch your step, cowboy, or this boss lady might put you to mending fence." She laughed at the chagrin that covered his face and reached for another drink of milk. She could get used to this.

Chapter Twenty-two

....

Christy Grey sat easily in her sidesaddle on the mare she'd rented from the big blacksmith, Ralph. He'd not wanted to take her money, but she'd insisted. She didn't care to be beholden to any man. He'd given good directions to Alexia Travers's ranch, and from her estimation, it should only be another mile or less. The mare covered the ground with an easy, long trot, and Christy set her mind to planning.

Much would depend on who happened to be home. She hated the thought of the sweet Travers girl hearing what she had to say, but she'd not been given a choice. Why did Alexia have to treat her with such kindness at the store the day after she'd arrived? It would've been so much easier had she slighted her.

Her mare snorted and shied to the side. Christy glanced around. All she saw was brush, towering trees dotting the sparse meadows, and the tinkling stream not far behind. The mare had crossed the fast-moving water without hesitation and didn't seem to spook easily.

She drew back on the reins. "Whoa, girl. Easy. That's right." The mare gave a soft nicker and flicked her ears toward the hill up ahead. Christy stroked the glossy chestnut neck, ruffling the long mane with her gloved fingers. "Nothing's going to hurt you." She felt the tense body relax under her hand, and the horse's head lowered a few inches.

A flash of something reflected for a moment on the hill above, and just as quickly it disappeared. She narrowed her eyes and peered through the brush but didn't see any movement. A rider? Probably one of Alexia Travers's hands.

She urged her mare forward and trotted up the trail but didn't meet anyone along the way. When she crested the ridge, she drew her horse to a stop and gazed down on the scene. A green plateau spread beneath her, dotted with horses and trees, and a meandering stream wove off to one side. A two-story, bat-and-board-sided house perched on the edge of a large grassy meadow, and a huge barn sat a hundred feet away. No buggy appeared outside the barn or house, but she discerned movement in a corral. A horse and a person—or two.

She searched the trail leading down to the house and glanced back the way she'd come. Nothing. Had she imagined that shaft of light? It could've been the sun reflecting through the trees. She glanced upward and shook her head. No, the sun was in the wrong position to have sent its rays over the hill and into her eyes.

Someone had been at the top of the hill—watching her? An unladylike word slipped from her mouth and she booted her horse. The mare jumped forward, rocking Christy against the high cantle. She righted herself and gripped the reins, slowing the mare. Stupid move. The last thing she needed was an injury.

Sometimes she hated what she'd become. *Sometimes? Most of the time.* She trotted down the trail and spurred the mare into a lope. The dangerous pace fit her mood. The sooner she got this distasteful chore behind her, the sooner she could crawl back in the hole she called home and pull a blanket over her head.

* * * * *

Toby shouted with glee as he sat up straight and gripped the reins. His short legs didn't reach the stirrups bouncing against the belly of the shaggy pony. "Giddup." He shook the reins and rocked in the saddle.

Alex watched the antics of the small boy in amazement. "He's smart and not a bit afraid. He's listened to everything you've told him."

Justin kept moving, leading the patient black pony around the enclosed corral. "I've not found much that Toby's afraid of so far. Except the dark." He ducked his head after he'd spoken the words.

"Has he always been that way?" She leaned her arms on the split-rail fence.

"Not till after his mother died. Molly let him sleep with her every night, and I guess he's not as used to me."

Toby's energetic bouncing caused the horse to break into a trot. "Go fast, Papa. Toby like to go fast." Justin turned and grabbed the boy as he nearly toppled from the saddle. "Whoa, there. You need to hold still."

Toby quieted, a serious look on his small face. He held a finger up to his lips. "Shhh. Toby be quiet and not scare the horsey. Go faster, Papa, okay?"

Justin laughed, and the transformation on his handsome face gave Alex a small start. Her mind replayed his words. Toby not used to his father? Wouldn't Justin have slept in the same bed as Molly?

The sound of hoofbeats on the hard-packed trail approaching the house drew Alex's attention, and she was surprised to see the redheaded woman she'd met at the store—the saloon girl who'd asked after Justin. Miss Grey loped her horse across the open space leading to the barn. Alex had forgotten she'd invited her to visit. She lifted her hand and waved as the woman drew near, trying to muster a genuine smile. A pang of disappointment hit her, but she pushed it away, reminding herself that Justin was an employee—nothing more.

"Miss Grey, I see you found our ranch." Alex nodded at the woman sitting sidesaddle on the prancing mare. She certainly could handle a horse. "Would you like to step down and come in?"

"It's Christy, remember?" Something about her tone seemed sharp and unnatural. "No, thank you; I won't be here long." She turned her attention to the corral, and her eyes widened. "Is that Toby?"

Justin stopped his tedious circle and stepped alongside the boy. "Yes. And you are?"

Alex frowned and looked from one to the other. Christy knew Toby, but Justin didn't know her? She'd asked for him by name. It wouldn't be easy for most men to forget a woman like this.

Christy's eyes swung toward Justin and narrowed. Her horse snorted and sidestepped. "You know very well who I am, Justin Phillips."

He took his hat off and ran his fingers through his hair then slid it back onto his head. "I'm afraid you have the advantage." He turned to Alex. "You know this woman? You called her Miss Grey."

Alex pushed off from the wooden rail and frowned. This wasn't making sense. "We met at the store a few days ago. She came in asking for you. I invited her to come out. Maybe I should go into the house so the two of you can settle this." She took a step away from the corral.

"Wait." Both Justin and Christy spoke at the same time. Justin clamped his lips shut and nodded to Christy.

"Please don't go on my account," the woman said. "I'm not staying long. I've just come to get Toby."

Justin clutched the pony's reins, his eyes blazing. "I beg your pardon? Who do you think you are?"

Alex stepped into the corral, drew the whimpering boy off the pony, and held him close.

Christy sat back on her horse and settled deeper into her saddle. "I'm Molly's sister, Christy. Half sister, actually, as you well know. I see you're trying to pretend you don't know me, just like you pretended a lot of other things."

Justin uttered a low growl and drew himself up. "I've never met you before in my life, and I never heard anything about Molly having a sister."

"Ah, just like you supposedly married her?" She gave what sounded like a forced laugh. "What you really did was move in with her, get her with child, and then desert her when she told you about the baby. Why'd you come back when she died, Justin? Did you think Molly had money stashed that would go to Toby?"

Justin gaped at the woman, seemingly at a loss for words.

Christy bent over and dropped her voice. "I want my sister's boy. You have no right to him. You barely know him, and you weren't even married to her."

He sprang over the fence and landed a few feet from her horse. "Get off this property."

Christy's eyes narrowed. "From what I understand, you don't have the authority to be giving orders. You're just a cowhand here."

Justin gave Christy a hard look, his voice firm. "Miss Grey, I don't know what your game is, but I married your sister—that is, *if* she was your sister."

She reined her horse back. "Then I want proof. And until you give me that, I want the boy. I won't take a chance of you disappearing with him."

Justin jerked his head up and glared. "Over my dead body, lady. He's my son and no one's taking him away from me."

"We'll see about that. I'll be talking to the sheriff when I get back to town."

Toby whimpered and reached for Justin. Alex patted his back and pulled his head down on her shoulder then stepped forward, her eyes flashing. She raised her hand and lifted her voice, not bothering to keep the anger from her tone. "Miss Grey, I don't think your current living conditions are acceptable for a child."

Justin stared at Alex as though trying to understand the direction her words were going. "Living conditions?" He spun back toward Christy. "Where do you live?"

She remained silent and bit her lip.

Alex walked up beside Justin. "She works at the saloon as a dance hall girl. She told me so when I met her at the store."

Christy's face hardened as she straightened and picked up her reins. "We'll see what matters and what doesn't." She pushed her horse around with her heel and clucked to the mare.

* * * * *

Christy cantered off the property and spurred her horse up the hill, feeling as if a pack of hounds bayed and nipped at her heels. Dirty—she felt dirty and disgusted with herself. Alexia Travers had been decent in the store and hadn't shunned her, even when she'd heard where she worked. Christy couldn't blame her for using that information now— she'd have done the same in Miss Travers's place.

Her thoughts turned to Molly's boy—she'd only seen him a few times as a baby, when Justin was gone on cattle drives. A branch lashed her face as she drove her mount under the trees, heedless of the trail or what might be coming.

Truth be told, she hadn't known what kind of a father Justin was— until she saw him with Toby just now. But it was too late—the damage was done. She'd just threatened to destroy the man's happiness, and she'd succeeded in destroying any chance of friendship with the only decent woman who'd been kind to her.

* * * * *

Alex handed Toby to Justin and headed for the house without a word.

"Alex, wait. Please." Justin's frustrated voice floated toward her, but Alex kept moving. "I'd like to explain—"

She stopped but kept her back turned. "There's nothing to explain. It's not my business what my employees do—or have done—as long as they're not running from the law."

Solid footfalls sounded behind her. Toby fussed and demanded to get down. "Want to ride the horsey more. Please, Papa?"

"Later, Toby. I need you to be quiet, son. All right?"

"All wight." The child's plaintive voice reached Alex's ears. "What's wrong, Papa? Why you frowning? You sad?"

Alex's heart started to melt. She drew a deep breath and turned to face them. "I'll listen to what you have to say, but not now. Maybe later. I don't think it's something Toby needs to hear."

Justin hoisted the boy higher on his hip and nodded. "You're right. I'll put the pony up, and then I need to get to town to send a wire. You'll find out the truth, Alex." He stared at her for a long moment before turning toward the barn.

Alex felt rooted to where she stood as her mind ran in circles. The accusations Christy had leveled at Justin were ugly. Alex wanted to believe him, but the logical side of her mind urged her to take it slow and discover the facts. She'd only known him for a couple of weeks, after all, and a lot of questions about his past remained. First, there were the accusations at the church when he first rode into town and the problems plaguing her horses since he'd arrived. He'd come back to the ranch an hour before Carter and his hand rode in—and if she remembered correctly, he'd been in the area not far from where the fence had been cut. He claimed to have been scouting for stray horses.

And although Justin had also claimed he'd been married and had called Toby his son, something didn't add up where Molly and the boy were concerned. Why would Christy think she could claim Toby and get away with it? Could it be possible that the accusations were true? If Molly had the same type of background as her sister, it was certainly possible.

Then there was Christy. Something about her had seemed fragile and genuine when they'd met in the store. In today's encounter it had been like Alex was seeing a different person—hard, cold, and scheming. But what did Christy have to gain if her story weren't true? Why would a lone woman working at a saloon be anxious to have the care of a child only three years old? None of it made sense.

Justin returned from the barn with Toby and stood to face Alex. She felt her eyebrows rise. "So you can prove your claim. You weren't just saying that so she'd leave." She felt awful asking him, but she felt a deep need to know the truth.

Justin's face turned a dusky red. "I'm not a liar, Miss Travers, whatever else I may be." He stroked Toby's hair and cleared his throat. "I hate to ask you this, and I guess I can take him with me…."

"Of course I'll keep Toby. Go. It's fine." She reached for the boy, and he came willingly into her arms. "Let's go read a story, Toby."

"All right. Toby likes stories." He patted her face with a grubby hand and smiled. "Then ride horsey again?"

Alex couldn't help it; she had to laugh in spite of the circumstances. The child didn't give up. "Not today. Maybe another day, when we have more time. Papa has to go to town while we read a story."

He heaved a deep sigh and settled his head on her shoulder. "Okay."

Justin leaned over and kissed his son on the cheek. He raised his eyes to Alex. "Thank you." He didn't step away but stood close, grim determination covering his face. "I'm going to prove she's lying, whatever it takes. I can't stand—" He broke off and turned his head then spun on his heel and strode to the barn.

Alex stared after him, not sure what she believed. She'd wanted to keep her distance when she'd heard he'd been recently widowed, and now she was being told he'd never been married. Had he loved Toby's mother and married her—or used her and discarded her when the baby came along? The latter didn't seem to fit the type of man he appeared to be, but what did she really know about him?

Very little. She turned back toward the house, carrying the quiet boy on her hip. And at this point, she wasn't sure how much she wanted to know.

Chapter Twenty-three

Justin swung into his saddle with Durango already in motion. The plunging stallion hadn't been out of his pen since yesterday and was anxious to run. Justin didn't look back but leaned forward and loosened the reins. His mood suited the fast pace of his mount—driving and dangerous. He wanted to yell, punch someone, or shoot something—anything to fix the mess he'd had no part in creating.

The doubt evident on Alex's face scorched his insides. The seeds of mistrust had been sown, and he wasn't sure how he could squelch them. Even if the preacher who'd married him and Molly remembered the ceremony and produced a letter, what proof would he have that the letter was genuine? Any friend could send a letter by stage claiming to be a preacher.

He wanted to rail at God for letting this happen. God could have protected him—even rewarded him for staying with someone like Molly and taking her problems on his shoulders. But for some time after he'd married her, he'd struggled with being tied to a woman who'd proven she didn't love him and only wanted to use him.

Did God even care what happened to him? A pious mother and father had taught him right from wrong. He'd regularly warmed a church pew when he was younger, but he'd drifted away when he reached manhood. Beads of sweat trickled into Justin's eyes and he swiped his forehead with the back of his sleeve. That could be the problem now. God might not look kindly on someone who'd ignored Him all these years.

His horse headed up the steep slope, and Justin shook himself out of his thoughts. No sense in laming his horse on the rocks littering the trail.

The stallion still teemed with energy and fought the bit, unwilling to settle his gait. Justin sat deep in the saddle and gave another hard jerk on the reins. The black shook his head but slowed to a steady trot.

Recent tracks showed plainly in the soft earth under the fir trees, and Justin leaned over to peer at the ground. One set looked like the tracks of the mare the woman rode, but another set of hooves had traveled the same area shortly after hers. The prints were imprinted over the top, and from the spacing of the strides, it appeared the rider might have been following at the same pace.

He thought back to the last hour. He hadn't noticed anyone riding up this hill, and this wasn't a frequented path. Could the rider have been waiting in the trees? The Grey woman could have a partner, but if so, why follow instead of ride with her? There was plenty of room in this section for two horses side by side. They'd surely want to discuss the recent confrontation.

Justin decided it would be a good idea to follow and see where this second set led.

He kept an eye on the trail for the next couple of miles, and the tracks didn't vary. He reached the edge of the rocky area and headed down the trail leading toward the fast-moving stream. The tracks continued to overlap, and the mare hadn't slowed or pulled to the side to allow the second rider to catch up. The woman must not have been aware someone followed her. Interesting. It looked like this could be more complicated than he'd assumed.

One quiet word to his stallion and Durango surged ahead, eager to run. Justin kept his mount reined to a steady lope, not eager to overtake the Grey woman yet. At the stream crossing he slowed and bent low from his saddle. Looked like the tracks following her headed upstream, away from town. Justin sat for a moment and considered, but then he decided to keep to his original plan. If they didn't get another shower, he'd follow the tracks on his return—assuming he had enough light.

He'd keep his eyes and ears open in town, but with so many miners working claims in the vicinity, it wouldn't help to ask about strangers wandering through. Besides, he was enough of a stranger to raise a few eyebrows if he started digging for answers. Better to keep quiet and see what he could find out on his own.

* * * * *

Christy stood back in the shadows of the saloon and watched Justin Phillips ride past on his tall black stallion. Dried lather covered the horse—it looked like Phillips had run him for a while before slowing down and cooling him out. She didn't blame him; she could imagine the torment and anger that must have chased him down the trail. Nor was she surprised that he appeared in town on her heels. She'd half feared he'd jump on his horse and spur after her, overtaking her by the time she reached the stream. Thankfully her mare loved to travel at a fast trot. They'd covered the ground at a rapid pace and crossed the rushing stream without incident.

All the way to town she'd sensed something pursuing her. She'd kept looking over her shoulder, wondering if *he* were closing in. She didn't fear Phillips, but she deeply feared the man who'd summoned her here. She breathed easier now, knowing the man behind her must have been Phillips all along. He'd probably had no more desire than she to meet on the trail and had held back when he'd spotted her up ahead. She'd barely had time to slip into her work clothes and take her place in the saloon.

A voice already slurred by drink sounded close behind. "Hey, Christy. You gonna get me another beer or stand there peekin' out the door?" She swung quickly, not wanting whoever it might be to grab her arm or bare shoulder. More than one man had felt the back side of her hand when he'd gotten too familiar and she'd not been in the mood to tolerate his touch. Tonight would be one of those nights.

"Hurry up, would ya? I'm thirsty." The sound of heavy footfalls drew near.

"Give me a minute, all right?" She tried to smile and headed to the bar, wanting nothing more than to be out of this place. A grubby miner reached for her skirt as she passed, and she pushed his hand aside. "Now, Calvin, you know better than that." She winked and kept moving, sensing the bartender's hawk eyes honing in. No need to give him an excuse to squeal to the boss.

The clamor of bottles clinking against the rims of glasses sounded around the room. The place had filled with miners when the day shift ended at the nearby New Caledonia mine. She'd heard the rumor that a group of townsmen had formed a temperance society, but it didn't appear as though the miners cared to take part. It would probably be short-lived, regardless. She'd seen few towns that could persist in their decision to remain dry.

She leaned over the bar and placed the order for the thirsty miner awaiting his drink. The bartender shoved it the couple of feet to her open hand, and she plucked it off the bar. "Sam?"

The dark man scrunched heavy brows over brooding eyes and scowled. "Yeah? What'cha want?"

Christy did her best to smile, but it felt more like a grimace. "Can you get word to Mr. Sanders that I'd like to speak to him? Soon?"

Sam's face was blank for a moment before realization dawned. "Sanders, huh? Sure. I'll get word to Mr. *Sanders*." His laughter conveyed anything but a sense of mirth and sent a shiver over Christy's bare skin.

Christy dropped her eyes and kept her face passive. "Thanks." She swung away from the bar and hurried back to the waiting miner. He reached out a meaty hand and she placed the drink into it without looking at him.

The rest of the evening dragged by, with the rotgut whiskey flowing from the bar almost faster than she could serve it. The piano found in most saloons was noticeably absent. Instead, a man who'd had a little too much to drink swayed on his feet and played a mouth harp, while another man tapped out the tune on the base of a wooden bucket. It didn't appear that anyone cared whether there was entertainment or not, as long as the drinks held out.

After traveling the treacherous, steep canyon trail from Michigan Bluff, Christy could understand why a pack mule driver wouldn't burden his animal with a piano. She shuddered, remembering some of the trails where she'd chosen to walk behind the animal, too frightened to ride. One misstep on loose rocks could easily send a mule—and its rider— over the edge to their deaths at the bottom of the ravine.

Maybe that would have been a better end for her than coming here. Quick and simple—but painful. No, she'd take her chances with Sanders, or whatever he called himself here. If only she could climb back on that mule and disappear.

* * * * *

Christy scrubbed the last table then leaned her fists on the counter and rocked backward, hoping to relieve the tension in her lower back. What a rotten job. She'd give anything to get out of the mess her life had become.

"Christy." Sam beckoned from behind the bar and pointed to a door at the back of the room. "Get over there. Someone to see you."

She straightened her back and dropped her hands to her sides. Finally. She couldn't see the man's face hidden in the shadows beyond the open door, but she hoped it was Sanders. A loud *thump* made her flinch and she turned. Sam picked up another chair and turned it upside down onto the table. She'd better hurry. He'd be cussing at her to get back and start sweeping if she took too long.

A quick glance told her that the stranger was no longer standing at the door. She hurried to the rear of the smoky saloon and placed the palm of her hand against the rough wooden door, giving it a slight shove. It squealed in protest but finally swung open. She slipped through. The darkness in the small storeroom was almost complete. Only the little bit of dim light from the main saloon penetrated into this hovel. She sniffed, not liking the odor that assailed her nostrils. Sweaty clothing and damp, earthen walls. The back of the building must be up against some type of hill, or else a cellar lay beneath.

"Is anyone here? Mr. Sanders, is that you?" She stepped another foot into the room, willing her eyes to adjust to the dim light.

"No, Mr. Sanders ain't here, but I am." A low voice spoke from a nearby corner, sending chills up Christy's bare arms. "Now ain't you a pretty thing." The leering voice drew closer, and Christy took a step back.

"I asked to see Mr. Sanders." She tried to stand her ground and keep her voice level. This type of man preyed on the fear of others, and she didn't intend to feed that lust.

A sharp bark of a laugh came from a few feet away, and a shadowy figure loomed in front of her. "Don't matter what you want, missy. It's the boss what calls the shots, not you, and you'd do well not to fergit it." He rubbed his hands together then wiped them down the sides of his pants and leaned closer, staring into her face. "What you want with him? He tol' me to talk to ya and bring him word, so spit 'er out whilst you got the chance."

She drew back a short step then froze at the gleam of satisfaction on the man's face caused by her nervous gesture. "I want him to let me out of our deal. I tried to do what he asked, but it's not working. Tell him I'll help him in some other area."

"So yer sayin' you won't do what he tol' you? That what I'm hearin'?" The leer on his face changed to a snarl. "Yer playin' with fire, girl."

"No." Christy blurted the word then drew a deep breath, rubbing her hands over her bare arms. "I tried. Tell him I tried, but the man says he has proof that I'm lying. I'll do whatever Sanders wants me to do, if he'll just let me slip out of town and forget this."

"I'll tell him for ya, but he ain't goin' to like it." The man stepped back in the shadows and a floorboard squeaked. Christy heard his hand rattle what sounded like a doorknob. Light flooded the dank room, and just as quickly the door shut behind the man, leaving her once again in the murky dark.

* * * * *

Justin exited the tiny telegraph office with a paper clutched in his hand. The answer had come back sooner than he'd expected from the sheriff in Auburn. He dreaded opening the missive, as he'd expected a reply from the minister.

He glanced up the street, thankful to see few pedestrians lurking on the streets or boardwalks. As much as he wanted to rip into this message, he'd rather find a quiet spot. It looked like there might be a small clearing below the blacksmith and livery stable, from what he could see through the scattering of oak and small pine trees.

He struck out up the street and cut behind the dry goods store, going across the narrow, sparsely wooded area to the side of the smithy. He headed down the slight embankment and into the clearing that encompassed at least two acres. A sparkling pool of water lay on the east side. A fallen log drew him, and he sank onto its rough surface.

The telegram lay in his lap. Its contents could protect his right to keep Toby and clear him with Alex, or it could once again turn his world upside down. It had been hard enough being married to a woman who didn't love him, but the way she had tried to keep Toby from him had cut deep. He'd fight to keep this boy—he'd done so with Molly, and if need be, he'd do it again with this woman claiming to be her sister. Time to face whatever this small scrap of paper might contain. He held it up to the sunlight filtering through the trees and carefully unfolded it. It contained just a few terse words.

Preacher died last year. Courthouse burned three weeks ago. All records lost. Sheriff Jeffers.

Justin let the paper flutter to his lap and groaned. Maybe he should pack up Toby and hit the trail. Go somewhere Molly's sister wouldn't think to look. But what about his promise to Travers? No matter that the man no longer lived—Justin's promise extended to Travers's daughter.

Alex.

He dropped his head into his hands and rubbed his eyes. Even without the promise to Ben, he'd have stayed at the Circle T after meeting its new boss. Classy, that's what she was—classy, smart, beautiful, and capable. Never would he have believed that a woman could take up the challenge of running a ranch full of wranglers and succeed, but she appeared to be making progress. No other wranglers had quit since he'd arrived, and the ones who'd stayed seemed to respect her position as boss.

If only he could talk to Alex about his past. But why would she care? She wouldn't. Sure, she might feel sorry for him and the boy, but he didn't want any woman's pity. Would she believe him if he told her the truth? If the courthouse hadn't burned…if the minister had lived… But wishing wouldn't make it so. Alex had no reason to trust his word over anyone else's—and if she ever discovered that he'd come at her father's

request and not told her, she'd send him packing.

It looked like God had abandoned him this time for sure. He'd prayed for help when he came into this town, and look what a mess he was in now. A solid wedge of bitterness settled into his soul, and this time he didn't push it out. Hadn't he cleaned up his act after Toby was born? He'd never darkened the door of a saloon again. Stayed away from women. Done his best to raise his son. So why was God still against him?

Justin pushed to his feet and jammed the telegram in his front pocket. Time to hit the saddle and get back to the ranch. He'd left Toby in Alex's care long enough. He didn't want her resenting the boy. No. He needed to care for Toby—regardless of whether the law acknowledged Toby as his. He'd fight for the right to keep his son, and no one would stop him.

Chapter Twenty-four

....

Three days later Justin stepped off his horse in front of the sheriff's office and looped his reins around the hitching rail out front. A full day at the ranch had brought him to town late, and he'd put Toby to bed early after Martha offered to keep an ear tuned for the boy.

The last two days had been frustrating. Alex ignored him when he got back from sending his telegram, seemingly lost in the book she was reading to Toby. The two dark heads bent together over the colorful pictures, and Toby's chubby hand pointed at the book as he tried to follow the words. The image of his little boy snuggled on Alex's lap had wrenched his heart. Would his son ever know the love of a mother again, or would he always need to depend on housekeepers and caretakers?

He'd attempted to talk to Alex since then, but she hadn't seemed interested. She'd been acting like a driven woman, putting work first and foremost. This evening was the first time Justin had felt comfortable heading to town.

He raised his hand and reached for the doorknob of the sheriff's office when it swung open from the inside.

Sheriff Ramsey stood in the dim light, a surprised look on his face as he stared out at Justin. "Just headed home, but I have a few minutes, if you're lookin' for me?"

"Thanks, Sheriff."

Carl Ramsey drew the door back farther and motioned Justin inside. "What's on your mind, son?"

"More trouble at the Circle T." Justin stepped across the threshold and heard the door click shut behind him. He sank down into the chair in front of the desk as the sheriff took his seat behind it. Ramsey rocked back in his chair and crossed his arms, his gray eyes boring into Justin's. "Go ahead; I'm all ears."

Justin nodded. "Thanks. You already know about Alex's missing horses and the fence being cut."

"Yeah. You, Frank, and Alex followed the tracks and lost 'em."

"Never found the horses, either."

Ramsey nodded and placed a booted foot up on the corner of his desk. The other foot joined it, and a chunk of dried mud fell to the floor. The sheriff scowled and glared at the offending dirt. "Sarah's not going to like that." He snorted and waved a hand. "No matter, I'll clean it up 'fore she comes. Go on."

Justin crossed his arms and leaned back. "Carter Foster called on Alex a few days after he brought word about her cut fence. Stayed for dinner and said he'd picked up the contract Alex lost with the cavalry. I don't trust him, but I can't prove he's not on the level."

"Huh. Ben told me that Foster was some kind of distant relative. He got his ranch from his daddy, along with plenty of money to run it. His herd is big enough to fill more than one army contract. Never figured out why he didn't get it instead of Travers." He rubbed his chin. "Never cottoned to him myself, but it wouldn't surprise me none if he's sweet on Alex—and he'd not be the only man in the mountains to feel the same." He narrowed his eyes and leaned forward, his back rigid and his voice low. "You think she suspects who done it?"

Justin shrugged. "I'm the new man on the ranch. Not much gets discussed with me. She may have spoken with Joe; I don't know. None of it makes sense."

"Hmm. It don't, at that. I don't want to see Alex get hurt, if there's trouble brewin'." He leaned back and seemed to relax. "Makes you wonder if someone's out to cause trouble for Alex and Joe or if it's just some young'uns what had too much to drink that cut the fence. I'm guessin' you're here because you think it's the first case."

"I do. I can't prove anything, but I have a bad feeling." He hesitated, wondering if he should tell about the episode with Christy Grey. No, that was personal and had nothing to do with the ranch. No reason to burden the sheriff.

Ramsey leaned forward. "Wish Alex had come to me right after the horses disappeared. She mentioned it to me not long ago, and I've been keepin' an ear to the ground. I'll keep nosing around and see if I can turn anything up."

"Much obliged. I'll do the same."

"I'm glad you're out there. Alex know that her father sent for you?"

Justin winced and shook his head. "No. The subject hasn't come up."

Sheriff Ramsey trained a keen pair of eyes on Justin. "Might be just as well. She's a strong woman. Independent, with a mind of her own. Pretty and smart. She'd be a good catch for a man, but she'd be a poor enemy if she decided you couldn't be trusted."

Justin smiled and raised his eyebrows. "Yeah. But I can't see the man that catches her being someone like me. Alex deserves a man who's never been married, not one who'd burden her with a ready-made family."

"About that. I wondered—your boy—he don't look much like you. He favor his ma?" The shrewd gray eyes peered out from under the bushy brows.

Justin's gaze held steady. "He does." A few seconds elapsed and he plunged forward. "I'm not his blood father, but I married his mother well before he was born. If love makes a man a father, then he's one hundred percent mine."

"Ah-huh." The gray head bobbed in agreement. "Thought it might be somethin' like that. I agree, the boy's as much yours as his ma's. Any idea about his natural pa?"

"No, and I don't care to. The man got Molly in a family way and promised to marry her then disappeared the next day. If I were to discover his name, you'd probably have to lock me up for what I'd do to him."

Sheriff Ramsey squinted his eyes and rubbed his chin. "Doubtful. Kinda think I wouldn't be in town the day that happened. Sometimes a man's got to do what's right, if you catch my meanin'."

"I do. But it'll never happen anyway. The secret died with Molly."

"Mind me askin' what happened to your wife? A shame, a young woman like she musta been, dyin' and leavin' a little one behind."

Justin removed his hat and ran his fingers around the rim. "We lived over in Auburn. Funny, coming full circle like that. My pa's ranch lay between Sacramento and Auburn, and when I left home, I landed there. Met Molly and thought I was in love. Molly didn't love me. I thought she did when I married her, but I found out not long after that she was with child. And it wasn't mine."

"Good of you to take on her problem like that."

"She was still pining for the baby's father. I cared for her and I stayed. Guess I hoped she'd come to care for me."

"What happened?" Carl Ramsey leaned his forearms on the desk.

Justin settled back in his chair. "She started drinking. I think Toby was almost two before I figured out that drink was fueling her black moods. Bernie, the bartender where she'd worked, kept her supplied. When I found out, I laid him out cold on the floor of the saloon. A few days later, Molly was dead."

"Dead. Just like that? She take sick?"

"Not the kind you're thinking of. More like sickness in her soul." He sighed wearily. "When she found out what happened with Bernie, she threatened to take Toby and leave. The next day I came home to find Toby asleep and alone at the cabin. No Molly in sight. I figured I

knew where she'd gone, as I'd dumped out all her bottles a couple of
nights before. I knew she wouldn't go to the saloon, and I'd asked the
storekeeper to be sure she didn't get anything from him."

"But she got some anyway?"

"No. I think she tried. She went to the store and was on her way
back. Don't know if she was thinking clear. A boy came running to my
door, shouting that Molly was hurt. I told him to stay with Toby and
raced up the street. She lay in the middle of the road, her body crumpled
from a passing wagon."

Sheriff Ramsey winced and ran his hand over his chin. "Sorry to hear
that. What'd the driver say?"

"He never saw her. According to an onlooker, she ran in front of him
like the fiends of Hades were on her heels. The man never had a chance
to stop. Lead horse knocked her down right under the wheels of the
wagon." He shook his head, trying to clear the memory of Molly's broken
body. "After I buried her, I packed up the boy and moved to Truckee. Too
many people around town were talking—saying they thought she did it
on purpose 'cause she couldn't get anything to drink."

"What do you think?"

Justin wagged his head and closed his eyes for a moment then slowly
opened them and focused on the sheriff. "I wish I knew," he whispered.
"I'll never forgive myself for failing her."

"You loved her?"

"At first. But I failed just the same. I shoulda been able to make her
happy—or at least kept her from sinking so deep into the blackness.
I failed the boy, too. He lost his mama and didn't hardly know me, what
with me being gone so much. I shoulda been around more. Took my
place as her husband and Toby's father. Anyway, I swore the truth would
never come back to haunt Toby. He'll be told that his mama loved him—
that much is true."

A somber silence settled over the room. The sun dropped below the horizon and darkness increased. The lone lantern hanging on a wooden peg near the door cast its light over the two silent men, each lost in his own reflection.

A few minutes passed and Justin started to rise then settled back into his chair. "One more thing."

"Git it off yer chest, son."

Justin let his gaze rove the room for a moment before answering, trying to gather his thoughts. Dim shadows lingered around the barred cell in the back of the shack, and an air of expectancy hovered nearby. "Molly's sister turned up in town a few days ago. Name's Christy Grey and she's working at the saloon."

"Saw her. Pretty, nicely dressed redheaded gal?"

"Yeah."

"And you say she's your wife's sister? Come out for a little family visit?"

Justin bit back a laugh. "Hardly. I didn't know she existed until she showed up at the ranch two days ago."

"Hmm. Alex see her?"

"Unfortunately."

"What'd she want with you? Or did she come to see Alex?"

Justin shook his head and released a small groan. "Me. Or maybe I should say Toby. She's trying to take my son. Says I have no right to him."

The sheriff's forehead wrinkled and his head drew back a mite. "No right? You're his pa."

"She's claiming I never married Molly. That I abandoned Molly and Toby. Says she's blood kin, and she wants him."

"Does she know you're not Toby's natural father?"

"I don't know for sure, but I don't think so. Besides, I don't care to have Toby find out. Things like that cast a shadow on a child's life. I'm his pa, and that's all he needs to know. I just got to prove I married his mother."

"Should be simple. You got a marriage certificate or a family Bible that the preacher put the date and your names in?"

Justin leaned forward. "No. I wired the preacher in Auburn and got a reply from the sheriff. The preacher died and the courthouse where he recorded the marriage burned. I have no idea what happened to Molly's copy."

"Ah, tough luck." The sheriff wagged his head and tapped his fingers against the surface of his desk. "Alex know all this?"

"Miss Grey blurted it out in front of her. I haven't told her about the courthouse or the preacher."

"Ah-huh. Well, now." Sheriff Ramsey seemed at a loss for words but kept his eyes steady on Justin.

Justin pushed to his feet and extended his hand. The sheriff stood and shook it, then Justin stepped toward the door. "Thanks for your time, Sheriff. I appreciate you keeping an eye out for what might be going on at the ranch—and for the listening ear."

The man hitched up his belt and walked around his desk. "Sure thing. I should tell you that if the Grey woman comes to me with a complaint, I'll have to look into it. Not that I want to, mind you—but I've a sworn duty to uphold."

"Yeah, I know." Justin turned the knob and pulled open the door. He hesitated then swung back around. "I'm sure it goes without saying, but…"

"I'll keep your story about Molly and the rest to myself. Not anyone else's business."

"Thanks. Much obliged again, Sheriff. Have a good night."

"You, too. Guess I'll be gettin' on home, or Sarah's going to send the posse after me."

Justin pulled the door shut behind him and headed down the street to his stallion tied to the hitching rail. He'd hoped things would get easier after he arrived here, but life sure had a way of disappointing some men.

Seemed like God might take a hand in things just this once in his life. 'Course, he'd not been doing much along the lines of prayer or reading a Bible for some time now.

He stopped alongside his horse and paused then reached into his saddlebag, drew out an object wrapped in oilskin, and balanced it on his hand. *Mother's Bible.* He hadn't thought of it or looked at it since placing it here more than a year ago. Maybe it was time to start reading it again. It might not change anything, but he doubted it would hurt, either.

Chapter Twenty-five
·····················

Alex sat at her father's desk and stared at the remaining stack of
paperwork. Why hadn't she noticed the hours her father must've spent
in here? Most of her memories of him revolved around their rides,
shooting and hunting expeditions, and starting the young stock under
saddle. She'd had no idea how much time the business end of running
a ranch could consume.

As soon as she finished here, she'd take Hunter for a run down the
road. She leaned over and stroked the big dog's ears. "Want to take a
walk, boy?"

His tail began to thump and he lifted eager eyes.

"Soon. I'm almost done."

The contract for the small band of mares due to be delivered in a few
days lay on top. Ten mares shipping via the railroad in Auburn to a stable
in Sacramento. That meant sending a couple of men off the ranch for at
least three days. Justin? She shook her head. As much as she'd like to send
him, she couldn't do that to Toby. Davis and one of the other men would
do. The Foresthill sale would be a faster trip—maybe Justin could take
that one instead.

The bookkeeping end of things caused her the most stress. The theft
of the geldings a few weeks earlier and the resultant loss of the cavalry
contract cut deep. This small sale would barely pay this month's ranch
expenses, with nothing set aside against the bank mortgage.

The men had searched for the missing horses again, with no results.
She'd given up looking, and the weight of the note against the ranch
sat even heavier on her shoulders. Something needed to change, and

soon. She'd had to dig deep to pay for the new stallion and mares, and it would be more than three years before she'd see any income from them.

She glanced down at the books again. For some reason, the tally of her herd seemed off. She'd had the men count the mares, foals, and geldings over this past week, and the numbers didn't correspond with her father's list. It appeared that at least a dozen head were missing, or else her father's figures were off. "No way. Papa never made a mistake on a head count in his life." She muttered the words under her breath.

Footsteps outside the open door came to a halt, and Martha poked her head around the corner. "Need something, dearie?"

Alex smiled and shook her head. "I declare, you've got better hearing than I do." She reached her arms in the air and stretched. "The only thing I need is a new back and a few missing horses."

Martha's eyebrows shot up into the soft fringe of bangs feathered across her forehead. "More missing horses? What's this you're saying?" She stepped into the doorway and shot a sharp look at Alex.

"Unless Dad's numbers are off, we've got about a dozen head unaccounted for. A couple of mares that are open this year and the rest geldings."

"What in the world?" Martha braced her sturdy hand against the door frame.

"I don't know, but I mean to find out." Alex pushed up from her chair and bent her shoulders toward the floor. "After I get this kink out of my back. How anyone can ride an office chair for more than an hour I'll never understand. I'd rather sit a bad-tempered horse all day than sit in that thing for half that long."

"Your father, God rest his heart, used to say the same thing. He hated sitting in here away from the sunshine and fresh air. What *you* see in sitting a hard saddle being bounced all over creation, *I'll* never understand. A rocking chair with a pillow under your bottom and one behind your back is far nicer."

Alex laughed and put her arm around Martha's plump shoulders. "Martha, Martha, you have no idea what you're missing. But I must admit I'm grateful you feel more comfortable in your kitchen than in a saddle, or we'd all starve."

"That you would, dearie, that you would." The older woman's eyes twinkled and she patted Alex's arm then moved off to her chosen domain. Martha paused in the doorway and turned. "Best tell your uncle Joe about those horses and maybe Justin, as well. He seems like a smart, honest boy. I'm guessing he could help."

Alex rolled her eyes at the not-so-subtle hint. Why was everyone close to her determined to play matchmaker? "He might be smart, but I have no desire to confide my business to the man."

Martha swung around and marched back a few paces. "What's ailin' you, child? You've had a bee in your bonnet for days."

Alex avoided the older woman's eyes and dropped her gaze back to the account book. "Nothing. Just tired, I guess."

Martha snorted. "No, ma'am, I don't believe that. You're as healthy as a young colt turned out on new spring grass. Something's worrying you. You're no good at keeping things from me, missy, so you might as well spit it out." She tromped back to the desk and lowered her bulk into a chair.

Alex grinned and shook her head. "I've kept lots of secrets from you over the years. I'll bet you don't know I used to climb out my window and shinny down the oak tree so I could sneak off and ride my pony in the moonlight, do you?" She grinned at the shocked look on Martha's face. "Huh. What'd I tell you."

Martha crossed her arms and leaned back in the chair. "Have it your way. Keep your secret and go on being miserable all by your lonesome."

Alex's grin faded and she felt herself droop. The last thing she wanted was to keep the worry about Justin stored up inside. Alex knew that Martha was right. "Something happened while you were gone to Alice's for tea." With a sigh she launched into a description of the events of the past few days, from her first meeting with Christy Grey to their most recent encounter with Justin at the ranch.

"So you see, she claims she's Molly's sister and wants Toby. Says Justin wasn't married to Toby's mama and he abandoned them both while Molly was alive—that he has no right to Toby. She plans on going to the sheriff if she has to."

Martha gasped and placed her hand over her heart. "Toby? Over my dead body. Nobody's going to take that boy off this ranch or away from his papa." She turned a fierce look on Alex. "Don't care what the woman says. Justin loves that boy and he's his pa, pure and simple."

She got up and leaned over Alex, giving her a brief hug. "I'd best get back to my work." Martha paused before leaving the room. "You know, your papa's Bible might ease your heart."

Alex lowered her head. "You're right. I haven't been very faithful in my scripture reading since Papa passed away. He'd be disappointed in me." She looked back up at Martha. "Call me if you need me?"

"I will, dearie. But for now you try to relax."

* * * * *

Alex leaned over and patted her sleeping dog's head then reached for the Bible lying on the corner of the desk. Why she hadn't thought of her father's Bible before now shamed her. Where to start? She'd been partial to Psalms and Proverbs—maybe she'd find what she needed there.

The Bible opened to a paper folded in half bearing her name in her father's distinct script. She drew it out and laid the Bible aside then opened the two sheets. His precise handwriting flowed across the parchment. When she spied the date at the top, her eyes widened. Just three days before his death. He'd written her a letter but not given it to her? Why write it when he could speak to her instead?

She blinked her eyes, forcing back the tears collecting in the corners at the sight of her father's script. This wasn't the time to cry.

Alex,

I'm unsure of how much to share or whether to give you this letter. I'm not expecting anything to happen, but if it did, you might be put in a hard position. I'll leave this in my Bible and consider for a few days, knowing the Lord will lead me. But until that time, I'm going to record some things that have happened and what measures I've taken to protect you and all we hold dear.

A couple of weeks ago I found what looks to be a rich ore deposit on the far side of our property, near the boundary between our place and Carter Foster's. I've not shared this with anyone but Joe. He and I were speaking about it in my office. You know how I always keep the window open. I heard movement outside. I checked but found no one there. The next morning I found tracks, but it had rained and they weren't clear enough to follow.

I haven't told Joe the exact location of the deposit, although I plan on telling him and you after the assay results come in. No use in getting everyone stirred up with false hopes if I'm wrong. Since then, things have been happening around the ranch. The place I always visit when I want to think was tampered with. I was standing on the edge when it started to cave. I jumped back in time to avoid a nasty fall. I won't go on, but there's been more and it's got me worried. I plan to talk to Sheriff Ramsey when I take this next batch of ore samples to town.

Alex stopped at the bottom of the page and stared out the window her father had mentioned. Had someone really been listening outside their home, hoping to obtain details about the gold's location? She glanced back at the page. Papa had stated that there had been other episodes. Her gaze returned to the open window. Suddenly she bolted from the chair, drawing the window closed with a *thump*. Papa's revelation heightened the sense of unease she'd been trying to conquer ever since her horses disappeared. Had someone been sabotaging the ranch and possibly spying on her since Papa's death? She shivered and sank back into the chair, not liking the direction her thoughts had strayed. She turned her attention back to the letter, slipping the first page behind the second.

I made a decision to ask for help. I don't know if I ever mentioned my old friend Josiah Phillips to you. Some years ago I helped him during a rough spell. Josiah needed money to save his place, and I loaned it to him. He passed away without paying it back, and his son, Justin, wrote to say that his father's debt weighed on him. Fine boy. Said he'd pay it back any way he could. So I told him that if I ever needed help, I'd ask him to come and we'd be square. He didn't want to agree, but I insisted. I sent a wire to Justin Phillips yesterday. He should arrive in the next couple of weeks.

The letter continued, but Alex's vision blurred and the pages fluttered to her lap. Justin Phillips? Why hadn't Papa talked to her about the gold, his fears, his need of help, or sending the wire? Why did he feel he had to shelter her? Maybe all these years of training had been a sham. Maybe he didn't really think her capable after all. He chose to bring in a stranger instead of leaning on his own family.

And what about Justin? He knew her father and hadn't told her— and worse yet, took the job and never said a word.

Her eyes quickly scanned the rest of the letter. Only one
paragraph left.

> *I told Justin to keep quiet about my asking him to come until I hire
> him and introduce him to you proper. You'll like him, Alex. He's honest
> and fine. I heard he'd been married and lost his wife not long ago. In
> his younger days, his pa said he ran wild for a bit, like most young bucks
> will do, but he straightened up and made his pa proud before he died.*
>
> *Know that I love you, Alex, and I'm glad you're my daughter.
> You're better than any son the good Lord could've seen fit to give me.
> Hopefully I'll get to the bottom of what's happening soon and not need
> to bother you with this mess.*
>
> *Papa.*

Alex tipped her head back and closed her eyes. Papa had asked Justin
to keep quiet about the reason for coming—at least until he was hired
and introduced. Well, Papa died before Justin got here—so why the
pretense now? Why not come right out and tell her?

She tried to push down the irritation and anger she felt building inside.
She didn't care for the thought that her father had brought in outside
help without telling her. Between him, Uncle Joe, and Martha—and now
Justin—she felt like a grammar school child being protected from the
bullies on the playground. Or rather, she felt that they saw her that way.

She slipped the letter back into the Bible and closed it. Her desire
to read God's Word had faded. It might not be a wise decision, but right
now she felt betrayed by nearly everyone around her. She tried not to
lump God into the circle of blame, but if her father hadn't had a heart
attack, none of this would be happening. Was that so much to ask of
God—to keep her only remaining blood relative alive a few more years?

She bolted up out of the chair, tired of thinking and feeling a twinge of a headache starting. "Come on, Hunter. Time to head outside." The dog lying beside her desk pushed to his feet and stretched, yawning and shaking his head. She stroked his soft coat and rubbed his ears. "I'm sure glad there's someone around here I can count on."

Chapter Twenty-six

....

Christy shut the back door of the saloon near midnight, thankful to be away from the foul breath and pawing hands. A walk in the fresh night air might clear her head. A decision needed to be made, and soon. Disappointment and worry had troubled her sleep the past few days. After the message she'd sent with Sanders's flunky a few days earlier, she'd hoped he'd come—or at least send someone to respond to her request. His continued silence wrapped an ominous blanket around her shoulders. Hearing anything would've been better than hearing nothing.

She slipped around the corner of the building and headed toward a small patch of trees to the clearing down over the bank. The soft shafts of moonlight cast fingers of light through the branches of the cedars and pine. No small creatures rustled or called to one another this time of night. She pulled her cloak around her shoulders and shivered. The air was pleasantly warm, but dancing fingers of dread sent a shiver running along her skin.

She glanced over her shoulder, certain that she sensed someone following. No one. Maybe this wasn't such a wise idea, walking alone at night. She hesitated, took a few more steps, and turned again. Still nothing. *You're being foolish, girl.* It was only a short distance to the trees and down the slight grade to the meadow, where the moonlight shone bright and strong. She'd feel safer there, not so closed in and trapped.

"Goin' somewhere, missy?" A rough hand landed on her shoulder and spun her around, and another clamped over her mouth.

A second voice hissed into her ear. "Sure seems a shame to rough up such a pretty face, don't it, Mouse?"

"Shut up!" the voice belonging to the rough hand snarled. "No names, remember?"

The second man wheezed a laugh. "Don't matter. She won't be fit to tell no one when we finish."

Christy broke from her stupor. Standing here would bring her one thing—death. Sanders was behind this attack. She jerked the arm held in the filthy grasp of her attacker and swung her other fist backward, hoping to hit his face. At the same time her booted heel came down hard on his instep. A hard twist of her body, and she felt his grip loosen. Just another wrench and she'd be free.

The one called Mouse growled an oath and pawed at her arms as they slipped from his grasp. "Cain, grab her! She's gettin' away."

Cain leaped toward her just as she gained her freedom and started to run. His fingers tangled in her hair and he yanked. Christy yelped in pain. Her head flew back, and she felt strands of hair loosening from her scalp.

Cain's panting voice sounded next to her ear. "What now, boss? Want me to club her?"

"No, you id'jit. We're too close to town, and someone might hear. Come on, keep yer hand over her mouth—we'll drag her out of this clearing. We'll be dead our own selves if'n we mess this job up for the boss."

Christy fought down the panic rising in her throat and threatening to spew out beneath this foul man's fingers. She couldn't give way to fear. Now that she'd run and they'd caught her, maybe they wouldn't expect another attempt. Whatever she did, it had to be fast. They'd soon penetrate the deep gloom of a grove of mesquite a hundred feet away. She opened her lips beneath the man's hand and almost gagged from its taste and the smell. But it was no time for squeamishness. She drew back her lips and bit down hard on the fleshy part of his hand. Something wet and salty touched her tongue before the hand jerked away. Blood.

"She bit me!" The man yowled and dropped his hand.

Christy lunged forward, heading back toward town. If she screamed, would anyone hear? And if they did, would they care? Or would she just be another dance hall girl getting what she deserved? She'd better save her breath and try to outrun the mongrels.

Panting sounded behind her, and footfalls crashed through the low-lying mesquite brush. She hazarded a peek over her shoulder and saw shadowy figures drawing closer. *Blast this dress.* She hiked it up to her knees and stretched out her legs, determined to outdistance the pair.

She turned her gaze back toward town one moment too late. A large tree loomed directly in front of her, and she couldn't dart around it. She felt her shoulder strike the stub of a broken branch, ripping a gash into her flesh. She stumbled and almost fell but caught herself and fought to continue.

The sound of wheezing came close. "I'm gonna kill you now. Would'a just beat you before, but you bit me. Drawed blood, too."

Bile rose up in Christy's throat. Her breathing came in ragged gasps and she opened her mouth to scream.

A hairy arm clamped around her throat and jerked her from her feet. "No, you don't, missy. Not a peep out of you." He threw her to the ground and knelt over her. "Not one peep or I'll make this long and painful, you hear me?"

She whimpered and managed to nod.

"Get up." He grabbed her wrist and jerked her to her feet. "We're takin' you away from town so the good people of Last Chance can't hear you scream." His evil laugh smote her ears just before welcome blackness enveloped her mind.

Chapter Twenty-seven

....

Alex trotted her horse into town. No particular need pressed her today other than a need to escape the ranch and all the people who'd deceived her over the past few weeks. She'd decided not to share Papa's letter with Martha or Uncle Joe. They'd only try to assuage her anger.

But the last person she wanted to see was Justin. She'd asked Uncle Joe to send him, Frank, and Davis to Foresthill with the small group of geldings she'd sold. The men would be gone the entire day and possibly overnight—a good thing for her peace of mind—and probably safer for Justin than running into her sharp tongue.

She pushed open the door of Cramer's Dry Goods Store. The bell tinkled, but no one waited at the front. Strange. Elizabeth wouldn't leave the store unattended unless something happened, but why not turn the sign and lock the door?

"Elizabeth?" Alex walked across the wooden floor and peeked behind the high counter flanking the front. No one stood behind it tending the multiple drawers of goods for sale. She peered down the nearest aisle of leather goods, skirted around a table stacked with yardage, and stopped at the last row brimming with farm implements and kitchen utensils. "Elizabeth, Mr. Cramer? Anyone here?"

At the sound of the bell tinkling on the door, Alex whirled around and hurried back to the register. She found her friend standing just inside the door, leaning against it, with her eyes closed.

Alex stopped and bit her lip. "Elizabeth? Are you all right?"

Elizabeth's eyes flew open and her hand rose to her heart. "Alex! Oh, my. I didn't realize anyone was here. I guess I forgot to lock the door."

Alex walked over and touched her arm. "Something's wrong. What is it? Has your uncle worsened?"

Elizabeth shook her head. "Come sit at the counter and I'll tell you about it." A small shudder shook her slender frame. "But I'd rather not be interrupted." She walked quickly to the door, flipped the sign and the lock, and came back to sit at the counter.

Alex leaned her elbows on the hardwood surface and stared at Elizabeth. "What's going on? Why all the mystery?"

Elizabeth drew a deep breath and released it through parted lips. "You remember Christy Grey—the girl who came in that day asking about your new hired man?"

Alex winced and nodded. "I remember." She'd planned on talking to Elizabeth about her today. "Has something happened?"

"Yes, and it's not good. Ralph took two horses from the livery down to that spring in the meadow early this morning, and he heard someone groaning from somewhere in the brush. He looked around and found Christy dumped in a tangle of mesquite."

"Dumped? What exactly do you mean?"

"He found her body"—she shuddered—"covered in blood, her clothes all torn. No way did she walk there or fall. Someone had to have dumped her."

Alex's hand flew to her throat, and she felt the blood drain from her face. "Her body. Is she—dead?"

Elizabeth clutched Alex's other hand and squeezed. "I'm sorry. I shouldn't have put it that way. No. She's alive. Ralph carried her to the doctor's office. She's hanging on, but not by much. It appears she's been beaten. Doc thinks she has broken ribs and some damage to her insides. There's some bad bruising in her middle, like she got kicked, and she's lost a lot of blood."

"Does the sheriff know who did it?"

Elizabeth shook her head. "No idea. She's not conscious. It could've been someone at the saloon. Talk has it she doesn't give away favors the way some of the miners would like."

Alex leaned against the low back of the stool. "I can't believe it. Why would anyone hurt her, even if she didn't—you know?"

Elizabeth shrugged and slipped off the stool. "No idea, but I hope they catch whoever it is and string him up. No one should treat a woman that way." She headed to the door. "I'd best open." She flipped the sign and unlocked the door.

"What's going to happen to her?" Alex asked.

Elizabeth turned, her eyebrows scrunched down over her eyes. "What do you mean?"

"To Christy? Who'll care for her while she recovers? I can't see the saloon owner doing it, and Doc only has one bed. He can't keep her forever. She'll have to stay somewhere till she's better."

Elizabeth walked closer to the counter and peered into Alex's eyes. "If you're thinking what I think you're thinking…you'd better stop."

"What?" Alex slid down from her stool. Her feet hit the floor with a soft *thump*.

"That you want to take her home. She's not a lost puppy or a hurt horse. She's a dance hall girl who's been beat up, probably by a disgruntled customer."

Alex crossed her arms and tipped her head. "I didn't say I was going to take her home, but if I were, why would that be so terrible?"

"Because…because…" Elizabeth sputtered then drew a breath. "We're supposed to love people, even in their sin. But I don't think the Lord expects us to take the sinners into our homes."

"He entered their homes, sat with tax collectors and prostitutes. It's not like I'm worried about my reputation. Mind you, I'm not saying I'm going to ask her, but if I did, would you be angry?"

Elizabeth groaned and rolled her eyes. "Of course not, silly. I just don't think it's your place to provide for her."

"Then whose place is it?" Alex tapped her foot and narrowed her eyes.

"Oh, for goodness' sake, I don't know." Elizabeth planted her hands on her hips. "I doubt Martha or Joe would agree, regardless."

Alex's body stilled and she lifted her head. "It's my house. Not that I wouldn't care what they thought. But honestly, Elizabeth, you're making it sound—I don't know—like she's some type of criminal who doesn't deserve help. As Christians, aren't we supposed to go the extra mile when others won't?"

Elizabeth's head tipped forward and she stared at the floor. "Yes. You're right, of course." Her voice dropped to a whisper. "I'm sorry."

Alex wrapped her arms around her friend and drew her into a warm hug. "Nothing to be sorry for. You're looking out for my best, and I appreciate you. I do feel sorry for her. Even if she is trying to take Toby away from Justin."

"What?" Elizabeth pulled back from Alex's arm encircling her shoulder. "Explain."

Alex spent the next few minutes filling Elizabeth in on recent events, from Christy's arrival to the finding of her father's letter.

Elizabeth leaned her hip against the counter and crossed her arms. "Whew. It's a good thing the store isn't busy right now. I think I'd have shooed out anyone who dared to come in while you told that story. I can't believe she had the gall to ride out and demand that Justin turn over his son."

"She claims Justin wasn't married to her sister and that he abandoned them before Toby was born. As Molly's sister, she thinks she has a stronger claim to the boy."

Elizabeth huffed and pursed her lips. "You can't even consider having that woman on your place. Justin would have a fit, and I wouldn't blame him."

"It's not his call. Besides, how better to keep an eye on someone than to have them living under your roof?"

"But aren't Justin and Toby staying in your house? Wouldn't that be…awkward?"

"I agree, it could be. But like I said, I've not made any decision. You're the one who brought it up, not me. Maybe you should be the one to keep her." Alex hid a smile and turned a serious gaze on Elizabeth.

"I–I—" Elizabeth stumbled then fell silent.

Alex laughed and patted her friend's arm. "Don't worry. Your uncle wouldn't allow it, and I was teasing. Tell you what—you're always telling me I need to trust God and pray about things more. What if we both pray about Christy? I'm not thrilled with what she pulled on Justin, but I don't think God wants us to ignore someone in need, either."

"I agree, and I'll pray." Elizabeth sighed. "I wish I were as nice a person as you."

Alex hooted then clapped her hand over her mouth. "That's funny. You're one of the nicest people I know."

Elizabeth shook her head. "But it never would've occurred to me to offer Christy a place to stay, and I'm ashamed to admit that it's due to her livelihood. I'm just as guilty of judging her as some of the other women in town are."

"No, you're not. You may have let the thought slip through your mind, but you didn't let it take root—that's the difference. You were quick to see the error of your thinking and repent. Now if I can just do the same thing with the issues I'm struggling with. I'm having a hard time forgiving Papa for keeping so many secrets and understanding why God allowed all this."

Elizabeth nodded. "None of us is perfect. We often have to choose to trust God. When hard things come, it's our nature to want to fight or flee— or blame someone—but in the end I think you'll see God's hand in it all."

"I hope so. I'm heading to the doctor's office to see what he has to say." She held up her hand when Elizabeth opened her mouth. "Don't say another word. I'm going to see how Christy's doing, nothing more. At least not yet." She smiled and winked then headed to the door. "I'll stop by before I leave town." She turned the knob and then swung back around. "Thank you, Elizabeth."

"For what?" A quizzical smile lit the attractive brunette's face.

"For being my friend."

* * * * *

Alex hurried across the street, lifting her skirt a few inches. She didn't care if anyone saw her ankles or not. The need to discover if Christy Grey would live accelerated her pace.

What drew her? Why did she care, after all Christy had done, whether someone tended the woman or not? She'd like to believe that Christ's love shone through her, but she knew that wasn't the entire reason for her concern. Alex had felt an affinity with the woman the first time she'd met her. The longing for acceptance had burned in Christy's eyes, but she'd quickly cloaked it behind a shell of indifference.

How many times had Alex felt the same desire—been driven by the same need? Did she care what mean-spirited people thought about her? No, she did not. But being misunderstood by a handful of women who'd never taken the time to know her still stung.

Christy's lot in life must've been so much worse, considering her occupation. Had she ever longed for a different life or tried to break free and change? What drew her to live a way that brought such shame?

Alex could well imagine the life she might have had if Papa had died without providing for her future. So few options existed for women left alone and penniless. Some could fall back on sewing, teaching, or taking in laundry, but what if their skills were lacking or there was no work to be had? Alex knew that dance hall girls and other women of ill repute didn't always choose their line of work. Only by God's grace and care had she been spared such a life.

Alex shook her head. It wasn't her place to seek out the answers, but she couldn't abandon someone with a wounded spirit and broken body. She stepped up on the porch of the wood-slatted building and glanced at the sign. DOCTOR IS IN hung by the doorpost. She rapped and nudged open the door then slipped inside. "Doc? You here?"

A muffled voice answered from behind the curtain that hung over the doorway to the back room. "Just a moment."

A few minutes later Doc Stevens pulled open the dark green curtain and stepped through then yanked it closed again. "Miss Travers, what brings you in today? Not feeling well?"

"No, sir, I'm fine." Alex wondered if the poor man had slept lately. His broadcloth trousers and white shirt were rumpled and covered with dust. Fine lines branched out from the corner of his blue-gray eyes, and his mouth had a tired, pinched look.

The wiry man pushed his eyeglasses up the bridge of his nose and peered over them. "Martha doing all right, and your uncle Joe?"

Alex nodded and glanced toward the closed curtain. "Yes, sir. But I'm here because Elizabeth told me that Ralph brought Christy Grey in early this morning, hurt pretty bad."

"So he did." Doc nodded and a lock of light brown hair fell onto his forehead. He lifted his hand and pushed it back with a grunt. "Tarnation. Haven't so much as had time for a haircut in weeks."

"Is she hurt bad?"

"Huh?" He peered at her and then followed her gaze. "Oh, you mean Miss Grey? Yes, afraid so."

Alex kept a rein on her impatience. Why couldn't the man offer some details with his answers? She looked past the thick lenses in his eyeglasses and noted the red-rimmed eyes. "You been up all night, Doc?"

He ran his fingers through his already-mussed hair and sank into the chair behind his battered table. "That I have." He drew a deep breath and sighed. "Just a mite tired, I'm afraid. Now, what can I do for you?"

"I'm concerned about Miss Grey. Can you tell me what's wrong with her?"

Doc Stevens drummed his fingers against the table and frowned. "You a friend of the woman?"

Alex sat up straight and nodded. "Yes, sir. She came out to the ranch to visit a few days ago." She hoped the good Lord would excuse the slight shading of the truth. She had invited Christy to the ranch and she *had* come, hadn't she?

He nodded, his eyes not quite focusing on her face. "I see, I see. Well, now." He paused and stared out the window and his head began to droop.

"Doc?"

His head snapped up and his mouth parted. "Yes? What's that?" He blinked his eyes at Alex and frowned. "Oh, Alexia…I apologize. Miss Grey." A nervous twitch started in the corner of his left eye and he rubbed at it with the palm of his hand. "She's been badly beaten. Possible damage to her organs. No idea about internal bleeding yet. Fever. Broken ribs. Lots of bruising. Stitched a deep cut on her shoulder. I think she escaped without serious injury to her head, but I won't know till she wakes up. I think that about covers it."

Alex raised her hand and stifled a gasp with her fingertips. "Oh my. I had no idea. Do you think she'll make it?"

"If there's no internal bleeding and her organs aren't bad. Have to wait and see. I'll know more tomorrow." He pushed to his feet. "Come back then if you'd like."

Alex rose. "Thank you, I'll do that. It looks like you'd best get some sleep."

"Right. Ralph's coming in to watch Miss Grey while I rest. He'll call me if she wakens, but it's doubtful." He glanced back at the curtain.

Heavy footfalls on the steps outside sounded just before a tap on the door. Ralph shoved it open and poked his head inside. "You ready for me, Doc?"

"Quite. Come in." Doc Stevens motioned to the big man.

Alex smiled at Ralph and nodded at the doctor. "I'll be going. I'll see you tomorrow. I'd like to talk to you about Miss Grey's care."

"Quite so, good plan." He tipped his head.

"Good night, Doc, and thanks." She gazed after the man as he almost stumbled down the steps. She turned to Ralph. "Hope he makes it home before he falls asleep."

Ralph's deep-chested laugh rumbled from his throat. "Me, too. Looks about done in, if you ask me. I brought Miss Christy in around five this mornin', and the doc was just returnin' from tending a man who'd been hurt out at the Home Ticket mine. Must'a been up most of the night and goin' ever since."

"Well, I'm glad you found Miss Grey. She'd probably have died if you hadn't brought her in."

He ran his hand down his muscular arm. "Yeah. I'd like to break the head of whoever hurt her. She don't deserve that."

"I agree. It's just too bad more people aren't like you." She stepped outside and smiled back at the big man. "Take good care of her, will you?"

"You bet, Miss Alex. You can count on it."

Chapter Twenty-eight
....

Alex exited the barn after unsaddling Banner and turning him out to graze. A streak of color racing across the lawn caught her attention as she stepped into the bright afternoon sun.

"Lexie!" Toby's shrill voice broke the stillness of the early August morning. "You comed home!" His little arms pumped and his short legs carried him across the space between the porch and the barn.

A chuckle broke from Alex's lips and she bent over with outstretched arms. "Of course I came home, silly goose."

Toby threw himself into her arms and chortled with glee as she swung him around in a circle. She deposited the boy on her hip and gave him a hug. He grinned into her face and patted her cheek. "I not a goose, I a boy."

She laughed outright and kissed him. "Yes, you're a boy, and a sweet boy at that. Have you been good for Martha today?"

He nodded and his dark curls bounced in the light breeze. "Uh-huh. Uncle Joe gave me a ride on my pony."

Alex bit the inside of her lip. *His* pony. Well, she certainly couldn't ride it anymore. She tickled his ribs and he ducked his head against her neck and giggled.

"Let's go find Martha."

Toby wriggled in her arms and slid down to the ground. "Miz Marfa bakin' pies for Toby." He grinned and dashed toward the house then stopped and spun around. "Come on, Lexie, hurry. I give you some pie, too."

"Thank you, Toby." She tried to keep a serious face and almost succeeded.

The front door swung open at the same time her foot hit the bottom step on the porch. Uncle Joe stuck his head outside. "Toby…" His eyes met Alex's and he halted. "Ah—it's you. Thought I'd have to go pull that boy outta the barn again. He's been runnin' off to see the horses."

Alex took two long strides. She knelt down beside Toby and turned him to face her. "Toby?"

The little boy directed sparkling blue eyes up to hers. "Hmm?"

She gripped his shoulders. "You must never, ever go to the barn or the corrals by yourself. If you do, a big horse could step on you or hurt you, and your papa would be very sad." She smoothed his rumpled curls and tucked the tail of his shirt into his trousers.

He threw his arms around her neck and buried his face in her hair. "I be good, Alex. I not go to the barn no more."

Alex carried the boy into the house and set him on his feet. "Go tell Martha I'm home."

He nodded, grinned, and raced toward the kitchen, his high-pitched voice trailing behind him. "Miz Marfa…Lexie home."

Uncle Joe chuckled and tapped his cane against the floor. "You're good with him, Alex. You've got more energy than I do."

"He's such a sweet boy." She patted his arm and headed toward the office then paused. "When do you expect the men back from Foresthill?"

"Justin told me he planned on pushing and getting back tonight. Said he hated bein' gone overnight on account of Toby."

"Hmm. If he makes it before dinner, could you let me know? Or better yet, ask him to stop by my office?"

"Sure enough. I imagine they won't hit any snags with the sale. Justin seems like a capable man."

"I'm sure he is."

Joe peered at her from under bushy brows. "Somethin' on your mind, darlin'?" He gripped the head of his cane with both sun-bronzed hands and leaned against it.

She shrugged and turned her head away from his penetrating gaze. "Nothing I want to talk about right now."

"Uh-huh. Still sore at me and Martha for not tellin' you about the mortgage?"

"Not at all." She hesitated then rushed on. "I'm trying to sort some things out. I promise I'll talk to you soon."

He nodded and hobbled across the foyer toward the sitting room.

* * * * *

Three hours later Alex roused from her reverie at the sound of a man's voice. She'd spent the first two hours working on balancing the ranch ledgers and the last hour staring at the wall. So much had happened over the past few weeks that her head still felt muddled with the details.

She pushed aside the sash covering the window and watched riders pull up in front of the barn. Justin, Davis, and Frank swung down off their dusty horses. Alex sat back in her chair and clenched her teeth. She dreaded this meeting with Justin, but it couldn't be avoided. Not only did she want a report on the sale of the horses, but she also needed to know the truth about his relationship with her father and what brought him to the Circle T.

The dull thud of boots on the front porch and a rap at her door brought Alex back to the present. Her heart rate accelerated and she pressed her hand to her chest. Uncle Joe wouldn't knock. Justin still felt uncomfortable entering the house without knocking, although Martha had told him repeatedly to make himself at home.

"Come in." She sat up straight and made her expression as calm as possible.

Justin stepped inside and hung his hat on a hook. To her dismay,

Alex discovered that her heart still wouldn't behave. Why couldn't she react to him like she did to any other wrangler? Walter and Charlie didn't stir this type of feeling, and they openly displayed their desire to court her. As far as she could tell, Justin had never so much as entertained the idea. And now why should that thought send a pang of disappointment swirling through her mind?

He swung around, his dark brown eyes meeting hers with a direct, inquisitive gaze. "Joe said you wanted to see me?"

She nodded toward a horsehair chair on the far side of the desk. "Yes. Have a seat. I'd like a report on the trip to Foresthill."

His brows rose and surprise lit his face. "Why from me? Frank and Davis have been with you longer."

"I know, but I'd hoped to speak to you about another matter, as well. If you'd prefer I speak to one of the other men about the trip…" She leaned back in her chair and clasped her hands in her lap, trying to still the shiver that coursed through her at the look in his eyes.

He shook his head. "No need. Just wondered. I figured you'd been thinkin' about giving me my walking papers."

"I beg your pardon?"

Justin crossed one dusty booted foot over his knee. "Kinda thought Davis or Frank would be telling me in Foresthill that you were cutting me loose. 'Course, there's Toby, and I'd have to return for him."

She placed the palms of her hands on the desk and leaned forward. "If I ever decide to let you go, believe me, I'll do the telling myself, not send word through one of my other hands."

He gave a curt nod. "Fair enough. Now to answer your first question, the meeting with your buyer went well. The horses more than met his expectations, and he didn't quibble over the price. Seems the gold rush has increased the demand for horses and pack animals."

"You brought payment back with you?"

He shook his head. "I didn't care to handle it. Frank took charge, and I believe he delivered it to Joe before taking his horse to the barn."

"That sounds fine." She hesitated, and an uneasy silence settled over the room. The clanging of pots in the kitchen drifted in on the still air. She made a quick decision and started to rise. "I'm sure you're anxious to see Toby, so I won't keep you."

Justin didn't budge but fixed his intense gaze on her face. "He doesn't know I'm back, and while I do want to see him, I don't think we're finished."

Alex kicked herself for telling him she had something else to discuss. Too late now. But truth be told, she was glad for the nudge to pursue the subject heavy on her mind.

She settled back in her chair. "You're right, we're not. I'd like to know about your relationship with my father."

Surprise flitted across Justin's face but then quickly disappeared and was replaced by a flat stare. He didn't respond.

Alex bristled. "You knew my father before you came here. He sent for you, and you've kept that fact from me this entire time. It's been hard enough discovering that my father kept secrets from me, so please don't make it worse by denying it. You owe me an explanation."

He seemed to consider the request and come to a decision, as he nodded and the tension in his shoulders relaxed. "Of course. May I ask you a question first?"

She inclined her head.

"How long have you known that your father sent for me?"

"Just a couple of days." She laced her fingers together. "He left a letter for me in his Bible, explaining some of his actions." She didn't care to say more at the moment and sat back, waiting for his reply.

Justin brushed at a patch of dust on his trousers then looked up. "I'm sorry you had to find out that way. I wish I'd told you sooner."

"Why didn't you? Why all the secrecy? If Papa asked you to come and he'd known you in the past, why hide it from me?"

He drew a deep breath and released it between his teeth. "I probably shouldn't have, but I didn't arrive under the best circumstances."

She raised her brows and waited, unsure of his exact meeting.

"Getting flattened by Ralph at the church wasn't a good introduction, along with being accused of decorating a Wanted poster."

Alex felt the blood rush to her cheeks as she remembered the question she'd posed to the sheriff. "But the sheriff didn't appear worried about it. Besides, after I hired you, there was plenty of opportunity to clear the air and tell me the truth."

His intent gaze remained fixed on her flushed cheeks and then traveled to her eyes. "But you've had your doubts, haven't you?" He spoke softly but without the censure Alex expected to hear.

She started to shake her head but then paused. "To be honest, a few. I didn't see how you could love Toby like you do and not be what you claimed, but I also know there are evil men who love their children." She held up her hand when he started to speak. "Please, let me finish?" She waited for his nod. "When you arrived I figured you for a drifter—until I saw Toby. When I heard about your wife, I assumed you might be running from the pain and wouldn't be here long. Then when your sister-in-law showed up last week—"

Justin shot upright in his chair. "She's not my sister-in-law," he growled. "Well, I suppose she is legally, but I don't remember her. Molly had a half-sister who stopped by a couple of times after Toby was born, but she seemed to make a point of coming when I was gone. Besides, I don't look at her as family after what she tried to pull."

"I understand that, but you must try to see how it appears to me. Her accusations, combined with your not telling me that you knew my father and the mysterious things happening on the ranch—well, I guess I began to wonder."

"Whether I was honest or not?"

"My heart knew you were, but I've been feeling the weight of the ranch on my shoulders and my mind didn't want to trust my heart. Even my faith in God has wavered as a result of all of this. My father left me with a legacy of strong faith, and I truly want to trust God. But I'm still not sure I've gotten past the hurt and betrayal I've felt—the feeling that God somehow abandoned me. Does that make sense?" She leaned her forearms on the surface of the desk.

He gave a slow, thoughtful nod. "Yes, I suppose it does. And I've not helped by keeping quiet. I'm sorry, Alex. My silence was meant to honor your father's request, and then as time went on, I wasn't sure how to open the subject. I see now it's done you more harm than good."

She met his eyes and reached up her fingers to wipe a hint of moisture from her cheek. "Thank you. So you knew my father years ago?"

"Yes. He came by our place a couple of times and visited. Pa told me how Mr. Travers helped us out of a bad spot with some money a few years back, and it rode Pa hard that he never managed to pay it back."

"Papa said he told you the debt would be square if you came when he needed you."

Justin crossed his arms and frowned. "He did, but I have no intention of not paying back every penny Pa borrowed. Since your father is gone, the money will go to you. Feel free to start holding back my wages."

She sat back against her chair. "That's kind, but Papa was very clear— the debt is settled. I just wish he'd seen fit to take me into his confidence rather than leave me to find out by accident."

"I'm sure he'd have told you, if he hadn't died."

"True. But it still rankles that he felt the need to bring in help."

Justin settled his hands on his knees and leaned forward. "Your father wanted someone on the ranch who wasn't known around here— someone who could keep his eyes and ears open for trouble. It sounded like he thought he and the ranch might be in danger, and I'm guessing he didn't want to put you in the middle of it. Hiring a new hand wouldn't raise any suspicion to whoever was trying to sabotage his ranch, but keeping quiet about it was important if your father didn't know who he could trust."

She sat upright and frowned. "He could trust me. He could have told me about his plan."

"But he needed everyone, including you, to believe that I was just another hand. I'm guessing he wouldn't have kept it from you for long, but your father was a smart man. He'd have had a plan worked out."

"I suppose. I just wish he'd seen fit to let me and Uncle Joe know. We could've helped."

"I doubt he meant it as a slight to your ability. Remember, he was your father first and a businessman second. Knowing how I'd protect Toby with my last breath, I can only imagine your father felt the same about you. I imagine he thought I could help you, in case anything happened to him."

Alex sucked in a small breath and her eyes widened. Of course. She was, after all, his daughter—his only child—not his business partner. For so long she'd dreamed of following in his footsteps, making him proud of her ability to run the ranch. How long had it been since she'd thought of herself as his daughter—someone he'd want to protect? "I think you're right, and I won't say anymore about it. I shouldn't be upset with you for following my father's orders. Please consider the matter closed."

Justin nodded and smiled. "Happy to, Miss Alex."

Her eyebrows rose and she narrowed her eyes. "*Miss* Alex?"

He flashed a heart-stopping smile. "Well, you are the boss of a successful horse operation, and I'd hate to get too familiar."

She tipped her head against the high back of the chair and laughed. "I see. I'll have to remember that." She met his eyes and saw something there she couldn't quite identify. Need? Yearning? Or was her own desire driving her to see more than was truly there? "I won't keep you any longer." She pushed back from her desk and started to rise then sank into her chair. "Wait. One more thing."

Justin gave a half smile. "Sure."

"I'm not saying I'm going to do this, as I haven't spoken to Martha or Uncle Joe yet. But in case they agree and I don't have a chance to talk to you again, I don't want you surprised." She paused for breath, but when he didn't comment she rushed on. "While you were gone Christy Grey was attacked and badly beaten. Broken ribs, cuts, bruises, possible organ damage."

Shock showed on Justin's face and he leaned forward. "You don't think I had anything to do with it."

"Of course not! It didn't even occur to me." Shame swept over her at the haunted look on Justin's face. "The sheriff is investigating, but no one has suggested you. I'm sorry you'd think that."

He sat back with a groan. "No, I'm sorry. I shouldn't have assumed…." He ran his hand through his hair and looked up. "Is she going to make it?"

"Yes, the doc thinks so, but he'll know more in the morning. But there's one more thing…."

"Yes?"

She drew a deep breath and plummeted forward, her words nearly tripping over themselves trying to discover the correct route to take. "I'm considering taking her in until she gets well."

The words dropped into stillness so deep it felt bottomless. The flat expression on Justin's face gave nothing away. Had the shock driven the man dumb?

Alex pushed to her feet and stepped around the corner of the desk. She reached out a hand. "I'm sorry—I knew you wouldn't be happy, but I can't leave her to the wolves in town. She has no one. I know she's not my responsibility, but I felt sorry for her, lying there broken with no place to go." She was babbling but felt powerless to stop. "Please understand? I'm not trying to bring more trouble to you or Toby. But maybe it would be better to have her here and know what she's up to."

He brushed the back of his hand across his eyes and gave a small shake of his head. "Not my business what you do. Like I said, you're the boss." He started to rise.

"Wait. I forgot to ask…did you find a copy of your marriage certificate?"

His shoulders slumped. "No. The sheriff sent a wire saying the pastor died and the courthouse burned. I've no proof I married Molly."

"I see." She didn't, but the past few minutes had been painful enough without pressing the issue of his marriage or his right to Toby.

He pushed to his feet and a hollow smile appeared. "I'll go see Toby now, Miss Travers. Thanks for your time." He jerked his head in the semblance of a bow and turned to the door.

"Justin, if you don't want me to ask Christy—I haven't said anything yet." She reached out and touched his arm, but he stepped closer to the door and her hand fell to her side.

"Like I said, it's your ranch." He slipped out the door and closed it softly behind him, leaving Alex with numbness in the region where her heart had once resided.

* * * * *

Justin stomped from the house not caring that the scowl on his face reflected the tumult inside his chest. His conversation with Alex left a taste like bitter ashes on his tongue. Her decision to invite *that woman* to the ranch when Alex knew what a threat she was to Toby ignited fierce anger and protectiveness. Maybe he'd best leave this place, and the sooner the better.

His hand drifted to the spot on his opposite wrist where Alex's soft touch had sent a stab of longing through him. He'd almost turned and implored her to change her mind—almost, but not quite. He'd not beg favors of anyone—and especially not of Alex Travers.

How could the woman have gotten under his skin so thoroughly in such a short amount of time? He'd been married to Molly for nearly three years and never once felt the desire and longing that smote him now. And not only because Alex was a beautiful woman. No. It was so much more than that. Her independent spirit, intelligence, kindness to his son, and yes, even her desire to help the very dance hall girl who threatened his future—all these things made her more attractive in his eyes.

She was a wonderful woman—and he'd hurt her. By keeping Ben's secret for so long, Justin knew he'd been an unwitting participant in the pain she'd felt over the past weeks. He stood with his face toward a large oak tree, leaned his head against its rough bark, and groaned. Why did trouble seem to follow him wherever he landed? Why couldn't God make a way for him, the way He seemed to do for others in need?

He remembered Alex's words just moments ago—she'd been trying to trust God, to rest in Him. Could he do that? Did his childhood faith still exist, or had he strangled the life out of it over the years?

If he chose to hang onto his anger and bitterness, what effect would it have on Toby? More than anything, he wanted to be the example to his son that his father had been to him. Pa had lived his faith every day. Not in words so much as in actions. A harsh, judgmental word never passed the man's lips toward another human being, no matter how deserving. His generosity and willingness to help others had earned him the respect and love of his family and the community around him.

Justin closed his eyes and his shoulders slumped. "God, help me, please. I don't know what else to ask, except that You help me. Have mercy on me. Help me out of the hole I've dug. I have no one to blame for my poor choices but myself. Forgive me for blaming You. Give me wisdom and strength to fight Alex's battles, as well."

Justin straightened his shoulders and stepped away from the tree as a deep sense of peace swept over his spirit. For the first time in years he felt a connection to God and knew himself loved and forgiven. "Thank You, Lord—so very much," he whispered. "Help me make good choices from now on."

Somehow he'd have to let Alex know he'd support her, whatever she decided about Christy Grey. He still didn't like it, but he'd trust God with the outcome. Besides, if the woman had broken ribs, she wasn't too apt to scoop Toby up and run off with him. His feeling of triumph at the thought quickly turned to shame. "Forgive me, Lord." He raised his eyes to the heavens and shook his head. "Guess I've got a lot to learn." It would probably be one of the toughest things he'd ever attempt, but he'd find the strength to pray for Christy and leave the rest in God's hands.

* * * * *

Alex sat at her desk, her head in her hands, fighting tears. She hated to cry—it seemed like such a sign of weakness. All her life she'd striven to maintain tight control over her emotions—to be strong and make Papa proud.

Justin said her father saw her as a daughter to protect, not as a business partner. She could view that as something that stung—another slight from the man who'd raised her in his footsteps—or accept the freedom that came with the knowledge of his deep love for his daughter.

"*You don't have to prove yourself to be accepted, Alex.*" The sweet, quiet voice inside her heart spoke. It wasn't her own voice, she knew. Genuine tears welled up in her eyes and spilled over, making their way unchecked to her chin and dripping onto the papers on the desk.

"*Trust Me—come just as you are—you are My beloved.*" A deep well of love opened within, almost flooding her in its intensity. "Yes, Lord. Yes. I've missed You so much. Thank You for loving me, for accepting me." She bowed her head and sobs tore from her throat.

Her father had loved her, too. Her need to be perfect and make him proud had been her need alone—never his. He'd always demonstrated his love for her—in the multitude of times he took her with him when it must not have been convenient. His pride in her had been apparent, and she'd never suffered a harsh or unkind word. Why had she driven herself to please someone who didn't demand it? Was she trying to take her mother's place in his life? Give him back something he'd lost and be the son she imagined he'd wanted?

She raised her head and reached for the Bible lying on the corner of the table. Reverently she opened the leather book and carefully withdrew the folded missive inside. Her eyes traveled down the page to his final words. *Know that I love you, Alex, and I'm glad you're my daughter. You're better than any son the good Lord could've seen fit to give me.*

"Oh, Papa…forgive me. And heavenly Father, please forgive me as well." She placed the letter back in the Bible and closed it, suddenly sure of what she needed to do.

Chapter Twenty-nine

....

A subdued atmosphere blanketed the supper table, with Toby carrying most of the conversation. Although Alex had won a reluctant victory on the matter of Christy Grey, Martha still smarted from what she considered Alex's ill-advised decision and remained terse throughout the meal. Poor Uncle Joe sat with bewilderment blazoned across his face and escaped from the table as soon as he could. He had been easier to sway; he might be crusty on the outside, but he was a lump of downy feathers inside.

As Martha boiled water on the kitchen stove for the dishes, Alex stacked the plates in the dining room.

Justin reached for a mug then turned his intense brown eyes her direction and smiled. "Reckon I'll stay and help. Besides, I've got something to say and I won't sleep until I say it."

Her hand stilled over the plate she'd started to place on its mate. "I'd hate to keep you from sleeping." After the prayer she'd prayed, she knew she should've given a more gracious response, but her old stubborn streak was difficult to squelch.

A slow grin started at his finely chiseled lips and made its way up to his dark eyes. "Uh-huh. Figured that much."

She stopped and planted her hands on her hips. "What are you so smug about? I thought we were mad at each other."

He tipped his head to the side and his eyes narrowed. "Ah, now the truth comes out. And here I thought it was just me."

A rush of blood swamped her cheeks and she ducked her head. "Yes, well…"

A genuine chuckle erupted from his parted lips. "You know, you're beautiful when you're embarrassed. Or angry. Or happy."

Alex's hands flew to her face. "Is *that* what you wanted to say before you could go to sleep?"

It was Justin's turn to redden. "Nope, I didn't plan on that, but I'm glad I finally got it out." His smiling face sobered. "I wanted to say I'm sorry. What you said about making your peace with God? It hit home. I've needed to do that for years. Whatever you decide about Miss Grey is fine with me. I'll not stand in your way."

Her eyes widened and she sank down into the nearest chair. "You mean that? You won't be angry and leave the ranch?"

"Yes, I mean it, and no, I won't quit or be angry. I'm sorry I made you think that. I'd like to be…friends…if you think we can manage?" He stuffed his hands in the front pockets of his trousers and stood ramrod-straight.

"Friends?" Her voice sounded odd even to herself. He wanted to be only a friend—after he'd said she was beautiful? Disappointment washed over her and she struggled to keep it out of her voice. "Friends would be nice. Thank you for taking the time to speak to me about Miss Grey. I'll talk to the doctor tomorrow."

Justin nodded and took a step back from the table. "I'll be going now. Joe's reading to Toby in the parlor, and I need to put him to bed."

Alex rose and extended a hand, just touching the edge of his sleeve. "One more thing?"

He glanced down at her hand then raised his eyes to hers. "Anything."

"The church is having a picnic lunch down in the meadow after church this Sunday. Would you care to come?" She sensed the hesitation in his eyes and rushed on. "As part of our ranch family, of course. Most of the wranglers try to come if they're not on duty."

He pursed his lips and nodded. "Sure. Toby would like that. Will Martha and Joe be there?"

"Yes. Uncle Joe will make Martha comfortable in the wagon. She doesn't go to town often, but you couldn't keep her away from the combination of church and a social." Alex gave a small grimace. "I'm not much on the social part and would just as soon head home, but it means a lot to Martha."

His entire face transformed with a warm light. "Good for you." He pushed in his chair. "Guess I'd best go rescue Joe from Toby."

* * * * *

Alex swung off her horse in front of the doctor's office and wrapped the reins around the hitching rail. She shook herself free from the tantalizing thoughts of Justin's smile and the words he'd spoken the night before. Other men had told her they thought her beautiful, but their words didn't play havoc with her heart the way Justin's had done. *Friends.* She sighed. Why did that word disappoint her? Hadn't they made excellent progress lately?

She rapped on the doctor's door and pulled it open, slipping inside. It took a moment for her eyes to adjust to the dim light, but when they did, she spotted Doc Stevens hunkered over his desk and scribbling at high speed in a journal of some sort. "Doc?"

He jumped as though shot and his eyeglasses fell off the tip of his nose and hit the tabletop with a clatter. "Miss Travers. I didn't hear you come in."

"I'm sorry, Doc. I knocked, but I guess it wasn't loud enough."

"No, no—not your fault. I'm still catching up on my rest and not as attentive as I should be. What can I do for you?" He picked up his eyeglasses and perched them higher on the bridge of his nose.

"I wanted to see how Miss Grey is doing. And talk to you about her care." Alex slipped into the chair propped against the nearby wall.

"Yes, I see." He rubbed his chin and gazed with unseeing eyes at the top of Alex's head. "Care, you say?"

"Yes. When she's well enough to leave, I wondered if she has a place to go. Has she spoken of it?"

"No. I've had her on steady doses of laudanum since she arrived, and she's not said much at all. Seems to be aware of where she is but has no desire to speak." He leaned back in his chair and sighed. "I'm not too worried about her organs anymore. Seems she's just badly bruised and has a couple of broken ribs. Could've been much worse."

"Does she know who hurt her? Have they caught him?"

He shook his head and wisps of hair brushed his collar. "Sheriff came and asked her some questions, but she was none too helpful. Ralph checks on her often, but he's not brought word of an arrest."

Alex folded her hands in her lap. "How long do you think she'll need to stay?"

"That depends on where she'd be going. Can't go back to working in that saloon till her ribs heal, and that'll take weeks. But she could leave fairly soon if she's able to stay in bed and not move around much."

"I'd like to take her home when she's ready. If you think I'm capable of caring for her, that is." She sat up straight and planted her feet squarely on the floor under her chair, hoping he'd see her as the adult she'd become rather than the girl he used to treat for childhood ailments.

The doctor stared over the top of his eyeglasses again, seemingly at a loss for words or else drifting off to sleep—she couldn't be certain by the blank look in his eyes. He shook his head and ran his hand over his chin. "Sorry. You want to take her home? She's not a stray puppy, you know."

Alex almost rolled her eyes at the repeat of Elizabeth's words. "I'm aware of that, and yes, I want to take her home."

He leaned forward, his gaze suddenly sharp and focused. "But are you aware of what the young lady does for a living? I mean, do you really think it would be wise…." His words trailed off.

Alex pushed to her feet and clenched her hands at her sides, working to keep her voice calm. "Yes—to both questions. She's a person, Doc—a person who's been hurt and needs care. I don't care what she does for a living; she won't be doing it at my house, and she's too broken up to cause any harm."

"Not physical harm, no. But tongues will wag if you take a woman like her to your home. What do Martha and Joe have to say? Have you consulted them?"

Alex crossed her arms and raised her chin. "It's my home, but yes, I've discussed it with them. Martha isn't thrilled, but she's willing to help, as is Uncle Joe." She wanted to tap her toe and place her hands on her hips, but she willed herself to relax her stance and sink back into the chair. She knew that Doc Stevens cared about his patients—every one of them—and he would be remiss in his care for her as an old family friend if he didn't question her request. "I appreciate your concern, but I've thought this through. I'd like to care for Miss Grey, if you think I'm capable."

He clasped his hands and leaned his chin on his knuckles. "I do. Especially with Martha's help." He paused and rubbed the rough bristle covering his chin. "I must confess I'm pleased you're willing to do this. Not many respectable women would take on someone in Miss Grey's position. Your father would be proud of you, Alexia. He always loved the scripture about the Good Samaritan, and I must say you're doing a fine job in living up to that story." He tapped his fingers on the desk and pursed his lips. "I'll release her to you on Monday. Another four days in my care and she should be ready to go." A spasmodic jerk of his head and rapidly blinking eyes signaled a sudden thought. "I imagine you need to get her permission before we move forward."

Alex stifled a groan. Christy's desires hadn't entered into her figuring. She'd been so focused on helping the woman that it hadn't occurred to her that Christy might not want to come. "You're right. I'll speak to her. Would now be a good time, or should I come back?"

"Now should be fine. I'll see if she's awake and you can have a few minutes. Just don't tire her too much." He placed the palm of his hands on the desk and heaved to his feet. "I'll just be a moment."

He disappeared behind the curtain for several moments then returned and motioned Alex forward. "You can go in." He stepped aside to let her pass and pulled the curtain behind her.

The sound of his footsteps faded and a soft click of the front door signaled his departure from the office. The muscles in Alex's stomach clenched, and she drew a deep breath. She turned her attention toward the bed, unsure of what her reception might be. Christy lay unmoving, with her back to the room. The wayward tufts sticking out of the braided red hair evidenced an unpracticed hand. A light sheet covered the slender frame, not giving any indication of the damaged body beneath.

Alex took a tentative step and paused. Could Christy have fallen asleep so quickly, or did she not care to see a visitor? "Miss Grey? Are you awake?"

The figure on the bed didn't stir. Alex tiptoed closer and tried to peek over the still form, hoping to see Christy's face, but it was burrowed into the pillow. "I won't bother you, then. I'll come back another time, when you're feeling up to talking."

She turned away and took two steps to the curtained doorway when a soft noise arrested her attention. "Christy? Did you say something?"

"I heard you talking." The muffled words were barely discernible coming from the depths of the pillow. Her head moved and the red braid shifted. "I'm not going home with you."

Alex slipped across the short distance and reached a tentative hand toward Christy's shoulder then drew it back. No telling where she'd been hurt. "Can you turn over, or would you like me to help you?"

A slight shake of the head on the pillow served as her answer.

"All right, then I'll stand here and talk to your back. You've no place to go and Doc Stevens can't keep you here until you heal. We have an unused room on the ground floor, and I'm offering it to you for as long as you need it."

"No. I won't take your charity." The woman lay rigid and unmoving. Suddenly she raised a hand, placed it against the wall and pushed, rolling herself onto her back. A deep groan emanated from between her parted lips, and Alex saw beads of sweat break out across the pale forehead. "Look at this face. I'm a worthless saloon girl who got what she deserved. That's what all the townspeople are saying. Admit it."

She glared up at Alex out of red, swollen eyes that were only half open. Bruises shadowed her cheekbones and chin, where a hard object— probably a man's fist or foot—had landed repeated blows. The once dainty, clear complexion sported red, black, and blue splotches, and her forehead showed neat stitches just beneath the hairline.

Alex met the stormy gaze of the battered young woman but didn't flinch. She'd seen injuries like this before, when one of the wranglers had gotten into a brawl, but never on the face of a woman. But there was no way she'd allow Christy to see her dismay. "I don't care what you look like or what the townspeople think. It's not their concern who I invite to my home."

Christy lifted a shaking hand and tugged the sheet up close to her chin. "Then you're crazier than I thought. Besides, Justin Phillips works for you, and he's not going to want me on the place."

"I've discussed it with Justin, as well as Martha and Uncle Joe, and it's settled. You're coming. You have no place to go and no other choice, unless you're independently wealthy. But I'm guessing that's not the case, based on your occupation." Alex hated the need for the brusque words but saw no other way of penetrating the woman's stubborn refusal.

Christy's expression hardened and she turned her face away. "Fine. I'll come, but only because you're right—I don't have a choice. But the minute I'm able, I'm leaving. And I'll pay you for every scrap of food I eat and every day I take up space in your bed if it's the last thing I do. I won't be beholden to you."

Alex shrugged and tried to hide a smile as the sense of relief at her victory washed over her. "I don't have a problem with that. Doc says we can pick you up on Monday. And in case you didn't think of it, you'll be living in the same house as Toby. I don't think Justin wants to keep you away from your nephew, if you love him as much as you appear to."

Christy seemed to brighten at the words and nodded, but she didn't respond.

Alex took a step back then paused. "Is there anything you'd like Uncle Joe to get from your room?"

Christy drew in a sharp breath then coughed. "Ouch. These blamed ribs hurt—can't even take a deep breath without pain." She laid a hand over her chest and smoothed the sheet. "I'd love to say no, but the truth is, I'd like to have my valise. I can have the doc send someone to bring it over, if they haven't already tossed it."

"I'll have Uncle Joe get it. Christy…" She hesitated, not sure of the wisdom of her next question. "Doc says you don't know who attacked you, or why. That true?"

Christy's face drained of color and she struggled to shift toward the wall. No sound escaped her closed lips, but her stiff back shouted that she was through talking.

Chapter Thirty

································

The church buzzed with excitement following the shortened service. Parson Moser had dismissed them early, explaining that he'd never be forgiven if the ladies' covered dishes and pies wilted in the midday heat. Women scurried from their places and prodded their husbands out the door toward wagons and horses waiting behind the building.

Alex peeked over her shoulder at Justin and Toby standing along the back wall. Justin had declined Martha's invitation to sit with them in church, giving Toby's inability to sit still through the service as an excuse. Alex hoped his reason didn't disguise a deeper motive. His recent offer of friendship reassured her somewhat, but she'd hate to see them slip back into a place of mutual distrust and avoidance.

Toby spotted her and squealed. "'Lexie, I go to a picnic!" The high-pitched voice wafted across the open space, followed by a sweet giggle. Justin raised an amused gaze and met her eyes. Everything in the room seemed to come to a quiet standstill as the look deepened into a question.

Alex drew in her breath and bit her bottom lip, surprised at the nervous flutter in her stomach. She dropped her eyes and spun away, searching for Martha or Elizabeth in the chattering crowd. What had she seen in his eyes? Dare she hope he might want more than friendship? Would he think her bold that she'd held his gaze?

A gentle hand patted her arm. "Alexia, dear." Martha stood nearby with her eyebrows raised. "Are you all right? You seem to have a bit of color—did you get too hot? It is rather close in here today."

"It's a bit warm, but I'm fine." Alex turned away and ducked her head.

"Well, then, let's get the food from the wagon and find a place in the shade. Joe's spreading our blankets, so we'd best get a move on."

When Alex glanced back at the spot near the door, Justin and Toby had disappeared. He hadn't waited to walk with them. What if she'd imagined more from his gaze than he'd meant to convey? He'd made it clear that day in her office that friendship was all he desired. A dull disappointment settled inside, coloring the afternoon in a drab shade of gray.

She stepped outside and her spirit lifted at the sight that met her gaze. Families spread large, colorful quilts under the spreading bows of cedar and fir trees. The unmarried miners attached themselves to a variety of families, squatting on their heels and visiting. Squeals from small children erupted as they escaped the confines of their parents and chased one another across the clearing behind the church.

Delicious smells wafted on the gentle summer breeze, starting a low rumble in Alex's stomach. After her earlier disappointment, she'd thought she wouldn't be hungry, but the sight of Martha's heavily laden basket convinced her otherwise.

Martha lifted a covered platter out of the basket, which Alex knew contained deep-fried chicken. "Come here, child, and help me." She waved a wrinkled hand at the box near her knee. "You unpack that one. It has the dessert and cold-water jug. Too bad we couldn't get any milk yesterday, but you can't hardly beat the likes of our spring water, no-how."

Alex knelt beside the wooden crate and pulled off the lid. "If Mr. Elton finds out that you brought your famous apple pie, I'm afraid he'll leave his wife's side and sneak over here for a piece." The thought of the banker brought back the memory of her father's loan against the ranch, and a dull ache returned to Alex's stomach. Why did life have to be so difficult?

She gave herself a mental shake. Just a couple of days ago she'd turned her problems over to the Lord, and here she was trying to pick them up again. Best to leave them lay and not try to figure out all the answers. God had promised to see her through every difficulty with His grace and strength. Sure, the answers might not be exactly what she expected, but they'd always be His best. That's where trust came in— letting Him make the decisions when her fingers were itching to take the reins.

Martha peeked inside a large gingham cloth at an abundance of home-baked biscuits. "Clarence is more than welcome to a piece. I brought plenty. Never know who might come hungry." She pushed up on her knees and peered across the small throng of people gathered under nearby trees. "Where's my Toby-boy? Justin promised to bring him over. He didn't take him to sit with Frank and Davis, did he?"

Alex rocked back on her heels then pushed to her feet and shaded her eyes against the early afternoon sun. Elizabeth waved at her from a nearby blanket she shared with her uncle Larry, Sheriff Ramsey, and his wife, Sarah. Too bad Elizabeth didn't have a beau—with her sweet spirit and gentle nature, she'd make some man a wonderful wife.

Parson Moser strolled from one group to the next, apparently intent on greeting each person who'd come to share the festivities with the church family, regular attendees or not. His booming laugh rang out as he leaned over to ruffle Johnny's hair. The freckle-faced boy grinned up at the older man, but the chattering crowd drowned out his reply.

A small, dark-haired boy darted around a woman's wide skirt. Toby. Justin must be close behind, as he never allowed the boy far from his sight unless he was in the care of Martha or Uncle Joe. Justin's tall, lean frame and smiling face appeared a few yards behind Toby, and Alex relaxed. He'd kept his word and stayed for the picnic. Now if he'd come share their meal as she'd asked. She watched him wend his way through the crowd and noted that more than one set of female eyes appraised his movements as he passed.

Martha raised a plump arm and waved. "To–by," her high-pitched call rang out, carrying above the noise. "Over here, darlin'."

Justin grasped Toby's hand and steered him toward their blanket, releasing him when they arrived. The small boy scampered across the intervening space and launched himself into Martha's arms. "Miz Marfa, I hungry!"

Martha picked the boy up and settled him on her hip. "When aren't you hungry, little man?"

He wiped a lock of hair out of his eyes and peered into her face. "Never."

The solemn reply brought a round of chuckles from the three adults and elicited a big grin from Toby. "Miz Marfa bring chicken and pie?"

She nodded and patted his back then let him slip to the ground. "Yes, we have chicken and pie. We're just waiting for Uncle Joe and then we'll eat." She turned to Justin and motioned toward the box. "Won't you get out plates and silverware and take a seat?"

Justin didn't move. "How about the rest of your men? Aren't they joining us?" He looked at Alex with raised brows. "You mentioned joining your 'ranch' family. I don't think I should stay if the other men aren't coming."

She tucked her feet under her skirt and shook her head. "Davis, Will, and Frank are here somewhere. Martha packed them their own basket since they like to smoke with some of the hands from nearby properties. They'll stop by when it's time for pie."

He scooped up Toby and took a step back. "Maybe I'd best find their group."

Alex rose to her knees and held out her hand. "No need. Martha's been looking forward to having Toby, and we wouldn't want the two of you separated. You're both welcome. Please stay." She bit her lower lip to keep from proclaiming just how welcome they both were to her.

* * * * *

Justin sank onto the blanket a few feet from Alex. He'd been wandering the grounds for the last few minutes, gathering the nerve to approach. The last time they'd talked about their mutual decision to trust in God, he'd felt an intimacy he'd never experienced with a woman. Why hadn't he declared his affection for her instead of asking her to be his friend? But maybe it was just as well—she'd eagerly accepted the proffered friendship and didn't seem dismayed at not taking it further.

Then there was the added complication of Toby—his welfare must come first. Alex appeared to care for him, but would she want a stepson? Worse still, would she think the ranch drew his interest more than she did? A woman on her own with holdings the size of the Circle T had to be careful. Many men might court her in hopes of attaining control of her spread.

Toby plopped down in Justin's lap, drawing his thoughts back to the present. "Papa, Toby wants pie." The little boy reached up and patted Justin's face.

"Not now, son. We'll eat Martha's other good food first." He hugged the slim body against his chest and glanced at Alex. The expression on her face was unreadable.

Joe hobbled across the cleared area, stepping carefully over the large sugar pine cones in his path. "Save any vittles for me, Toby?" His weathered face lit with a smile and he sank down next to the boy.

"Uh-huh. Toby saved pie for Unca Joe." Toby scooted off Justin's lap and trotted over to Joe. "Papa says chicken first."

Joe hooted with laughter. "That's what Martha always says. I tell her you should eat pie first, case anythin' happens and you don't get a chance. It all ends up in the same place, anyhow."

Martha wagged her head and shook her finger. "Don't go givin' that boy any ideas."

Parson Moser raised his voice and called for attention. "Let's ask the Lord's blessing on this abundance so we can enjoy what our womenfolk have prepared." Silence settled over the crowd, and the parson offered a short prayer.

The next few minutes passed in companionable silence as Martha heaped each plate with a variety of mouthwatering dishes. Justin's stomach growled as he eyed the chicken, biscuits, beans, fresh greens from Martha's garden, apples from the nearby community orchard, and warm pies nestled in their box. "This all looks so good that I don't know where to start." He grinned up at Martha with his fork poised above his plate.

A pleased flush covered her face and a sparkle lit her eyes. "Ah, go on with you. Just grab a drumstick and dig in. I know a hungry man when I see one."

Alex bent over Toby, tucking a cloth into the neck of his button-up shirt and whispering something in his ear. The boy nodded, grinned, and drew a chicken wing to his mouth. She giggled and tousled his hair then turned her smile on Justin.

His heart stopped for a brief moment then rushed on, pounding an assault in his ears at the tenderness in her eyes. A rush of emotion nearly choked him. He pressed his napkin to his mouth to cover the sputter. How long had it been since he'd felt the desire that pounded through his veins? But this time it was different. Mixed with the physical attraction was a longing for a pure and holy relationship.

His parents had experienced that type of love—one that encouraged, protected, and sustained. Alex's integrity and depth of character called to something within him, making him long to love and cherish her in a way that transcended mere physical desire. All this flitted through his thoughts as he watched her interact with his small son. He couldn't completely grasp what he hoped might happen between them, but he yearned for so much more than what he had now.

He scraped his fork across his plate and lifted the last bite to his mouth then froze. Carter Foster wove his way around a nearby family, his gaze intent on Alex. Who had invited him? Did Alex know that Foster was coming? He frowned and reached for Toby. An urgency to hold and protect his son inexplicably drove him.

Alex's laugh broke and stilled as Justin drew Toby from her arms and onto his lap. "Justin, Toby's fine."

He tipped his head toward Carter, who stood silently on the edge of the blanket behind her. "You have company."

Alex's head turned in the direction he indicated. "Carter. How nice of you to stop by." Her voice expressed curiosity, but did it also hold a hint of warmth?

Carter swept his hat off his dark head and smiled, first at Alex then at Martha and Joe. "Ladies, you both look lovely. Joe, you appear in fine mettle." Justin didn't miss the man's lack of acknowledgment for himself and Toby.

Martha's brows rose, but she allowed a small smile to soften her lips. "Have you eaten?"

"I have, but I'd never turn down a piece of your pie." He stepped forward and gazed at the box of pies sitting near Martha's knees.

She reached for the box and drew out a pie tin. The golden crust was dotted with small chunks of apple juice that had oozed out the slits in the top. "Certainly. Take a seat. Alexia, would you pass Mr. Foster a plate?"

Carter knelt beside Alexia and smiled into her upturned face then reached across for a plate, his shoulder and upper arm brushing hers. She drew back slightly but didn't appear perturbed.

Justin frowned and tightened his grip on his squirming son. Had Alex invited Foster just as she'd invited him? She'd made it clear she was asking Justin only as part of their group of wranglers, not as a special guest. Had Foster received a more personal invitation?

Carter settled in beside Alex. "I'd have come sooner, but pressing business kept me at the ranch longer than I'd planned."

Joe leaned forward on the knuckles of his right hand. "Pressing business? Anythin' wrong?"

"Just a small mystery I hope to clear up soon." Carter accepted his slice of pie with a smile and a nod. "I'm finding a discrepancy in the tally of my cattle. Of course, they could easily have wandered into the deep timber or down in the breaks of a canyon. That doesn't worry me, but the few head of missing horses does."

Alex's head snapped up. "You've lost horses? When did that start?"

Carter lifted a forkful of pie to his mouth then paused as his gaze turned toward Justin. "Not exactly sure, but I'd say about four to five weeks ago. About the time you arrived, Phillips."

Justin dropped his fork and set his plate aside. "I don't care for what you're implying."

Martha reached for Toby and shushed the whimpering boy. "Now, Justin, I'm sure Mr. Foster doesn't mean anything. Do you, Carter? It's just an unfortunate coincidence that you discovered some stock missing around that time."

Foster gave a slow nod and a smile that didn't come close to reaching the eyes still trained on Justin. "Certainly, Martha. My apologies if I implied anything else." His smile grew as he turned toward Alex. "I expected your other men to be close by, seeing that your new hand is here with you. You don't typically invite your wranglers to the church picnic, I'm sure."

Alex started to answer, but Justin pushed to his feet. "Martha, I'll take Toby for a walk and let Miss Travers enjoy her time with her guest."

Martha's eyes widened, and her gaze darted from Justin to Alex and back. "Don't you go rushing off, young man. We invited you to eat with us, and you've only had one piece of my pie."

"And a perfect piece it was, Martha." He scooped Toby up in his arms and bowed toward Alex. "Miss Travers, I wish you a good afternoon."

Justin sensed more than saw Alex stiffen and start to reach out a hand, but he didn't pause. A deep sense of rage was building inside him, and he needed to escape before it ruptured. He'd beaten a man for less than what Foster threw at him, but his desire to honor the Lord had stayed his hand this time.

A rustle of skirts drew his attention. Had Alex decided to follow? He pivoted around, only feet from the Travers' picnic area. Lacey Bradford, the little waitress from the hotel, stood shyly staring up at him. "Ma thought you and your son might want to try some of her blackberry cobbler, Mr. Phillips. That is, if you aren't headin' anywhere else."

"No, ma'am, I'm not. And I'd be most pleased to try some of your ma's cobbler. Thank you for asking."

* * * * *

Alex watched Justin swing Toby onto his shoulders and start to walk away. Why hadn't she repudiated Carter's comments and urged Justin to stay? She'd seen the hurt in his face and heard the anger in his voice. He'd not gotten two steps when she'd pushed to her knees, determined to follow and set things right. But Lacey Bradford approached him, and her words carried sharp and clear to the silent listeners. As did Justin's reply.

Justin kept one hand on Toby's leg, balancing the boy on his shoulders, and offered the other arm to the blushing Lacey. Alex sank back onto the blanket and her breath escaped in a small groan. Justin hadn't seemed a bit reticent about accepting the pretty girl's invitation, and the smile that softened his face sank a shaft of jealousy into Alex's heart. She was glad she'd not gone after him—but if she'd acted on her impulse and reached his side before Lacey, would he have returned?

A slow anger built as she remembered Carter's words. Unfair, hurtful words, with no justification.

Uncle Joe cleared his throat and used his cane to hobble to his feet. "Think I'll go take a bit of a walk myself. Gettin' stiff sittin'. Hope you won't mind, Foster?"

Carter rose and shook the older man's hand. "Not at all, and I appreciate your allowing me to join you, sir. Let me know if you ever need any help on the ranch. I'll be glad to lend a hand."

"It's Alex's ranch, not mine. Ask her." Uncle Joe's curt reply didn't leave room for discussion. He swung around with surprising alacrity and stalked away with the aid of his cane then stopped and turned. "Martha, why don't you leave Alex to her guest and walk with me a spell?"

"I think I will, old timer." Martha ignored Carter's proffered hand and stood on her own. She dusted off her skirt and shook it out. "I'll help pack up when I get back, Alexia."

Carter sank down a few inches closer this time with his lips drawn back in a satisfied smirk. Alex wanted to smack the gloating look off his face, but making a scene wouldn't help her standing in Last Chance. The thought of her own missing horses rose in her mind, but she shook the thought away. There was no proof they'd disappeared at the same time Carter had lost his stock. And Justin wasn't a thief, no matter what Carter implied.

She turned toward him. "Why'd you say that?"

He drew back and crossed his arms. "Say what?"

"You implied that Justin might be involved in the loss of your stock."

He shrugged. "It's possible. He's a stranger who came at the same time they disappeared. That speaks for itself."

"Lots of strangers come through. That doesn't make them thieves."

"They don't all have knowledge of good stock or access to them.

Phillips has both." His stiff posture relaxed and he smiled. "Let's don't worry about one of your wranglers, Alexia. He's not important." He edged a little closer and touched her arm. "Have you thought any more about what I asked you?"

She drew her arm away and scooted back. "About what?"

"I've come to care for you more deeply than I realized. You're all I want in a wife. I hope you've had time to reconsider my proposal." A cunning expression nudged out the smile and made its way into his eyes. "You won't regret it, I promise you. I have much to offer a woman." He touched one of her loose curls and stroked the side of her face.

She jerked her head back and pushed his hand away. "You have no right to touch me. I haven't changed my mind. I have no desire to marry you, and you need to quit asking."

Carter's smile faded and something nearing a snarl took its place. "So all this time you've been toying with me?"

Alex scooted farther from his reach and crossed her arms across her chest. "I haven't toyed with you at all. In fact, I haven't encouraged your suit. I told you the first time that I didn't love you."

He glared. "You think you're too good for me? You have no idea what you're giving up." The last words hissed through his teeth.

She stood and took a step back, being careful to keep her voice low. "I think you need to leave, Mr. Foster."

A low growl erupted from between his parted lips and he jerked upright. "You're smitten with that good-for-nothing cowpoke, aren't you? He's nothing but a two-bit thief. You turn me down and you'll live to regret it."

Alex glanced around, glad to see the nearby families occupied. "I'll not regret anything other than allowing you to malign Justin Phillips in my presence. Leave. Now."

Uncle Joe approached from the side and laid his arm across her shoulders. "You heard Alex, Mr. Foster. You've worn out your welcome, and she'd like you to leave."

The man turned with a muttered curse and stalked away, but his final words continued to ring in Alex's ears.

Chapter Thirty-one

....

Alex and Uncle Joe stood at the end of the buckboard on Monday morning, waiting for Christy Grey to catch her breath after the long, painful drive to the ranch. Beads of perspiration covered her white face from the jostling along the way. Uncle Joe had done his best to prepare the bed of the wagon, lining it with Martha's heavy quilts, but the broken ribs were still causing her intense pain.

Uncle Joe hovered over the side panel, his brows drawn down in concern. "Young lady, you want I should pick you up and carry you?"

A small grimace flashed across Christy's face, and she shook her head. "No, thanks. If I can get on my feet, I'll make it into the house."

Alex placed her booted foot on a wagon spoke, swung over the sideboard and into the bed. She knelt in the tight space beside Christy's legs. "How about I slip my hand under your neck and help you sit?"

"That might help." Christy reached up, grasped the side rail of the wagon, and gripped it until her knuckles turned white. "I'm ready."

Alex slid closer and positioned her hand under Christy then raised her head as the woman pulled her weight up. A groan tore from Christy's throat, but she kept moving until she sat upright. "I made it." The words trembled and her breath came in short gasps.

"Put your arm around my shoulders." Alex gripped Christy's wrist with one hand and put her other arm across her back. "Uncle Joe, when I get her scooted forward, you take her arm."

The next few minutes passed on ponderous feet as they made slow progress to the rear of the wagon and down to the ground. Christy stood almost erect, with one hand pressed over her rib cage and the other gripping Uncle Joe's arm. Martha stood on the porch holding Toby in her arms, a silent witness to the woman's travail.

Uncle Joe shifted his weight onto his cane but retained a grip on Christy's arm. "Still think we should'a had one of the wranglers help. Could'a carried you right into the house. Afore my fall, I'd a done it for you. Blasted hip won't let me do anythin.'"

Christy shook her head, and her chin rose in a stubborn tilt. "I didn't want anyone else. I wish I didn't have to depend on any of you." She glanced from Alex to Uncle Joe then dipped her head. "Sorry. I don't mean to sound ungrateful, but I don't belong here."

Martha bustled forward and stopped a few feet away. "Go on with you. Anyone who's hurt and needing a helping hand is welcome— leastwise, they are till they prove there's a reason we shouldn't help them."

Christy took a tentative step and grunted then another. "Seems I've already proved that. I can't imagine why you're willing to have me here."

Martha patted Toby's back and hugged him. "Reckon you wouldn't be asking that question if you didn't see you'd done wrong. That's a good enough reason for this family to be willin' to help." She turned and hustled back toward the steps.

Christy gazed after her and gave a small shrug. "I don't understand, but I'm beholden to you, just the same."

Uncle Joe clicked his tongue. "Makes no difference now. Let's get you in to bed. Martha's got a room fixed up proper. If you're hungry, we'll have a bite to eat brought in; then you can sleep."

They moved at a slow pace from the wagon to the porch, somehow navigated the steps, and got Christy into her room. Uncle Joe plucked Toby from Martha's arms then slipped out and closed the door, leaving the women alone. Alex and Martha gently unbuttoned the back of Christy's dress and helped her into a nightgown. She slid into bed with a soft moan and straightened her legs under the snow-white sheet. "Thank you," she breathed in a soft voice. "I don't know what else to say." She closed her eyes and a single tear crept from under one lid and made its way down her cheek.

Martha patted the younger woman's hand. "No need to say anything else. 'Thank you' works just fine." She tucked the sheet under Christy's chin and smoothed a lock of red hair from her forehead. "Looks like you could use rest more than food right now. One of us will check on you later and see if you're hungry."

Christy nodded and turned her face away, but not before Alex saw another tear join the first.

Alex and Martha silently exited the room and closed the door almost shut. They moved by common consent to the kitchen, where Uncle Joe waited with a happy Toby. The little boy sat in the chair his papa had fashioned, munching on a piece of bread and jam.

Martha leaned down and kissed the plump, rosy cheek then faced Alex. "I declare. I understand why you felt you had to bring her. Poor lost dear—she don't think she belongs anywhere with decent folks. She's not at all what I expected."

Alex sank into a chair at the small kitchen table and nodded. "I felt the same way the first time I met her. She's trying to hide a lot of pain beneath that tough exterior."

Uncle Joe tapped his cane on the floor. "Uh-huh. I'd say it's our job to help her heal while she's here. God's surely able to fix what's ailin' her."

* * * * *

The next few days passed without incident. Christy kept to her bed most of the time with Martha and Alex taking turns helping tend to her personal needs. Justin had requested that Toby stay out of Christy's room, and no contact occurred between Christy and Justin. He'd hoped this arrangement could continue until she was well enough to leave, but common sense told him differently.

Saturday dawned clear, sunny, and hot. Martha rose from the breakfast table and leaned her knuckles on the smooth pine surface. "It's time for a change in this house. That Christy girl has kept to her room long enough. She may not want to come out, and Justin, you might find it uncomfortable, but she's not staying another hour in there. It ain't healthy."

Three faces raised to stare at her, distinct expressions on each. Justin tried to keep the displeasure from showing on his—after all, this wasn't his home, and he had no right to dispute Martha's wishes. He hazarded a glance at Alex and noted her lips curving in a soft smile. The comments she'd made over the past few days proved the tenderness Alex felt for the woman. He didn't get it—she'd threatened his son's security and been nothing but trouble.

Ever since the church picnic last week, the atmosphere had been strained between himself and Alex. It couldn't have set well with her when he'd accepted Lacey's invitation. He gave a mental shrug—what did he know, after all? Maybe she was relieved he'd left so she and Carter Foster could talk in private. He'd noticed that Martha and Joe didn't stay long and assumed they'd done so for Alex's sake.

Most of Alex's time had been taken with Christy the past few days, and they'd had no chance to talk. He'd stayed away from the house and taken on more of the outside chores, relieved that he'd not been asked to help with Christy's care. Alex had accepted his absence and even seemed to approve. No doubt she saw him as just one of the hands and chafed at his intrusion into her household. How could he have been thinking of marriage just one short week ago when he'd watched her loving attention to Toby? Stupid daydreams.

"Come on, Alexia." Martha beckoned before turning her attention back to the men. "I'll leave the two of you to care for Toby and clear the table. If we need help moving Christy to the parlor, we'll call."

She and Alex disappeared down the hall that led off the far end of the kitchen. Justin heard a soft chuckle and swiveled his gaze to Joe. "What's so funny?" His tone came out crankier than he'd intended.

Joe shook his head and grinned. "Don't blame you, son. This has been hard for you. I'm just laughin' at Martha. She'd go crazy if she didn't have someone to boss." He reached for a plate. "Come on. We'd best get this done, or she'll nail our hides to the barn door."

Justin matched Joe's grin and lifted Toby from his chair. "You go play now, son. And don't get in Miss Martha and Miss Alexia's way, you hear?"

The little boy nodded. "Yes, Papa, I hear." He scampered out of the kitchen, and the sound of his voice humming a tune floated back.

* * * * *

Alex stood in the kitchen and hung the pot she'd scrubbed and dried onto the rack above her head. The few days since Christy had hobbled to the main living area had passed with an uneasy peace attending them. Justin avoided the injured woman, and Christy refused to join the family at the table for meals. Only one bright spot shone in Alex's estimation, and that was the developing relationship between Christy and Toby. Alex remained the little boy's favorite, but he couldn't seem to resist the invalid, bringing her one of his storybooks from time to time and begging that she read to him. For some reason Martha didn't interfere, and if Justin was aware of the growing bond, he'd chosen to ignore it.

Christy had little to say around the adults, but the advent of the child into her life seemed to electrify her. Toby had been warned about not bumping her or sitting on her lap, but he'd wiggled his way under her arm and lay with his head on her shoulder. Any time he snuggled next to her with his book, her face lit up as if the sun resided within.

Alex tiptoed into the parlor, not certain if Christy slept. She found

Toby standing next to the woman, patting her face. "You still got a owie?"

Christy grasped his hand and planted a kiss on his fingers. "Yes, but it's getting better." Gripping the back of the sofa, she strained to pull herself into a sitting position.

Alex rushed forward. "You've got to ask for help when you want to sit up. You're going to hurt yourself worse if you try to do everything alone."

"You've done enough. You shouldn't wait on me all the time. I'm sure you have other things to do." Christy allowed Alex to wrap her arm around her shoulder and help her.

Alex sank onto the firm brocade surface beside Christy. "Uncle Joe's taking care of the ranch business, and the men know their jobs without a lot of direction. I'm just happy you're regaining some strength."

"Yeah. I'll be out of your way soon and back at the saloon." Bitterness gave a hollow sound to her voice.

Alex wrapped her arm around Toby's waist and pulled him close. "Uncle Joe's in the kitchen and he'll read you a story." She patted the small boy's back and shooed him toward the door then turned her attention to Christy. "Martha and I have been talking, and we don't want you to rush off. Consider this your home for as long as you need it."

Christy turned wide eyes on Alex. "Why in the world…? I don't understand you people. I'd think you'd be glad to have me off your property."

Alex bit her lip, wondering how much to say. Would Christy even listen? She'd never been good at sharing her faith, but her recent decision to turn everything over to God nudged her forward. "If it weren't for the Lord, we might be."

Christy's eyebrows rose. "So you're admitting it? You wish you'd never invited me."

"Not at all." Alex shook her head and clasped her hands in her lap. "I said if it weren't for the Lord—He makes all the difference. Does that make sense?"

Christy's lip curled. "No, it doesn't. Church people have been my biggest critics, said some of the cruelest things. Why would God make a difference in how *you* see me?"

"I'm sorry you've been hurt by people who call themselves Christians. They're either ignorant or they don't have an understanding of God's love. Whatever the case, they aren't allowing God's grace to shine in their lives." She leaned forward and locked her gaze on Christy's. "He loves you so much that He died to make sure you wouldn't perish. He wants to help you—and He wants us to show His love to you."

Christy's eyes dropped and her shoulders slumped. "He'd never love me. You have no idea what I am—what I've been."

Alex touched her hand. "It doesn't matter. He forgave and accepted thieves, prostitutes, murderers, and more—all that matters is your willingness to accept His love."

Christy stared into Alex's eyes, her expression grave. "I'd like to be loved like that—but I don't think it would work for me."

"I've known all my life that God loves me, and I still struggle."

"You?" Christy raised wide eyes.

"Yes. A couple of weeks ago I asked forgiveness for not trusting Him and for allowing bitterness to fester."

Christy nodded slowly. "And He forgave you?"

"Yes. I don't know how to explain it, but an amazing peace enters your heart when you accept that forgiveness."

Christy sat with her head resting against the back of the sofa. "Thank you," she whispered. "Thank you so much for caring enough to talk. I want to believe what you said, really I do."

Alex braced her hand against the arm of the sofa and stood. "I'll be praying for you." She touched Christy's curls then drew back. "You won't be sorry if you choose to believe and accept God's love."

Chapter Thirty-two

....

Three weeks had passed since Christy's accident, and her strength had continued to grow. Martha and Joe took a much-needed break and headed to town for supplies. They'd hesitated to leave Toby, but Christy had insisted that her ribs had healed sufficiently and that she could watch him. Even Justin hadn't objected. He, Alexia, Davis, Frank, and a couple of the other hands were on the far side of the ranch rounding up the mares with foals born earlier in the spring.

Christy snuggled into the cushions of the sofa, her feet propped on a nearby ottoman and her ears tuned for Toby. A board creaked in the entry near the base of the stairs and she perked her ears. "Toby? Come in and Christy will read you a book."

Nothing. Had she imagined the sound? "Toby—I need you to come in here." She tipped her head and listened but heard only the sigh of the wind outside in the fir trees. It must've been the old house settling and groaning.

Her head nestled against the back of the sofa and her hands relaxed on the pillow cradled on her lap. Justin had given Toby strict instructions to come straight to the parlor upon awakening, and the little boy rarely disobeyed his papa. Besides, he'd been begging for another story when put down for his nap, and only the promise of more when he woke had sent him off without protest.

She swung her feet up onto the sofa and stretched out full length. Her eyes grew heavy and she allowed them to drift shut. The strain of sitting for so long had set off a dull throb under her ribs. A few minutes' nap while Toby slept might do her good.

A fly zipped past her nose, buzzed her again, and landed on her cheek. She kept her eyes closed but roused enough to slap at the pesky insect. "Go away." A drowsy dreaminess settled in and she sank a little deeper into the pillow.

A rough hand slapped her cheek then covered her mouth. "Keep still."

Shock screamed through Christy's mind and her eyes flew open. She struggled against the tightening grip and fought to breathe.

The leering face of Dick Sanders leaned close. "Not a word, or I'll kill the kid."

Toby. He knew Toby was here. Her back stiffened and she lay still, but she couldn't quite stop the trembling that seized her hands.

"Anyone else here?" He hissed the words close to her ear and loosened his grip over her mouth.

"No." She moved her head to the side, hoping to escape the suffocating stench of that hand.

"Get up, and don't try to scream or run." His hard eyes locked on hers, sending a chill down her back. "Where's the kid?"

Christy's thoughts raced upstairs to the small boy she'd come to love. "He went with Martha and Joe to town."

Sanders smacked her with the back of his hand and Christy tasted blood on the inside of her cheek. "Don't lie. I watched them pull out and he wasn't there." He jerked his head toward the door. "He upstairs?"

Once more the hand raised and Christy flinched. "Why do you want Toby?"

"He's insurance, my dear. He'll accomplish what you weren't able to."

"You're trying to hurt Justin. Why? What's he done to you?"

His harsh laugh rang in the small room. "What hasn't he done? He claimed what was mine when he married Molly."

"You threw her away! She cried buckets over you, and you didn't return. Why would it matter to you that she married Justin?"

His mouth twisted into a snarl. "What's mine remains mine—forever. I'm not in the habit of sharing. He kept you from doing the job I assigned—you in love with him, too?"

Christy's laugh sounded hollow, even to her own ears. "Hardly. He has eyes for one person—Alexia. No decent man would look twice at a woman like me."

Sanders reached out a finger and drew it down her cheek. She snapped her head back, feeling as though he'd branded her with an iron drawn from the deepest red embers. His hand snaked out and he gripped the back of her neck. He leaned in close, dropping his voice to a whisper. "Don't pull away from me." A finger traced its way down her cheek again. "I've looked at you more than twice."

She recoiled but didn't jerk from his touch. "I'd never marry you."

A deep chortle broke from his lips. "I said nothing about marriage. That's reserved for little girls like Alexia who own land, horses, and gold—not tramps like you. No—women like you are good for only one thing."

The open door leading into the parlor drifted open another foot. "Christy?" Toby stood in the doorway holding the knitted blanket Martha had made him. "Want my story now, 'kay?"

Sanders drew in a sharp breath. He placed the palm of his hand on Christy's chest and shoved, hard.

Her side struck the edge of the small table next to the sofa and she hit the floor. A shaft of pain shot through her chest and radiated down her arms, clear to the tips of her fingers. The ribs that were just beginning to heal throbbed, but she managed to roll over and prop herself on the palm of her hand. "Toby. Come to Christy."

The little boy put his thumb in his mouth and stared from Sanders to Christy.

Sanders's frozen stance suddenly thawed and he leaped for the boy.

"No, you don't. You come to Papa." He swept the sleepy boy up in his arms with a triumphant grin.

Toby braced his hands against the large man's chest and strained to get free. "You not my papa. My papa workin'."

Christy stared at Sanders. The leering grin changed to a gloating, almost crazed smile. Had Toby's answer pushed the man over the edge? "Justin Phillips is his pa, and you know it. You sent me to lie to Miss Travers about Justin's marriage to Molly, but you can't pull that on me. I know they were married because she told me."

He turned a burning gaze her way. "Oh, they were married all right. What she didn't tell you was that Justin married her *after* she was with child, not before."

Christy held her burning side with one hand and pulled herself to her knees. "My sister wasn't loose."

His laughter barked and Toby started to cry. He clapped his hand over the boy's mouth. "Shut up, kid."

The wails ceased and Toby's eyes widened. He held out his hands to Christy and whimpered. "Christy hold Toby?"

She shook her head and tried to smile. "Just be good, Toby, and don't cry. I'll read you a story later if you'll be quiet, all right?"

Toby nodded but his lower lip trembled.

Sanders took a long step toward the door. "Tell Alexia she gets one chance to save the boy. She marries me and sends Phillips packing and I'll release him. Not that I'd have to—seeing as he's *my* son."

Christy gaped at the man and finally found her voice. "You're lying. Molly would have never…" Her voice trailed off as she stared at his face. The man had lied many times in the past, but this time she sensed he'd spoken the truth. A burning lump of bile rose in her throat and threatened to spill out. She placed her hand over her mouth and retched.

"That's right—*my son*." His sneering voice filled her ears. "Molly loved me, you know. She told me so, over and over. I'll give her credit, though; she wasn't easy. I had to work hard to convince her we'd be married the next day. If you don't believe me, ask Alexia what my middle name is. It's an old family name. Molly named the boy after me."

Christy wiped a shaking hand across her lips and came away with a bloodstain. "Why would Alexia want to marry you? She doesn't even know you."

"Oh, but she does, my dear. Just tell her that Carter Foster stopped by and extended his offer one last time. She'll understand." He slipped out the door. Toby's whimpers drifted back, lifted to a wail, and then mixed with the sound of hoofbeats heading down the lane.

Christy didn't care that she'd gotten hurt—right now she welcomed a little pain. If only she hadn't got caught in this mess. If only she hadn't taken money from that man when necessity had pressed her. If only she'd kept her mouth shut when she'd needed someone to talk to and hadn't told him her worry about her sister's child—then Toby would be safe.

Shame and sorrow engulfed her, and she wept.

* * * * *

Alexia drew her horse to a stop in front of the house and stepped down from the saddle. What a long day—only two hours until sunset. Most days she loved to spend riding, but today she ached all over. Trailing horses into the deep canyons and pushing them out was treacherous work. She'd sent Justin, Frank, and the rest of the men in pairs to some of the steeper canyon country, and she'd covered the end of Deadwood Canyon alone. More than likely the rest of the hands wouldn't return until well after dark, if then. The two pairs farthest from the ranch would spend the night if they didn't get out of the canyon prior to dusk.

She tethered Banner to the rail and hobbled up the porch stairs.

That's what she got for spending too many hours in the office lately and not enough in the saddle. Christy must be tired, with Martha and Joe gone and Toby's care falling on her most of the day. The house seemed quiet, but maybe they were cuddled on the sofa with a book.

She pushed open the door and slipped inside. "Christy? You downstairs?"

A small cry sounded from the parlor and drew Alex forward. She stepped into the doorway and stopped. Christy struggled to push herself from the sofa, a protective arm wrapped around her ribs. A look of pain flashed across her face, but she pressed her knuckles into the fabric and came to her feet. "Alex. You've got to stop him."

Alex hurried toward the panting young woman and gripped her arm. "Whoa there. You've hurt yourself again. Sit back down and tell me what's wrong."

Christy shrugged off her hand and shook her head. "No. I won't sit down until you listen. He came and took Toby. You've got to stop him." Her shoulders shook and tears flooded her eyes. Wrenching sobs erupted from her lips and she covered her face with her hands.

Alex felt as though she'd been struck, but she had no idea which direction the blow came from. "Get hold of yourself and explain. Who took Toby, and where? Did Justin come back and take Toby away? Is that what you mean?" She grabbed the sobbing woman's arm and squeezed. "Stop it, Christy! Talk to me."

Christy sank onto the sofa and turned tear-drenched eyes up to Alex. "No, not Justin. It was Dick Sanders. He came a couple of hours ago. Said you had to marry him or you'd never see Toby again. He pushed me against a table, grabbed Toby, and left." The sobs turned to cries and she buried her face in her arms. "I'm so sorry. If I'd never come, this wouldn't have happened."

Alex stared at the bent head, trying to make sense of Christy's words.

Who in the world was Dick Sanders and why would he demand that she marry him? "Stop crying and make sense. Who is Dick Sanders?"

"He said to tell you that Carter Foster stopped by to extend his offer again, and that you'd know what he meant."

"Carter Foster? *Carter* took Toby?" Alex's head whirled. "He's proposed to me twice, and I've turned him down. But what would he want with Toby?"

"He says he's Toby's father. Molly knew him before she met Justin, and Sanders—Carter—whatever his name is—promised to marry her but left. I guess he's kept an eye on Toby ever since. But he doesn't care about him. He's the one who sent me here and told me to lie about Justin." She stared at Alex with wide eyes. "I think he's been after your ranch the whole time and is using Toby to scare you."

Alex sank onto the edge of a nearby chair. "You said Justin hasn't come in yet. How about Uncle Joe or any of the other hands?"

Christy shook her head. "No. I've been alone all day except for Toby." Tears started again at the mention of the little boy. "What can we do?" She swiped at a tear with the back of her hand.

"I'm guessing he's gone to his ranch. He won't leave all that behind. But why take the chance of grabbing Toby? He's got to know the sheriff would arrest him, and I'm certainly not going to marry him."

"Sanders said he's Toby's father and has a right to take him. I guess he thinks the law won't touch him."

Alex pushed to her feet. "I'm going after them. Carter was angry when I turned him down at the church picnic, but maybe I can talk some sense into him."

Christy reached out and gripped Alex's hand. "Get the sheriff, or wait for Justin. Don't go over there alone. Please? You don't know him." She shivered and dropped Alex's hand, her voice dropping to a harsh whisper. "He's killed men—shot them in the back. I'd never trust him with a woman."

"All the more reason I can't wait for help. Toby's alone with him, and for all we know, the man's mad. If he's as dangerous as you say, I won't take a chance with Toby's life." She spun on her heel and headed for the door. "I promise I won't go into the house without help, and if there's a problem, I'll go after the sheriff. Let Justin know when he gets home."

Chapter Thirty-three

. . . .

Alex swung into her saddle and laid her spurs into Banner's sides. The tired horse surged forward and swung into a canter, his hooves sending gravel and chucks of dried dirt flying. A sense of urgency leaned her forward over her horse's neck, her hands gripping the reins and her feet firm in the stirrups. Banner seemed to sense her mood and increased his gait from a rolling canter to a full gallop. He dodged manzanita brush and jumped a shallow wash, his breathing steady and ears pricked forward, intent on his mission. Alex pulled him down as he started up the hillside leading to the ridge. He'd worked hard today and the last thing she needed was a lame horse.

If only Justin or Uncle Joe had been home when Carter had visited the ranch. But chances were he'd been watching and knew that Christy and Toby were alone.

She still couldn't comprehend that Toby could be Carter's son. Justin never once hinted that he wasn't the boy's father. What did Carter hope to gain? Could he possibly care for the boy? It didn't seem possible he'd be so desperate to marry her that he'd stoop to kidnapping. The ranch had value, but with the loss of some of her stock and her father's gold never having been found…

She sat back so hard that she threw Banner off balance and nearly brought him to a halt. "Sorry, boy. Come on—let's go." A nudge with her heel sent him forward at a hard trot, and she returned to her startling thoughts. She'd nearly forgotten that her father had found gold not long before he'd died. He must have meant the loan to be short-term—until he'd staked a claim and developed his mine. Carter must have known about the gold. The words of her father's letter returned. Papa had heard someone outside his window when he'd talked to Uncle Joe about the gold. There didn't seem any other logical reason the man would pursue his suit. Would he stoop so low as to steal her horses and try to throw the blame on Justin?

She suddenly remembered Christy's words. Carter—or Sanders, as she called him—was responsible for the deaths of others. Horse theft would be nothing to a man like him. Her stomach clenched and fear rose in her throat, but she pushed it down. No time for that—Toby's safety must come first.

Banner snorted and slowed at the fork in the trail, and she swung him away from town. Carter's ranch lay another mile away, its nearest line touching the edge of her property. They traveled at a fast trot as the sun sank in the sky. She approached a dense thicket of mixed cedar and pine and hesitated. Just beyond this grove lay Carter's ranch house. She clucked to Banner and urged him forward, renewed determination pushing her on. A low-hanging branch slapped her cheek, and she felt a welt begin to rise. A quick pull at the reins brought her horse to a slow walk, and she ducked under another limb.

"That'll be about far enough." The words were barked in a short, staccato growl somewhere off to the right. "I've got a gun trained on your back and my finger's jest itchin' to pull the trigger. Name yer business and make it quick."

"Alex Travers. I've come to see Carter Foster."

"Ha. Mouse and me had bets on whether you'd show up. Looks like I win." A figure stepped out of the heavy brush with a rifle balanced on his arm, its muzzle pointed at her. "Get off yer horse." He motioned with his gun. "Now."

She slid to the ground and flipped the reins over Banner's head.

He emitted a grunt. "You walk ahead of me, missy, and don't try nothin'. I got orders to bring you in, but the boss didn't say nothin' about what kinda shape you had to be in."

Alex moved forward and heard a branch break behind her. A rough hand snatched the reins out of her grasp and the butt of the rifle prodded the middle of her back.

"Get movin'. The boss is tired of listenin' to that screaming brat, and he's in a foul mood. You'd best be able to shut the kid up, if you want him to see his next birthday."

* * * * *

Justin lashed his stallion's flanks with the end of his rawhide reins, pushing the horse to extend his stride and dig his hooves into the hard-packed trail. Christy's account of the past few hours had planted a knot in his chest that wouldn't unfurl. Toby's abduction by Carter Foster, coupled with Alexia's rash decision to ride off without help, roused both fury and fear. The thought of losing Toby terrified him. He loved that boy and couldn't stomach the thought of harm coming to him. Alexia's promise to wait for help and not approach Foster alone offered slight reassurance. Hopefully she'd headed for the sheriff when help hadn't arrived soon.

As he guided Durango around brush and under branches that threatened to tear the skin from his face, he shot up a prayer for safety, wisdom, and guidance. Only God knew the reasoning behind Carter Foster's actions. Somehow he had to trust the Lord to guide them through the pitfalls ahead.

Gratitude welled in his heart toward Frank. He'd wondered over the last few weeks if the man was part of the horse-theft ring plaguing Alexia's ranch, but today that fear proved unfounded. Frank had overheard Davis and his old pard, Tim, talking at the saloon. Davis had had too much to drink and was boasting about the theft of Alexia's horses. After relaying the news to Justin, Frank returned to town with orders for Sheriff Ramsey to corral Davis and then head to Foster's place.

Justin gritted his teeth and tightened his legs against the stallion's sides. The big horse hadn't started breathing heavily yet and seemed anxious to move. He'd not hold him in this time. The rocks and brush flew past as the horse lengthened his magnificent stride and settled into a steady run. Justin leaned forward over his neck and ran a hand under the length of his mane. "Come on, boy, you're racing for Toby and Alex. Keep it up; we'll be there soon." Seconds turned into minutes and Justin trained his thoughts on the coming confrontation, continuing to pray for protection.

Lights glinted through the heavy trees and he reined Durango back to a walk then drew to a halt when he neared the edge of cover.

A pressing desire to launch himself through Foster's front door drove him forward. He reached the final row of mixed pine and cedar and stopped, breathing deep. What would he accomplish if he kicked in the door? Judging from what Frank had overheard Davis saying, his boss was ruthless and not above putting a bullet in his enemy's back. Justin didn't lack confidence in his ability to face a man with a gun, but the odds of coming out unscathed in the dark—and against several armed men— weren't good.

No. Better grit his teeth and wait for backup. No sense in getting killed and leaving Toby an orphan. Or worse yet, leaving Toby at the mercy of the murderous thief who claimed to be his father. He'd expect Foster to have a guard posted outside the trees. He swung off his mount and looped the reins around a low-hanging branch back in the shadows.

Silence settled in a deep hush over Justin's hiding place, igniting his memories. All these years he'd built a wall around his heart because Molly had betrayed him. He'd judged all women alike and determined he'd not trust any. Alexia had broken through his rigid barrier. Her forthright personality had drawn him from the first, as had her beauty, but he'd learned from experience that those could be false. Her work ethic rivaled that of most hardworking men, and her love for her family equaled any he'd known. But the crowning point came when he saw her surrender to the Lord and her affection for his son. The patience and kindness woven through her actions drew him like a bee to a newly opened flower.

Her voice, her smile, her intelligence—all the things he'd come to appreciate over the past few weeks—had woven themselves into the fabric of his being, fostering an intense love and a deep longing. Losing her wasn't an option.

Nor was losing Toby. A fierce protectiveness lashed at him, and he nearly bolted out of the trees to rush the cabin. He couldn't lose his son. He sat back down with a groan, knowing he had to wait for help. Memories of Toby as a baby flew through his mind—his first smile, his first steps, the first time the little tyke said "Papa." Toby had made up for all the love he'd wanted and hadn't received from Molly.

If Sheriff Ramsey didn't arrive in the next few minutes, he'd go in alone. Frustration at the delay pushed him to his feet.

Soft hoofbeats sounded behind him, and Justin spun around to face them.

"Phillips? That you?" Sheriff Ramsey's voice whispered a few yards away.

Justin heaved a sigh of relief. He kept his voice low and walked away from the light. "Yeah. Get off and tie your horse. We're close to the house."

"I left Frank at the jail to watch over Davis. Don't want him gettin' away. Had a time corralin' him, or I'd a'been here sooner."

"Good. Wasn't sure but what he'd give you the slip. You get any information?"

Ramsey looped his reins around a broken stump and tied a slipknot, giving it one final pull. "Sure did. Told him he could avoid hangin' by spillin' his guts. Faced with turning in his boss or stretching his neck, he chose the former. He admitted to cutting Alex's fence at Foster's orders and helpin' to steal her horses. Said Foster helped with the first theft then backtracked and met Alex out on the range to throw suspicion off himself. Carter Foster's our man, all right. Goes by several names, one of them Dick Sanders."

Justin nodded and tipped his hat back on his head. "That's what Christy told me. I've wondered about Davis ever since I met him." He scratched his chin and looked the sheriff in the eye. "Think I know why he seemed so familiar to me."

"You meet him sometime?"

"For a while after Toby was born, a stranger hung around town. Seemed to be watching our house, but I never could be sure. Now that I think about it, it was Davis. Must'a been spying on Molly and me for Foster. Any idea what Foster's angle might be, grabbing Toby?"

"Not sure, but Davis claims Foster's after the gold Ben found. Figured he'd marry Alex to get it. Guess when she turned him down, he decided to force her hand by takin' your boy."

"Does Davis know if his story about being Toby's father is true?"

The sheriff wagged his head and frowned. "He didn't know for sure but says Foster bragged about Molly a couple of years ago. Says Foster spent a night in Molly's room at the saloon, 'bout the right time of year to be Toby's pa—so I'm guessin' it could be."

Justin drew a deep breath and let it out with a grunt. "Doesn't matter. He's my son. Molly gave him my last name and left him in my care."

"I agree. The law'll see it that way, too. Far as I'm concerned, this is a case of kidnappin', pure and simple."

"What now?"

Ramsey slipped his rifle out of its sheath. "We call Foster out and see if he'll give up the boy. Where's Alex?"

"She promised Christy she'd wait for help. I figured she headed back toward town when no one showed up. You see her?"

"No. You don't think she came here alone?"

Justin felt a trickle of fear run down his spine, and his heart rate sped up. "If so, where is she now?" He shook his head. "I haven't searched the area, but surely she'd have seen me along the trail, assuming she didn't get this close to the house."

Ramsey swung his rifle under his arm and jerked his head toward the dim lights glinting through the trees. "Come on, let's find out."

Justin loosened the gun he'd slipped behind his belt and nodded. "I'm right beside you."

Chapter Thirty-four

....

Justin stopped on the edge of the timber and waited for the sheriff's next move. He didn't want to believe that Alexia might have stumbled into a trap. The girl had too much courage at times. He could only pray it hadn't landed her in a dangerous situation.

No sounds emanated from the cabin—no cries from Toby or raucous laughter from ranch hands that might be typical on a normal night.

The sheriff leaned his rifle butt on the ground and straightened. "Sure wish we had some light, but I don't want to strike a match. No help for it. Guess we'd best let 'em know we're here." He drew a deep breath and let loose with a bellow. "Ho, the house. This is Sheriff Ramsey. You in there, Foster?"

The light winked out and nothing moved, but the rising moon cast a glow over the front of the house.

The sheriff hollered a second time. "Step on out the door and show yourself."

The hinges on the front door squealed as it swung open and a tall figure stepped out. He reached back inside and drew out a shorter figure. Justin caught his breath. Alex stood straight and tall, her chin lifted and arms by her sides.

"I'm here, Sheriff. What do you mean by coming here this late at night?"

"You got Justin Phillips's boy in there." He leaned forward and peered at the house. "That you, Alex?"

"It's me, Sheriff."

"You all right? Is Toby inside?"

Carter's voice cut across her first word and his hand grasped her arm. "She's fine and so's my son. Alexia has agreed to marry me and care for the boy. You've no call to worry. Everything is under control."

Justin took a step forward. "Toby is my son, Foster. Bring him out. Now."

"He's asleep. You can come say your good-byes tomorrow."

"Like—" He bit his tongue and stopped. *Forgive me, Lord, and help me, please.* "Alex? Did you agree to marry this man?"

Carter put his arm around her shoulder and drew her close. "You have my word that she did, Phillips. Now get off my property." He took a step backward and drew Alex with him, reaching for the door.

Justin started forward, but Sheriff Ramsey laid a restraining hand on his arm. "Wait." The sheriff raised his voice. "Carter. Talk to me. Tell me what you want, and let me try to help."

"I want the lot of you off my ranch. Go back to town and don't come back. Me, Alexia, and my kid are riding out of here and heading to Auburn. We'll get married there."

"Tell me why you want the boy, Foster. I don't believe Alex wants to marry you, but even if she does, why take Toby away from the only pa he's ever known?"

Carter emitted a sharp laugh that ended in a snarl. "Molly belonged to me before she married *him*. I used to visit Molly at the saloon in Auburn whenever I'd travel there. She was different from most dance hall girls. Carried herself with pride. I actually thought twice about marrying her." He shrugged. "Then Phillips came along and stuck his nose in where it didn't belong. He owned that place on the edge of Auburn. I saw how he'd look at Molly whenever he saw her. She was mine, not his. She didn't love him, not even when he married her. Then he tried to lure Alexia away from me, just like he did Molly. But he won't get her—or Toby."

Justin gripped the sheriff's arm and spoke close to his ear. "No way is Alex there on her own hook. And I'm not leaving here without my boy. Foster won't turn him over without a fight."

The sheriff shifted the rifle to the crook of his arm and directed his voice toward the pair on the porch. "Davis gave you up, Carter. I could see you hang for horse thievin', but I'll ask the judge to go easy on you if you turn Alex and Toby loose. Don't add to your crimes by keepin' them here against their will."

Foster uttered an oath and jerked open the door then reached back and dragged Alex forward.

Justin noticed for the first time that she was clad in her customary pants, with riding boots on her small feet. One foot lifted in the air and came down—hard—on Carter's instep. The man let out a yelp and leaned sideways. Alex shoved and started to run, but Carter's arm snaked out and grabbed a handful of her hair.

"Get back here, you…." He yanked hard, and again she fell to her knees in front of his legs. "That'll be about all." His hand reached inside his vest and the light of the moon reflected off cold steel. The muzzle of a pistol pressed against her temple. "No more games!" he yelled to the men in the brush. "Get off my ranch before I pull the trigger."

Justin pulled his gun and lunged forward, but Sheriff Ramsey lay hold of his shoulder and dragged him back. "Hold it, son," he hissed. "Give me a minute." He raised his voice. "You don't want to do this, Carter. It'll get you hung."

"I'd rather be shot or hung than go to jail. No one is taking my freedom from me. I swear I'll kill her and the boy if you don't back off."

The sheriff drew Justin into the edge of the trees and dropped his voice to a whisper. "I think he means it."

Justin nodded, raised his gun, and leveled it. "I'm not letting him hurt either of them."

Ramsey raised his rifle and stared down the barrel. "And I'm not letting your boy grow up knowing that his pa shot the man who claimed to have fathered him. Put your gun up, son."

Justin's gun wavered, then dropped. "But I can't let him—"

"You leave it to me." The sheriff swung toward the cabin and cupped his hands around his mouth. "Carter, don't do something stupid. Drop the gun and let them go. I'll recommend the judge go easy on you if you do."

The muzzle of Foster's gun didn't move but seemed to press harder against Alex's temple. "I don't think so. She's mine, and so is the gold her old man found on his place. He found it on my boundary line. I tried to talk him into mining it together, but he was set on having it all for himself. For her future, he said. Ha. I fixed him. Now her future and the gold belong to me." He wrapped his fingers around Alex's hair and gave a yank, tilting her head. "You'll marry me if you want the boy to stay alive."

Alex yelped and in the light of the moon, Justin saw her face blanch. "Carter?" Her voice came out in a loud, husky whisper that barely reached the woods but then gained in strength. "You can have the gold. I'll give you the rights to it if you'll let me and Toby go."

"Not likely. You'd turn on me, same as everyone does. I don't trust you any more than that stupid Grey woman."

"What does Christy have to do with this?"

"She turned on me, and you'd be no different. No. You'll marry me in Auburn then sign the mining rights over." He gripped Alex's arm and drew her to her feet then yanked her back to the front door. For a second, he released his grip and shifted the gun, fumbling behind him for the doorknob.

Suddenly, Alex fell flat on the ground and rolled, and the sheriff's gun roared out a blast. Carter Foster dropped to the ground like a felled tree, face down in the dirt, and lay unmoving.

Justin and Sheriff Ramsey ran across the wide clearing toward the house, guns extended, keeping an eye on Carter's body. They slid to a stop next to him and waited.

Alex pushed to a sitting position and stared then covered her mouth with her hand. "Is he…?"

The sheriff nudged the body with the toe of his boot and picked up the gun that had fallen out of Carter's grasp. He leaned over and gripped the man's shirt then rolled him onto his back. "Best you go inside, Alex. This ain't nothin' for a lady to see."

Justin took three long strides to Alex's side and helped her to stand. He shoved his pistol into his belt and wrapped his arms around her, drawing her close. Her shoulders started to shake, and muffled sobs came from the vicinity of his heart. "Shh. It's okay now, Alex. You're safe. What about Toby? Where is he?"

Her voice choked, but she forced the words out. "He's asleep in the house. He's safe."

His sigh of relief came out close to a groan. "Thank God." He tipped up her chin and looked into her wet eyes. "Are you hurt?"

Her hands crept around his waist and tightened on the back of his shirt. "I'm fine. I was so scared." The words spilled out between her sobs. "I'm sorry I came ahead and didn't wait for you."

"It's over now." He tipped her head back and brushed the hair away from her face. A slow tear wended its way down her cheek, and he used his thumb to gently wipe it away. "You scared me half to death. When I saw that gun to your head…" He shuddered and choked. "I thought I'd lost you for sure."

One hand cupped her cheek and the other tightened around her shoulders. "I couldn't have stood it if he'd hurt you." He ran the back of his hand down her face, wanting to soothe her fears and drink in the feel of her soft skin.

Alex raised a tearstained face in the moonlight, her wide eyes meeting his and her soft lips parting. Her hands moved from his back and crept up to his neck, slipping behind his head.

Justin stared into the upturned face, barely able to believe the love he saw shining from her eyes. Slowly he dipped his head toward the trembling lips and softly kissed them before raising his head. He could hear his heart hammering in his chest and felt the answering beat of hers. Placing gentle hands on her shoulders, he drew back a half step. "We'd best go get Toby," he whispered.

The sound of a throat being cleared a few feet away preceded the sheriff's voice. "I think that'd be a right good idea," he rasped. "Not that I have anythin' against kissin'—I do it regular with my Sarah—but this might not be the best time."

Justin jerked up straight and dropped a hand to his belt. "Foster's men. Why didn't I think of that? Alex, are they inside the house?"

She shook her head and took a short step away. "No. They cleared out when Carter came back with Toby. All but one that was standing guard in the trees. He took me to Carter when I rode up and put my horse in the barn. When the sheriff called out to the house, I saw him slip out the back door. Carter was peering out the front and I don't think he noticed him leave."

Sheriff Ramsey gazed at the house and nodded. "Looks like we'll have some cleanup work to do. No tellin' how many of Carter's men were in on this deal, but we'll see who we can round up and bring them to trial."

Justin settled his arm back around Alex's shoulders and drew her close. "Let's go get Toby and take him home."

Alex put her arm across his chest and hugged him. "I wasn't sure I'd ever get another chance to see you or care for Toby. I'm so thankful God gave me one last chance." She gave another squeeze then slipped her hand through his arm. "I'm ready to go home."

Chapter Thirty-five

Alex sat in a wingback chair in her office with her chin resting on her hands, her eyes locked on Uncle Joe's somber ones.

"There's something I hope you'll tell me."

"Uh-huh." He took a step and sank into the adjoining chair. "You want to know if the sheriff learned any more about your father's death."

"Yes." She clasped her hands in her lap. "I'm almost afraid to hear, but I need to know the truth."

He stroked his gray mustache and nodded. "Only right. Davis said Carter shot at your pa that day on his way to town. Didn't hit him, but it spooked his horse and threw him. The fall must'a triggered his heart givin' out. Carter came back later and found the gold your pa tried to hide."

Alex dropped her head and bit her lip then raised steady eyes to Joe's. "But why would Carter want to kill Papa?"

"He hoped to spook him into selling the ranch and leave the area by settin' up a few 'accidents.' When Ben refused, Carter took a shot at him. Worked out even better for him when your pa died from what appeared to be natural causes."

"But why? Carter's father left him plenty of money, and he owned his ranch."

"According to Clarence over at the bank, Carter's been in trouble for a long time. His little gold mine petered out and his herd's been dwindling. Mostly poor managin', as well as gamblin' and spendin' money over at Auburn and Sacramento like there's no tomorrow. Guess he thought hirin' Tim might help him put the ranch back in the black but it was too late. The gold your papa found would'a saved him. Taking Ben out of the picture left you as the owner, and he figured he'd marry you and get the ranch and the gold."

"Till Justin showed up."

"Yeah. Justin and Toby. When you started carin' for the boy, Carter used Toby to get to you. He had some of his men steal your horses; then he sent for Christy and blackmailed her into trying to drive Justin off." He shook his head and grunted. "He's a consarned idjit. He didn't take into account that you're a fighter and that Justin truly loved the boy, even if he wasn't his blood-born son. Not to mention the two of you bein' sweet on each other."

"Christy told me that Molly named Toby after Carter—Carter Tobias Foster." She gave a rueful smile. "That bothered me at first."

Joe leaned forward and patted her hand. "I reckoned it might. How 'bout now?"

"I prayed about it, and God changed my mind. I love that little boy, and his family roots don't matter. I realized I was guilty of the same type of attitude some of the women in Last Chance had about Christy—and me, for that matter."

"Toby's a wonderful boy and I reckon he's goin' to make you a right fine son, once you and Justin get things settled amongst yourselves."

Alex felt the color rush to her cheeks. "Uncle Joe, Justin hasn't asked me yet."

"He will, darlin', he will. And if he don't hurry up and do it soon, then he's not as bright as I thought." He chuckled and pushed to his feet. "Bless you, my girl. I'm proud of you."

* * * * *

Alex savored the feel of Justin's arm around her as they sat on the porch swing after tucking Toby in bed. His arm tightened and she laid her head on his shoulder. "Did Uncle Joe tell you that Sheriff Ramsey discovered Papa's leather pouch of gold hidden at Carter's house?" It was hard for her to believe that the events of the previous week had even happened.

Justin nodded. "I'm glad. You'll be able to pay off the bank."

"I'm thankful for that, but I'm still angry about Carter stealing my geldings and selling them to the cavalry. From now on I'm branding my stock when they're weaned, not right before they're sold."

"At least the cavalry's giving you another chance, now that they know the truth."

Alex sighed. "Yes. God's been good to me." She snuggled a little closer and entwined her fingers with his. "I still can't believe this is real—having you and Toby here, knowing you care for me."

A deep chuckle rumbled in his chest and vibrated into her ear. "I'm the one who's having a hard time believing it. A beautiful woman like you with everything she needs, loving a man like me."

"What do you mean, a man like you? I think you're pretty special."

He pulled away a few inches and reached out to tuck a strand of hair behind her ear. Serious brown eyes met her own. "But I'm bringing along a family—and I've been married before. Not to mention that I've not always lived an upstanding life. I should probably tell you…"

She sat up and slipped her hand over his mouth. "No. I don't need to know anything about who you used to be. You're a man who loves God, your son, and me. Those are the important things."

He placed a soft kiss on her forehead and drew her head back down. "That I do."

"There's just one thing I'd like to know."

"Sure. Anything."

"Tell me about Molly. Did you love her a lot? Was it terribly hard for you when she died?"

She felt his chest heave, and he was quiet for a long moment. A feeling of panic nibbled at her heart, and she fought down the notion that Molly's name stirred memories that gave him pause. Was it possible the love he'd had for his wife hadn't been put to rest and might hang between them the rest of their lives?

"I'm ashamed to say that's one of the things that's been hard for me to forgive from my past."

She struggled to sit up and look into his eyes in the soft light of the moon. "Forgive? Why?"

"Because I don't think I ever really loved her. And when she died, I didn't grieve. At least, not for us. I did for Toby, and for the life Molly wasted on drinking and poor choices, but not for myself."

"Then why did you marry her?"

"I guess she was the first woman who really showed an interest in me. She must have known she was in a family way when she met me. I had a steady job, a little cabin, and a fairly good reputation. I'd only known her a couple of weeks when I asked her to marry me. I thought I was in love with her, but I think it was more the idea of a woman caring for me that drew me—and rescuing her from the pit she called a job. It didn't take me long to figure out she didn't love me, and my love began to die just a few weeks after our marriage."

Alex sank back against Justin's shoulder. "Poor Molly. Carter must have hurt her deeply."

"He did. Now I understand that's one of the reasons she started drinking. She believed he planned to marry her. When she realized he'd used her and left, she must have been so ashamed."

"Did it get better when Toby came?"

"Not much. The baby's needs were all that got her out of bed in the morning. She pushed me away—didn't want me near her or the boy. Screamed at me if I tried to hold him." He shook his head as the memories came crashing around him. "I didn't know what to do. Offered to bring the doctor, but she told me no. I started working longer hours, thinking maybe my presence hurt her somehow."

Alex nodded encouragement. "But it didn't. She wasn't mad at you for being a man, she was mad at herself for making a mistake with a man."

Justin's head jerked up. Why hadn't he thought of it that way before? "You think so? I always figured…"

"Yes, I do. You figured she hated you because of what a man did to her. No." Her voice was steady. "I think she couldn't forgive herself." She shook her head. "That's sad. No one but God can fill that empty place in a person's heart. You couldn't have fixed Molly's hurt. God could have helped her, if she'd given Him a chance."

Justin's arm tightened around Alex's shoulders. "Then why didn't He? Why didn't He keep her alive for Toby's sake?"

"It doesn't work that way. God doesn't make us do things—we aren't puppets in a traveling show, dancing whenever the master pulls the strings. God wants us to make good choices, but He won't force us. It's sad that no one helped her to see God's love and care for her life. She only saw the darkness and despair that came with her poor choices."

"And I did nothing to make it better, other than pour out her booze and scold her for the way she was living."

"Justin, you didn't make her choices for her. You might've helped point her to God, if you'd had a close walk with Him at the time. But you couldn't take her pain away or fix her. God gave her a way of escape through Jesus, but she had to accept Him."

Justin drew in a deep breath and slowly let it slide out through his parted lips. "I know that much. Ma loved God with her whole heart and raised me to believe in Him. I've drifted away over the years and grown hard inside. Molly knew the truth, too, but she couldn't accept it. She talked about it one time. Said she knew Jesus came to forgive sinners, but she didn't think He'd want her in heaven. Said she'd done bad things and didn't believe the preacher knew what he was talking about when he promised forgiveness to anyone who'd ask."

"It's so sad when anyone turns their back on the free gift God gave us through His Son, but it happens every day." Alex wrapped her arm across his chest and hugged. "I'm sorry—for your pain, and for hers. I had no idea."

Justin stroked her hair and laid his cheek against her head. "I know. I should've told you sooner, but it never seemed like the right time. Besides, I didn't think you were interested in me, so it wouldn't have mattered."

"Weren't interested? Did you happen to see the jealousy on my face when you walked off arm in arm with Lacey at the picnic?"

It was his turn to stare. "You were jealous of little Lacey? But you were having a good time visiting with Carter. After he called on you at the ranch then joined us at the picnic, I assumed…." His voice trailed off, and he shook his head. "Guess that's what we both get for assuming. That reminds me. I assumed a lot about Christy, but I still don't understand what hold Foster had over her."

Alex nodded. "It all centered around Toby. A few months after the boy was born, Carter befriended Christy—probably because he had been keeping tabs on Molly and figured Christy would be a good source of information. Christy was in a hard spot and needed money, and Carter gave her what she needed, convincing her he just wanted to help. He started asking questions about Molly and Toby, and she answered them." Alex sighed. "Poor Christy. After Molly's death, Carter told Christy she'd better do what he wanted, or he'd take Toby and she'd never see him again. Between that threat and the hold he had over her from the money she'd taken, she believed she didn't have a choice—even when it came to trying to take Toby from you."

"But that was playing into Foster's hands. If she'd taken Toby from me, who knows what Foster would have done with him?"

"She thought she could take Toby and disappear. Now she realizes that she wasn't thinking clearly—that Carter would have hunted her down. It's just a blessing that God intervened and saved Toby—and the rest of us—from that man."

Justin laced his fingers through hers and stroked the side of her hand with his thumb. "One more question?"

She tipped her head and smiled.

"Are you at all curious about the gold your father found? Will you and Joe hunt for it?"

Alex took a moment to think and then replied, "I don't think so. Having you, Toby, Martha, and Uncle Joe safe is what matters the most. Maybe someday if we need it…I suppose it will still be there, but right now it doesn't seem important." She squeezed his fingers and smiled up into his eyes. "That's settled, so what comes next?"

He sat bolt upright and a strange look flitted across his face—part consternation, part anticipation. He tenderly stroked the side of her face before slipping off the porch swing and dropping down on his knees in front of her. One hand reached out to grasp hers, and the other covered his heart.

Alex smiled when her eyes met his. Such intense love radiated from the brown depths. Her smile faded and her heartbeat quickened as she felt herself drawn into that gaze.

"Alexia Travers, I love you more than words can express. God brought us back to Himself and then brought us together. I can't imagine life without Him or you. More than anything, I want a marriage that centers on God. You are the woman I want to spend the rest of my life with. Would you do me the honor of agreeing to become my wife?"

Her free hand reached out and stroked his hair. How good the Lord had been to them both. He'd brought them through so much these past few weeks—delivering them from danger and depositing love into their lives. A deep joy welled in her heart at the adoration shining on Justin's face. "Only if you kiss me again—and don't make me wait too long to say 'I do.' "

He jumped to his feet and whooped. "I'm the luckiest man on earth." He pulled her to her feet and swung her around in a circle then set her down. Two strong arms circled her waist, and she slipped her hands up around his neck. "How about next week?"

A smile curved her lips and she nodded. "That's fine, but you haven't sealed the other end of the bargain."

The grin on his face faded and his lips parted ever so slightly. One hand tipped up her chin and the other cradled the back of her head. Slowly his lips descended on hers. Warmth stole through her body and a flood of love enveloped her heart. Her world was complete, at last.

* * * * *

One week later, Alex stood in front of the long mirror in the back room of the church and straightened her linen waist. The folds of her pale yellow skirt draped in billows to the floor, and the fitted white waist accentuated her slender figure. "I guess it would be asking too much to get married in trousers."

Elizabeth rocked back on her heels and planted her hands on her hips. "I can't believe you, Alexia Travers. You've roped the best-looking man in Last Chance, and all you can think of is getting married in trousers."

Alex laughed and smoothed the tiny edging of lace encircling her hips. "Trust me, I'm having a hard time believing this is happening. Thinking about normal things makes it seem a little less like a fairy-tale. How in the world did the black sheep of this town lasso someone like Justin?"

Elizabeth pulled Alex's hair back and ran a brush through the long brunette curls in strong strokes. "You're far from an outcast. I'd say more of a hero, once word spread that you'd gone to Carter's ranch to rescue Toby. The women around here think the world of that little boy, and that's all they've been talking about the past few days. That and the fact that Carter lived dual identities."

"According to Christy, probably a lot more than two."

"That's another thing you're being praised for. The tide of opinion is turning in favor of Christy, after you took her in and she got hurt trying to save Toby from Carter. I still find it hard to believe he fathered Toby and abandoned Molly. It's a good thing Davis talked, or you'd probably never have known the truth."

"I guess that proves God can use even the evil intentions of people to bring good into His children's lives. What Carter planned as destruction, God turned into something beautiful for Justin, Toby, and me."

Elizabeth paused in her brushing. "I know what you mean. And speaking of Christy, how's she doing?"

"Good. She's healing quickly, and with Carter no longer a threat, she gave the sheriff the name of the men who attacked her. One went by 'Cain,' and he called his companion 'Mouse.' Sheriff Ramsey thinks he'll be able to find them both."

Elizabeth gave a soft whistle. "That's great. They should pay for what they did."

"I agree. By the way, Uncle Joe's bringing Christy—I asked her to attend my wedding. After all, she's Toby's aunt and deserves to be part of his life."

"I'm glad. I talked to her for a few minutes when I stopped by the ranch to see you. She seemed changed somehow. I'm not sure quite what's different, but something is."

Alex nodded, tugging her hair out of Elizabeth's grasp. "Oops, sorry."

She stood still and tipped her head back. "She's been asking a lot of questions about the Lord, and I think she's very close to making a decision. Martha talked Miss Alice into letting Christy move into the boardinghouse until she can find her own place. She'll help Alice cook and clean for her room and board. It'll be the perfect arrangement, and I'm guessing Alice won't want to let her go after she's been there for a while."

"You've been a wonderful influence. If it hadn't been for you, there's no telling what might've happened to Christy. Besides," a sly smile curved Elizabeth's lips, "I'm guessing she won't be at Miss Alice's too long, if Ralph Peters has anything to say about it."

Alex grinned. "Did you know he's been out to see her three times in the past two weeks? He's been smitten with her since the day he carried her trunk to the saloon. That man has a tender heart, and he'll be a healing influence in her life."

"She deserves some happiness. Ralph loves the Lord, and I imagine he'll be encouraging her that direction, as well." Elizabeth took a step back and surveyed her handiwork. "You hair looks wonderful, with your gorgeous curls down your back. I think you were right to not put it up."

"I was afraid Toby wouldn't know me. He's never seen me with my hair up." Alex sank onto a short bench and fluffed her skirt. "Would you hand me my locket?"

Elizabeth plucked it off the small desk in the corner of the room and draped it around Alex's neck, hooking the clasp in the back. "Did you get a photograph of Justin?"

Alex nodded and smiled. "Yes, but it's an old one that his mother had made before she died. When we're in Sacramento for our honeymoon, we'll have new ones taken." She touched the locket and tears thickened her voice. "Mama would have loved Justin and Toby. I wish she and Papa were with me today."

Elizabeth wrapped her arms around Alex's shoulders and gave her a long hug. "I think they know, and they're happy," she whispered. "Now wipe your eyes and put on your biggest smile. It's almost time." She peeked out the door into the main gathering room of the church then turned back to Alex. "Well, I'll be."

"What?"

"Didn't you say you expected a handful of people? Your family, the sheriff and Sarah, Miss Alice, and Christy?"

"Yes, that's right. I didn't think many others would care to come, so I didn't make a point of inviting anyone else."

"Well, you were wrong. I think most of the town is coming in the back door!"

Alex placed a hand over her heart. "All because I tried to save Toby from Carter?"

"Maybe the women finally woke up and realized your worth. I'm guessing this is their way of saying they're sorry for the way they've treated you." Elizabeth peeked out again and stifled a gasp.

"What?" Alex tried to see over her friend's shoulder.

Elizabeth shut the door and turned, enveloping Alex in a hug. "You're not going to believe it, but Mabel and Clive Gurney are sitting in the third row, looking pleased as punch." She shook her head. "I'm guessing that's the end of your struggles with the gossiping women." A mischievous grin tugged at her lips. "Of course, they might just be relieved that you won't be a threat to their menfolk, now that you've caught a man of your own."

Alex gave a weak chuckle. "Let's hope you're right. It's going to take some getting used to. Are Uncle Joe and Martha here yet? And do you see Justin and Toby?"

"Yes. They're all here. Uncle Joe's headed this way."

Joe tapped on the door and slipped inside. Alex flew across the intervening space and lost herself in the older man's hug. He gently grasped her shoulders, taking a long moment to look deep into her eyes. "I can see it in your face, darlin'…you're truly happy."

"Yes, Uncle. I'm happy and at peace." She lifted her face and kissed his weathered cheek.

"I'm glad, darlin'. You deserve the best." He patted Alex's shoulder and motioned toward the door. "Speakin' of which, they're waitin' for you out there, and I reckon we'd best get a move on." He offered his bent arm. "I seen Justin, and he's sweatin' bullets watchin' for you to come down that aisle."

Alex slipped her hand into the crook of his elbow and smiled. "Let's not keep him waiting."

Elizabeth opened the door and stood aside for the two of them to pass then slipped out and closed it softly behind her. Joe and Alex walked to the front of the church with Elizabeth following.

Alex raised her eyes as they moved between the crowded aisles, and her gaze met and held Justin's. His deep brown eyes didn't waver but burned with an intense passion that ignited something deep in her spirit. This man and his son would be her world for the rest of her life. Together they'd accepted the challenges presented by Carter Foster—and won. They'd both received a last chance at love, and with God in the center, they'd make it through whatever their future held.

Author's Note
....

Last Chance, California, is now a ghost town with only one small shack and a cemetery attesting to the thriving mining town that once existed. My husband, Allen, and I flew to Sacramento, drove to Foresthill, then ventured on a two-hour drive through the winding canyons and steep slopes leading up to the spot in the forest that once sheltered Last Chance. Now the area only comes to life when the annual Tevis Cup, a one-hundred-mile endurance race and the yearly marathon, brings runners, riders, and horses here, using the wide spot in the road as a checkpoint.

The bustling town is almost totally obscured, and the encroaching forest hides the remnants of cellars. Careful searching revealed a number of one-hundred-year-old fence posts with the original square-headed nails, broken pieces of ancient glass, and a handful of tombstones. We may have found the location of the blacksmith shop, based on the square configuration of posts not far from the meadow and spring, and a building looked to have been close by. You can still see the spring and the nearby glade, but a few years ago vandals cut down the ancient apple trees that still bore fruit for the forest creatures.

We researched the area and the history with our wonderful guide, Nolan Smith, a Forest Service archaeologist who loaned me books and maps, pointed out landmarks, and gave us insight into some of the people buried in the small cemetery outside of the original town site. The reference in my book to Allen Grosh, the man who originally discovered the Comstock Lode, is documented in history, and his headstone is located in Last Chance where he died.

I discovered an old diary entry from the 1860s that referenced a large, treeless plateau a mile or so out of town that stretched for three miles. We located that plateau while we were there, but over the past 130 years trees have grown up and completely taken over. That section of land could have easily housed a horse ranch, even though deep canyons and steep hillsides cover much of the balance of the surrounding vicinity.

While Alexia and Justin's story is purely fictional, the area, history, and surrounding towns are real. Foresthill, Deadwood Canyon, Auburn, Robinson Flat, and the rugged, deep canyons all exist today. A small museum in nearby Foresthill contains pictures and remnants of that era. The old Wells Fargo station in Michigan Bluff, one of the stops for the mule trains headed into Last Chance, has been transformed into a private home, but you can still see much of the original building as it was over one hundred years ago. The trail from Michigan Bluff to Last Chance is well-marked and can be transversed by foot, horseback, or mountain bike, and historical markers exist on many of the trails. It's an area filled with fascinating history and stories of tragedy and triumph, as well as likable, friendly people. I hope you've enjoyed this small peek into yesteryear and my take on what might have been. You can see the pictures I've posted on the Summerside Press blog at http://lovefindsyou. wordpress.com/2008/06/19/photos-of-last-chance-area/.

Miralee Ferrell
www.miraleeferrell.com